Snakebite

Ruby –
Thank you for always
being there for me.
You are my hero.

love,
Kris

Snakebite

❖

Book Two of the Chronicles of Reality

K. M. Outten

To order additional copies of this book, contact:
Xlibris Corporation
1-888-795-4274
www.Xlibris.com
Orders@Xlibris.com
16642

PROLOGUE

Before Roxanne Black ran into Mongrel and found her way into a new and exciting land; before the three Chosen stood together to face the Betrayer in an attempt to save the land; and, before the Lords had a hope of finding the answers, Snake was made.

During the land's darkest hour and its greatest time of need, three Chosen people rose to the calling of hero. But, one of them had not always been who she was then. Snake had a dark and secret past. A past that haunts her, drives her, and refuses to let her go. In our first meeting with this reluctant heroine, we see hints of who she really is but much is left to supposition and guesswork. We know that there is a great deal more to her than even her own mind reveals, but we are kept just outside the gates of the house where her truth lies hidden.

Snake is a tortured soul, who comes through, despite her past, to help save the land. And, although we wonder, we never truly know why she is who she is.

This is her story . . .

CHAPTER 1

The pounding of hoofs raced past the sleeping girl's head and sent her reeling to her knees. As the terror of her dreams faded, she focused on the world around her, and the terror of her new life stabbed her painfully in the heart. Tears flooded her tender eyes as she lifted a dainty hand to her left cheek and touched the symbol of her betrayal; the symbol that was to be her doom. She shook her head and wiped the tears from her eyes. *Be strong, Jenny. You can't keep crying all the time. You have to take care of yourself now.* With that thought, the tears started like a river. She had lead a life of pampered privilege; she had no idea how to take care of herself.

A flash of silver caught her eye. She controlled the waterfall that was coming from her eyes long enough to focus. It was one of the king's guards. Jenny slid further under the bush where she had been sleeping and held her breath. *Please don't let him see me. Please, please, please.* The guard took a couple of steps in her direction, she closed her eyes. If he saw her, it would be all over for her soon. That thought almost gave her comfort.

The guard heard strange noises coming from the bushes near the castle gate, so, like the trained soldier he was, he investigated. He was only a couple of feet away when he saw the huddled form; eyes closed, and body shivering. He knew at once that it was the Princess. He also knew it was his duty to apprehend her, by order of the King. He took a couple more steps toward her, but the gut-wrenching sound of her sobs stopped him dead in his tracks. She was so small and so scared. He remembered the silent dignity on her face as the Prince carved into her dove-white skin. That she had been reduced to this huddled mass nearly broke his heart. He could not help her, for that he would loose his head. But, he would not harm her either.

Jenny heard the footsteps moving away from her. Slowly, she opened her eyes. The guard was gone. *He didn't see me!* The relief nearly overwhelmed her, and the tears started anew. For a few moments she sat and sobbed, but, then, her eyes started to ache, her head started to pound, and her senses started to return. *I can't sit here crying forever. I've got to find out what to do.* A rumble in her stomach told her exactly what she had to do; she had to find some food. But, with no money and no servants that wasn't going to be an easy task. Still, she couldn't stay where she was. Pulling the hood of her cloak down over her scarred face, she climbed up on her weak legs and started the longest journey of her short life.

With courage she didn't know she possessed, Jennifer moved her tiny frame forward into the crowds surrounding the castle. The world around her was bustling with life of every shape and size. There were food dealers, cloth dealers, wine makers, farmers, gypsies, and other various merchants pedaling their wares. Children ran from one booth to the next, grabbing little pieces of whatever they could get their hands on, and adults laughed and argued with each other. In the midst of all the confusion, the terrified little princess pulled her cloak tighter and pressed her hands to her heart to try and stop the constant ache. A single thought kept pushing against her mind, *These people all look so much smaller from by bedroom window.* A window she knew she would never look out of again.

Once again, the tears began to course down her cheeks. *This is getting ridiculous. I have to stop crying!* The smell of warm bread drew her attention. She shifted her head and followed the smell, tripping through the crowd like a newborn babe learning to walk. Her stomach ached and her head was pounding so hard she could barely see. Still, she moved on in the direction of food until, through bleary eyes, she saw the object of her desire. Almost in awe, she reached out to grab a loaf of bread but was stopped short by a strong hand and a gruff voice.

"Money first then you can touch," growled the burly owner of the hand that held her.

Startled and confused, Jennifer looked up at the man, "What? I don't . . . "

But, it was too late. She had made a fatal mistake. The man was no longer interested in the bread; he was staring at the bloody mark on her face and fumbling with his thoughts.

"The Princess . . . That's who you are." He turned his head to search the crowd for a royal guard. There was already a price on her head, and he wanted to collect.

Jennifer realized all too late what she had done. Panicked, she tried to break free from his grasp. He felt the pressure of her pulling away and turned to face her.

"Oh no you don't, girlie," he growled, "You 'ain't going nowhere until I get what's coming to me." He tightened his grip.

Despair seized her heart. She screamed out, "Let me go! Please! Let me go!"

The man just laughed down in her terror-ridden face and yelled out to the soldiers.

"Guards! Hey, guards! I've got her! I've got the Princess!"

The guards, hearing the screams, turned and started through the throngs of people to investigate. The frantic former regal lady cried and begged for her life, and the dark figure in the corner, who was as yet unnoticed, waited. He had been watching for sometime. He had watched as the small mass wrapped in the dark cloak had stumbled through the people. He had watched as she had reached out for the bread. And, he had watched as her face had been revealed. Now, he waited for just the right opportunity to claim what he felt was rightfully his. After all, he had waited patiently for her to show herself. Now, as the guards closed in, he knew that he had to act. And, so he did.

Silently, he slid to the front of the mob that was rapidly growing around the bread vendor. Reaching the front, he pulled a little black ball out of his pocket and tossed it gently into the air. Timing every movement, he stepped behind the trembling girl just as the ball hit the ground with a horrendous **BOOM!** The guards drew their swords, people fell to the ground in terror, women screamed, and the dark stranger hit the Princess on the head with the hilt of his knife, threw her over his shoulder, and disappeared into the cloud of black smoke that promptly followed the explosion. When it was all over with, the bread vendor found himself face to face with the king's guards and nothing in his hands but a loaf of bread. The Princess was gone.

*   *   *

Complete blackness began to fade into shades of gray as the sound of voices reached the tattered girl's ears. She strained to make them sound more coherent. That only added to the ringing she now realized was coming from inside her ears. Feeling searing pain, she changed tactics and attempted to open her eyes. That only made her head pound and her swollen eyes ache. *I feel like I've been crying for days.* As she slowly began to regain consciousness, the memories of the past two days came flooding back. *Oh, that's right. I have.* For a moment, Jennifer resisted consciousness—reality only brought pain—but her mind was already alert and asking questions. *What happened? Where am I?*

She pulled her hands to her face to rub her eyes clear, but they never made it there. A shot of fear ran down her spine as she realized her hands were tied. Further attempts to move told her that her feet were also tied and that she was gagged as well. The panic that she was growing so accustomed to seized her once again. She had to calm down and pull herself together. *Okay, think Jenny. What happened?* Her mind raced for answers. Slowly, the picture began to form in her muggy mind. She remembered the bread, the vendor, the explosion, and smoke. She concentrated until her head pounded. *The vendor let go of me. So, how did I get here?* Try as she might, the bedraggled Princess could not remember past the smoke.

The sound of voices getting louder drew her out of her mental torture and brought her back into the world of physical pain. She listened to hear what was being said, but all she could hear was the beating of her heart echoing in her ears. Suddenly, a door flew open. Had she not been tied down, Jennifer would have jumped through the ceiling. As it was, her heart leapt into her throat. She was momentarily blinded by the burst of light that filled the room. However, her eyes quickly adjusted and she was able to take in her drab surroundings.

All too quickly, she realized that she was in a bedroom. That was obvious by the huge bed in the corner. It was a majestic looking bed, covered with dozens of fluffy pillows and what appeared to be silken blankets. The wooden bedposts were full of elaborate carvings and a canopy covered it all. The rest of the room paled in comparison. There was a dresser against the far wall, a wooden chest at the end of the bed, a table with a wash basin that looked as though it would fall apart at the slightest touch, and a stone fireplace directly in front of her. Oh, and there was the red-velvet chair that Jennifer had been tied to. The whole thing appeared to her as a mockery of a royal bedroom. She shuddered as a memory ran through her mind.

"Don't tell me you are cold, my dear. You can't get much closer to the fire."

Jennifer jerked her head back toward the door and the source of the voice. What she saw intrigued and terrified her. There were two men strolling across the room toward her. One seemed vaguely familiar, like a figure once met in a dream. He was tall, slender, and dressed all in black. A sinister smile curled his lips on his gaunt face as he eyed the young Princess. She shuddered again and pulled her gaze away from his ghoulish face only to find herself locked in the stare of the other man. Her heart stopped briefly. His eyes were crystal blue and twinkled mysteriously as he grinned at the Princess. They terrified her; she averted her eyes. Quickly, she took in the rest of his features. He had the smooth skin of royalty, jet-black hair curled around his square face, and muscles stretched the fabric of his clothes. He was beautiful and sinister all a once. Jenny tried to take a deep breath and nearly choked on her gag.

Gently, the blue-eyed man reached forward and removed the gag.

"Don't suffocate yourself, my dear. You made it this far alive; you don't want to die now."

As she felt her lips let free, her first thought was to scream, but she didn't have the strength. Taking in as much air as she could, she realized that she didn't have the strength for much of anything. She thought she might cry, but she had no tears left after all that she had been through. Instead, she made a timid plea.

"Water?"

The blue-eyed man gestured to the lean man, "By all means, bring her some water."

The lean man filled a glass with water and brought it over to Jenny.

"Don't be an idiot, Lucas. Can't you see her hands are tied? Here, give that to me!"

Abruptly, the blue-eyed man grabbed the glass from Lucas and held it up to Jenny's lips. "Go ahead, take a drink." Gingerly, she took a drink.

"Tastes good, doesn't it? I apologize for the uncomfortable position you are in, but it was the only way to be sure that you wouldn't hurt yourself by trying to run off. After all, you have had quit a couple of days."

He pulled the glass away from her lips and hunched down in front of the haggard Princess. Slowly, he lifted a hand and touched the mangled scar on her cheek. She flinched and pulled away. His hand followed her face and traced the scar.

"A snake. How unbecoming of someone so young and innocent. Look, Lucas. She has child-like blue eyes and golden blonde hair. Hardly the look of a serpent. In fact, except for this hideous scar, I'd say she is a perfect beauty. Wouldn't you?"

Lucas grinned from ear to ear. He looked so completely evil that Jenny gasped. Blue-eyes laughed.

"Don't fear him, little one. Lucas can't talk—that's what makes him the perfect thief. Noise isn't a problem." Lucas sat back, folded his arms across his lean chest and smiled proudly. "In fact," continued the sinister man in front of her, "I'd say he's the best thief around . . . next to me of course."

Jenny's head was swimming in confusion. *Where am I? What is going on? and . . .* "Who are you?" she stammered in a weak voice.

The large man stood to his full height and took a deep bow, "I am Stephan the Great. Perhaps you have heard of me?"

The Princess shook her head.

Stephan shrugged his muscular shoulders, "No matter. You will soon know me well enough. What does matter is that I know who you are, Princess."

The way he said *princess* sent chills down Jenny's spine. There was something so evil about this man. She wasn't sure why, but she was terrified of him. Trying to hide her fear and keep from crying all over again, Jenny mustered all the false bravado she could and confronted her jailer.

"What do you want with me?" she eeked out.

Stephan smiled and leaned over her, bringing his face within inches of hers. The hair on her neck stood on end in response. He reached out and lightly stroked her scar again. "Why, my dear, I want nothing with you. What I want is what the soon to be king will pay for you. But," he smiled and dropped his hand to her breast, "I may find use for you until I can negotiate the price I want."

Jenny's entire body jerked at his touch; it was so violating.

Now, when she spoke, she spoke with a fire that was real, "Get your filthy hands off me."

Stephan pulled back in mock surrender, put his hands in the air, and let out a hearty laugh, "You see, Lucas, there is some life in her still. And, I thought our future king had taken it all from you. "

Her eyes widened and her face flashed ghostly white. Her heartless jailer leaned back down into her face and dropped his voice to a whisper.

"That's right, my dear, I know what the Prince did to you. I have friends in his personal guard. But, I'm not going to let that stop me from making a profit off your soul."

With that he stepped back, turned, and left the room, his henchman close on his heels. As suddenly as she had been overtaken by the bandits, the former princess had been abandoned to her own fear and imagination. *Profit on your soul . . . Use for you . . .* echoed over and over in her ears.

"My God," she whispered, "I've got to get out of here. But how?"

Her terror mounted as she pulled at the restraints around her wrists. She was securely tied to the chair and lacked the strength to pull away. But, the more her fear overcame her, the more she tugged and pulled, until she felt the ropes cut into her wrists. After several moments of straining, she finally stopped and began to sob in exhaustion.

"Why . . . why is this happening to me? What have I done?" she cried out to the darkness. No one answered.

*   *   *

She wasn't sure how long it had been since she quit sobbing. And, she was even less sure how long she had been sitting in that nasty, red chair, dancing in and out of consciousness. But, she was sure of one thing; she was too tired to go on this way. Silently, she murmured a little prayer. "Please, just let me die. I can't suffer like this anymore." Her heart ached even as the words crossed her lips but she couldn't see any other way out. "I'm just not strong enough on my own."

She was so caught up in her world of self-pity that she didn't see the figure that had entered the room until it was upon her. She nearly jumped out of her skin when the piercing voice hit her ears.

"Oh my lord, do you look the frightful sight!"

Jenny lifted her head and brought her eyes to focus on the speaker. She was an elderly woman with soft, round eyes and a plump face. Her hair was tattered and tied back with a torn cloth. Her clothes looked as though they were the only she had. And, though she was filled with concern at the moment, her mouth looked as though it had rarely worn a frown. The woman took Jenny's face between her gentle hands.

"I declare child, you look like you've been walked on by a team of horses. What happened to you?"

Tears burst forth from Jenny's eyes, "I've been doomed to hell on earth. Please, let me die."

The old woman was taken aback by those words, "Now, listen here child, there isn't a thing bad enough in this world to make you give up on living. What kind of talk is that?"

The battered princess felt that she had to make this woman understand how horrible things had been; how unfair life was. But, before she could utter another word, the woman was in motion. She ran to the door and pulled in a large basin full of water, threw some clothing over her shoulder, and began to untie Jenny, and lectured all the while.

"Now, I can tell by the look of you that you have had it rough, and I know you think you should just give up, but that's not right. Just remember that no matter how bad it is for you someone else has had it worse. What kind of crazy talk is that? You are stronger than that. Everyone's stronger than dying."

"Not me," murmured Jenny as the last of the ropes fell from her body.

The woman shook her head and began to remove Jenny's clothes. "Even you child."

Gently she removed the last shred of Jenny's dress and helped her up into the basin. To her amazement, the tired young girl found that the water was warm and relaxing.

"Who are you?" she mumbled.

The old lady stood back and laughed, "Well, I suppose I did forget to introduce myself. I am Flora. I work for Stephan as his house-cleaner, cook, and caretaker."

As she began to relax, Jenny let her questions go, "Why would someone like you work for someone like him?"

Flora actually managed a frown, "Now is not the time to concern yourself with that. Let's just leave it that I owe him a favor and that you are not the only one who has had a hard life."

Jenny felt pain at the frown on Flora's face, "I'm sorry." She also felt shame at herself.

"That's quite alright, little one. Let's just say that I know what I'm talking about when I say there is no pain that is worth giving up on life for. The things that don't kill you outright only make you stronger."

"Yeah," quipped Jenny, "then, I'm about to become the strongest person in the world."

For a few moments, neither woman spoke. Then, Jenny realized that if she was not going to drown herself, which she couldn't bring herself to do in Flora's presence, there were a million little things she needed to know.

"What is Stephan going to do with me?"

Flora looked deep into the young girl's pleading eyes. She knew she shouldn't tell, but she had never been one for lies.

"All I know is I'm suppose to clean you up, feed you, and keep you in good condition for as long as you are here."

"That's really no answer."

"I know."

Jenny squared her shoulders and thought, "Well, where is he now?"

Flora shrugged, "I heard some guards saying that he had gone to the palace, but I wouldn't know why."

Jenny's heart leapt into her throat. She knew he must be making a deal with the prince. *I'm dead for sure.* Oddly, that thought did not bring the comfort it had earlier. Somehow, the thought of the prince getting away with all he had done upset her. Instantly, she knew that she didn't want to die. Sitting straight up, she grabbed Flora's hand and looked her in the eye.

"Listen to me very carefully. I am the Princess who has been banished. Stephan has gone to sell me to the Prince. If that happens, I will die. You have got to help me."

Recognition and terror flashed in Flora's eyes, "Oh dear god."

Searching the eyes of the child before her, Flora knew she was hearing the truth. What's more, looking at the beauty and innocence in her face, she knew that the prince was the least of the princess' problems. She had worked for Stephan far too long not to recognize his tastes. One thing was for sure, this little girl was going to be used and abused even more before Stephan was done with her. Flora's heart broke and shattered into a thousand pieces when she realized all that was about to happen and that she was powerless to stop it. She closed her eyes against the pain. But, when she opened them, the princess was still pleading with her.

"Please. I'm so scared and alone. I don't know how to do anything myself."

Flora mustered her strength and squared her shoulders, "Now, listen very carefully child. You will survive this. There is a strength in you—I feel it. But, you will have to get through most of it on your own. That is a reality you will have to face sooner or later, just as well it is sooner."

Tears pulsed against Jenny's eyes, "Won't you help me?"

Flora felt as though her heart was being ripped from her chest, "I can't, child. Much as I want to, I am bound to Stephan in ways that you will never know. To cross him would go beyond my life and hurt those closest to my heart."

Scared and desperate as she was, Jenny could hear the torment in the older woman's voice and see the truth in her eyes. "Then, what am I to do?"

Flora straightened her back and put her hands on hips, "Well, the first thing you are to do is get cleaned up dressed, and comfortable. Then, when you are calm, you can think things through."

Jenny looked up with tear swollen eyes, "If I am to end up dead at the hands of the prince, what reason could I possibly have to go on living?"

"That, my dear, is something you will have to find for yourself. Now, get out of that bath and move forward."

Even as she made the command, the gentle caretaker knew she may be asking too much of the beaten girl. She looked liked she had already faced death and lost. *This one may not make it on her own. But what can I do?* Slowly, an idea slipped into the back of her mind and begin to take shape. It was crazy and desperate, but possible. The old lady banished it from her thoughts. But, it was too late. She knew that, no matter the risk, she wasn't going to let this child die. *But now is not the time for such thoughts. I must prepare the poor girl for what is to come.*

Gently, Flora helped the fallen angel into clean clothes and brushed through her golden tresses. Jenny never uttered a word and scarcely lifted a finger to help. She had the look of someone totally defeated. Chills ran down Flora's spine, as she thought of this child alone with Stephan and his plans.

The last thing had come and Jenny still had not even muttered. The last thing. The injury to her face. Using a dark rag so that the young girl could not see all the blood, Flora scrubbed the gaping wound. She concealed her shock at the horror of the uncovered scar with a false coughing attack. Then, like the caretaker she was, she rubbed healing salve into the tender skin. Even this torture brought no response from her ward.

Jenny felt all the touches, but they meant nothing to her. She had gone completely numb. Just when she had decided to live, she had been condemned to die. *Isn't that ironic?* At first she had toyed with the idea of escape, but she didn't know how or where to go. She realized that she would probably be caught and killed immediately, and so she gave up and settled into a state of numbness. There was an odd comfort in that state. But, as Flora rose to leave, something flickered inside Jenny. From some deep fire in her soul came one last burst of desire. There was one thing she wanted to see before it was all over. Her voice eeked out of her throat.

"Wait. Do you have a mirror?"

Flora turned in shock, "A mirror?"

"Please," Jenny stretched out her hand, "I need to see it."

Flora hesitated, "Are you sure?"

Jenny's voice became firm, "I am sure."

"Very well."

Reluctantly, the older lady handed the mirror to the young woman before her and cringed as she waited. For a moment, the former princess stalled. *Do I really want to do this?* She took a deep breath and put the mirror in front of her face. What she saw made her want to vomit. On her left cheek, where once dove-white skin had shone unmarred, was a raised, purple mass of skin and blood that looked like a coiled snake. It was made even more grotesque by the bruised black and blue skin that served as a background.

"I'm hideous . . . " she whispered like a small child standing over the corpse of a rotting animal.

"It isn't as bad as that," offered Flora. "In time, the bruise will vanish and the swelling will subside . . . "

She stopped cold as the wounded girl's eyes flashed upon her. "No. The damage has been done."

Jenny turned her eyes back to the mirror—trapped by the horror of her own reflection. She stared long and hard at what the prince, her cousin, the future king had done to her and began her journey into hate. She thought back to the way he had trapped her. The hate began. She felt the pain of him forcing himself inside her—raping her. The hate grew. She felt the stab of his lies about her that lead to her banishment. The hate grew. She felt the point of his knife on her face. The hate came alive. She felt her fear and self-loathing. The hate consumed her. *Now,* she thought, *now, I have a reason to live. That bastard is going to pay for this.* With the single glance in a mirror, Jenny had seen the reflection of the darkest part of her soul and given herself a reason to live. She was resolved to never let the prince, her cousin, enjoy a moment's rest.

"Now, I am ready to live."

The fury in the princess' voice made Flora's skin crawl and she feared the worst for her new ward. *I've got to help her soon before she loses her mind completely.* She gathered her belongings quickly and left—leaving the mirror behind. She somehow knew she would never see it again.

*   *   *

Jenny was still looking into the mirror when Stephan crept into the room. Her resolve to live to seek revenge coursing through her veins. The scene made no impact on Stephan. He tossed it aside to woman's vanity.

"Admiring your cousin's handiwork, Princess?"

Jenny looked up at the once terrifying man and found she was unafraid. Her resolve did not falter.

"Why don't you give me the mirror," he took it from her hands, "and I'll tell you all about the day I've had?"

Jenny locked her jaw tight and did not speak. Her resolve did not falter.

"Oh, have you lost the power of speech? No matter. You won't need your voice for what I have planned."

Here Stephan grabbed her by the arms and threw her on the bed. Then he pulled out a length of rope and quickly tied her hands to the posts. She made no effort to fight him, but her resolve did not falter.

"You see, the prince very much wants you returned to him and he has agreed to pay most handsomely for your return. So tomorrow, you will be home and I will be rich. But, I wouldn't want this time to go to waste. So, before you are his tomorrow, you will be mine tonight . . . as many times as you can take without dying on me." The sinister man let out an evil chuckle, but her resolve did not falter.

Even when he raped her over and over, her resolve did not falter. With each violation, her hatred of the prince increased. If not for him, she would not be in the pain she now was. She blamed all things on him; her hatred grew into a beast; and, her resolve increased. One thought pounded in her brain as the torments of her body ran throughout the night. *I will live and you, dear cousin, will pay.*

*   *   *

CHAPTER 2

The city streets were empty and cold and shone with an eerie glow as candlelight reflected off a light mist that had rolled in from the sea. All around were shadows and silence. The night air weighed heavy on the souls that inhabited the streets of the city as they scurried from place to place, never looking up and never looking at each other. It was the city of angels by day, but, now, it was the world of demons. Nothing good was to be found.

A lone figure worked its way down one of the cold, damp streets as though running for its life. At the end of a dark alleyway, it stopped and looked left then right as though uncertain of which way to go. A breeze swept along the alley, knocking over a bottle. The sound caused the figure to jump and turn quickly. Silently, it searched the path behind for any hint of movement. None came. But, that brought no relief for the figure knew that if a thief was following there would be no way to know until your throat had been slit. Spinning on its heels, the figure moved on to the right.

A few feet down this passage, the nervous figure found what it had been searching for; a small opening hidden behind the piles of trash. The figure moved rapidly now. Time was running out and nerves were running thin. The figure parted enough of the rubbish to squeeze its large frame up to the opening. It was shut tight. The lone explorer didn't even slow down. Reaching into its flowing robes, the figure produced a long dagger and used it to pry the door open. Only now did the person hesitate. There was no way to know what lay hidden in the darkness beyond. This was the last moment to turn back. Once it entered the portal ahead it would be do or die. The figure took a deep breath and stepped into the realm of no return.

Nothing. Not even the sound of its own breathing penetrated the blackness. Then, the lone person let out a long breath . . . and all of hell came raining down.

Before the figure could cry out for help, it had been knocked to the ground and a black cloth thrown over its eyes threatening to make the now labored breathing impossible.

"What have we here?" whispered a sinister voice.

Cold steel made contact with the prisoner's next. "I need to see the Reverend," the prisoner gasped.

The blade pushed hard against the struggling figure's throat. "Oh, don't worry, you are definitely going to see the Reverend."

With that, the blade was moved and two sets of powerful arms dragged the desperate soul down the dark corridors. This journey was just beginning.

*   *   *

The Reverend looked down at the mass that lay huddled before him. Whoever this person was, he had found the entrance to their lair entirely too easily, for that he was still alive. He had to know how he had been found and if anyone else was following close at hand. But, as he viewed the hooded person his men had claimed as a prisoner, he felt no fear. There was something odd about this man . . .

"Remove the hood!" he boomed.

One of his men stepped forward and yanked the hood off the prisoner only to reveal the gentle face of an old woman. Everyone stepped back in shock. The Reverend stood emotionless and confronted the woman.

"I know you, don't I." It was more of a statement than a question.

Flora looked into the penetrating brown eyes of the strong face framed by long dark hair that hung just past his shoulders. Blinking furiously to adjust to the light, she managed a smile.

"Yes. I am Flora," she took a deep breath, "and I work for Stephan."

Swords came out of everywhere and found their way to her throat and heart as the Reverend men reacted to that name. "A spy!" they cried. The Reverend never took his eyes off Flora's scared face. He dismissed the swords and cries with a wave of his arm.

"Stand back. She is hardly in any kind of shape to do us any harm."

A young swordsman spoke, "But what if she has lead Stephan right to us?"

The Reverend cocked an eyebrow, "Yes, there is that. Have you old woman? Have you lead that monster right to my doorstep?"

Flora faltered, "I . . . I hope not, but cannot be sure. I am, after all, an old clumsy woman and not a master thief. Frankly, this hiding in the shadows bit is a little annoying."

So, you have come on your own, eh? But why? But, that thought could wait. First, the Reverend needed to make sure his hiding place was still safe.

"T, Sam, and Rock, take your men and secure the alley and the tunnels. No one gets in, understood? Stand firm on those orders until you hear from me."

T hesitated, "No one, Reverend?"

"We don't know how she found us, get it? No one!"

T nodded, all hesitation gone from his huge, dark figure. The glow of the candles reflected off his dark, bald head as he charged down the tunnels. "You heard the man, let's move!"

With his men on their way to guard the palace of the underground, the muscular man turned his attention back to the stranger who had taken him away from a good night's entertainment by showing up on his well hidden doorstep. *How the hell did she find me?* He took a seat at one of the solid wood chairs surrounding the long table in the meeting hall. Motioning with his hand, he instructed Flora to do the same. He studied her very carefully as she took her seat. He had spent years learning how to read every inch of a person in jut seconds, so he looked for her secrets. Yet, all he could see was honesty in her being and sadness on her face. *Who is this woman? If she is how she seems, why is she working for Stephan?* The Reverend leaned back in his chair and crossed his legs on the table. He looked something like a pirate in his tight black leggings and billowing white shirt. Flora could not help but admire him. Without warning, he spoke.

"How did you find my humble abode?"

Flora flinched at the thought of getting someone in trouble, but could not lie, "The barmaid who keeps you company . . . I have nursed her through many an abusive night with Stephan."

This sparked the Reverend interest. *She shares a bed with Stephan? Remind me not to send her flowers.* "She has been blindfolded each time she has been brought here."

"Yes, but she could smell the trash and knew the entrance was hidden and I followed your men as they escorted her away tonight."

The Reverend let out a low chuckle, "So it seems you have been something of a thief this night."

Flora smiled nervously, "Yes, well, I'm not very good at it as you can see." Then her thoughts turned to the poor girl she had just betrayed. "Do not blame poor Gwen for what I have done. She didn't want to give you away. It was only after I told her why I am here that she told me anything. She took much convincing . . . "

The Reverend put his feet firmly on the floor and leaned over the table toward the sputtering woman, "And why, exactly is that?"

Flora went silent. She stared back at the Reverend without uttering a word, as though she was weighing things in her mind. After several moments, she began to speak.

"What I'm about to suggest could get me and my daughter killed. The fact that I'm even here may have already accomplished half of that if I have been discovered. But, there is too little time for it to be any other way. It is getting late and time is becoming an enemy."

The Reverend felt dizzy, "Speak straight, woman. You aren't making any sense."

She inhaled deeply to calm her nerves, "I'm talking about the life of the Princess."

A shock wave ran through the Reverend's body, "*The* Princess? As in the one who has been banished for life for seducing her cousin the Prince?"

"The one and the same. Only, one look at her gentle eyes will tell you that she is incapable of that crime. There is talk among the palace guards that the Prince raped her and banished her to cover his own sin. Whatever the truth, the poor girl is in trouble now and needs our help."

"Our help?" asked the Reverend, "Why should I want to get involved in a tiff between two royal brats?"

Even as he said the words, he knew that he did want to get involved. He loved a good adventure, and, deep down, he had a heart . . . although he would never admit it.

Flora's upper lip stiffened, "I'm not asking you to get involved for the Princess; I'm offering you Stephan the Great's head on a platter. If you help me to rescue the girl, you will get the chance to eliminate Stephan forever. You see, he has the Princess and I will take you to him."

Light flared in the Reverend's eyes. This woman was about to give him everything he had always wanted for a long time, and all he had to do was save a spoiled brat in the process. *What a deal. But wait . . . there is always more.*

Calmly, he asked, "What's the catch?"

"Two things," she replied, trying to sound tough, "One, should anything go wrong, you don't know me. If Stephan knows I have betrayed him, he will torture and kill me and my daughter."

The Reverend wondered how Stephan was holding this woman's daughter over her head and why, but did not ask. He could see that she did not care to share that secret. "You have my word."

"And, second, you take the girl to safety. She is all but helpless and will never be able to get out alive on her own."

Great, babysitting duty. But still, she is probably small and easy to carry around. "Okay, I'll get her to safety. Anything else?"

Flora shook her head, "No. But we must hurry. Stephan is to deliver the Princess to the Prince at dawn."

"She must be something to get you to risk all this for her?"

Flora smiled, "Maybe I have just been waiting for a way out."

"Perhaps," he muttered.

"She is special. I can feel it."

The Reverend stood, "Then we begin now!"

As the echoes of his voice traveled along the stone corridors, the Reverend had a sinking feeling that he had just sold his soul.

*   *   *

The sounds of the night echoed through the underground lair of the self-proclaimed master thief. Everything as it should be in this evil place. Drunk men snored loudly in their beds and on the floors, mice scampered through the half eaten food on the tables, women tossed and turned under the men, and Lucas' breath grated in his own ears. Once, he had thought he had heard a door open, but it had been a cat wandering in for the night. And, once, he had heard the dainty little girl in Stephan's room scream. He smiled. But, that was to be expected. Now, the familiar sounds of the night took over and he kept guard over all. Shifting silently, he stared on into the night.

Down the hall, in the dark of Stephan's room, a small figure thrashed about wildly within the confines of the bed. Had she not been tied down, the Princess might have thrown herself from the bed. But, she was still secured to the bed; forgotten by the selfish and evil man passed out beside her. Safe. As safe as she had been in the last three days of her young life. Suddenly, her head snapped up and her eyes popped open as the violence of her nightmare ripped her from her troubled slumber.

Sweat poured down her face as she struggled to remember where she was and forget what she had been dreaming. As the ropes cut into her wrists, the knowledge of her surroundings flooded into her mind. *Oh, that's right . . . I'm in hell.* But the memories brought to life by her nightmares refused to release her tattered mind. She shook her head violently and looked at the pathetic mass in the bed next to her. If she had been untied, she would have clawed his eyes out. Anger rushed through her veins and warmed her against the coldness of the world she now faced. A single thought controlled her mind. *Revenge!!* Quickly, another thought crept in next to that one. *Escape.* She had to get out of this place, now.

Think, Jenny. There has to be a way. She scanned her surroundings for something, anything that would help her break free. The room was dark now and she had trouble making out objects in the darkness. In frustration, she pulled against her ropes. Her left hand moved. *What the?* She pulled again. The rope loosened some more. *This can't be.* But, it was. Apparently, in his hurry to tie her down, Stephan hadn't secured the rope quite tight enough. *Or, maybe it just loosened during . . . her* thoughts faltered, but she drew on her anger . . . *all the fun we were having*. She bit into her bottom lip until she tasted blood. Holding onto this anger was going to have one hell of a price.

She took one last breath and pulled with all her might. Her hand came flying forward as the rope broke free. She almost shouted in glee . . . almost. Instead, she pulled her lip back between her teeth and used the pain to keep focused. *I've got to be quiet. I can't wake him.* Slowly now, the brave beauty reached up and began to work on the knot that held her other wrist captive. A snort from Stephan nearly stopped her heart and sent her diving for cover. It seemed like an eternity passed as the terrified girl listened to him breath and felt her heart pounding against her chest.

But, the evil thief never opened an eye or made a move. He simply slept soundly. Gathering all of her courage, Jenny began, once again, to labor with the knot. She worked quickly now as the tie began to loosen. She could see her freedom just inches away. Her pulse quickened and her breathing became labored, as though she had been running for days. Anxiety filled her. Then, with one last pull, she was free. Perhaps if she had had any tears left, she would have cried in joy. However, she had long since used her last tear. The well of her emotions was running dry; she tapped into the abundance of anger and made a move for the floor.

*   *   *

The Reverend crouched in the darkness and listened for the sounds of a trap. He had heard many people say that he could smell a trap a mile away. That wasn't entirely true. He always heard them. There would be anxious breathing, uneasy shuffling, and an unnatural calm. He didn't hear those sounds, but still . . . He waited for T to return with verification of what he felt to be true.

A shivering next to him drew his attention to the woman who had brought him here. Flora looked like she was about to explode. His heart, the one he kept so carefully hidden, went out to her. Even if this was a clever trap, it had taken a great deal of courage for the old woman to do what she had done. To cover up his sympathetic nature, he leaned over to her ear.

"If this is a trap, I will kill you myself."

Her eyes widened, but she said nothing. For a split second, he felt a pang of guilt. But, then it was gone and the master thief turned back to the night and his waiting. He didn't wait long.

T's form materialized out of the darkness and slid up next to the Reverend.

Quietly he whispered, "No trap. One entrance. About forty men passed out all over the floor. About fifteen women, all bought and paid for. Stephan's room must be down the hall like she said. Only one person standing guard." T paused and took a deep breath. "It's Lucas."

Damn! With Lucas standing guard there was no chance of taking him out quickly and then taking the others at their leisure. Lucas had, no doubt, positioned himself right in the middle of the room, facing the entrance, and was wide-awake. *Hell, he might even already know we are here.*

"Did he see you?"

T shrugged, "Didn't seem to, but it's Lucas."

"Great. We might have to call this party off. If we go in there full force, which we might have to, to take care of Lucas, we are risking waking all the rest. Stephan will definitely have time to . . . " The Reverend voice trailed off into the night as his eyes fell on the huddled form of Flora. Suddenly, a new plan came to life.

T, use to his friend's odd behavior, waited patiently for the next sentence he knew had to be coming.

"You know," began the confident leader, "it's only when you are all out of options that you find a way out. I've got an idea."

T smiled, "I knew you would."

*   *   *

Lucas stared at the entrance and listened. Had he heard breathing? He stopped his own and filtered through the sounds that were familiar to him, until there was nothing between him and the entrance. Minutes passed as he held his breath and concentrated. Then . . . there it was, a breath beyond the door. Allowing his own breath to begin again, he pulled a dagger from his belt and hefted it into position. Then, the breathing became footsteps. Moving calmly and fluidly, Lucas crouched close to the floor like a panther about to attack. A shadow crossed the threshold and the hidden figure stepped forward. Lucas stood to throw . . . at the last second he stopped and the figure shrieked in fright.

"Aaaah!" Burst out Flora as she grabbed her chest. "Oh mercy, Lucas. You scared me right out of my skin."

Lucas eyed the old housekeeper carefully. *What the hell is she doing out at this hour?* He gave her a questioning look. She responded.

After years in this community, she knew what that look meant. "Have you seen a cat come through here? You know, I always go to sleep with that darn tabby at my feet. Drives me crazy. But, he must have slipped off in the middle of the night. Anyway, I woke up, he was gone, and now I can't sleep. I keep worrying about the cat. I know it sounds silly, but I was hoping to find him so I could go back to sleep."

Lucas felt like covering his over-sensitive ears. If anyone could talk for hours without saying a thing it was Flora. He often amused himself with the idea that she had gotten his voice along with her own. He put his hands up and motioned for her to be quiet. Then he motioned for her to look around the room. He had seen the cat earlier that evening. He bent down to look under the table when a thought hit him. *Why hadn't he heard Flora leave her room?* All of his senses came to life and he hit the ground, hard. Suddenly, all hell broke loose.

The Reverend and his forces had waited until Lucas was finally distracted, then they stormed. In an instant, fifteen men had taken out all those asleep on the floor and were working their way down the halls. It was only a matter of seconds before the fighting began. As soon as it did, Lucas sprang.

He had slid beneath the table as soon as the first man had come through the door. Calmly, he had watched them pierce hearts and slit throats, and, as they moved down the halls, he had realized one thing, Flora had lead them here. *You die old woman.* But, his desires were torn. He had to warn Stephan and protect him above all else. The old woman would have to wait, unless he could hit her first. He looked at her huddled against the wall and decided to chance it. Moving like a snake, he crawled to the edge of the table, pulled his dagger from his sheath, and sprang.

The Reverend had waited patiently for this moment. He knew better than to go looking for Lucas on his own territory. But, he knew Stephan's right-hand man wouldn't hide for long. When he saw him spring he started into motion. But, the Reverend had misjudged. Instead of going for the bedroom, Lucas went for Flora. The Reverend only had a split second to react. The dagger flew from Lucas' hand, straight toward Flora's chest. Grabbing a nearby chair, the Reverend threw it in front of the scared old woman. Metal, wood, and flesh collided. Lucas didn't waste another second; he sprinted down the hallway toward his master's bedroom.

The Reverend took off after him, pausing only long enough to see if Flora was alive. She was, but the dagger had found its way to her gut. Instantly, he knew that she was going to die. That secret heart of his spasmed in momentary pain. He couldn't just leave her. Her smiling eyes looked up at him, filled with pain.

"Well, what are you waiting for?" she smiled, "Go get the girl."

"It will be alright," he tried to assure her.

She smiled meekly, "Sure it will. Now go."

The powerful man needed no further urging. He leapt to his feet and started after Lucas. It was, after all, personal now.

*   *   *

Lying against the cold, stone floor, the battered princess thought she heard the sound of fighting outside the door. *Probably a bunch of drunks beating on their whores.* Her stomach turned as she swallowed some more anger. Was she going to have to take on everyone's pain to get through this? She couldn't shake the feeling that she was about to sell her soul for revenge, but that was all she had now. She pulled her legs underneath her and crawled toward Stephan's clothes. She had to find something to wear.

The sound of footsteps stopped her dead in her tracks. Her heart began to race again. Was someone coming? Was it that cold-hearted mute? If he were to see her now, she would be finished. She had to think. *How do I get out of here in one piece?* An idea flashed in her mind. She shook her head. *Be realistic, Jen. You can't do that.* Or could she? She heard the footsteps getting louder and felt her heart pounding harder. She had to do something. And, so, for the first time in her life, she made a violent move and felt her soul slip into the darkness, replaced by a cold, hollow feeling.

Scurrying quickly to Stephan's clothes, Jennifer hoped she could pull this off. Frantically, she searched his clothes for the weapon she knew had to be buried somewhere in the folds. The footsteps were right outside the door. Her heart pounded and sweat blurred her vision. She kept searching. The footsteps were at the door. Her heart stopped. Then, she felt the cool steal. Desperately, she pulled the dagger from the folds of the shirt and ran toward the bed. But she was too late.

The door burst open, and there stood Lucas. It took him less than a split second to see what was happening. He jumped on the princess and knocked her to the floor. All the air burst from her lungs and the dagger flew from her grasp. Stephan jumped from his sleep, yelling, and grabbing for his sword.

"What the hell is happening here?"

He looked down at Lucas struggling with the princess. Confused and still half-asleep, he screamed at his man.

"What are you doing? Why is she on the ground? Why aren't you at your post?"

Lucas knew there was no time to explain. He grabbed the princess and slammed her head against the ground, rendering her unconscious. Then, he jumped to his feet, threw Stephan a robe, and made the sign that sent a chill down Stephan's spine. He put one hand to his throat and saluted. The Master of this lair faltered.

"The Reverend? He's here?"

A wall torch came flying through the room and knocked Lucas flat on his back in response. Then, the majestic figure was in the doorway.

"Hello, Stephan. Did you miss me?"

The Master thief remained composed as he brought his sword to bare before him.

"Why, Reverend, you've aged . . . badly."

"At least I'll live to get older. You, I'm afraid, have seen your last birthday."

"We shall see."

The Reverend smiled, "Indeed, we shall."

Stephan prepared for the attack that was about to begin. The Reverend ran full steam at his adversary and took a swing at his legs. Stephan blocked the thrust and brought his sword back into play, but the Reverend was no longer engaged. He ran right past Stephan and brought his sword down on the unconscious figure of Lucas, neatly removing his head from his body. *You're not so tough when you are on your back.* That move cost him. Realizing what was happening, Stephan lunged for the Reverend's back. Only his instincts saved the seasoned fighter.

The Reverend spun to one side, but took a hit in his right thigh. Blood burst everywhere as the Reverend brought his sword back into the battle.

"Looks like you are getting slow, old man," chided Stephan.

The Reverend's eyes became slits and a smug grin crossed his face, "Old age and treachery will always overcome youth and skill . . . or lack thereof."

Stephan took another swing at his worst enemy and the fighting encompassed everything. Blow after blow was dealt. The Reverend was careful to stand between Stephan and the lifeless form of the princess on the floor. He wasn't convinced she was still alive, but, if she was, he had to protect her. He had given his word. As Stephan's sword lunged at him yet again, he began to wonder if that promise was going to be the death of him. He couldn't shake the feeling that it was.

Sweat poured into Stephan's eyes as he struck wildly at the massive monster of a man before him. He knew that, if he held his ground, he could beat the Reverend. There was no doubt that he, Stephan, was a better sword fighter, and the Reverend had another weakness; he was trying to protect the princess. *Looks like youth and skill win.* With that thought still fresh in his mind, the master thief screamed in pain and hit the ground as an arrow pierced his shoulder. It was quickly followed by another in his back. He dropped to the ground in shock.

The Reverend dropped his sword and called out, "Well, it's about time T. I was beginning to wonder if I was alone in this damn place."

The faithful right-hand man stepped out of the shadows of the doorway, "Sorry, boss. You just looked like you were having so much fun."

T walked into the room and joined the Reverend as he stood over Stephan. "What should we do with the Great One?"

The Reverend smiled, "Kill him, of course."

"Wait," Stephan mumbled. "I could be of use to you . . . "

The Reverend ran his sword through Stephan's heart, "I don't think so."

Then, he and T turned their attention to the fragile form on the floor. She looked like a broken porcelain doll. *I hope she's alive.* The Reverend bent down and touched her soft neck. A tiny pulse of blood answered his fingertips.

"Well, she's alive. I guess we'd better get her back home and cleaned up."

T nodded. "Boss, the old woman didn't make it."

The Reverend kept his attention focused on the princess. He didn't want T to see the guilt surfacing in his eyes. *If only I had found another way.* No. He cleared his head. Everyone is responsible for their own actions. He could not, would not, accept the blame for Flora's death. But, he would make it right.

"See to her burial. Make sure her grave is marked. Throw me a blanket and let's get the hell out of here before the troops show."

"Right," T nodded. He knew the Reverend all too well. He was the kind of man who suffered alone. He headed out the door to gather the rest of the men.

Gently, the Reverend wrapped the naked girl in the blanket and lifted her from the floor. *My sword weighs more than this waif.* As he carried her out of her prison, a single thought ran through his tortured mind. *You had better be worth it.* Somehow, he knew she was.

*   *   *

CHAPTER 3

Gray mists surrounded her head for the millionth time in the past few days. *Am I ever going to wake up peacefully again?* Jenny groaned and pulled her hands to her aching head. *I feel like I was run over by horses.* Now knowing better than to open her eyes at this point, the tired princess slowly began to reconstruct the events that brought her to this new awakening. She cringed as her mind painfully skimmed over the rape, the betrayal, Stephan, Flora, the night of torture, and her decision to sale her soul by killing Stephan. *But I didn't. So what happened?* She pushed the palms of her hands against her temples as though she could force the memories to surface. Still, the world remained gray and fuzzy.

The Reverend leaned back in his favorite chair and puffed on his favorite pipe as he watched the tiny figure suffering in his favorite bed. She had tossed and turned all-night; crying out against the world. More than once, he had restrained her to keep her from hurting herself. And now, as she started to come around, he wondered if she could make it past her memories. Well, there was only one way to find out.

"It will help if you open your eyes."

The princess flinched at the sound of the male voice. She was sick of waking up to men. She had come to realize that her life got worse each time.

"You'll forgive me if I don't agree."

The Reverend smiled at the dainty girl's attempt to sound cynical. *You need practice, my dear.*

"So, keep them closed then. But, it will make it hard to eat all the food I've had prepared for you."

Food, huh? Slowly, Jenny opened her eyes and allowed them to adjust to the room around her. She was lying in the middle of a huge bed covered with pillows and soft blankets. She was wearing a silk sleeping gown that hung on her small frame. The room was well lit by candles and torches. At the end of the bed there was a huge green armchair, and in it sat a massive figure of a man smoking a pipe. His square jaw, flowing hair, and beautiful brown eyes took Jenny by surprise. Under other circumstances she might have found him attractive . . . but those days were long gone.

Cautiously, she spoke, "Where am I now and who are you?"

The Reverend stared straight into her liquid blue eyes, "You are in an underground stronghold for the dregs of society and I am their leader; they call me the Reverend."

Jenny eyed this man for a moment. She saw scars and wrinkles that revealed years of fighting and hard living. Yet, despite his harsh appearance, she felt little fear. *Maybe I'm just beyond fear anymore.* With all that she had been through, it was very possible that the battered beauty was no longer capable of fear. She had just accepted that the worst would happen. She took a deep breath and engaged her new captor.

"And what do you want with me?"

The Reverend grinned, "I want nothing with you. In fact, I would have been happy living my life without you in it."

Confusion crossed Jenny's face, but she held her ground, "Why am I here, then?"

The Reverend put his pipe on the table beside his chair, stretched out is legs, and folded his arms behind his head, "You are here, my dear, because I made a deal with the devil."

"What are you talking about?" *Wait a minute! I'm not tied down. I could escape.*

The Reverend saw realization cross the princess' face. *Ahh, at last she sees she is free.* He decided to let her work through this on her own. He feigned ignorance and moved the conversation forward.

"I was given a chance to destroy my enemy, Stephan in return for retrieving you and bringing you to safety. Being a good business man, I accepted." *She's going to make a break for it any second.*

Glancing to her left, Jenny noticed that there was nothing between her and the bedroom door. If she bolted, she could make it. *What if the door is locked? What if he's faster than I am?* Memories of the past few days pulsed against her head. *I can't do that again.* It was worth a try. In order to try and distract him, Jenny asked another question.

"Who gave you that offer? Was it the Prince?"

The Reverend stifled the desire to laugh at the bold little girl. The past few days had given her courage. Knowing that she was trying to keep him busy, he played along.

"No. I don't deal with royalty. I . . . "

Jenny jumped from the bed and made a mad dash for the door. Her heart was racing as the sheer panic of the moment consumed her. *I'm going to make it!* The pounding of her heart echoed so loudly in her ears that she almost couldn't hear the laughter from behind her. It wasn't until she hit the door that she heard it. *Why is he laughing like that?* As she pulled at the locked door, she understood. He had her trapped and that was funny to him. Anger replaced panic. *You have no right to play with me like this!* She turned to confront her happy jailer.

As the young princess whipped around to face him, the Reverend was startled by the fire in her ice blue eyes. *Uh-oh, she looks pissed.* Now his senses came alive. She was probably about to do something very rash and stupid and he didn't want to hurt her. He sobered up and prepared to move.

Fire and ice shot from her eyes, "You have no right to torment me like this," grated across her teeth.

Oh boy, this could get complex. The massive man stood, hoping his towering frame would defuse some of her anger. By the way she squared her shoulders and glared through soulless eyes, he could tell she wasn't impressed. Thinking fast, he tried the truth.

"Okay, Princess, calm down. No need to do anything stupid," he said in a deep soothing voice.

She didn't budge. She had had enough, but he had a point. She didn't want to do anything stupid. She tried to edge her fury and let him speak as she began to contemplate her next move. Slowly, she let some words drip from her mouth.

"I'm not a princess."

The Reverend decided to take this small opening and run with it. *Why the hell am I doing this, again?* Flora's face flashed in his mind. *Damn.*

"Okay. But I don't have anything else to call you."

Her name approached the tip of her tongue, but she bit down on it. *I'm not Jenny anymore either. Who the hell am I?* She knew she could never be a princess again and her given name was given to a sweeter more innocent child. All that had been lost in the past three days. She didn't know who she was. All she had left were some painful memories and a scar on her cheek. She fought the urge to touch it and stared at the man they call the Reverend.

He watched the girl before him struggling. *So this isn't working.* He wasn't going to get a name from her so he quickly moved the conversation forward.

"Alright then, let's think this through. If I really wanted to hurt you, I could have done it by now."

Recognition flashed in her eyes, "Maybe you just want to sell me back to my former cousin and make a profit."

Very good, princess. "I told you, I don't deal with royalty."

The tone of his voice tempted her to believe him, but the pain of the recent past prevented her from trusting him.

"I guess I should believe you, then. After all, when have I ever been deceived by a man."

He felt the sharpness of the sarcasm in her words. This was getting tedious. He fought back the desire to tackle her and beat some sense into her. *That would be a brilliant way to gain her trust, genius.* But, he was stuck. This creature before him had been through too much and he had agreed to get her to safety. He sat back down, crossed his arms behind his head, and tried to look nonchalant.

"Fair enough. You don't have to believe me. But, since I have your attention I'm going to tell you a few things. One, I hate royalty and wanted nothing to do with the spoiled little princess," he held up his hands to stop the protests on her lips, "I now know that you lost your royal lineage days ago, okay. But, as the story goes, Flora approached me and . . . "

A moment of gentleness flashed across the angry girl's face, "Flora came to you? But she said I was on my own."

The softness in her voice reached out towards the Reverend's heart. She was still a hurt and confused child. "Yes, Flora came to me. She promised to deliver Stephan to me if I would only rescue you and take you to safety."

"Where is she?"

The gentle giant hesitated, "She died during the attack."

Jenny slumped to the floor and put her head in her hands. And, just when she thought she had no tears left, she started to cry. *No, no, no . . . This can't be happening.* She had just finished building the walls that cut her off from the rest of the world; she had just learned to accept that she was on her own; she had just sold her soul to solitary confinement; and, she had completely given up on kindness. She could not, would not, accept that someone had cared enough for her to die for her. The torment was too much. Once again, her world fell apart. Her emotions churned inside her stomach. She felt sick.

The Reverend's carefully shielded heart threatened to break as he watched the scene being played out in front of him. He saw the poor child's strength melt away and felt her world coming to an end. He wondered if she would break. He waited and watched. Slowly, the sobbing ended and she lifted her head. She wiped the tears from her eyes, pushed her hair back from her face, and took a deep breath.

With all the strength she had left, she spoke, "How do I know you didn't kill her?"

Well, my dear, looks like you are stronger than I thought. But, this is getting old. He leaned forward in his chair, "Because I don't murder little old ladies for fun. No matter what you think about me I am not an evil assassin. Now, you can go on and hate me and the rest of the world. I can't stop that. But, sooner or later you will have to learn to see the truth when it slaps you in the face. As for me, I just want to get you out of here and to safety like I promised Flora. Then I can get my dark existence back to normal."

Thoughts and emotions crowded her head. Nothing made any

sense anymore. She felt as though she was no longer in the room, just watching from a safe distance. *Will I ever be safe again?* Her thoughts jumped from place to place until they suddenly came to the end and the beginning. All she could see was the face of her cousin, the Prince as he threw her to the ground. She could feel the pressure of his body on hers. She could smell him. She could hear her screams echoing in the dark. Those screams changed into silent screams of her night with Stephan. Slowly, those screams turned into a death scream from the gentle Flora. Fury erupted in her soul as she took on the guilt of the old woman's death. *Why? This can't be happening again.* But it was. She was back to rock bottom and found herself trying to dig a way out. Her hatred for the man who started this all consumed her again.

Then, she heard what was being said, "Wait. What do you mean get me out of here? Where are you taking me?"

"I'm going to have you escorted to Vale in the south. I have friends there who owe me some favors. They will find a place where you will be taken in and kept safe."

Her tears were gone now, replaced by the anger she had become accustomed to feeling. She sat up straight and looked Reverend in the eyes.

"It doesn't matter where you send me, I will never be safe again. I have too many scars."

The Reverend found himself staring at the hideous thing on her cheek; the only black mark on her beauty. She saw his eyes looking intently on her face and fought the urge to cover her mark.

"Indeed you do have scars. But scars show character that was built by the healing of the wounds. In time, they become just another part of who you are."

She felt her heart break, "Who I am? I can't even tell you who I am. My scars have consumed my identity."

The Reverend felt as though he was banging his head against a brick wall. It was clear this child before him was not ready to heal.

"Be that as it may, I made a promise to get you to safety, and that is exactly what I intend to do."

Although she was now wrapped in a mental battle with her identity, the former princess knew she had to stop this. The only clear thing was that she had to take revenge on her cousin for all the horrors that had happened to her in the past few days. It was that thought, the thought of vengeance, that had helped her through the night she had endured with Stephan. It was that thought that had allowed her to forgive herself for Flora's death. And, it was that thought that gave her the strength to breathe. She would have her revenge. But, if the Reverend sent her away, she might never have the chance. She had to stay. A crazy thought crept into her head.

"I'm not leaving."

The Reverend sat up straight in his chair and gave a confused look, "Come again?"

The girl in her almost felt like smiling at the loss of composure she had caused. The fast growing woman prevented it. Slowly, she pulled herself up to her feet and drew in a deep breath.

"I mean it. I am not leaving."

Leaning forward in his chair, the majestic man tried again, "And you think you have a choice in this because . . . "

She could see this was not going to be easy. The very look on the Reverend's face told her that he truly did hate royalty. Maybe her insight was improving, for she could see that he just wanted to dump her down south and forget she existed. She was going to have to give him a reason to let her stay. *But what am I going to say?* Mustering all her courage, she looked into his piercing eyes, and knew she had nothing left but the truth. Taking a deep breath to calm her nerves, she opened her soul for the last time before sealing her feelings in stone.

"Because I owe my dear cousin at least one lifetime of pain. Because Flora died for me. Because all I am is my pain. Without my anger I am numb. I would be dead already if I didn't hate him so much. So, I'm not leaving until I find a way to repay him for all he has done to me. You don't have to help me, but I'll never let you stop me."

The Reverend watched in horror and pity as the girl spoke. Her entire frame trembled as she bit through each and every word. Even now, she was still afraid. But, as he watched, he could almost see her soul slipping away. That was what horrified him. He had been afraid that he would loose his soul in this mess; now he was certain. *There has to be a way to stop her.*

"I am quite powerful, you know. I have friends in places you don't even know exist. I would have no problem sending you away and keeping you there," he said as nonchalantly as possible.

She knew that. Quickly, she bluffed, "But you won't."

A confused grin crept across his face, "And why not."

This was it; all she had. *Here goes everything.* "Because, if you do, you will be sentencing me to die and you "don't kill old ladies for fun", remember?"

As soon as she had said it, she was sure she had stepped across the imaginary line in the sand. The Reverend's face flared with a look of anger that sent shockwaves down her spine. At that moment, she knew she was dealing with a cold-blooded killer. *I may have gone too far. Oh well. The worst thing he could do is kill me.* Her fear began to subside and she held her ground.

That last remark had been too much. She had thrown his words of comfort right back in his face; exploited a moment of weakness; destroyed a small thread of trust; and . . . and . . . *Made me look like an ass using anger and sarcasm. Dammit! Now I know I like her.* His anger faded into a warped sense of pride, as though he had taught her how to be bitter. He knew, at that instant, that he was going to let her stay, but he sure as hell wasn't going to make it easy on her.

Carefully, the Reverend began to speak, "Oh, I remember. I also know who is responsible for her death. And, that person will pay. But, you? I don't know if I have any use for a spineless royal brat."

The fury in her face made him chuckle inside. *Hit a nerve, your highness?* Three days ago, she could have had him killed for that remark . . . Today, she could almost do it herself.

"I am not spineless," she bit down on each word, "and I am not royalty."

The Reverend leaned forward and stared into her eyes, "Then what, exactly, are you, and why should I keep you around?"

She nearly faltered. His questions were merely echoes of her own that were screaming through her head. She fought every urge to use her name. *I'm nobody, dammit! All I have is my anger. All I am is my scars!* Once again, when she thought she was trapped, her desire for vengeance found a way. She mustered every ounce of her strength, stepped forward, and looked the last man she would ever trust deep in the eyes.

"I am a willing pupil for you to teach and mold, who can read and write, and has first-hand intimate knowledge of the royal palace and all its secrets."

Though her voice was strong, her hands trembled. All the cards lay face-up on the table. There was nothing left. She had no more tears and too much anger. But, she would die before she would leave and let the prince go on living a happy life. She held her breath.

The Reverend spoke slowly, thinking about each word, "That's a fascinating proposition, your former highness." *Best offer I've had since last night.* She was right. He could definitely use her knowledge. *But, do I really want to baby-sit?*

"Here is my offer. You stay, if you tell me everything, and it is reliable, and if you train as a thief. Everyone pulls their weight around here. Hell, even the mice work. You will do what I say, without question, and I, in turn, will let you stay and teach you all I know."

For a split second, Jenny's heart experienced the forgotten feeling of joy. It was quickly numbed when she realized that her happiness came only at the thought of destroying another human being. *He's not human, girl. Don't let him be.* She pulled her lower lip between her teeth and stared at her momentary savior.

"Agreed."

The Reverend smiled a beaming smile at the conflicting emotions on her face. Somewhere deep inside, the tiny person in front of him remained an eager, loving child. *I wonder if her soul can be salvaged?* His, he knew, could not. So, he stood, stretched, reached over her, and opened the mysteriously unlocked door.

"Good," he replied, as he pushed her through the door. "Find some clothes for her T," he said to his friend who was waiting outside, "she's training, now."

T grabbed her shoulder, "No problem, Boss," he said in his most nonchalant tone as he herded her forward.

"What the hell?" he muttered when she seemed out of range.

"Go with me on this," murmured the Reverend.

T knew his friend had lost his mind. *Maybe he's just bored now that he managed to kill his mortal enemy.* "You have lost your mind."

The Reverend nodded. *And my soul . . .*

T knew there was nothing to be done. He followed the pathetic looking recruit down the hallway. She walked with a silent dignity and determination. Soon, he was back in the lead, shaking his head and questioning everyone's sanity. As he went to direct the child to the training gear, he realized he had no idea what her name was.

"Hey," he said, "What is your name anyway?"

She brought her hand to her face and the scar that had consumed her identity and simply replied, "Call me Snake."

And so it began.

*   *   *

Dusk crept slowly into the town as the people finished their daily business and began to prepare for the end of the day. Women yelled last minute orders for food for dinner, children cried in exhaustion, and men filtered into the nearest taverns. All around, people let down their guard and began to relax. It was the perfect time of the day for an eager thief.

The Reverend strolled calmly down the center of the street, head held high, nodding to ladies as he passed by. Most often, consumed by their own duties, they simply ignored him. He smiled at being invisible in plain sight. *Sometimes they make it so easy.* But, it wasn't him that was out on the prowl today. Today, he was merely a supervisor, a distraction, and an easy way out for his men. Stopping to check the price of a chicken, he quickly scanned the area for his army of ghosts. He picked them out one at a time, as though running down a checklist.

T was two dealers down filling his cloak with bread from the booth and coins from pockets. He only took a couple from each, so they could not be sure they were robbed. Sam, long done with his food gathering, was investing in weapons at the city gate checkpoint. Rock was leading a group of his soldiers back toward home; each looked a little fatter under his cloak. And, then there was Snake. The Reverend scanned the tavern front where she was supposed to be picking the pockets of drunks.

Although she had learned with incredible speed, Snake was still the newest recruit and was therefore given the easy assignment. Not to mention, the Reverend was still protecting her safety. He scanned swiftly. No Snake. He looked closer this time. Nothing. *Dammit!*

This wasn't the first time she had gone against orders. *She is going to be the death of me.* Trying to look like nobody in particular, the tower of a man moved away from the poultry and started on a subtle search mission. Like a man without a care in the world, he reached down and scooped up a pebble, whistling a little tune as he went. Playfully, he tossed the pebble in the air and strode forward.

T placed a couple more coins in his bursting pouch and smiled at himself. *Damn, I'm good.* As he moved toward his next victim, his highly tuned senses picked up a faint whistle. He immediately recognized the tune. Turning, he saw the pebble being tossed into the air. *Oh, hell. She's done it again.* Quickly, the seasoned man of cunning changed courses and began to search for signs of the missing girl. This was becoming too much of a habit for the little pain in the ass, and, if she wasn't such a good thief, he'd ring her neck himself. But, now was not the time for thoughts of death; now was the time to find Snake. The task was made harder by the fact that she was so small that she simply disappeared. *And, she was trained by the best,* he thought with a smile.

Moving on instinct rather than senses, T walked toward the castle. Snake seemed to be drawn there by some inner plan. He had found her nearby, searching the windows, and sweating many a time. While he knew she had reason, he had never understood why she would risk getting so close. Her scar, after all, would give her away in a heartbeat, and now that the prince was King, her life would not be spared. T hurried his pace.

Searching the area with his eyes, he spotted a small shadow disappearing into the bushes near the side gate. *Idiot! You will be seen for sure.* He knew better than to draw attention to her by chasing after her. Instead, he signaled for the Reverend.

"Hey! Jack! Is that you, you old bastard?" he yelled in his best drunken voice. It wasn't subtle, but it blended in.

The Reverend stopped, "Byron? Why you old swindler . . . How the hell are you?"

Quickly, he made his way to his friend. While they exchanged pleasantries, T motioned to Snake's location. The Reverend gritted his teeth and motioned him forward.

"Come on over here and sit a minute," he said as he moved T to a nearby bench. "How is the wife?"

"Same old sow," muttered the drunk as they moved to solitude.

"Okay, where the hell is she?"

T kept his voice low, "She disappeared into those bushes. Looked like she was heading straight for the castle."

"Has she lost her mind?! She'll be executed if she's caught, and the bastard will probably make a kingdom wide holiday out of it. I knew she was going to be a pain in the ass, but I didn't know she was going to be stupid."

T fought back the urge to chuckle. In the three years since they had taken the former princess into the fold, she had become skilled, increasingly bitter, a royal sized pain, and the center of the Reverend's world. T wasn't sure if it was a kind of love or just a sense of responsibility that held his boss to the blonde beauty, but he was sure that the Reverend needed her. He liked her, too. It was hard not to. There was a strange mystery to her that grabbed you and sucked you into her world.

"Okay. So we've established the fact that she's an idiot . . . "

"An idiot disobeying orders," interjected the Reverend.

"So, what do we do?"

"Absolutely nothing," answered a soft voice behind them.

Both men turned to see the hooded figure of Snake standing, smugly smiling, in the bushes. Her face was cloaked from view, but they could feel her icy eyes staring at them. T stood and shook his "old buddy's" hand, uttered a drunken good-bye, and headed home. The Reverend urged him on and then returned to the figure in the bushes. Pretending to be looking for something lost on the ground, he addressed the rouge element he called Snake.

"And just what the hell do you think you are doing?"

Her voice came back sultry and calm, "Just looking."

Maintaining the calm for which he was famous, the Reverend spoke, "And if they had seen you, you would be killed. You might have jeopardized us all."

There was a long pause. But, he could hear her breathing. *She needs to work on that. If I can hear her, others can as well.*

Finally, she responded, "If you would have just gone back to base, you would not have put yourself in this spot."

The Reverend picked up a coin and gave an "ah-ha" for the benefit of those around. Putting it in his pocket, he muttered, "We never leave a man behind."

With that, he headed back to base, as he knew she would, too.

Snake closed her eyes as he walked off and took a deep breath. She was pushing him to the limit, of that she was certain. But, she couldn't allow herself to forget why she was still here. She made these trips to the castle to watch and remember. Especially now, as she was growing comfortable with the thieves, she needed to keep her hatred ablaze. So, she came, watched, and remembered and, occasionally, took more than her memories away. She reached into her pocket and patted the key she had taken off a sleeping guard. With an evil grin, she headed home.

*　　*　　*

"Coming in late again, huh?"

Snake nodded to Mikel as she slid through the entrance, "Last minute shopping."

Despite her never-ending coldness, Mikel liked her. They all did. She was kind of the adopted daughter of all these low-life scum, a reminder that they were still human. Mikel handed her a candle, took her loot, and let her enter the underground castle. In three years, she had grown a lot. He smiled to himself as she floated away.

Snake knew he was smiling as she moved down the corridor, and so she walked faster. She didn't really want more friends. Everyone she ever trusted either betrayed her or was murdered, so she fought against her nature and tried not to care about anyone. Yet, these dregs of society had taken her in, trained her, and helped her survive. At first, they had all protested. "She's a spoiled brat. She'll get us killed. I 'aint a nursemaid," echoed through the halls for months. But, she concentrated on her anger, and learned. She built up muscles she didn't know existed, learned how to handle a sword, picked up knife throwing, and learned the art of being invisible. Slowly, they came to accept her. Now, it seemed, they even liked her. The thought made her queasy. *I don't want to do that again.*

The Reverend, despite his complaints, had been the leader of her training. Every day, he and T had woken her with cold water and hard training. Even now, though she felt she was trained enough, they continued their daily torture. Snake accepted it as the Reverend's way of getting back at her for staying around. But, she had kept her end of the bargain, mostly. She trained and she gave them inside information on the palace that had paid off big more than once. (But, he never let her go with them to the palace . . . she knew why.) The only problem she had was the following orders thing. She just couldn't get that one quite right. Her own agenda was too overpowering for that. She slid the key into her shirt and entered the main chamber. One look at her "boss" told her she was in trouble, again. *Well, here we go again.*

Snake stepped into the chamber and joined the feast that was going on around her. Everyone was eating, drinking, and sharing stories of the day's adventures. The Reverend sat at the head of the table, pipe in hand, and surveyed his land. He looked as cool as ever, but Snake knew better. Something in his eyes let her know she had not been forgotten. But, he would never handle it here. That was not his style. He would wait until most were passed out for the evening. Then, she would find herself face to face with the man himself, while T waited patiently in the background. *And all of this before bedtime. Lucky me. Maybe I should try to . . .* She let that thought die. It meant being more human, and she wasn't about to try that. Not with *the* day being less than a week away. No, she'd just have to take her punishment like a man.

So, with a pulsing brain, she began to eat and wait.

The Reverend smiled a joyous smile as he watched Snake slither into the room. By the look in her eyes, he could see that she knew what was coming. *Good. She can suffer for awhile for a change.* But, he knew she really wouldn't. As time passed, her heart hardened more and more. Nothing seemed to touch that part of her that was still human anymore. And, with *the* day fast approaching, he knew she would only get worse before she got better. Something similar to compassion pulled at his heart, but he pushed it away. She was one of his troops and she had screwed up, again. She would be dealt with. Now, however, was not the time for punishment. Now, was the time for food, wine, and merriment.

So, with a pulsing heart, he continued to eat and wait.

*   *   *

CHAPTER 4

Lord Ambrose inhaled deeply as he walked through the temple gardens. This was by far his favorite place in the land. Flowers, trees, and creatures of every kind could be found here, existing in perfect harmony. This was the way it was suppose to be. This is what the fairies had trained the Lords to do. It was their job to try and keep this balance across the land. And, the gentle Lord had embraced this duty with enthusiastic hands and a loving heart. Balance had to be maintained; life had to go on, even now . . .

Lord Ambrose kneeled on the path, placed his hands in the earth, and slowly began a healing spell. It was an ancient chant designed by the fairies to spread healing energy to all living creatures the source could reach. After a few moments, he looked around the garden to see, but there was no healing, there was only sorrow. Quickly, he pulled his hands from the earth, sat down, and closed his eyes against the hurt that surrounded everyone and everything in the temple.

"Why? Why is this happening? We have tried so hard to serve faithfully."

A tender voice behind him answered his fruitless cries of desperation. "It is not us who have done anything wrong, my friend. But, we will be the ones to set it right."

Lord Ambrose looked up into the glowing eyes of Lord Earin.

"How? I don't know where to begin."

"I do."

Then, as suddenly as he had appeared, Lord Earin was gone. Ambrose felt a slight chill in the air and a sense that his fellow Lord

49

was holding something back. He shook his head to clear it. *You are getting old, Ambrose. No one has any secrets here.* He stood and followed Lord Earin to the meeting that had been called. Now, they had to decide how to save High Lord Brennen.

*   *   *

General Sabastian stood at the back of the meeting hall and tugged at his flowing red beard. His broad shoulders were set squarely against the anger he felt within and the people that surrounded him. The strong lines in his face and many scars defined him, as the war hero all knew him to be. He waited patiently for the Lords to begin; his mind set firm that he would take any course of action necessary to save his friend.

"Are they going to start this party anytime soon, or do they want to risk completely losing the trail?"

The General glanced at his right-hand man and understood his impatience. *Still, what he doesn't know . . .*

"Patience, Commander. Believe it or not, they know what they are doing."

Commander Gabriel, the most brilliant military leader since the General himself, chose not to believe it. In all his time here, he had yet to see the Lords do anything that led him to the belief that they knew what they were doing. To him, they seemed puppets being played with by a highly talented and invisible master. *Probably the same guy that stuck me here.* He pondered that thought as he gently fingered the pendant tucked inside his shirt. It was a silver dragon that ended in a claw wrapped around a crystal ball. He never took it off.

The General watched the Commander's hand fly to his shirt like an old habit. His fierce brown eyes glowed with a private pain as he played with that damned dragon around his neck. Silently, Sabastian wondered why that thing was so important, but that was a thought he kept to himself as he and his cocky Commander waited for the Lords to begin. They didn't wait long.

"You all know why we are here, so I shall get right to the point. We have to find a way to locate High Lord Brennen." It was Lord Anjalina who spoke. Her fire red hair and emerald eyes gave her a majestic look as she stood before them all. She seemed so young, yet so powerful. It was still hard for the Commander to believe that she was the second in command. *How can she know anything when she is so young?*

I know more than you will ever understand, and I'm decades older than you think.

Damn! Gabriel quickly closed his mind. *God, I hate it when they do that!* He knew with the Lords around he had to shield his thoughts better. *Never let them know more than you want.* He had been thrown off-guard, but did not stay that way for long. Instead, he plastered a "what-I'm-about-to-say-will-irritate-the-hell-out-of-you" grin on his face and asked a simple question.

"Excuse me, but what if he doesn't want to be found?"

The General threw up his hands and muttered, "Oh, shit. Here we go again."

"Commander," something painfully dangerous coated Anjalina's voice as she spoke, "there are certain things you just don't understand."

His smile never faltered, "Then enlighten me o' ancient one."

Before he ever got the chance to know whether or not he had hit a sore spot, Lord Earin jumped in between the flying insults.

"We know he wishes to be found, Commander, because he has made a brief and weak link with the rest of us."

Commander Gabriel looked into the innocent eyes of this truly young lord and wondered how he had even made it so far. Yet, he sensed something else there, something almost secretive. He waited.

"The High Lord has been taken. Someone loyal to the evil rising in the Land, that can only be the return of the Betrayer, has taken him against his will and intends to sacrifice him. We have very little time and less knowledge . . . " Lord Anjalina faltered as she tried to complete the information.

"I understand you are all suffering, but with no where to begin, there is no real way to find him," replied the Commander.

There was silence in the hall as the Lords held a mental discussion. There was no doubt that the brazen soldier was right. They had no starting place. They had very little hope, and they needed the High Lord more now than ever with the apparent return of the

Betrayer close at hand. Panic and pain filled the room. Finally, the General could take it no longer. High Lord Brennen was his oldest and dearest friend. They had walked into hell and back together, and he knew he had to do something.

"I will not sit back while the Lord High Protector of the Land is executed. There must be something else, something we are all over-looking. If you have nothing else to offer, I'm sending my men out searching and I'll be in the High Lord's chambers looking for clues."

Commander Gabriel put a restraining hand on his boss' arm. "Calm down, boss. There are other ways to handle this. We can't just send all the troops aimlessly wandering the Land in hopes of stumbling onto Lord Brennen."

"But we **must** do something!"

"Yes," came the calm voice of Lord Earin, "General, you are right. We must do something. And, I believe I know where to begin."

Complete silence engulfed the hall, even the mental conversations died. All eyes were now upon the young Lord. He took a deep breath for courage and began to speak with inward glancing eyes.

"There is a prince, one who has long proven himself loyal to the evil in the world. He is known for holding ritual sacrifices of all those who represent good. He has killed so many children . . . " He faltered, but did not fail. "He is powerful and would have all the resources required to have done this. It is even rumored that he has studied the dark magic of the Three Sisters. I believe, with all my soul, that if we begin there we will not be disappointed."

The room stood silent and wondered how Lord Earin came to have such knowledge. Question clouded everyone's eyes. But, Lord Ambrose felt the pain within the tender Lord and came to his aid.

"Tell us which prince this is, so that we may begin."

Lord Earin raised his eyes, "Prince Jordan of Bodicia."

"Bodicia, huh? All right. We shall start our search there. I will assemble a team to . . . "

" . . . No, General. You will not."

The fierce red-haired warrior turned to answer the command of the fiery Lord Anjalina. It was an epic struggle of red-haired, hot-blooded passion for just a moment.

"And why not?" demanded the General.

"General Sabastian, if we fail to find the High Lord, you are the only one who has ever encountered this threat we now face. You fought with Lord Brennen before. We will need you to fight again. There are no others to replace you."

He knew she was right, "Then let me send my men."

"No. You will need them. We must also consider that this may be an attempt to separate our forces and slow down our preparations for whatever battles we may soon be facing. The fact is we have no idea why or how the evil in the Land is growing and organizing. Without the High Lord, we might not recognize the truth before it is too late, and, without you and your men, we will not be able to defend against it."

She was really starting to get on his nerves. "Who then? Certainly not you Lords, not alone. You will be spotted, captured, and killed before you even get close enough to ask stupid questions."

She knew he had a point, but she couldn't see many other options. Quickly, she conferenced with the other Lords. The answers had to be somewhere in their thirteen minds. But, all she found were more questions and a sadness that seemed to pour from Lord Earin. She would pursue that later, they had more important problems at the moment. It felt like an eternity that they searched for answers from within, but none came. It was a small voice that brought them hope; an outside voice, the voice of Lord Brennen's young page.

He spoke with uncertainty and respect, but what he had to say captured them all.

"I-I think I know where you can find assistance."

Sensing his fear, Lord Ambrose took him gently by the hand, "It's alright, young Quain. Please tell us what you know."

The small page clasped his hands together, shut his eyes against his uncertainty, and began to speak carefully, "There is a man that High Lord Brennen has mentioned to me on several occasions in my training. He speaks of him to remind me not to over-look the true nature of a person even when their outward appearances contradict your beliefs. The man is a great leader of an underground group. He and the High Lord have some kind of bond. The High Lord has said, many times, that this is a man he would call on in time of need, and that he would come. He is a thief called the Reverend."

The room, that had sat in spellbound silence as they young voice echoed in their ears, now blazed to life. Cries of confusion, outrage, concern, and debate filled the air. Quain never looked up. He simply kept his hands folded, head down, and eyes closed against the noise.

"A thief?! Has the boy lost his mind? The High Lord needs help, not scoundrels."

"We must send trained men at once. We can't search for both this 'Reverend' and Lord Brennen at the same time."

"This whole thing is folly. We don't have any true answers. All we have are more questions. Is there no sanity?"

"That is enough!" boomed a calm voice from the back of the room. Everyone stopped at turned to stare at the Commander. *I love it when they do that. Looks like I've got their attention.* Sometimes he hated these people so much, for he knew he was trapped here to help them whether or not he ever agreed with them. Not that his other options were much better. He just couldn't understand how such "brilliant" Lords could turn into fighting children at the drop of the hat.

"You are here to assist in tactical decisions, not to . . . "

The Commander cut Anjalina off, "I'm trying to assist."

He sauntered up to the front of the room with his "I'm-about-to-be-clever" grin plastered firmly on his face. "Look, kids. This really isn't such a bad idea. Think about it. You won't let the General go, and God knows you guys can't do it alone . . . so, enter a Master thief. Here we have a person who, if loyal to the High Lord, can walk right in, under everyone's noses, and find our precious leader. All he needs is a little guidance. I think that a couple Lords and myself would have no trouble locating the Reverend and talking to him. And, should he choose not to help us out, we can just carry on ourselves." Before anyone could object, he turned to Quain, "Did the High Lord ever mention where this Reverend might be?"

Sadly, the young man shook his head. *Just great. Now what the hell am I going to say that is clever?* The Commander didn't have to say anything.

"This is not a worry. We can use a location spell to try and find this man," said Lord Earin.

"A location spell? Pardon me, but does someone have a really good reason why we didn't just try that one on the High Lord?" asked Commander Gabriel.

"We did," shot back Lord Anjalina. "We were blocked."

"Fine. Run the location spell, pick a couple of you to come with me, let the General run the preparations, and let's get this party started."

Lord Earin shook his head. Sometimes he just did not understand a word the Commander said. The terms he used and the manner of his speech was unlike any he had ever encountered, but now was not the time to try and figure out that one. Now was the time to find the High Lord before it was too late. So, he joined the others in the location spell and prayed for their souls.

CHAPTER 5

The Reverend spun quickly and looked over his shoulder for the person he knew had to be there, but there was nothing. He peered long and hard into the corridor, still nothing. Yet, he was certain someone was watching him. Years of living in the shadows had given him that ability. He carefully scanned the room, all the hairs on the back of his neck at full attention. But, there wasn't anyone there.

"You okay?"

The Reverend turned his attention back to Snake. *Oh, that's right, I'm working here.* The feeling of being watched was gone but not forgotten. There was definitely no one in the room except Snake and himself. He shook his head to clear it.

"I'm fine. Just a chill in the air, probably."

Snake looked at her boss like he was losing his mind. He had reacted like an entire army had been standing behind him, and he wanted her to believe it was a chill in the air. Not likely. Was there something he wasn't telling her. She looked at the tall, powerful, broad-shouldered rock of a man and wondered.

"Look, if there is something going on here, I'm a big girl and think you could let me in on it."

The Reverend eyed his young trainee. Actually, she was beyond that now. She had learned so much so fast. She was his most eager pupil, but he feared her motives for training. To be sure, she was beautiful and kind somewhere deep inside. But, now she was deadly, cynical, and bitter. He had long feared her heart lost forever to the darkness she had suffered in her life. He searched her ice-blue eyes and found a faint glimmer of concern. That was rare and he found he cherished it. But, would he have laughed out loud if he knew the rest of his men thought he was falling in love with her?

"I had the feeling that someone was watching me."

Snake grinned, "I was, remember? It's called training as a form of punishment."

He felt the sarcasm oozing, "Punishment? Why, whatever do you mean?"

"Look, you haven't let me out of here for three days. Are you really that pissed at me for not following orders or is there something else?"

Tread carefully here. Yes, he was punishing her, but he was also trying to protect her. Today was the yearly anniversary of her banishment and he wasn't about to take any chances. It wasn't that he had a problem with her desire for revenge, he had often thought of killing the King for what he had done to Snake, he feared her methods.

"No, nothing else. Just mad at you for being a pain in the ass."

"Sure you are."

Snake knew better. He did this every year. She knew he was trying to keep her from attempting revenge on her cousin. The very thought of him made her blood boil. It was her hatred of this evil man that had given her the strength to live, train, and even breath. For years, she had dreamt of killing him in so many different ways. Slowly and painfully. But, she had never been ready. But, now, after hearing that he was King and knowing that he felt complete joy and that his life was wonderful, she knew she was ready. She could not stand the thought of his happiness for even one second. She gritted her teeth against that thought and returned to her training.

The Reverend watched as pain and anger flashed in Snake's eyes; emotions too old and ingrained on someone so young. She had lost her youth years ago. Now, she was a seasoned thief and fighter. He watched each of her knives hit the target precisely. She threw with better accuracy than he did. *Now you're getting scary.* As chunks of wood began to fall from the target, he decided the training was over for the day, but he still had to watch her until this day was over.

"That's enough for today. Get cleaned up and meet me in my

quarters for lunch and a tactical meeting. We are going out tomorrow for the festival, and we are going to need everybody."

With that, he was gone. She sighed and picked up her gear. Holding on to all this hatred and keeping everyone at arm's length was exhausting. She didn't know how long she could carry on like this. There were brief moments where the human side of her longed for the closeness that can only come with trust. There were times when she managed to remember what love felt like. And, there were seconds when she wanted it all again. *What the hell am I doing?* She shook her head, allowing her long, blonde hair to fall in her face. No, it just was not possible. To feel all that again would mean the chance of complete hurt and betrayal all over again. That was something she could never face. The pain she had already endured was enough for a thousand lifetimes. *Well, it was a nice fantasy for a second. Back to the real world.* She took a deep breath, put up her emotional stronghold, concentrated on her anger towards the man who had taken away her life, and moved forward.

*   *   *

Commander Gabriel sat on his majestic horse and waited patiently. *Where in the hell are the Lords?* Patiently for him. He was a man of training, planning, and timing. So, much of life was simply a matter of timing. He had often wondered what could have happened if he had been a minute later or earlier. How different would his life really be? *Easy, Nitro. No need to do this right now. There will be plenty of time for nightmares, later.* Instead, he checked his gear for the thousandth time, looked at the other **empty** horses, and stared at the setting sun.

"Are we going to do this or not?" he muttered to his horse, who snorted in reply.

He turned and gave the corridor leading back into the castle one last look. Finally, he saw two Lords approaching. *Surprise, surprise.* There was no mistaking the determined strut and forward gaze of the lady Lord. Nor, could you fail to notice the burdened walk of the young Lord Earin. This was going to be harder than the cocky Commander had originally envisioned.

Lord Anjalina drew a deep breath as she focused on the strong figure before her. There was no doubt that Commander Gabriel was a powerful man and a successful leader. But, his arrogance was overpowering and she sensed that, despite his position, he didn't care much for the Lords. She mentally prepared herself for the argument that had to be coming. He wasn't about to let her just waltz into this mission. She looked at Lord Earin for support. His gaze was focused and sure, and she could sense that he, too was preparing to have a battle of wits with the Commander. It almost made her laugh that one man could hold the Lords of the Land at bay. *We are the leaders and protectors, are we not?*

She reached into her robe and squeezed the pendant that reminded her who she was. The tiny dragon. The twin to the one the Commander wore around his neck. The one thing he had kept hidden, but they knew it was there. He was Chosen and did not know it. They had debated long and hard, but in the end, High Lord Brennen had told them to wait. No, now was not the time to reveal to the Commander who he was. They would wait until they were able to locate the others. There were two more Chosen. *But only one pendant. Where shall we find the third?*

Lord Earin sensed Anjalina's uncertainty. "Is there something wrong?" he asked as they rapidly approached the waiting horses.

"I'm contemplating the mystery of the Chosen."

His next question caught her off guard, "You have the pendant with you?"

He smiled, "I have eyes. I see things. You did bring it, didn't you?"

She returned his smile. There was no need to fear Lord Earin, he was a Lord. "Yes. I have a feeling . . . "

She trailed off as they reached easy hearing distance of the Commander. Lord Earin nodded in understanding.

"Don't worry, kids. I'm really not interested in your high and mighty secrets. All I want to do is get moving. We've wasted enough time already," said Commander Gabriel.

The two Lords looked at each other in relief. Perhaps there wouldn't be a nasty exchange of words after all. They mounted their horses swiftly and prepared to depart. Before they could start in motion, the Commander made one last comment.

"Oh, and don't think I didn't notice that the Lord in charge and the secretive Lord who knows all about Prince Jordan are the ones making this trip. So, if we fail, guess who I'm gonna hold responsible?"

The twin white-robed riders sighed. Of course. There would be no denying the Commander his bitterness. With that, two very different souls each slyly clasped their hands around their pendants, said a little prayer, and rode off into destiny with a melancholy Lord close at their heels.

*   *   *

"Sorry I'm late, I couldn't find a thing to wear."

The Reverend simply nodded and pointed at a chair, "Take a seat." *You could have come naked. Whoa. Where did that come from?* He knew exactly where that came from and it scared him. As he watched Snake slide into a chair and pick up a mug of ale, he couldn't help but notice the shapely curve of her hips, the muscular tone of her legs and arms, and the shine of her freshly washed hair. *God, you take my breath away.* He forced himself to change his focus to her scar, but even that added to her beauty. It gave her character and strength. He had to stop that, now. She was not the kind of woman to fall for, or to even entertain those types of thoughts for. After all she had been through, she deserved to never be touched again. She deserved to be left emotionally isolated, too if she wanted. *Just like me.* Somehow, his conviction of his own solitude was slipping.

T reached over and patted her shoulder, "Looking good there, Slick. You been doing those arm exercises I taught you?"

Snake almost smiled, "Why do you think I couldn't find a thing to wear? It's 'cause I'm so damn muscular."

T slapped her on the back and let out a loud laugh that indicated how much he'd already had to drink. Sam and Rock joined in the laughter. The Reverend leaned back and puffed knowingly on his pipe. Snake let herself be part of the group for a moment.

"Looks like I'm behind. How many barrels do I have to consume to catch up?"

Rock picked up his empty glass and sadly turned it upside down, "Didn't they tell you? It's bring your own ale night?"

The laughter erupted again. The Reverend considered letting this childishness continue to occupy some more of the night. He had to keep Snake distracted until this day had passed. But, it was too out of character for him and there was business to attend to tonight.

"If you all don't mind, I thought we might maybe discuss tomorrow's little festival and our role in it. That is if it 'aint too much trouble."

T could feel the sarcasm flooding the air. He grinned from ear to ear. Whether the Reverend knew it or not, his friend could see right through him. He had always known there was a heart in there, but, now, he saw it beating. *Oh well. I'll play his game, if it keeps him sane.*

"I guess so, boss," T turned to his cohorts. "Sober up, boys. We got a mission to plan."

"That's just great," kidded Snake, "I'm suppose to sober up and I'm not even drunk yet."

"Well, I could beat you upside the head and it would be the same effect," said Sam.

"Or I could spin you in circles until you throw-up," suggested Rock with a grin.

"Hey, I know. Let's pour ale over her head and knock her unconscious," added T.

"I'd like to see you try it," replied Snake—sounding a little too serious.

So would I. The Reverend smiled at the thought of his prodigy kicking their asses. But, this was getting them nowhere, and he was feeling unusually edgy.

Snake studied the oddly quiet Reverend. *What? No sarcastic remark? Are you feeling okay?* She suspected the cause. He was watching her. There was no denying what this day represented. Every year, she felt the pain stronger. Every year, she wanted to act. And, every year, he had watched her every move. Sometimes she wondered why he cared. But, she knew. He was a man of his word, and he had promised Flora that he would protect her, and that was exactly what he was doing. *I almost feel sorry for what I have to do.*

Almost sorry. Her mind was made up. She had to act. She had to rekindle the anger that was keeping her alive. She had to give her life meaning by punishing the monster who had created her. She owed him a lifetime of pain. She smiled in her resolve and thought of her debt repaid.

All the others in the room caught her evil grin and shuttered as a definite chill ran down their spines.

"Okay. Playtime is up. We have to plan, now!"

With that command, an amazing thing happened. Everyone in that room became a professional and focused soldier of the underworld. The glaze over their eyes disappeared, the haze on the brain vanished, and total control returned. The Reverend cleared a spot on the table and laid down his worn map of the city. The other four leaned in and followed his plan.

"The festival has brought hundreds of people into the city. Merchants, buyers, royalty," he shot a glance at Snake. She seemed fine, so he continued, "performers, and general riff-raff."

"Yeah, like us," said Rock proudly.

The Reverend grinned, "Yeah, like us. We should have no problem blending in with the crowds. Everyone will be out tomorrow. We will work in five groups, each member being responsible for all members of his or her group."

Snake took the emphasis that was directed towards her. *Yeah, yeah. I get the point, already.* "I'll be good."

"I'm sure," said the uncertain leader. He considered holding her out of the coming days activities, but he knew he needed her so he continued. "Okay, five groups with each of us in charge of a group. I'll take my men here," he pointed to Area 1, the castle gate. "Snake, you will take your group here," he pointed to the city gates, Area 5, as far away from the castle as possible. "T, I want your gang to cover the entire region, here," he placed his hand on Areas 2 and 3, the merchant booths and local taverns. "Sam, take your group to Area 4," he indicated the location where visitors had set up their living tents for the festival. "And, Rock, your group will cover visiting performers," he looked for acknowledgment from them all.

"As always, if you see any outside competition, eliminate them.

The last thing we need is more security because of some idiot traveling thief. Watch your amounts. It will be tempting to go crazy with all the wealth out there tomorrow, don't. And, stay away from the ones that have very little or that are constantly counting. Any questions?"

"Yeah. Do we need more weapons, or do you just want my gate group to concentrate on funds?" asked Snake. She took her position very seriously for she knew that if she failed she would be gone.

The Reverend did a quick mental inventory, "No, no weapons. Besides, they are too hard to bring through the gates during the festival. We'll take any off people who manage to smuggle them through, but let's leave the ones at the checkpoint there. Anyone else?"

T grinned, "Yeah, how many barrels of ale do you want?"

Sam jumped on that one, "How many do they have?"

The Reverend laughed, "As many as you can fit in the front of your shirt. Tell them you have huge breasts."

T grabbed his crotch, "Howz this for huge?"

"A poor excuse."

The whole room erupted in laughter. Everyone but Snake. She was too wrapped up in her own plans for revenge to really notice what the juveniles were doing. She was drawing mental maps, plotting time frames, working out back-up plans, and packing her supplies in her head. This was not going to be an easy task, but it was going to be rewarding. She smiled to herself and let the others be idiots.

The Reverend, while bonding with his men, kept an ever-watchful eye on Snake. It was painfully obvious that she was somewhere else mentally. It was also obvious to his trained eye that she was planning something. He had to put a stop to that. Once a plan was conceived, there would be no stopping her. The seasoned leader decided to take action. *Well, here goes nothing.*

"We have a long, hard day ahead of us. You should all go pass out now. The crack of dawn comes early."

"The crack of dawn! Man, this sucks," said Sam as he stumbled out the door.

"Come on Rock, I'll point you in the right direction," T said.

Snake stood up to follow the others out the door, but was stopped by the Reverend shutting the door behind T's dark figure. He could almost hear T's grin through the solid oak door. Trying to maintain the calm for which he was famous, the Reverend took a deep breath.

"What's up, boss? More punishment."

He flinched at her words. *I hope not.*

"Have a seat, Snake."

She stared intently at him, trying to read his mind. *What is it that you want from me?* He hadn't been himself all night, and now . . . Had he figured out her plan? Was he planning on keeping her locked in here with him all night. That's a little too far to go for a promise. Still, she was intrigued. She sat down.

"Make it quick. The crack of dawn comes early, remember?"

He sat down next to her, "Yeah, I remember. Look, we need to talk."

Oh, boy. Here it comes. "I already told you, I'm all about following orders tomorrow. No reason to worry about me. Besides, you have me stationed as far away from my 'family' as humanly possible."

The Reverend leaned back and pulled out his pipe, "Oh, I have no doubt about that. You are a great thief and I trust you will carryout your duties with perfection tomorrow. But, it's not tomorrow that I'm worried about. It's tonight."

Fuck. She knew it. He'd figured it out. She had to think of something clever, fast. "What are you talking about?" That wasn't it.

He raised an eyebrow. "Don't play stupid. We both know what I'm talking about. Your lovely cousin, our new king, the man you have sworn to repay. I don't want you going off like an idiot and getting yourself killed by doing something stupid."

She was beginning to feel trapped. She hated that feeling. So, she got nasty. "What I do with my hatred for that man is my business. I have never dragged you into it and I don't want your advice on it."

Fire flared in his eyes, "What in the hell are you talking about?! I'm in this everyday. Since the second I let you stay, I have been dragged in this. And, every time you run off into the damn castle grounds you pull me in. So don't you get self-righteous with me."

Her voice turned to ice, "You don't have to follow me. If you just let me wander around the castle as though you didn't know me, you would have no worries."

"I told you," he said in a dangerously calm voice, "we don't leave anyone behind."

She couldn't take this anymore. She was tired of his play sympathy. She was merely a burden to him, they both knew it. He was not going to keep her from her goal. She had to get revenge. It was all she had where a heart used to be.

"Let's stop playing games, Reverend. You've done enough. You let me stay. You're debt to Flora is repaid."

Real pain flashed in his eyes as her words hit his ears. Snake's pulse skipped a beat at the sight. Was he human after all? Instead of getting angry, he stood and quietly walked over to the fireplace. For a few moments, he simply stared into the fire as though he were trying to grasp a thought long forgotten. She didn't know why, but Snake followed him. After what felt like an eternity of silence, he spoke.

"Is that what you really believe this is all about? A debt to a dead woman? Oh, you are so wrong. I repaid that debt the second I picked your crumpled form up off the floor. I could have sent you out on your own any time after that and been done. I didn't owe anymore than that. That's what I could have done. That's what I should have done. That's what I would have done . . . " he faltered.

She watched him close his eyes for strength as he stared into the fire. She had never seen this side of him, it scared her. But it scared him more.

He opened his eyes and continued, "But, there was something so powerful in your eyes when you said you were going to stay, and I have no choice but to let you. I didn't know it then, but it was your ability to let me feel my own heart again that over-powered me. You showed me something I thought I had sold with my soul. I denied it as long as I could. But, watching you grow . . . "

Snake covered her ears and called out in pain, "No! Stop! This can't be happening, not again. Don't show me any kindness . . . You just can't. I can't bear it."

He turned on her at the sound of the pain in her voice. It was that deep, soul-penetrating pain that echoed his own. He grabbed her hands and pulled them away from her ears.

"I'm so sorry. I know this is painful, but you have to hear it. If there is anything I can do to make you give up your pain and anger, I have to try. I won't risk letting you kill yourself for revenge. Not now. Not with you having given me part of my human side back. I . . . "

The stone-cold lady felt her walls cracking and their foundations shake. She didn't want another reason to live. It was too much to ask. She tried to cling to her hatred. It had been so easy when she believed that this powerful, heartless man was merely watching her a as a matter of honor. The simple thought that someone as strong as him could be brought to fear by her was destroying the world she had carefully designed for all these years. She couldn't take it, and, for the first time in three years, tears began to flow from her eyes as she pleaded with him for her sanity.

"Please, please stop. Don't say anything else. I can't stand it."

At that moment, the Reverend lost all that was left of his emotional wall. The sight of her pain was more than he could stand. He let go of everything else and let himself fall. With all the tenderness of a father holding a newborn babe, he wiped the tears from her cheeks and kissed her. It wasn't the harsh kiss born out of passion, but a gentle kiss born out of love. Her heart nearly stopped a his warm lips covered hers. For the first time in her life, she felt the kind and loving taste of a man's lips. They weren't harsh and violating. They were warm and passionate. Safe.

Pain disappeared. She melted and gave herself to an emotion she had craved for so long but given up on. She had no idea it could taste so sweet or feel so powerful. And, so, it was thus that two people without hearts, and who had sold their souls long ago, found a few moments of love. He carefully took her in his arms, carried her to his bed, and made love to her until they were both physically and emotionally drained. Then, they held each other as though it were a dream from which they would wake any second.

Suddenly, a thought crossed Snake's mind. There was something she had to know, "What's your real name?"

The Reverend was startled. For nearly fifteen years, that word had not crossed his lips. It belonged to someone who had passed away a long time ago. But, after all he had taken tonight, he could not deny Snake this.

"Alex," he whispered, and the last of him was revealed.

"Alex," she repeated. He almost liked the sound of his forgotten identity on her lips.

"Your turn," he said as he realized she had never given her name.

She struggled in silence. That was a name and identity that had been erased. She did not know if she now dared to resurrect it. *What have you got left to loose?*

"Jenny."

And now, he understood. Jenny was the name of a younger more innocent girl. It was a name that belonged to someone who had never felt pain, someone with soft hands that had never known work and kind eyes that had never seen reality. It was a name she could never have again. He knew at once that he never should have asked.

"I'm sorry," he murmured.

"It's okay. Go to sleep. The crack of dawn comes early," she said. He obeyed.

But, it was not okay. She had read his thoughts as plain as day. She had felt his pain and remembered her own. The joy she had felt in his arms tonight only made the pain worse. Her cousin had robbed her of her youth, her identity, and these feelings that she had experienced tonight. He had made it impossible for her to feel joy without pain. The flood of violations to her young body came pouring back. She could not even love without remembering hate. He had ruined her life, killed her joy, and stolen her soul. The anger flared back to life. She looked at the sleeping form of Alex. *No, we will never be Alex and Jenny. We are doomed to only steal moments of their lives. For that, as all else you have done to me, you will pay 'my king'.*

With thoughts of hatred and revenge coursing newly through her veins, Snake slipped out of bed. Quickly, she slid down the hall past the sleeping T like a shadow. She stopped only long enough to dress herself in black and collect her knives before she stole out into the darkness. The taste of love still fresh on her lips gave her anger a new source of strength, and so she sought revenge.

* * *

The market place was packed, yet completely deserted. It was an odd mixture. So many merchants, performers, and visiting buyers had set up their various booths that you couldn't move without tripping over one. *I hate these fucking things.* Yet, no one was awake, moving about. Aside from the random cat sneaking through the darkness, *or the random Snake slithering around,* the city had a dead look. It was as though someone had put all the belongings of the dead in one room to be dealt with later. It was the perfect atmosphere for revenge. Snake smiled.

Cautiously, but quickly, the experienced thief moved through the crowded streets like a shadow. She became one with walls, blended into darkness, and hid in the very stillness surrounding her. She was impossible to see if you weren't looking for her and more impossible to see if you knew where she was. Her small frame and strong resolve made her a perfect thief. Snake relished her life of invisibility; it was as though she wasn't even there. She could move around without the pressure of peering eyes, nosey mouths, and open hearts. A vision of the Reverend flashed in her mind. She froze and pushed it out. She could not afford those emotions. *I'm going to be sick.* Until that night she didn't even know those feelings were possible, so pure and kind. No, those feelings were for innocent lovers in the moonlight, not for her. She shook her head and forced those thoughts out of her mind and heart. They belonged to someone else's life.

From the safety of the shadows, she looked up at the ominous figure of the castle. The gates seemed to be jaws that would pull you in and crush you, while the windows in the towers that had once belonged to her seemed to be evil eyes trying to see right through you. She shuddered. The thought that this place had once held her childhood dreams and her bright future made her stomach turn. Her increasing anger toward the king doubled at the knowledge of what she would never be. She sucked in the pain and anger, letting it course through her veins and give her new strength. Eyes fixed ahead, she slid through the surrounding gardens and up to the back kitchen entrance.

Hunched in the shadows, she watched and waited. There would be guards. There were always guards, even when she had been a part of things. So, she waited and counted the moments that passed. Before long two guards approached the back door.

"All clear?" asked one.

"All clear," replied the second.

Then, as she had longed suspected, they relaxed.

"Are you working the festival tomorrow?"

"Yeah, right. I'm stuck back here like always. Man, I hate being one of the new guys. I get to spend my day watching cooks go in and out. The only bright spot is that daughter," he grinned an evil grin.

The second man joined in, "Oh yeah. The girl with the huge tits. I'd love to get a hold of her."

They laughed. Snake tensed. *Yeah, I'd like to get a hold of you. I've got a sword I'd like to try out.* She controlled herself and waited patiently as they droned on and on about meaningless things. *Don't they ever shut up and do their work?* One thing was certain, they were poorly trained. If she had to confront them, she could take them out easily. But, she was certain that wouldn't happen as they were about as alert as a passed out drunk. Still, she needed to get in that door. She needed them to move.

After what felt like a lifetime, they finally moved.

"Well, guess we should make another pass of the grounds," said the first one, stretching.

"Yeah," agreed the second one, picking up his sword. "See you in a few."

Slowly, they moved off in opposite directions. Snake contemplated letting them get around the building, but decided time was of the essence, so she moved. She laid herself flat on the ground and "sank" into the grass. Then, she slowed her breathing. The Reverend had told her at least a thousand times that slow kept her quiet and calm. She concentrated on the calm, waiting until she could scarcely hear her own breath. When she finally felt invisible, she crept out into the open. She pulled herself slowly across the ground, inch by painstaking inch. As she moved away from the safety of the bushes, she could hear the sighs of the guards' breaths and feel the vibration of their footsteps on the ground. Plotting their positions in her head, she concentrated on the door and moved forward.

The vibrations continued to move at a steady pace away from her and she continued at a steady pace toward the door. She was nearly there when a sudden flurry of movement from her left stopped her breathing completely. She pulled herself closer to the ground and listened. An excited guard was rushing back this way. Had he seen her? She chanced a glance. The smile on his face told her he had not. But, he was gesturing wildly at his counterpart.

"Hey! Hey, Justin. Pst! Check this out!"

He spoke in a half whisper, half yell. It was an awkward attempt to be quiet while yelling across a field. As he got closer, Snake slid a hand to the hilt of one of her knives. Her heart tried to pound loudly against her chest, but she controlled it. *This could get ugly.* He got closer; she pulled her knife out of its sheath. Then, movement from the right and the soldier on the left stopped in his tracks. He was close enough to her that she could reach out and touch his leg. But, he wasn't the problem. His attention was elsewhere. The other soldier was the problem. He would be looking or moving this way, and paying attention. She let all the air out of her lungs and pressed her body into the ground. *Don't breath. Don't sweat. Don't let your heart beat.* The Reverend's words pulsed through her brain so hard she was certain they could be heard by the outside word. She waited.

"What the hell is so damn important?" asked 'Justin' sounding annoyed.

Without looking, she could tell moron number one was grinning, "Shh. Just come on. You have got to see this."

"I'm not moving until you tell me what it is that I've "just gotta see.""

Great. My life hangs in the balance and they want to play a round of 'I know something you don't know.' Snake felt the weight of her knife still in her hand. *Well, now what?*

"I'm telling you . . . "

There was silence as he trailed off. No one moved. Then, . . .

"Fine. About half of the maids are bathing totally naked in that little pond. Tits and ass everywhere."

What an idiot!

Justin nearly stepped on her as he jumped forward. "Well, why the hell didn't you say so?"

The two dumb perverts took off in the direction of the probably not so unsuspecting maids at a run, and Snake breathed again. Her lungs ached with the pressure of pushing and keeping all air out. She gave herself a couple of minutes to let everything return to normal. She breathed, her heart started to beat at a normal pace, and a drop of sweat rolled down her face. She put her knife away. *Guess they're lucky.* Then a realization hit her like a boulder had been dropped on her skull. She'd never actually killed anyone before. She shook off the chill that ran down her spine. *Guess I'm lucky.* Her thoughts turned back to her reason for being here. *He won't be.*

With the bumbling idiots otherwise engaged, Snake moved quickly now. She ran to the door and slid into the surrounding shadows. Quickly, she pulled out the key she had taken from the guard shack three days earlier. In her rush, she nearly forgot to listen. Nearly. She paused and listened to the world inside that door. Nothing. Maybe the odd scraping of a mouse as is scurried across the floor in search of food, but nothing else. She put the key in and slipped inside.

Standing in the dark, she waited for her eyes to focus. It didn't take long. She looked around and knew instantly where she was, where he was, and how to get there. She slipped into the hallway like an old glove and made her way toward the king's chambers. The castle was exactly as she had remembered it. The same pictures hung on the walls next to the same tapestries. The same statues stood in the corners, and the same sounds echoed through the night. Yet, it was different as well. It no longer felt like a sanctuary, it was a cold and unyielding dungeon.

Then, she saw the door. Not the door to his room, but the door to hers. Her heart skipped a beat, and Snake the hardened thief became Jenny the scared little girl for a instant. Tears found their way to her eyes and blurred her vision. *Goddammit! I don't have time for this shit! I need to be able to see.* She brushed the tears back, inhaled deeply, and fought the urge to open the door and return to her past. As fast as she could move without drawing attention to herself, Snake, *That's who I am!!! I am Snake, not . . . ,* moved down the hall, leaving her bedroom and the final piece of her alternate identity far behind her. *Now my journey is complete.*

The lady of ice forced all of her attention to the other door, the one he hid behind like a coward. And, she knew that she still had one step left. *I still have to face Gregor.* Then she was there. Nothing left between her and her reason for living for the past three years except a solid oak door. She listened carefully. She heard three distinct sets of breathing. *Guards?* She listened more closely. *If they are, they're asleep, too.* She did some quick thinking. *No need for guards. Then maybe . . . female companions?* She decided to chance it. With trembling hands, but steady nerves, she opened the door and slid into the darkness.

*   *   *

It seemed like an eternity had passed and a new one had begun since the lady in black had first taken her perch on the dresser across from the soft, royal bed. Shadows moved, mice scampered, and the three figures in the bed tossed and turned. Still, Snake simply sat, bottom lip pulled between her teeth and one finger tracing her scar, and watched like a panther stalking its prey. Only, even now, she did not move. Her thoughts pulsed in her brain, threatening to drive her insane.

At first, it had all been simple enough. Quietly slip in, slit the son-of-a-bitch's throat, and return home before anyone knew what happened. But, that had changed the second she saw his miserable little face. Sleeping soundly, snug in the warmth and safety of his silk sheets with a self-satisfied grin plastered on his face, his two whores sleeping at his side. He was the perfect picture of warped and depraved happiness. Her anger had inflamed to a million times its former strength the moment she laid eyes on him. Yet, she no longer wanted to kill him. Oh, no. She wanted to wipe that smug grin off his face. She wanted him to suffer. She wanted him not to feel safe. No, she wanted him to never feel completely safe again. She wanted him to feel like she had when she was huddled under that bush three years ago crying her eyes out. That's what she really wanted. *But, what to do now?*

Two eternities had slowly come and gone, she was aware that daybreak was dangerously close, and she still hadn't reached a final decision. *I've got to get out of here before they see me.* Then, it hit her. She wanted him to know. She needed him to know what he had done to her and what he had created. With that, the Snake slid off her perch and made her move.

Quickly now, as time was gone, she knocked out the two bimbos, tied them up, and dumped them in the corner. *No need to have anyone verify his soon to be crazy story.* Next it was on to him. What was left of her heart pounded hard against her ribs in excitement. Finally. After years of dreaming, planning, and plotting she was about to get what she needed, his blood.

She slithered up to the edge of his soft and safe bed. Using the ropes hanging from the curtains, she tied his hands to the bedposts. *Now for the fun.* With cat-like agility and speed, she leapt onto his chest and put her hand over his mouth. He woke with a muffled yell.

"Shh," whispered Snake as she leaned close to his confused face, "you don't want to wake anyone."

He struggled to move, but the ropes held and she had him pinned. Watching him squirm made her smile. But that wasn't enough. He had to realize who she was and what she could do. She leaned in close.

"Don't fight so hard, you'll only hurt yourself. What's a matter? Aren't you glad to see me? Didn't you miss me?"

Snake turned her face and lightly traced her scar with her free hand. His eyes widened with complete recognition. She could feel his lips trembling under her hand. She grinned an evil grin that let him see the glare of her teeth.

"I just love family reunions, don't you?" her voice was only a whisper, but it echoed in his ears like she was yelling.

The feeling of control elated her, she took it as far as she could stand, "I'll bet you want to know why I'm here, where I've been, and what I'm going to do to you. Nod your head if you agree."

Slowly he nodded his head. She reached down and pulled one of her knives out. She put it to his throat.

"Now, I'm going to remove my hand because I can't stand the feel of your stinking breath on me, and you're not going to make a peep. Not one single squeak or I will cut your tongue out after I open up your throat. Do you understand?"

The petrified king nodded. Snake slowly pulled back her hand while applying pressure to his neck with her knife. She looked her destroyer in the eye and nearly laughed out loud. What she saw was so pathetic. *I was afraid of you?* He was nobody. Fat, old, ugly, and stupid. Fear coursed through his entire body. She would have felt sorry for him if he hadn't ruined her life. She shoved a pillowcase in his mouth.

"I just stopped by to thank you. You see, if it hadn't been for you, I would have never learned to hate or how to kill." Panic surged through his body. She did laugh. "Oh, no. Not tonight. I'm saving that. I just wanted you to know that I can kill you, whenever I want. That day will come, I promise, but not tonight. Tonight, I came to say hi. Now," she placed the tip of the knife against his skin on his face, "I need a little of your blood." She pierced the skin on his face, drew a straight line, and let the blood flow.

Muffled screams oozed out from behind his gag. "Shh," she reminded him with a smile, "if you make too much noise my hand might slip and I might have to kill you tonight. And, we wouldn't want that."

He managed to stop his whining, but the tears were flowing. *Nice try, asshole, but you've got rivers to go before I'm repaid.* She pulled the knife away and looked at the wound. An idea struck her joyful mind. She dipped her finger into the blood, leaned over is head, and wrote a message on the wall—**BOO!** Admiring her handiwork, she sat back and looked at her timid little victim. The power, the anger, the fear, the pain . . . it coursed through her veins like tainted blood. She didn't know whether to laugh or cry. She knew one thing, though, the last part of her that was a child died at that instant. She could never go back. The path was set. She could never be anyone but Snake ever again.

"Okay, this is only the beginning. I will haunt you like a ghost. When you see a shadow, I will be in it. When you think you are safe, you won't be. And, when you try to sleep, I will haunt your very dreams. You can never escape me. You made me."

Before he could even react, she was gone. One second she had been sitting on his chest with a knife to his throat, the next, she was nowhere to be found. Frantically he searched the shadows for any sign of her, his mind racing. *It's not possible. It can't be her. She has to be dead. This can't be happening to me.* But, she had the scar, and the face was the same under the anger. He knew it had to be her. His world came crashing down. He started to scream as loudly as he could through the pillowcase. *Where are those fucking guards? Someone is going to die for this!* He had a sinking feeling it might be him.

Outside the door, Snake listened to is muffled and wasted cries for help. *No one can help you now. I sold my soul and took yours to replace it.* She moved into the shadows of the hall and headed home. Tonight was over, but the game was only starting. *Good, god, what have I done?*

*   *   *

CHAPTER 6

The Reverend turned his head as yet another flash of silver caught his attention, it wasn't the good kind of silver. *Another palace guard? What the hell? There can't be any at the castle at this rate.* Since he and his hoards had hit town, he had spotted about fifty guards, *forty-nine to be precise.* And, they were looking for something, there was no mistaking that. In the pit of his stomach, he had a sinking feeling he knew what or rather *who* they were looking for. He let his gaze wander down to the main gate and the shadowy figure of Snake. *Why am I certain you have something to do with this, my dear?*

When he had woken this morning, she had been no where in sight. That had not surprised him. He knew he had crossed the line and taken more from her then she could stand to give . . . and given more than he could risk. The brief moment they had shared as their old selves had nearly killed them. But, as much as he wanted to, he could not bring himself to regret it. He shook his head. When he had found her, she was outside, suited up, ready to go, and colder than she had ever been before. There was no warmth in her eyes and an evil grin found its way to her face every now and then. He had wanted to reach out to her, but she was completely gone. That, at least, he did regret.

Now, as he searched the crowd for her and the rest of her team, he was certain that she had managed to do something last night that they may all regret. *You have made the king nervous, my dear, and I want to know how.* But, now was not the time for this. He had to concentrate on the crazy world around him and gather as much as he could before the day was out. So, he carefully bumped into a gentleman, removed some of his heavy coins, excused himself, and returned to his work. All the while, vowing to figure Snake out if it killed him.

Knowing, it would.

Snake turned toward the castle. She felt like she was being watched, but she knew who it was long before she ever looked. *Keep to your work there, Reverend.* It was obvious that he was watching her and that he was more than slightly confused by her behavior. *Give him a minute . . . he'll figure it out.* He had to know that it was too much for her to ever try to care for anyone again. The hurt and betrayal ran too deep through her blood and coursed through her heart. And, he had been kind enough not to ask, not to pry, not to pretend that things were different. Yes, he had seemed to understand that theirs was merely a moment that they could never repeat. Especially, now.

The vision of her helpless cousin pinned beneath her, terrified, danced across her mind. It sent an evil grin to her face and a shiver down her spine. She both loved and hated what she had done and who she had become last night. *So, now I really have no soul. I guess I'll just have to get over it.* One thing was certain, she had scared him to death; that was apparent by the endless parade of soldiers searching the crowd for her. *Time to get back on the job.* Snake reached down, grabbed some horse dung, smeared it on her cloak and face, to cover her scar, and motioned her team in.

Silently and with amazing skill, the attack began. People of all shapes and sizes were relieved of their wealth as they walked through the gates. And, yet, they all failed to take notice of the one woman the whole world was looking for that day. She had disguised herself in plain sight as a lowly beggar; there was no better way to insure that no one would look at her. Eyes averted, they moved forward. The rest of the team worked through the crowd as roaming dealers, buyers, common folk, and drunks. They all might as well have been invisible. With great ease, the lords and ladies of the underworld waltzed through their kingdom, taking what they pleased and smiling all the while.

All in all, the festival made for an easy workday and Snake was quite grateful for that. She was exhausted. She had barely made it back to the lair in time to suit up and be outside when the others woke. *Revenge takes a lot of energy.* She wondered how long she could keep this up. She watched her men gain weight, watched the guards swarm, and knew that the Reverend would signal an end to this soon. He was too smart to be too greedy. When they had enough, they would leave the rest to the lesser thieves. Besides, the hot sun overhead made people quick to anger and guards quick to interfere. Stifling a yawn, she snatched a few more coins and waited.

T looked around for his boss. *Come on, boss. It's getting a little too crowded around here.* He counted another three guards around the taverns. As he and his team had made their way through the gold mine, he had watched guard after guard materialize. One thing was for certain, this had to have something to do with Snake. *That damn girl is going to be the death of us all.* He was sure that she had already done in the Reverend. The tension between them this morning had been thick enough to serve for dinner. And, there was something different about Snake, something sinister. *Paranoid much, T? She's just Snake . . . I think.* No, he was certain there was something more. At this point, he just wanted to get home, drink some ale, and forget to try and figure it all out. Helping himself to yet another cask of wine, he concentrated on the newest batch of castle guards and waited.

Sam had had enough. *I swear if one more small time, nowhere, loser thief bumps into me and tries to take my loot, I'm gonna slit his throat.* It had been a long day of amateurs. In fact, he had failed to score any supplies himself. As soon as he and his team were in position, the idiots had materialized. So, he left the supply gathering to his team and spent the day disposing of the less than competition. At first, it had been fun watching the panic in their faces as they were caught and revealed or just simply knocked over the head and dragged to the nearest bush. But, now, he was hot, tired, and just plain annoyed. The fact that the place was crawling with guards was not helping either. As he watched them move through the crowd, he was certain they were looking for someone. Instincts told him that someone had to be Snake.

Sam scanned the throngs for Rock, hoping to see the signal. Quickly, he spotted his friend. It was amazing to watch him remove treasures from those around him. There he stood in plain sight and yet they never even saw him. Sam grinned. *So many idiots, so little time.*

However, Rock was merely attending to his duty and showed no signs of "retreat." Sam sighed and returned to trash duty. *Come on, Reverend, let's go home.*

"I beg your pardon, Miss," smiled the charming man as he accidentally brushed against the noble lady.

She was taken aback by his dashing manner and deep, brown eyes, "That's quite alright."

He couldn't resist playing with her, "An incredible festival isn't it."

She tried to retain her regal nature, but the blush on her checks gave her away, "Very nice, I'd say."

"Just nice, huh? Why does my lady disapprove?"

She obviously enjoyed being asked to pass judgement and did so freely, "Well, for one thing, all we have seen of the King are his hideous guards. He hasn't made an appearance and the day is half over. I dare say it is rude and borders on an affront to the nobility such as my self. You know . . . " She turned to face the striking man, but he was gone. "Oh really!" She exclaimed. "How rude!"

But, the Reverend hadn't heard any of her self-serving remarks. He was halfway across the market; it was time to go home. *The King is nowhere in sight.* She had uttered the words that he should have thought hours ago. It was a festival to celebrate his coronation and he, who loves lavish parties and the grandeur of society, was nowhere to be seen. It was so wrong it should have slapped the master thief in the face; but it hadn't because he had let himself be preoccupied with the very woman who had probably caused this situation. It was time to go home and beat some answers out of her. He hit mid-market and signaled the retreat.

Snake yawned deeply and shook her head. *Snap out of it! I've got to stay awake.* She surveyed the scene, searching for the signal. She had looked for it so often this afternoon that she almost missed it. She double-checked. Sure enough, the entire group was on the retreat, nonchalantly excusing themselves and disappearing into the hidden world beneath the streets. It was such a subtle withdrawal of people you never even knew were there in the first place, that no one took any notice of the army of darkness. Snake smiled and signaled to her team. *At last, I'll get some rest.* A glimpse of the Reverend moving through the crowd said otherwise. He shot her a look that said he knew she was behind the increase in guards and that he wanted to know why. *Ah hell. Looks like I'm not going to get that nap after all.* She shrugged. There was nothing she could do about it out here. So, she made for home.

At least she would have headed straight home, if she hadn't spotted the three figures on horseback entering the city. It was as though a light shone upon them from out of the sky and made them a little more radiant than the world around them. Snake knew better. It was merely a trick of the sunlight reflecting off their white robes and shiny gear. The two in flowing white were Lords, of that she was certain. They dressed the part, carried no weapons, and yet did not appear the least bit afraid. The redheaded lady looked almost naive, while the other one seemed so sad. The third figure must have been a guard of some sort. Although, he didn't look like he took orders. He sat high in his stead, eyes constantly scanning, and a deep, penetrating stare fixed firmly on his face. Snake couldn't resist. *What are they doing here?* Lords were not known to visit meaningless little kings like her cousin.

That would be funny right now. Snake grinned to herself, this time without the shiver. Was that a good thing? *I wonder what Lords keep in their pockets?* Now, she knew better than to think that thought, and she certainly knew better than to act on it. But, as soon as she had thought it, she almost couldn't help herself. She was drawn towards that female lord; almost compelled. As she moved through the crowd, she heard the Reverend's voice in her mind, *Never steal from the poor, the church, or a Lord.* She heard him, but she couldn't listen.

Snake was beside her horse, now. Invisible to the world. She caught the glimmer of something in the folds of the robe. It was a necklace. Swiftly, she reached in, removed it, slid it around her neck, and was on her way with sweat pouring down her face before the Lord ever even knew she had been there. Her heartbeat so hard against her chest she thought it would burst at any second. *This is stupid. That was too easy for me to be so nervous.* But that was it, it had been too easy. She shrugged off the chill that ran down her spine and headed back to base. The fun was only beginning.

The Commander glanced back behind Anjalina at the beggar

that was stumbling away. Was she walking just a little too smoothly? Had he seen her touch the Lord? He looked at Anjalina; she appeared undisturbed. *God, I'm getting paranoid. I don't even trust beggars. Still . . .* He couldn't let go of the feeling that something wasn't right.

Lord Anjalina saw the unease of the Commander. It comforted her in an odd way. As a matter of habit, she reached in to touch the pendant. It was gone. Yet, this did not concern her; it simply brought her comfort. For, she knew that only the Chosen can touch the pendants. That meant the other Chosen was nearby, waiting. Then, she realized something a little more disturbing, that also meant the next Chosen was a thief . . . and a good one. *Ah, Lord Brennen, perhaps this quest for your friend was not a mistake after all.* She shifted in the saddle and faced the gates of the city. Lord Earin took and deep breath and the three "missionaries" continued on their quest.

* * *

BANG-BANG-BANG!

Snake rolled over, face to the wall, and covered her head with her blanket.

BANG-BANG-BANG!

She put the pillow over her head.

"Open this door or I'm gonna knock it down!"

Wow! He sounds serious. Maybe I'd better get up and . . .

CRASH!

Too late.

Snake sighed deeply and sat up to face the angered Reverend. She looked at the broken door.

"You know you're just gonna have to fix that, don't you?" she said calmly.

The Reverend knew he had lost his composure, something he hadn't done in years. *Dammit! I hate it when she does that to me!* He pulled himself together and sat down on her bed as calmly as the day he'd first met her. *Better play this one nice and easy.* She suddenly had the composure of a saint.

"Oh, I've always hated that door. It never went with the place. I've just been looking for an excuse to replace it," he said as he leaned against the wall.

Snake shook the sleep from her head. Carefully, she copied the pose the Reverend had taken.

"You needed something?"

"No, I was just busy going down the hall, breaking down doors, and . . . Oh, that's right. I did need something." He leaned toward her and smiled a little smile, "If it's not too much trouble, would you mind telling me WHAT THE HELL YOU DID TO THE KING!"

The force of his voice blew her hair back. For a moment, she considered denying anything and everything. She thought of all the many clever things she could say and do to get out of this one. But, no matter what she said, he would know the truth. He would know because he was the last person on earth she had dared to trust; he would know because she had nearly dared to love him; and, he would know because he knew who she really was. She could either end this "friendship" completely by stalling and lying, or she could try a little honesty one last time. The choice was not an easy one for her.

He could see the battle in her eyes, "Well?"

Snake pulled her lip between her teeth and thought about what she had done and what she had become. Was she ready to admit it to him; was she ready to admit it to herself?

"I did what I had to do. I repaid him."

"What is that suppose to mean?" Panic grabbed at his heart. "You didn't kill him, did you?"

Snake grinned a malevolent grin, "Of course not; don't be ridiculous. That would never have been painful enough."

This should be good. "Well, then, what exactly did you do?"

Snake hesitated. This was so private for her. It was something she wanted as her own, something she did not want to share with anyone else. But, she knew that if she did not tell him, he would never let her back out on the streets. Worse than that, he would never trust her again. *And I need his trust because?* Because she did.

"That man stole my entire life. He took all I had and made me nothing but the scar on my face. For the past three years, all I have done is hate him in new and creative ways each day. I wanted to make him suffer the way I have; I wanted to make him feel terrified, helpless, and alone."

The Reverend could see all the years of anger in her eyes and hear the suffering in her words, "And did you?"

That evil smile again, "Oh yes I did. I snuck into his safe little bed, tied him up, gagged him, and let him know that I could kill him at any moment. Who knows? Maybe someday I will."

The Reverend was torn between his urge to congratulate her and throttle her with his bare hands. He somehow understood how badly she needed that—she needed to force her cousin to trade roles with her. Yet, at the same time, she had just walked up to the sleeping dragon and slapped him across the face. He took a very deep breath and played this one out slowly and carefully. He was, after all, a genius . . . just ask him.

"Do you have any idea what you have done?"

Snake coiled herself into a defensive position, but he stopped any reply.

"I'm serious, Snake. Do you have any idea what a huge mess you have created? We are talking earth shattering. The King is now terrified," she smiled, he ignored it, "and being too manly to admit that, even to himself, he will find another outlet for that emotion. And, which one do you think he will choose? My guess would be anger. Now, if our lovely little monarch is angry and looking for you, don't you think this might just increase the number of guards patrolling our pleasant town? I don't know, what do you think?"

Snake let the sarcasm hang in the air for a few moments as she carefully chose the words for her 'brilliant' reply. It took longer than she thought for a great idea to pop into her head and the sarcasm quickly mutated to tension. *Okay, girl. Now would be the time to say anything.* She held his gaze with her ice-cold eyes and thought it through. He maintained his calm pose, his brown eyes locked with hers in mock boredom. When she finally spoke, it relieved them both.

"Okay, you're right. I did wake him up and I know he will act out his fear through anger. But, I think you're missing something here. I think I've actually done the criminal element a favor."

He couldn't wait to hear her logic on this one. "A favor how? Perhaps you think I'd like to loose my head or get hanged or maybe slowly tortured?"

"Are you finished?"

"I don't know. How many methods of execution does the king have at his disposal?"

Snake lifted an eyebrow and bit down on her bitterness, "Do you want to hear this or not? Because I'm perfectly happy getting back to my nap."

The Reverend ran his large fingers through his long brown hair and nodded, "You know I do."

"Look, the King has been running around believing that his darling cousin was dead or long gone, right? Truth be told, he's more right than he knows, but that is not the point. Now, his world has been shattered because she popped up like a demon that won't die. On top of that, she told him that one day she would kill him. So, where do you suppose he will be concentrating his energies? Yes, there will be more guards looking around, but they will be looking for me! They will be so consumed with that hunt that they won't be paying attention to what the rest of you are doing."

The Reverend carefully contemplated what she had said. Snake waited patiently for a response. Though she hoped for the best, she knew that she wouldn't like whatever he would say. When he spoke, she knew she was right.

"That might be true, but that's not a chance I'm willing to take. Fortunately, we cleared enough at the festival that you're little stunt won't cripple us. However, we are going to have to bring operations down to a bare minimum for now, and you are not to leave this compound until further notice."

He stopped there, but so many other things ran through his mind. He wanted to make her talk to him and explain what had happened between them. He wanted to know if he had killed that last part of her that was human, if she hated him, if she would ever trust him, or maybe even . . . *No! That is best left unthought.* Instead, he maintained his role as leader and stood firm.

She knew that would happen. And, no matter how much it

inflamed her anger, deep down she knew he had to do it. There was no other way for him to maintain the integrity of the society. For a brief moment, she felt a twinge of guilt. But, it passed quickly. There was no room for guilt in a heart of stone; guilt implied compassion and she couldn't afford that. Still, there were other questions that remained unasked and unanswered between them. Questions that surrounded that shared human moment they had . . . *No! Some things are better left unasked.* And, so, the two who had once tried to be human, wrapped themselves up in their solitude and moved forward as though there was no other way they could go.

Snake turned her thoughts back to the problem at hand. Letting anger tint her voice, she spoke, "And just how long will that be, oh great leader?"

Her anger hurt him in new and painful ways. He fought back, "It will be as long as I make it. Now, I'm going to go back to my duties. You can go back to your nap."

With the bite of his words still hanging in the air, the Reverend stormed out into the hall,

Snake threw herself back down on the bed, and both fumed long into the night.

CHAPTER 7

Lord Earin looked out the small window of his room at the inn; a room, he had been informed, they were lucky to get at such short notice during the festival. An excuse the innkeeper had tried to use in order to charge them double. If it had not been for the Commander, they would have paid it, too. He sighed deeply and took in the world from his window. The inn was one of two on the main street of town, the other was directly across from them and served as a perfect reflection of this old, wooden, two-story building. The rest of the street was lined with taverns, food stands, a blacksmith, a couple of traders, and what seemed like hundreds of temporary booths set up for the festival. It was dusk now, and the number of people on the streets was diminishing as people returned to their homes or made their way to one of the many taverns.

Earin watched them with envy, for the burdens on their souls were so small. Tonight they would sleep without the nightmares of the end of the world, the return of the Betrayer, and the guilt. He stepped closer to the window and peered toward the castle. It was a huge, somber place, surrounded by more guards than he had ever seen in his life. The gardens were lavish to the point of extreme, fountains sprang up all around the dark fortress, and bright flags flew from the towers. Yet, it seemed so dim and depressing. A shudder ran through him. No, they would not be visiting this king.

Footsteps on the wood floor behind him turned his attention to Lord Anjalina.

"Wondering where to start?" she asked.

He shook his head, "Watching the world. It simply keeps going in spite of everything."

She nodded an understanding. "What else do they have?"

"I know. Somehow, it just doesn't seem real."

Anjalina touched him comfortingly on the shoulder, "The necklace is gone."

This, at last, shook him from his silent contemplation. He turned to face his confederate.

"Gone? How? When?"

She smiled soothingly, "It was taken without my knowledge as we entered the town."

Lord Earin felt the full weight of her words. It was no secret that only the Chosen and the Lords could take possession of the pendants. That meant that it must have been removed by one of the Chosen. But, it meant something else as well.

"A thief?"

"A thief."

A light sparked in Earin's mind, "Could it be this Reverend that we are looking for?"

Anjalina shook her head, "I don't know. He is a friend of Lord Brennen's, though and the magic that binds us together works in mysterious ways. We can only hope it is that easy."

"Easy? We are looking for an unknown thief in the middle of chaos, and you dare to use the word easy? I wonder what you think hard is."

The voice of Commander Gabriel sent both Lords reeling around to face the sturdy man. The look of shock on their faces made him smile. *Damn, I'm good.* He could sense the strain as they mentally debated how much he had heard. Truth be told, he had only heard the last couple of statements, but he wasn't about to let them know that. He smiled a big "I'm-God's-gift-to-the-universe" smile and waited for them to respond.

"Commander, we didn't realize you were back," said Anjalina calmly. "Did you have any luck?"

Nice cover, sweetheart. Hate to catch you in bed with my best friend.

"Well, that all depends on your definition of luck. If you mean, did I find the Reverend or anyone who would admit to knowing him, the answer is no. On the other hand, if you mean, are people now rushing to tell him that someone is looking for him, then the answer is yes. Hopefully, he will come looking for us. If not, we are almost certainly doomed to fail."

The Commander plopped himself down on the hard bed, which was scarcely more than a wood frame with a couple of blankets thrown on top. He stared at the Lords as they held yet another mental discussion, *I hate it when they do that*, and waited for a response. Before long, Anjalina spoke.

"I suppose we could try another location spell, but I'm afraid it would be horribly inaccurate with only the two of us," she said.

"There is also a good chance it would drain us for a long while," added Lord Earin.

All these Lords, so little real power. Tell me again why I do this job? The Commander left those thoughts unguarded just in case they wanted to probe his thoughts. The flash of fire in the feisty female lord's eyes told him they were. He grinned a satisfied grin.

"Makes no difference. We won't find him unless he wants to be found. I suggest we wait out the night. If he doesn't find us tonight, I'll try again tomorrow. If that doesn't work, then we'll resort to your limited magic."

Lord Earin ignored the word "limited" for the time, "And, what should we do in the meantime?"

"In the meantime, I suggest food, ale, and sleep."

The Commander heaved himself off the bed and headed back toward the door, stopping only to slide a brace of knives under his tunic, just in case.

"I'll be downstairs drinking some dinner if you need me."

The twin white-robed figures watched him leave.

"Such a bitter man," sighed Earin.

"Yet he is one of the Chosen," replied Anjalina as she sat on the bed.

Lord Earin turned back to the window and his haunted mind.

"Yes, and that is part of what terrifies me," he muttered as he watched the sun set behind the monstrous castle. *That is most definitely part of my fear.*

*   *   *

Snake flew down the stone corridor of the underground stronghold of thieves, nearly knocking over the torches that lit the way. She knew she needed to calm herself, but she didn't know how. It felt as though all her calm and rational thoughts had left her body when she discovered that the necklace wouldn't. Of its own volition, her hand wrapped around the cold metal dragon that hung from her neck; the necklace she had mistakenly stolen from the redheaded lady lord. She had been warned, and she had ignored that warning. Now, she was scared, a feeling she despised. And, so, she raced down the hall toward the only man she thought could help. *I don't know how I'm going to talk my way out of this one.*

It had all started simple enough. After tossing and turning for a few hours, Snake had managed a couple of hours of fitful sleep. Her nightmares shook her from slumber just after sundown and the smell of roast pig wafted in from the dining hall. Tired and hungry, she had risen and decided to take in a good meal with the others. But, something kept tugging at the back of her mind, and she suddenly remembered the necklace.

Carefully, as though it might bite her, she had pulled it from her shirt and examined the tiny dragon in fine detail. It was a silver figure with a small flame jutting from its open mouth and tiny teeth that appeared razor sharp. Its face and form were perfect until you reached the lower body. Halfway down, the reptilian form curved forward and mutated into a single claw grasping a crystal ball. So perfect was the detail, that Snake almost believed you could see things in the ball. She shuddered and tried to pull the cord over her head. That was when it began.

The necklace wouldn't budge. She pulled harder; it only felt heavier. Quickly, she pulled out a dagger and attempted to cut through the cord. Nothing. Panic had seized her at that point. *What kind of damnable magic is this?!* Had the lords placed a spell on this necklace? Could they use their magic to find her now with their stolen property? Had she gone too far this time? *What the hell is going on?!* Sensing she was trapped, she swallowed some pride and took the only path left. She went in search of the Reverend.

Snake turned the last corner at full speed, spotted T on duty outside the Reverend's door, and slowed herself to a walk. She tried to slow her breathing and calm the beating of her heart as she approached T. He smiled a greeting. For a second, Snake saw something besides friendship in that grin. *Does he know about the other night?* No, the Reverend would never betray that secret. She decided she was being paranoid due to her current situation.

"Reverend in?" she asked in mock calm.

T nodded, "Hope so. Otherwise I've been standing around like an idiot for no reason."

She tried to smile, but sensed it came out like a grimace, "I need to see him, okay?"

T felt her tension. *Guess it's about time the two of 'em talked about that night.* He had known the minute he left the room what would happen, and by their silence he knew he had been right. The strain between them since then had been too much and he was all too happy to let her talk to him now.

"Go on in. I'm sure he'll be happy to see you."

"Thanks," she said as she pushed open the door.

The room was filled with the sweet smell of his pipe and the soft glow of candles surrounding the walls. An immediate warmth came over her from the small fire that was ablaze in his fireplace. Shadows danced on the silk surface of his gigantic bed and human memories played themselves out in her mind. For a moment, as she stared at the emerald sheets and feather pillows, she felt the pure rapture of holding him inside her that night. She remembered the pleasure of being innocent one last time; he as Alex and her a Jenny. Then the pain of that life lost overwhelmed her and she thought she would cry out. Swiftly, she turned her eyes away from the past and back toward the rest of the room and her reason for being here.

The Reverend sat comfortably in one of his huge cushioned chairs near the fire, his muscular legs resting on the oak table in front of him. He seemed to be staring at nothing as he puffed on his pipe. Snake took a deep breath and made her way forward. Without waiting for an invitation, she sat down in the chair beside him.

He had caught her out of the corner of his eye as she entered the room, and the sight had sent chills racing across his body. It took all his resolve to stay seated as though she wasn't there. Desire tried to take control as he remembered the last time they had been alone together in this room. His body ached for another taste of her. He thought he would groan outloud in agony of desire as she crossed the room. But, he held on to his sanity with all his might and let her sit beside him.

"I have something to tell you, and I'm pretty sure you're not going to like it," she blurted out in an attempt to keep herself from falling into that chasm of warmth and desire. *All I am is my anger; my scar. I can't afford to feel that way again.*

The Reverend simply nodded, "What is it this time?" *God, you smell good. Maybe we could try again?* He knew the response to that thought before he even had it; certain things just weren't possible for her.

She took a deep breath, "Well, you know how when I started training you gave me a list of certain things we just don't do? And, you know one of the rules is a list of people you shouldn't steal from?" She hesitated and looked into his eyes for a hint of how he was taking things so far. He simply puffed on his pipe, trying to look disinterested.

"Go on," was all he said.

Snake knew it was best to get this over with as soon as possible, but she didn't like the thought of how angry he was going to be this time.

"It seems that this morning I kinda stole from someone on the list."

The Reverend did not like the sound of this, nor did he care for the total sense of panic that oozed from his ever-calm, ever-bitter companion. Yet, she had shaken him one too many times, and he would not allow that luxury again. Instead, he focused on the flames and urged her forward.

"Want to tell me who, or should I guess?"

Too worried to deal with his sarcasm, Snake simply said, "A Lord."

The man of ice nearly burned himself with his falling pipe as he shot out of his calmness and his chair. As he leaned over Snake's figure, he hissed out with all his fury, "You did WHAT!?"

Despite herself, the normally detached woman shivered, "I stole a necklace off a red-headed lord this morning at the front gate."

The Reverend was pacing now, arms waving in the air, "What in the hell possessed you to do something so utterly stupid and against the rules? How could you be so stupid?"

His words wounded her deeply, and her safety net of bitterness resurrected itself, "Don't you think I know it was stupid? I don't need any help with that. I can't explain it, but it was like I couldn't help myself. It was like I had no choice."

The Reverend stopped pacing and sat down in his chair. His eyes were flashing with thoughts as they ran through his brain. After an eternity, he spoke.

"What else?"

Who said anything about something else? She shrugged, "I can't take it off."

Snake watched as the color drained from the Reverend's face and flooded his burning eyes. He looked like he had been stabbed through the heart by an old ghost. She knew that look all too well. *Mirrors don't lie.* Slowly, he composed himself.

"Show me."

Gingerly, she pulled the demonic thing out of her shirt. He reached over and took it in his hands. He half expected it to burn him, but it just sat in his hand as he examined it. Somewhere from the back of his mind, he pulled up the old legend his friend had once told him. *Three sisters and three necklaces. They used them to destroy, and we used them to preserve. Now, that old lore is hidden away, and the three amulets are all that remain. We could not destroy them, so we altered them to aid us in times of need. Should that time ever come, they will find their way to three kindred spirits meant to protect us and our world; the Chosen. We can only hope that we succeeded in driving the evil from the necklaces or, in our attempt to save ourselves, we will be damned.* The Reverend turned the tiny dragon in his hand. There was no mistaking its form. This was the necklace from the long forgotten legend.

He looked with new wonder and amazement into Snake's eyes and dropped the amulet back to her chest. *Could she really be Chosen?* The thought of there being any kindred spirits for one as troubled as her sent icy chills down his spine. Yet, he had long sensed there was so much more to her . . . He shook his head in an effort to clear it and addressed her confusion.

"I know of no way to take it off, and, if it is what it appears to be, it won't be coming off."

Fire sparked in her eyes, "What the hell are you talking about? What do you mean 'if it is what it appears to be'? Look, you had better tell me what is going on before I . . . "

She never got a chance to finish. The Reverend cut her off with a whisper, "It's designed to stay on so that it won't be lost before its purpose is served." He could see confusion, anger, and pain building up inside her. *I always knew she would be the death of me.*

Gently, he leaned over and took her hands in his. "Listen very carefully to what I am about to tell you. There is a part of my past that no one here knows; one that I have kept hidden from even my own thoughts. But, it seems to have finally found me after all these years and refuses to let me go."

Snake pulled back, "You're starting to scare me, boss. I'm not up to another revelation like our last one. I'm not that strong."

He stood and faced the fire in contemplation, then said, "You have no choice. From the moment you laid your hands on that pendant, the choices were already made. You are going to have to be that strong." He paused only to see that she was listening. "In what feels like another life, I once served the Lords of the Land as a personal body guard. I was assigned to a Lord named Brennen. It was an incredible honor as he was to be the next High Lord after the passing of High Lord Beariam. For a great time he and I worked together. In time, we even became friends. He shared legends and lore with me, and I served him with all my heart and soul."

Again, he paused, as though searching for the strength to continue, "One of the legends he shared with me was that of the Three Sisters and their necklaces. The short version is these three sister witches used evil magic to try and take over and destroy the land. Each had forged a pendant for herself out of black magic and the fires of hell. They wore them as necklaces and used them to join their spirits and combine their powers. In the end, it was Lord Brennen who found a way to use those very necklaces against the sisters and banish them from the Land. But, unable to destroy them, the Lords altered them to help in times of crisis. It is said that these necklaces will now join three kindred spirits intended to come to the aid of our world and our very lives. And, they don't come off."

Snake sat silently as all she had heard sank into the black pit where her heart and soul use to be. *Evil magic . . . times of crisis . . . kindred spirits . . . don't come off . . . What the hell is this!? I can't handle this! I'm no fucking savior! I'm a walking, talking scar! I have nothing else! I can't do this! They can't make me!* The hopelessness of her situation swirled around her head until she felt like she was drowning. She began gasping for air. She shook her head from side to side. *This is not happening.* But it was, she felt as frail and defenseless as that lost little princess she had once been. It was too much. Just when she had managed a firm hold on her world, someone had changed the rules. She barely heard her own voice.

"This is not fucking fair. It's not happening."

His heart ached as the Reverend watched the torment Snake was going through. He wanted to reach out to her and comfort her, but he couldn't. There was more she had to hear, and he had to tell her. He had been contemplating the message all day. *A military commander in town with two Lords is asking all over about you,* Sam had said. *What could they possibly want with me?* he had wondered. He had nearly talked himself into ignoring it, but, now, he knew that wasn't possible. Something important was happening; as much as he hated to be a part of it, he had a feeling he had no choice. He sat back down beside Snake.

"There's more," he said as gently as possible.

She fell back with a totally defeated look in her eyes, "More? How could there be any more?"

"Apparently, those Lords you stole from came to town looking for me."

This tugged at her troubled mind. Snake reached for it as though it were the path back to sanity. "Why would they be looking for you? Do they know you?"

He shook his head, "No. I parted company with the Lords long ago. Lord Brennen was one of the youngest."

"Then how . . . "

"I have a debt to repay to Lord Brennen, perhaps he is calling it in."

The weight of that statement was painfully obvious. Snake wasn't sure she should push it, but she felt if she didn't she'd loose her grip all together. She used this to help her fight her way back from the brink.

"What kind of a debt?"

He looked like a man who had aged ten years, "I owe him my life."

Shock ran down her spine. *Your life?* Not even in her deepest, darkest imagination had she ever envisioned the Reverend needing help from anyone. He was as strong as granite and as sure as death. The thought that someone would ever have to save his life disturbed her to the very core. *How much worse is this day going to get?!*

"How is that possible?" she asked.

He shrugged at her question, but his eyes held a different story, "One day I failed and he did not."

She knew there was an endless amount more to that story, but, as much as she wanted to know, she refused to ask. It was obvious that he didn't want to share the information, and she had undying respect for private thoughts. A person with the kind of scars she had knew no other way. Not knowing how to continue without causing pain, she waited for him.

He bit down hard on the words that he had managed to say and chewed over the memories of his failure in his mind. He wasn't shocked to find the shame of so many years ago was still fresh. *How many times do I have to live this?* Still, he knew this day would have to come, he had sworn an oath to his friend and he would never fail him again. Stirring himself from his chasm of guilt, he remembered that Snake was in the room and waiting for answers. *Aah, hell!*

"Look, he saved my life, and I promised to return the favor some day," he explained, knowing that he wasn't really explaining anything.

"Did you quit after . . . I mean, why are you here now and not there?" *Great, genius. That was smooth.*

This, at least, was not his fault. "No, I didn't leave because of my debt. But, the Lords soon discovered their own powers and had little use for private guards. So, they formed a regular army to protect and serve the Land. And," here he actually smiled, "I just didn't fit into the structure. It was after that, that I left."

Snake nodded her understanding and breathed a sigh of relief that she hadn't pissed him off with her last question. Now, however, her mind raced with all the implications of what he had told her. Quickly, she pieced together the string of information until it formed a complete picture. Then, she outlined what this all meant. *Aah, hell!*

"So, let's see if I'm following this. There are Lords looking for you, carrying around a sacred pendant, and Lord Brennen is probably the High Lord by now. You owe him your life, and I'm supposed to be one of three saviors. The Lords are more than likely aware that their necklace is missing, yet they haven't come looking for it. If you ask me, it sounds like we are all in one hell of a mess."

The Reverend nodded. "Something else bothers me, too. Lord Brennen is not one of the Lords who is here."

She followed his logic, but didn't want to deal with it.

"Isn't it possible that they just don't send High Lords out to do this kind of thing?"

"Could be. But, he knows that I wouldn't trust anyone but him, and he knows how to find me. These guys, obviously, don't. I'm afraid something has happened to Lord Brennen."

As little as she knew about what was going on, Snake knew one thing for sure, if he was correct, they were screwed.

"Okay. So what do we do now?" she asked.

"I'm going to find these Lords and talk to them, and you are staying here."

Snake grinned a sly grin, "Oh, but you forget," she held the pendant dangling before him, "I am one of the Chosen. Looks like I *have* to go, too."

Protest after protest rushed through his mind. Yet, none seemed a good enough excuse. Still, he couldn't give in that easily.

"You are too great a liability right now. If I take you out there with every guard and his brother looking for you, I'll be hanging us."

She was firm, "I need to know what is happening to me, and they are the only ones who can tell me. So, even if you lock me in a dungeon, I will find a way. Wouldn't it just be safer to take me with you so that you can keep an eye on me?"

She has a point. "Suit up. We are leaving in five." *I just know I'm going to regret this.*

Snake spun on her heels and headed for the door. As much as she wanted to believe she had won some sort of battle, she had the sinking feeling she was wrong. Without knowing why, she wrapped her fingers around the demon on her neck and walked on toward the unknown.

*   *   *

The knowledge that there was someone else in the room woke the sleeping Commander with a jolt, but his years of training kept his body still. The only part of him that moved was his mind. *Okay, there is definitely someone here who is not supposed to be. How many?* He listened intently and decided it was just one, although the hair on the back of his neck stood up as though he was completely wrong. Slowly, he opened his eyes a crack and allowed them to focus in the dark.

After a very brief period, he was able to make out a single figure sitting in one of the two wooden chairs in the room. He had placed himself between the small company and the window. *Not bad. Looks like you have yourself an escape route.* But, he didn't look as though escape was his plan. He was a large man, over six feet easily, and very muscular. He sat at ease yet ready to strike at any moment. His tight, dark tunic and pants tucked into black boots revealed his identity to the Commander. Cautiously, he wrapped a hand around a dagger and then addressed the stranger.

"The Reverend, I presume."

The giant of a man was hardly surprised at the sound of Commander Gabriel's voice. In fact, he appeared to have been waiting for him to speak. *That's the problem with thieves, you can't sneak up on them.* Despite that fact, the Commander remained still.

A broad grin covered the Reverend's face, "In the flesh. You were looking for me?"

Gabe sat up quickly, keeping his eyes fixed on his target.

"Yeah, so it would seem."

"And now you have found me. Lucky you."

Gabe felt the truth behind that statement. Walking steadily, he placed himself between the slumbering Lords and the master thief. *How can they still be asleep with all this noise?* The Reverend smiled at the Commander's obvious move.

"What are your intentions?" asked Gabriel.

Oh goody, a direct one. "To find out what it is that you need so badly that you are willing to walk into the lion's den to find me."

Although he could sense no real malice coming from the Reverend, and he considered himself a fabulous judge of character, the Commander could not get the hair on the back of his neck to stand down. *I feel like I'm being watched through a microscope.* He decided to wake the Lords so he could examine the situation better.

It was all too easy to see that the Commander was uneasy. He knew he was being watched but he couldn't find the source. The Reverend suppressed a chuckle. *Damn, I'm a good teacher.* He glanced toward Snake's hidden location, and soon discovered that he couldn't see her either. *Now, that's scary.* He only hoped she was where she was supposed to be. He turned his full attention back to the military man, who was now speaking.

"I'm going to wake the Lords. They'll give you the low-down on the situation. However, I feel I should warn you that simply because High Lord Brennen has thrown your name around, does not mean I trust you. Make no mistake; if you attempt to harm these two, I will kill you."

The cocky thief became somber for one moment, "Then, my friend, that makes us even."

Resisting an urge to throw cold water on him, Gabriel shook Lord Earin.

"Get up! We have company."

As he roused from his sleep, Gabriel moved to wake Anjalina and the Reverend moved to light a fire. Gabe allowed him to do so as he welcomed the extra light to search the shadows. The Lords rose quickly and faced the stranger now confidently seated in front of the fire. Both collected their staffs and walked silently forward until they stood in the glow of the firelight. As they inspected him, the Reverend inspected them. The female had bright red hair, emerald eyes, and a look of grave responsibility and defiance on her face. The other looked old for his young age, as though he carried a special burden in his deep eyes. Both appeared solid as rock and pure. *Yep! They're Lords.*

After a long moment of mutual examination, Lord Earin finally spoke.

"Forgive our silence, I'm afraid we do not wake as crisply as the Commander. We must . . . "

"Restore the energy of your magic. Yeah, I know," interrupted the thief.

Lord Earin seemed taken aback, and the Reverend waited patiently as the Lords held a mental conversation. Finally, the female Lord continued.

"Well, then. I am Lord Anjalina, First Lord to High Lord Brennen. This is Lord Earin, and that," she pointed her staff in the direction of "Mr. Military" who was scanning every inch of the room, "is Commander Gabriel, Second in Command to General Sabastian. We welcome you and hope to call you friend."

He smiled, "And, I am the Reverend . . . King of the Thieves. Now, sit down and tell me what it is you want."

The Lords shared an uneasy glance, then Anjalina sat. Lord Earin remained standing at her side. The Reverend watched closely as both searched him for a sign of the necklace. *Oh, so you think I have it.* He suppressed the smile that begged to be shown, and leaned back into the chair. He was in no danger from these two. Although they were strong, they were in obvious need of his help and at a complete loss as to how to get it. The Commander, on the other hand, was very dangerous. But, he was busy surveying the shadows for whatever it was that was making him nervous. The Reverend knew that if he couldn't find Snake, the Commander never would.

After failing to find the pendant, Lord Anjalina spoke, "We are in time of great need, so I will be brief. We have come to find you in hopes that you remember your friend High Lord Brennen."

Her tone told the Reverend that she knew nothing of his connection with Brennen; in fact, it seemed she scarcely knew more than his name. *Okay, this is bad.*

"So he is the High Lord, now. I had a feeling," smiled the great man of mystery. "How is old Brennen anyway?"

Lord Anjalina frowned at his informal use of the High Lord's name, but did not have time to argue that point.

"We fear High Lord Brennen is in grave danger," she said.

"You fear? Don't you know?"

Lord Anjalina lowered her eyes and sighed, "No. We can only feel."

The Reverend leaned forward, "Why don't you tell me everything, from the beginning, before we are all confused."

She raised her head, "Yes that is a good idea." She sounded like a child who had been given a way out of some horrible punishment. "A few days ago, High Lord Brennen was taken from the Lord's Palace, presumably against his will. The moment we knew he was missing, we searched for him with all the magic we possess, but we were blocked. We did, however, receive a brief and weak message of distress from the High Lord, letting us know he was not gone by choice," here she shot a dangerous look towards the Commander, who ignored her.

There is something deep going on there. This was serious, very serious. "And, I come in where?"

"There is an evil rising in the Land; an evil that has been felt before," she paused as though she were uncertain how much she should reveal. Lord Earin jumped in where she left off.

"We fear the return of the Betrayer," he said with conviction, "and only the High Lord knows how to defeat him."

The Reverend hid the fear that rushed over him from head to toe. *The Betrayer?! Again!? I thought that was impossible. Oh, shit. We are in trouble.* While he reeled mentally, he asked calmly, "Where do I fit in to this?"

The two Lords looked to each other for guidance. Then, Anjalina spoke in a pleading voice, "We need you to help us find the High Lord. We can't use magic and we don't have enough men to . . . "

The Reverend interrupted, "And I do? Unless I have a place to start, this could take years. I have informants in every town throughout the Land, and I haven't heard word one about the High Lord. Whoever has him has the power to hide him."

Lord Earin stepped closer to the Master Thief, "I think I know where to start. I suspect that we will find him in Bodicia under the control of Prince Jordan."

Never did like that guy . . . far too charming. "King Jordan. He's been promoted."

The Commander had finished his search, but come up empty handed. Still, he felt as though there were eyes in the very walls. But, this discussion was getting to be too much for him. So, he called off his search and joined the "intellectuals."

"Look, I don't care if he is Lord High Executioner of the Universe, I just want to know if you are going to help us find the High Lord. 'Cause if you are, we need to get moving, and, if you're not, we need to get moving. I have a world to protect and limited resources. Right now, all I want to do is find the High Lord so we can get back to work."

The Reverend smiled. Despite the total distrust, he liked this man. Yet, if he honored his debt, it would be the end of the world as he knew it. And, if he did not, it would be the end of him. He had already given up too much of the man he was, he could not afford to let this go as well. He sighed and took the only course of action possible.

"I am a man of my word. I will find my friend Brennen if he is possible to find."

The Commander smiled. *I kinda like this guy . . . I don't trust him, but I like him.* The Lords sighed and glanced at each other. They looked as though they had something pressing on their minds. The Reverend knew what it was and opened that door for them.

"There is something else you need?"

The Lords exchanged a nervous glance, looked towards the Commander, back at the Reverend, and then gave in. Lord Anjalina spoke. "Do you have the necklace?"

You are so predictable. I could have had this conversation without you. Now for some real fun. "Not exactly."

"What do you mean?" asked Earin in a panic. "Either you have it or you don't."

"What necklace?" asked Gabriel, his heart leaping to his throat for reasons he could not understand.

The Reverend grinned, "Why, the necklace of the Chosen, my dear Commander."

The necklace of the Chosen? He had heard stories, of course, but had never paid attention. Now, as his hand itched to grab his secret pendant, he wished he had. He had a sinking feeling this was about to get interesting.

"And what, exactly, is the necklace of the Chosen?"

"Have your faithful Lords neglected to fill you in on such a fascinating aspect of the Lore of the Land. Shame on you Lords. Wouldn't he be better prepared to fight if he knew?"

The surge of panic that came from the Lords set the Reverend's devious mind into overtime, and the tension from the Commander nearly knocked him out of his seat. There was another chapter to this story that had not been told. Within seconds, it hit him. *Oh, shit! The Commander is one of the Chosen and they haven't told him.* He felt satisfaction and compassion all at once. Why hadn't they told him? This was a life-shattering thing, and they had kept it from him. That was wrong, and it was about to change.

Lord Anjalina saw the light in the Reverend's eyes, and read the only thoughts of his that she had been able to. *Either you tell him, or I will.* She attempted to stall.

"Perhaps. But, we are still waiting for an answer from you. Do you have the necklace?"

The Reverend grinned, "Like I said, not exactly."

Lord Earin couldn't stand it anymore, "If you don't have it, do you know where it is?"

"Ahh, at last we have a question that makes sense. Yes, my dear Lord, I know where it is. It's in this room right behind the other one."

At that moment Snake materialized out of thin air. The Commander whirled and brought a dagger to bear on her silent form. She smiled and looked down. He followed her gaze to the dagger she was holding on his groin. For a few seconds they held each other in a stalemate of epic proportion. Neither spoke, yet they felt no real fear or anger. Gabe searched her face for a hint of who she was. All he saw was strength and determination and a scar that marred her otherwise perfect beauty. *That has to be an interesting story.* She saw his eyes settle on her scar; she nearly laughed. It was a comfort to her that no one could get past that wall. She looked into his deep brown eyes and discovered that she felt no fear. He reminded her of another man that stood only a few feet away. It was the Reverend who ended the stand-off.

"Allow me to introduce Snake," he said with warm tone to his voice.

The two Lords stared in amazement. Then the mental words began to fly. *Can this really be the second of the Chosen?* Asked Earin. *If she has the pendant she has to be,* responded Anjalina. *Still, we have entered a dangerous area for the Commander is not going to be happy with this.*

The Commander slowly withdrew his dagger and placed a cocky grin on his face, "So, Snake, you're the one who has been giving me chills. Gee, and I hardly even know ya."

The Reverend flinched at that remark and prayed it wouldn't be poorly received by Snake. She might kill him for that. Instead she lowered her dagger and grinned.

"Can I help it if you are blind?" She turned to the Lords. "I have your necklace and I'd love to give it back but it refuses to come off, so . . ."

Lord Anjalina, who had finally regained her composure, interrupted her, "I'm afraid it won't come off until its purpose has been served, Chosen One."

Snake cringed at the title, "My name is Snake."

"So be it, Snake," replied Anjalina, "It still will remain. May I see it?"

The Commander, whose heart was pounding with the certainty that he was about to be a part of this, jumped on this one, "Yes, let's see this necklace."

Lord Earin felt the threat in the Commander's voice. He knew the man would be angry and that he could be very dangerous when he was angry. He locked minds with Anjalina and held his breath. Snake pulled the necklace from the confines of her shirt. The world crashed to a halt.

As he looked upon the all too familiar form of the dragon and crystal ball the Commander's heart sank to the pit of his stomach. *Oh my god. What the hell is going on here?* He reached into his shirt and pulled out his own pendant. Snake gasped in surprise as the Reverend's words echoed in her ears. *Kindred souls . . . save the Land . . .* Her stomach began to ache and her head started to spin. The Commander turned upon the Lords with a vengeance and the Reverend grinned from ear to ear.

The fire in the Commander's eyes caused both Lords to take a step back as they fought to maintain their composure. "I assume you have a fabulous explanation for this," he growled through clenched teeth.

Anjalina looked at Earin, he stared back blankly. He had no idea how to handle this one. He had always believed that the High Lord would be around when this revelation was made. Now there was no High Lord and he was unprepared for this battle. He returned indecision as his answer.

It had only taken a split second for Snake to figure out what had just happened. *He didn't know.* If she had been capable she would have felt pity for the strong man as his world came crashing down. As it was, her head was still reeling from her own predicament. She decided to pursue it further.

"Don't you think you had better answer his question?" she asked the Lords. "I'd love to hear how this one turns out."

Lord Anjalina recovered her composure and motioned for them all to take a seat. They stood their ground, she sighed. "Very well, I shall start at the beginning. First, it is not our decision who the Chosen are, so place that blame somewhere else. Whatever we are guilty of doing, we are blameless in that matter."

"I don't like explanations that start with disclaimers," responded the Commander. "Just tell me what this all means."

Anjalina frowned but continued, "You have heard of the sister witches. They were the three Lords who sought out dark and powerful magic against the will of the other Lords and the wisdom of the fairies. It was they who created the Betrayer and the three pendants. They used the pendants to join their souls and increase their individual powers. It was Lord Brennen who found a way to drive the Betrayer from the Land and banish the three sisters. Yet, the pendants remained. Unable to destroy them, the Lords altered them to save the Land in a time of need. They join kindred spirits of those who have the power to save the Land. They find the Chosen and they do not come off until their purpose is served."

The Commander listened patiently and let the words soak into his brain. Several questions pulsed through his brain along with visions of how to kill a dozen or so Lords. *That's not very nice, Gabe. But it sure would be fun.* "Okay. Let me get this straight. Snake and I have magic pendants that we can't get rid of, we are destined to save the Land, and there is still one more pendant floating around out there. Does that about sum it up?" *And, how did this one make it to my reality and bring me here?* He kept that question to himself, not wanting to share anymore about himself than was necessary.

"Correct," said Anjalina.

The Reverend watched the Commander carefully. He sensed there was more to the man than met the eye. There was a past, a secret, a dark side. He let it go. There was too much of that in this room. He looked at Snake as she struggled with the enormity of what had been laid upon her. Immediately he knew she was cursing the moment she had stolen the necklace. After a few moments of uncomfortable silence she spoke.

"So what you are saying is the only way to get rid of this necklace and any magic ties that come with it is to save the Land?"

Lord Earin attempted a gentle smile, "Yes."

Snake stared right through him, "And what are we suppose to save the Land from?"

"The Betrayer."

The Reverend jumped to his feet, "That's impossible. The Betrayer is gone, destroyed by Lord Brennen and company years ago."

Lord Earin hung his head, "I'm afraid he has found a way to return. Our magic tells us that he has returned to the Land, preserved by faithful followers such as King Jordan. He is weak but builds his strength with each passing day. That is why we must find the High Lord. Without him to guide us and the Chosen I feel we are doomed."

The Reverend quickly regained his composure, "Well then, I guess we had better find him."

"Not quite yet," said Commander Gabriel. "I'm still curious as to why no one bothered to tell me about my necklace and the fate that seems to be attached to it. This isn't exactly a small oversight. This is a secret and deception of epic proportion."

Everyone in the room felt the danger in the Commander's voice. Snake echoed his concern mentally as she searched for another way out of this. The last thing she needed or wanted was to be responsible for any fate but her own. *Why does my life always get complicated just when I'm getting use to reality?* Somehow it didn't make sense. There were far too many good people suffering in the world. *I guess that's why I want to be so bad. Being good causes headaches.* Lord Anjalina's voice brought her out of her contemplation.

"The decision was made by High Lord Brennen. Whatever his reasons he most assuredly had the best interest of the Land in mind when he made that decision."

"Nice to see we rank so high as the Chosen," mumbled Snake.

Gabe could have laughed. *I kinda like that one.* "Well we better get moving then."

"That's it?" asked Earin.

The Commander smiled a chilly smile, "Of course. I need to find the High Lord before someone kills him so that I can beat the ever-lovin' crap out of him for this latest gift."

The Reverend's hands itched to strike the Commander. *Not while I'm around.* Although he had to admit that was a pretty lousy thing to do to a person. But, it couldn't be changed now. All that was left to do was move forward, find Brennen, and keep Snake from stepping over the last line in her sanity. *By the look on her face I can see that's not too far away.*

Snake started to feel trapped; she hated that feeling. There appeared to be only two ways out of this one. She could ignore the necklace and go about her life as though this didn't exist or she could search for this Brennen guy and save the world. Neither plan was doing much for her disposition.

The Reverend turned to the Lords, "I will return in two hours, be ready to leave."

Oh yeah, there is that. If he was going, she knew she would too. He was the closest thing she had to a family, a friend, or even a person she could trust. She would not be left behind. "You mean we, of course."

It wasn't a question. "Of course," answered the Reverend.

The Commander answered for the Lords and they didn't have the courage to challenge him. "We will be ready."

With that, the thieves were gone and history was about to be made.

CHAPTER 8

"You are going to do what?!" yelled T at the top of his lungs.

The Reverend held up his hands, "Whoa, calm down would you?"

"No I will not calm down. I have stood behind you on a lot of crazy things, but this is over the hill and around the bend." T looked at Snake, "Talk some sense into him."

Snake shrugged, "I'm afraid I can't help you on this one . . . I'm going with him."

T threw his arms into the air, "That's just great. The boss has lost his mind and taken the prodigy child with him. Can I at least ask why?"

The sarcasm in the air was downright painful, but there were better things to do than play verbal war with T. Right now the Reverend needed him on his side.

"Look, years ago this guy did me a favor and now it's being called in. It's an honor thing. I have to go," said the Reverend.

T sighed. There was no arguing against that with the Reverend on these matters. But Snake? "Okay, but why take Snake?"

Snake shot a split-second pleading glance toward the Reverend; it wasn't needed. He was not about to add to her burden. "So she doesn't get into trouble while I'm gone. You'll have enough to worry about trying to keep this place running efficiently."

The mere fact that Snake didn't look like she was going to kill the man told T that there was a lot more to this story than he was being told. The chill in her expression told him he wasn't going to be let in on it any time soon. So, as he did so often when Snake was involved, he let it go and turned his full attention to the Reverend.

"So while you two go play hero I get to run this place, lucky me. What should I tell the men?"

The Reverend smiled, "The truth, of course. But, T . . . "

T didn't need directions for where the Reverend was heading, "Don't worry, no one in the world will know you are gone. It pays to keep your name attached to what is happening. When are you coming back?"

Fuck if I know. "When I'm done."

T shrugged, "I guess there's nothing else, then. Except, don't get killed or anything stupid like that, boss."

The Reverend grinned, "You don't get off that easy."

T turned to Snake, "I don't know why you want to be all wrapped up in this crap, but don't go dying either, okay?"

Snake had a sudden flash of memory of the time she had actually prayed for death. That time had long since faded into oblivion. All she wanted now was to be in control of her own life. For that to happen she had to go on this quest and she had to live. She set her jaw and stared intently at T who was watching the battle raging in her eyes.

"I have no intention of dying. I've just got a few loose ends I've gotta handle, then you'll have my undivided attention."

T smiled, "Great. Just what I need, you with nothing else to do but drive me insane."

The Reverend surveyed the chamber. Everything was ready and time was running out for him and Snake. There would be no delays and no reprieves.

"Time to go," he said.

Snake shouldered her pack and another burden she didn't want, "Yeah, let's get this party started quickly."

T felt the weight of the world all around him. *Damn this sucks.* "Hurry back."

They looked at each other one last time with unspoken messages on their minds and then they were gone and T was alone. He let it bother him for about ten seconds before he had, had enough. Shaking his head he said, "Time to go inform the troops and keep this boat floating."

*   *   *

The Commander slid into his saddle. Two hours had nearly passed since the Reverend and Snake had left and since the weight of the world had been truly dumped on his shoulders. *Well, technically some of that weight is on Snake's shoulders, too.* As he thought of Snake, he wondered for the millionth time if these damn necklaces weren't broken. He knew he wasn't exactly the savior type and he sensed that Snake had issues of her own. He slid his hand around his pendant and held on for dear life. Any way he looked at it, things were about to get interesting. Still he couldn't help but wonder how this one ended up with him and where the third one had got to. *Probably some poor sap back at the castle who the Lords haven't informed yet. Where are those two?*

As if in answer to his unspoken question the two Lords emerged from the inn packed and ready to go but nervous as a graveyard shift worker at a convenience store. Silently they mounted their horses beside the Commander and looked around for the newest members of the group. They did not wait long.

"Ready whenever you are," said the Reverend's voice from behind them.

The two Lords nearly fell off their horses the Commander stifled a chuckle and Snake let a brief grin of amusement cross her face. The Reverend merely sat calm, composed, and cocky upon the stead he had recently "acquired" for this trip. Anjalina was the first to regain her composure.

"Nice to see you are a man of your word. We are ready to depart as well."

"Good," replied the Reverend," now follow me the back way." Snake was a very wanted woman and though she wore a hood that covered her face, she would not pass the tight scrutiny at the front gate. Fortunately, the Reverend was aware of a secret way out of the city. *If they haven't sealed it to prevent people from sneaking out.*

"Why the back way?" asked Earin, shifting uneasily on his horse's back.

"For the entertainment value." The confusion on the Lord's face prompted the Reverend to expand, just a little. "Because we are low life scum and someone might recognize that fact and retain us. We wouldn't want any unnecessary delays now would we?"

Earin shook his head. He had an odd sense that there was more to it than that, but he knew he would never get the answer he wanted. It appeared that the best way to handle it was to let the Reverend take the lead from here. *I wonder how much the Commander likes having his toes stepped on?* He looked at Snake and sensed a tremendous amount of hatred and something close to desperation from her. Perhaps she held the answers. Now he was certain he would never know the truth. He sighed and motioned for the Reverend to lead them on their way.

The Commander stepped in, "Okay. You lead and I'll bring up the rear until we are out of the city. Do you know a quick and easy way to Bodicia, or should we follow the map?"

The Reverend eyed the Commander carefully. This was a cat and mouse game that would have to be played very carefully. Both men were use to leading and neither would relinquish control unless absolutely necessary. The Reverend shrugged.

"I know the way, but no better than the average traveler."

"I know a path," piped in Earin. When all eyes focused on him he wished he hadn't said anything, but time was of the essence.

The Commander sensed, yet again, that there was a lot more to Lord Earin than this Lord gig. He let that go and simply nodded. "Good. When we get out of town, you lead and we'll follow . . . mostly."

The Reverend took the lead and started in motion, Snake close at his heels. *She doesn't say much, does she?* thought Gabe. The two Lords rode side by side behind the thieves and the Commander brought up the rear. Soon the rag-tag band was on its way into history.

*   *   *

They had been riding for half a day with hardly a word among them. Each member of the party seemed to be immersed in their own personal thoughts of what might await them ahead. Snake was comfortable in the uneasy silence. When those around her were uncomfortable she felt an odd sense of control in the situation. She surveyed the group. The Reverend appeared completely disinterested in the world around him as he followed the path marked out by Lord Earin. Snake knew better. His sharp senses were picking out details no one else would notice and he could come to life in less than a split second should danger arise. She turned her attention to the Lords.

Lord Earin had an uneasy manner. He looked as though he was constantly doing battle with a desire to bolt and run, yet he seemed totally dedicated to his position as a Lord. He was definitely a haunted soul; she knew that look best of all. Lord Anjalina, on the other hand, was the firm figure of strength and unwavering determination. She had a purpose and an almost desperate need to find High Lord Brennen. Then there was her fellow Chosen.

Snake turned her attention to the Commander only to find him studying her as well. *Keep trying. You will never figure me out.* His attention didn't bother her; she was use to prying eyes. She knew that he was looking for clues to her identity just as she was looking for a hint of who he was. His mannerisms and arrogant air suggested that he was the younger more immature version of the Reverend. *You still need to grow up, little boy.* As she stared at his eyes she sensed a hidden past and wondered, yet again, if these damn necklaces weren't broken and where the third one was.

As though he were reading her mind, the Commander turned his gaze to the Lords and asked, "So, where is necklace number three?"

Lord Earin seemed to jump at the chance to break the long, uncomfortable silence, "We are unsure but believe it to be with the third and final Chosen One."

The Commander did not seem to like that response. He looked like a man who needed more; he seemed to be searching for something. "That's not much of an answer. You might as well have said it was dancing in oblivion."

Lord Earin shrugged, "It is the only answer I have to give. We must trust that the necklace will find its way to the proper soul in time."

For the first time in nearly a day Snake spoke, "What makes you so sure these things will find the right people? Isn't it possible that we are stuck with them because we are the fools who picked them up and put them on?"

Lord Anjalina spoke, "Only the Chosen and the Lords can handle the pendants and only the Chosen can put them on. Since you wear them you are the Chosen. It is not our place to question the choices made by the magic. We are simply the protectors of that magic."

So much for that avenue . . . "Okay, let's assume they are working properly. How did we end up with them and what happened to number three?" asked the Commander.

Lord Earin sighed, "Perhaps it would be best to start at the beginning."

"There's a concept," muttered Commander Gabriel.

"Yes," piped in the Reverend, "as long as we are to be a part of this plan why not fill us in on all the details."

After some consideration Lord Earin began his tale. "After the banishment of the Betrayer and the altering of the pendants they were stored within the castle of the Lords in the main library. There they remained safe and undisturbed as no one who visited the castle had the ability or desire to take them from their resting place. And so many years passed. But, as I have said, the evil that was the Betrayer would not be so easily destroyed. Those loyal to his power began to grow in power and spread throughout the Land. Soon, many began to resurrect his dark magic. One such person was the wizard Mengle.

Mengle was a powerful court wizard, interested only in increasing his own power. At first, he was neither good nor evil; he was simply ambitious and curious. He wanted to know more and more magic and the dark magic offered a swift path to knowledge. Unfortunately, dark magic always consumes its users in the end and Mengle soon found himself a slave to the magic and the dark powers beyond. It was only a matter of time before he became a servant to the returning figure of the Betrayer. He became the twisted old man known as Mongrel."

The Commander nodded, "Yes, I have heard of Mongrel. He is a very powerful wizard indeed. If he is working to return the Betrayer to power we need to pick up the pace."

The Reverend grew impatient, "This is all very fascinating, but what does it have to do with the pendants of the Chosen?"

"I am coming to that," replied Earin. "As I have said, Mongrel grew very powerful with the dark magic, but he was also a slave to the wishes of the Betrayer. The Betrayer knows as well as the Lords that the fate of the Land is tied to the pendants and the Chosen who will bare them.

In his weakened state he knew he would never be able to gain possession of them, but he thought that Mongrel could. So, he gave Mongrel the necessary magical knowledge to take possession of the pendants and return them to him within the depths of his fortress and he continued to rebuild his strength.

One night, about five years ago, Mongrel snuck into the library and began his spells. But, he was careless and we Lords sensed his presence. We came upon him just as he was removing the first of the pendants. He fled, taking the pendant with him. At that moment High Lord Brennen realized the pendants were no longer safe. Having greater knowledge than the rest of us, he performed a spell designed to connect the pendants with the Chosen immediately. One disappeared and was not seen again until the arrival of you, Commander. The other would go only to the hand of Lord Anjalina, however she could not wear it. Thus, it was decided that she was to keep it with her until such time as it could find its way to the Chosen. That is the one you wear now, Snake. Since these two made it to the Chosen we can only surmise that the last pendant will find its way to the third and final Chosen."

"That's a hell of a leap of faith even for a Lord, don't you think?" asked the Commander.

"Perhaps. But it is all we have."

The Reverend searched his memory, "Have you guys tried a summoning spell?"

Lord Earin nodded, "Up to this point all attempts to summon the third Chosen have failed."

Snake didn't like the sound of that, "What does that mean?"

Earin looked helpless and so Lord Anjalina's voice came to his rescue, "It means that the Chosen is not yet in possession of the pendant because the spell is designed to bring them both when they are together. It is the same spell that brought the Commander and his pendant to us many years ago."

Gabriel felt his world shake and crumble yet again, but he said nothing. *They called me? Of course you moron. How else were you going to get here? It's not like there is a bus or anything. Great, now I'm yelling at myself. This is clever, now I'm sure the necklaces are broken.*

"So the last person doesn't have theirs yet. And what if they never do get it? What if this Betrayer guy still has it?" asked Snake.

Lord Anjalina shrugged, "It matters little. If he has it there is nothing we can do to change that. We must believe that the connection spell worked for the last pendant as it has worked for the first two and that the Chosen will soon be in possession of it."

Such a warm and cheerful person. She almost makes me look friendly . . . almost. "I'm afraid I'm going to have to agree with the Commander on this one, that is a hell of a leap of faith."

The next comment nearly knocked Snake off her stead, not because of the content but because of its source.

"Sometimes faith is all we have," said the Reverend. Seeing the shock register on Snake's face he added, "Besides, the Lords are correct. It doesn't matter right now, nor does it change the path we must take."

Snake simply nodded and tried to digest the slight change in the Reverend. She was certain the change had to do with the Lords, especially Lord Brennen. There was a lot to the Reverend's past that she did not understand. She shrugged. *Keep it. Your secrets are yours to live with. I have enough of my own.*

The familiar yet uncomfortable silence was descending upon their shoulders again. Earin searched his mind for something to say. He was nearly mad with seclusion and silence. He felt as though he would go crazy if once again left alone to filter through his own thoughts and worries. Rather than risk madness, he chose to risk injury in order to keep some sort of a conversation going.

"And what of you, Snake? I would be most interested in knowing something of our newest Chosen One," said Earin.

Me too, thought the Commander, although he was wise enough not to ask. The Reverend shot a warning glance in the direction of the Lord. He missed it but Lord Anjalina was not so dense.

A sly look crossed her determined face, "Yes, it would be best if we knew something of you background."

Snake's heart tried to beat its way out of her chest, her grip tightened on the reins, and she stared intently into the Lord's eyes. At that moment Lord Earin realized he had made a mistake but it was too late now. Snake grated out a response.

"I am Snake and I am a fabulous thief who works with the Reverend."

"Yes, yes. Of that we are aware. But what were you before? You haven't always been a thief have you?" Earin pried.

Before I was a sweet, naive, weak, crying little girl. That person is dead. All I am is Snake. I will kill you before I let you make me claim an identity that is not me. Snake held her thoughts inside. Slowly she said, "There is nothing else. I have always been Snake. Nothing exists before."

"What about that scar?" asked the now thoroughly annoying Lord.

Here the Commander put a restraining hand on Lord Earin, "Let it go," he whispered.

The Lord tried to pull his arm away, but the Commander would not let him. He turned to Anjalina for guidance. She smiled.

"We are simply trying to gather some information on those who would join and aid us," responded Anjalina.

Snake's ice blue eyes flared with an old fury, "Let's get one thing straight, my life and my past are my business. Pry as you might, you will never get that information. I joined you because I want to get this damn necklace off and to watch the Reverend's back. I'm not in this for you or your ideals. As long as the Reverend needs me I will be here and loyal. That's all you need to know. As for my scar . . . it is me."

The Reverend watched Snake's inner walls fortify themselves with old anger resurrected. He saw the pain in her eyes. He felt the threat of her fury. And, he felt his heart break once again at the sight of the human side of her buried alive. It took all his strength not to strangle Lord Earin, but he saw the Commander had that matter in hand. He looked to Lord Anjalina and saw her curiosity welling up and ready to overflow from her lips. He jumped to her rescue.

"I recommend that you not ask any more questions Lord Anjalina. My friend has a low tolerance for annoying people."

Lord Anjalina turned to face the powerful figure of the Reverend, "We have a right to know about those we trust."

The Reverend shook his head, "That is where you are so very wrong. Trust comes in the form of accepting on face value what you don't completely understand. It's a lot like faith. We take it on faith that this Chosen One thing is what you say and you take it on faith that Snake is as she says, or else we can call this whole party off."

He's got a point. "Fine. We shall trust that you and Snake will aid us in recovering High Lord Brennen and you shall trust that our magic is right."

The Reverend smiled, "Fair enough."

The Commander released Lord Earin's arm. *Nothing hurt but his pride. I hope Snake doesn't kill him in his sleep.* The Commander turned to say something to Snake and realized she was gone. Brief panic surged through him.

"Uh, I hate to bring this up but Snake seems to have disappeared."

The Reverend held up his hands to ward off the Lords' cries of panic, "Don't worry. She has just gone ahead to scout. It's routine. She'll be back." *Fuck! Where the hell has she gone now!?* He feigned calmness as his heart pounded. *I didn't even see her leave.* He suspected that she had snuck off to collect herself. He prayed she'd return, and he knew that she would never be found until she wanted to. *This sucks.*

The Commander searched the surrounding trees for a sign of Snake. Nowhere, but her horse remained. He had no choice but to accept what the Reverend had to say. Still, his instincts told him something was very definitely rotten in Denmark.

"Well, let's get moving. I'm sure Snake will catch up to us if we stay on the same path," said the Commander. The rest of the group nodded and slowly they continued on their mission.

∗   ∗   ∗

The Reverend was going to be pissed, she knew that, but she really had no choice. Snake needed time to regroup and reestablish her walls. There was so much about her past that had to be repressed, so many painful memories, and so many pleasant ones, too. Those were the ones that killed her. All the happy times that had been taken from her, all the joy that had been erased, and all the comforts she would never feel again. Those were the memories that threatened to destroy her sanity. They just didn't fit in her new reality. *Get a grip. There is a lot to be said for my new life.*

That was true. She was now strong, self-sufficient, talented, and in control . . . mostly. If she had, had even half her strengths *then*, she would have never ended up a victim. *But, that's the tradeoff, isn't it? Strength and knowledge for innocence.* Snake pulled her bottom lip between her teeth and leaned back against the trunk of the tree she had perched herself in. She was going to have to get over this. She was out of her domain, now. There would be questions, stares, and prying curiosity. She was going to have to deal with real people, not her fellow thieves with secrets of their own to protect. The safety of those who refuse to pry would soon be replaced with those who have no respect for private thoughts that haunt us. Snake sighed. *I guess I get to grow up again.*

She jumped from the tree and landed silently on the ground, walls and wisdom intact. *Let them ask . . . I don't have to answer.* With that she decided to scout on ahead so that the Reverend would not be wrong.

*   *   *

Mongrel closed his eyes and let the darkness surround him; it was calm and soothing. In the darkness there was no struggle for power, no pain of ineptness, and no control by the Betrayer. Yes, the high prince of darkness was alive and nearly well. It was only a matter of time before all his strength was regained and he would once again seek dominance of the Land. At first, that thought had mattered little to the ambitious magician. All he had wanted was power and knowledge of his own. Now, he had it, but there was a price to pay. For his powers that now consumed him he had given his soul and his freedom over to the control of the dark lord. He sighed and opened his eyes. He missed his freedom.

"Well?" questioned a misty voice out of the shadows.

Sweat poured into the wizard's eyes as he concentrated on the pendant before him. "I have located another pendant. It has been removed from the safety of the castle. A Lord must have taken it in search of the next Chosen."

"Where is it?" demanded the shadow's voice.

Mongrel inhaled deeply, "I last felt its presence in the town of Valedon just to the south of Bodicia."

"And where is it now?"

Mongrel felt the very real danger in that question but had nothing to dispel it with. "I do not know. I have lost its connection."

Silence. Long and painful silence was the response. Both he and the Betrayer knew that if the Chosen One had taken possession of the pendant they would no longer be able to locate it. That was one of the special properties of the pendant, it prevented the wearer from detection. It was also possible, however, that the Lords carrying it were merely invoking a protection spell. It was a chance that would have to be taken. The Betrayer needed at least one more pendant to keep the circle from becoming complete. If the other two were placed, he would have no choice but to find the third Chosen, give up his pendant, and trust in the prophesies. The silence was broken by his disturbing voice.

"Take some men, travel to Valedon, and bring me that pendant."

Then he was gone and Mongrel sat alone in the darkness with all the powers of the universe and no control of their uses. If his heart were still intact he would have wept.

*   *   *

T stretched his legs out onto the table in front of the Reverend's fireplace as he sank into the comfort of his boss' favorite chair. *I could get use to this.* The Reverend and Snake had been gone for nearly five days now. By his estimation they had to be rapidly approaching the town of Bodicia. He smiled. Only he knew where they were headed. It was that way for the safety of the Reverend and Snake. Not that there seemed to be many threats, it was just a standing order. T let his eyes close as he relaxed from the strain of a hard day's work. Almost as a reflex, he listened to the world outside the Reverend's chambers.

He heard laughing, eating, and drinking in the main hall. He heard men and women having hard sex in the many rooms, he heard Rock breathing outside his door, and he heard a sudden uneasiness in the air. His eyes snapped open and his heart began to pound. He sat still and listened intently. Nothing. *No wonder the boss is crazy. It takes a lot of energy to be paranoid . . .* Just as he thought it, he knew it wasn't true. There was the sound again. The sound of a million soldiers holding their breaths as they prepared to attack. He leapt for his weapons, realizing the entire time he would be too late.

Almost as though his thoughts held prophetic force, the sounds of a massacre began. As he rushed for the door, he heard the outer doors burst. As he threw it open, he heard women scream. And, as he and Rock ran down the hall in shared panic, he could hear the failing breaths of dying men. He grabbed Rock as they approached the end the hall and stopped him in his tracks. He slammed his body into the wall.

"How many?" he whispered.

Rock blinked, hesitated, then nodded. Silently he disappeared. Only seconds passed before he returned. His face bore the look of a man who had danced with the Reaper. T felt his own heart sink.

"Well?"

Rock faltered, "All of them. There's an army in the main hall . . . There are so many . . . "

T shook his friend, "Pull yourself together. How many of our men are dead?"

Rock looked blankly into his face, "All of them."

"Oh dear God."

Panic surged over him. *All of them!? How the fuck can all of them be dead? This is our home. We are safe . . . Fuck, we have a traitor.* T snatched the useless man in front of him and dragged him back down the hidden hallway to the Reverend's chambers. Quickly he bolted them inside. Then he slapped Rock to get his attention.

"Listen to me. We have been ambushed in our own home, do you know what that means?"

Rock was regaining his composure and his shock was being replaced by the desire for vengeance. He cleared his mind and focused, "A traitor."

T nodded, "That's right. Some son of a bitch has turned us over for money. Which means we are only safe here for moments longer. As soon as that person surfaces, those men will be coming down this hall looking for us. Got it?"

Rock was filled with a new kind of fury. The only place he had ever belonged was being pulled out from under his feet and the only people he had ever trusted were either dead or had betrayed him. Fire filled his belly. "Yeah. I got it."

T watched as Rock took on a look he had seen so many times in Snake's eyes. It sent a shiver down his spine, but he didn't have time for that now. He had only what felt like ancient instructions to follow. The chest had to be destroyed. *In the chest, under the bed, are all the records of our life, our network, and our souls,* the Reverend had said so many years ago. *If there ever comes a need, burn it. Never let anyone get their hands on it.* T rushed to the bed as the old instructions pulsed through his head. Rock watched in confusion.

"What the hell are you doing? We have to get out of here, find the Reverend, and figure out who to kill?"

T shrugged, "You have a point, but I have orders."

"What orders?"

T pulled the chest out from under the bed, "Destroy this."

Rock heard the sounds of feet rushing down the corridor. "Here they come, let's get out of here, now."

T shook his head as the banging of the door commenced. He could hear the man in charge ordering the door broken down. "I have to destroy this. Reverend's orders."

Rock heard the giant door creak at the burden of being pounded on. He saw it begin to crack. He heard the grunts and screams of the men outside the door. And he knew that T was not going anywhere until the Reverend's orders were carried out. With all the fury of his newfound hatred, he swung his broadsword at the wooden chest. It cracked down the center. Another blow broke it in two and all the papers spilled to the floor. Realizing that Rock had not, in fact, lost it, T began tossing papers into the fire as Rock continued to beat the chest into splinters.

It was a battle of wills as the soldiers strove to break down the great wooden doors, the doors tried to remain intact, and the two men rushed to destroy the evidence and make it out alive.

Rock stopped swinging. Sweat poured from his face and his chest heaved with the effort of heavy breathing, "There. Can we go now?"

T threw the last pieces of paper into the fire, "Just waiting on you."

Rock ran for the back door but T stopped him. "Traitor, remember?"

Rock stopped cold. A traitor would know the planned emergency escape route. "What the hell are we going to do?"

At times like this, it's good to be number two in charge of the world. "Follow me."

T lead Rock to the fireplace and, as the massive doors groaned and gave away, the two men disappeared behind the fireplace and into the Reverend's greatest kept secret. It was a small chamber, just big enough for three or four men, but completely hidden from without. The best part was only the Reverend and T himself knew of its existence. No traitor would find them here. Silently the two men listened and waited.

The sounds of people rushing into and ransacking the room reached their highly trained ears. Suddenly the noises subsided and they could hear voices.

"There is nothing here, sir," said a military voice.

"Keep searching. It has to be here somewhere," said an old yet oddly powerful voice. "Besides, your King said you should bring everything else you find to him . . . but he does not know how much is here. Why not make the most of the afternoon? But, remember, bring all pendants to me."

Apparently greed ran rampant among the King's men as well. *If he's not working for the King, who is the guy in charge?* T listened closely to for the sounds of anymore conversation. He was not disappointed.

"Sir," began a new voice, "our scouts from within the town tell us they have found a tavern owner who claims to have had two Lords staying with him during the festival. He said they left nearly five days ago with three other companions."

"Did he say where they were headed?"

"No."

"Maybe I can be of help there as well."

T's heart sank at the sound of the latest voice to enter the conversation. It was one he knew far too well. One he had laughed with. One he trusted. What was left of his hardened heart broke as he listened to Sam give away the man who had given him everything.

"I know of a back way out of this town. If they left, that is most likely the path they took. They can be trailed from there."

"I'll break his fucking neck," muttered Rock from the shadows.

T nodded in silent agreement. *Only if you beat me to him.* So, the traitor is revealed. All that remained was to kill him, leave town, and find the Reverend. *Just how the hell am I suppose to do that.* T searched the darkness for an answer. The sound of another voice drew his attention.

"We have secured the area, sir. There is no one left alive."

T listened as Sam gave them away, again. "No. There are two missing, and if you don't find them soon, they will find you."

The older voice that was obviously in charge returned, "So, where are they?"

Sam sounded shaken, "I have no idea. They were here, but they did not take the planned escape route. They probably deduced a traitor and are looking for him right now."

"Well, my friend," responded the man in charge, "it would appear that you need us just as much as we need you."

"It would appear so," agreed Sam.

"You had better fucking believe it," muttered Rock.

T put an elbow in Rock's ribs to remind him to be quiet. Rock bit down hard on an angry reply.

"If the Lords have left town then the pendant will no longer be here. Lead us to this back way and then you will be paid," said the old voice.

Sam remained a smart thief, mostly. "No. Pay me now and then I'll lead you to the back way."

There was a long pause then the sounds of money exchanging hands.

"Good," said the leader. "Now let's get started. We have wasted enough time already."

"Yeah, but leave a few men behind in case those missing men resurface. I don't want them following us until I'm long gone," said Sam.

"As you wish," hissed the leader.

The sounds of a massive retreat combined with the grunts of men dragging what was obviously the stores of treasure toward the exit echoed throughout the underground world. For T and Rock it felt like hours, though it was only a matter of minutes before they were alone in the darkness. Still, they waited and listened to the silence. Soon they heard what they had been waiting for, voices. There were two men in the hallway outside the room.

"Why is it they always leave me on guard duty?" asked a very young voice.

"I don't know why you're whining, I'm stuck here too, you know," came the reply.

T whispered, "Young and easily distracted."

"Good," said Rock.

"Man, this really sucks," said the whiner.

"Hey, I have an idea. Instead of just standing here until they decide to come and get us, let's see if we can find any left over goodies," said the second guard.

"You are a genius."

The footsteps retreated. T struggled with the notion that they might be smart and just pretending to leave, but soon decided that was highly unlikely. Carefully he crept out into the Reverend's chamber and let his eyes adjust to the light. Rock was right behind them. As their eyesight returned they surveyed the room. It was utterly destroyed. The massive bed had been torn down and turned over. The pillows had been ripped apart. The Reverend's favorite chair had been sliced open, anything breakable lay broken on the floor, ashes from the fire smeared the floor, and the giant doors sagged against the doorframe.

"The Reverend is going to be pissed," muttered T.

Rock shrugged and asked, "Do you think Sam has them guarding the escape route?"

T had not thought of that. *Damn!* "Doesn't matter. We can't risk it. I guess we have to leave through the front door."

"There are probably guards there, too," responded Rock.

"Yeah, but they are more likely looking for people coming in than people going out. Anyway, it's our best bet. Unless you have a better idea."

Rock shook his head, "Just keep an eye out for guards. They are liable to do something stupid like trip on us."

T smiled and started down the hall. Being a thief had its advantages. Although he couldn't disappear as completely as Snake, T could be invisible in plain sight as could Rock. Quickly, they navigated their way down the well-known passages of their stronghold. The stench of death filled the air and threatened to strangle them. To keep their sanity, they avoided the bedrooms where people they had known would be dead. But, they were rapidly approaching the main dining hall. There was no way around it; it stood between them and the entrance. T stopped at the entryway.

"Are there guards in there?" whispered Rock.

T shook his head,"No."

Rock nodded in understanding. There would be the lifeless bodies of their friends covering the floor. There would be death all around them. This was about to be the most horrible event of their lives.

"Let's do this quickly," whispered Rock.

"Right," replied T. "Just move through and don't look down."

"Straight for the other side."

The two hardened criminals searched each other for strength and started forward. What they saw stopped them in their tracks. There was blood everywhere. It oozed along the floor like a river, dripped down the walls, and was smattered across all the bodies. The bodies. The bodies of their friends and companions lay strewn about the hall. Some contorted in hideous positions, others missing limbs, still others sliced in two. Eyes of the dead stared at them with pleading agony. Hell had risen and filled the room with horror. The two men shuddered. T shook himself from his trance and pulled Rock forward.

"Straight through, remember?"

Rock pulled his eyes up from the death and nodded slowly and painfully. He had not been prepared for the site of so much carnage. He hadn't see death like this since the Great War against the Betrayer. But, those had been men ready to fight and die and enemy trolls. That had been a thousand times easier to handle than the sight of cold and calculated murder of the innocent. Rock took his eyes off the door to look down at where he was placing his feet and nearly vomited at the sight. Quickly, he snapped his eyes forward and followed T's unwavering back across the room. *That man is made of stone.*

T fought back the tears that welled in his eyes as he marched silently forward through this morgue. His stomach turned and he ached to cry out, but he had no time for suffering now. Now, he had to get through the room, out the door, kill Sam, and find the Reverend. He knew it would not be an easy task, so he could not allow himself the time to weep for the dead. *I'm sorry, my friends.* He prayed he would be able to return to bury them, but knew that by then it would be too late. That thought only infuriated him more and pushed him that much closer to the edge. The Reverend was going to have to wait.

T turned to look in the pale face of his friend. Rock stopped short with a mild look of confusion on his face. T whispered through the gloom.

"They deserve better than this. Grab a lantern."

Rock needed no coaxing, he could read T's mind. Swiftly and skillfully both men retrieved the oil lanterns from the dining table and began dousing the room and the bodies. Oil mixed with blood to form a disgusting, slick, red film across the room. His lantern empty, T pulled a torch from the entrance hall and waited for Rock. Rock was instantly at his side.

"Once I start this there won't be much time before the guards sound the alarm. I say we go full steam out the front door, kill anyone in our way, and run like hell."

Rock replied, "I'm right behind you."

With that, T tossed the torch and waited only for it to spark before turning on his heels and running. Flames flared up behind him and a burst of heat nearly knocked the two men to the floor, but they stumbled forward down the passage. Around the corner was the entrance. The sounds of men talking filled the air. They could smell smoke. As T burst out the entrance two men were heading in to investigate. T drew his sword and charged.

He sliced through the gut of the first and elbowed the second man in the face. The rest of the guards turned to face him. He braced himself. Then, Rock bounded from behind him, rushed the men, and knocked three to the ground. T seized the moment to slit the throat of one of the others. Rock picked himself up, ran his sword through the belly of one of the soldiers, kicked one in the face, and threw a knife into the throat of the third. Seeing that they were clear, T yelled, "Let's go."

Rock checked his fury and followed as T lead them toward the back exit and the traitor.

*   *   *

Mongrel looked into the crystal black waters of the tiny cauldron he carried with him. The misty face of his master appeared and his voice oozed forth.

"Well?"

Mongrel drew a breath to steady himself. "The Lords have left Valedon. They have the pendant with them and are heading in the direction of Bodicia."

The cauldron was silent as the source of evil contemplated what he had heard. The Lords were not searching for the Chosen, they were searching for the High Lord. They had to be stopped. His followers needed time to break the High Lord's protection spell and sacrifice him.

"Find them before they reach the High Lord. They must be stopped. Do not fail me."

Then, he was gone and Mongrel was left alone with the weight of the world of darkness upon his shoulders. Quickly he wrapped the cauldron into his pack, left his shelter of trees, and returned to the anxious men awaiting him just beyond the secret exit.

"Can we go now?" asked Sam who had decided to stay with these armed men until he was well away from Valedon and the reach of T and Rock.

Mongrel scowled at the impatient thief, "Yes, and we must hurry. We will be joined by my troops soon and then we will easily find and dispose of this problem."

The small band of the king's men shifted uneasily in their saddles. They had no real idea who this man was or why the king had insisted that they help him, but they were certain they were not going to like whatever troops a warped wizard like himself would command. Thoughts of blood thirsty mercenaries and soul-less trolls danced through their heads as they prepared to follow this evil little man through the forest and in search of the Lords, a couple thieves, and some damned necklace. If they had known what they were up against, they would have deserted. As it was, with blind stupidity intact, they started forward with Sam leading the way.

Watching the king's men being lead away by a traitor only made sense to Rock. Still it took everything in him not to rush the group and hack Sam's head off his shoulders. But, he restrained himself with what felt to him like the patience of a saint. T slipped up beside him on the ground to watch the last of the men start down the forest path. *Straight down the center, huh? You are idiots.*

"That head guy is a wizard of some sort. He was having a conversation with someone through a magic cauldron. He's after the Lords," whispered T.

Rock nodded, "And expecting reinforcements. Maybe we should ambush them now, save ourselves some trouble."

T had thought that one over a thousand times but knew it just wasn't feasible. "No. If we failed there would be no one to warn the Reverend. Besides, if they are meeting up with more troops, won't the troops get suspicious when they don't show up? No, our best bet is to find the Reverend first."

As much as Rock hated to admit it, T was right. *I guess that's why the Reverend left him in charge.*

"Okay. But let's hurry. If I don't kill Sam soon I'm going to loose my mind."

T understood. Shouldering his anger, he lead Rock forward in search of the one man who might still save them.

CHAPTER 9

The Commander searched the tree line yet again for the illusive figure of Snake, but just couldn't find her anywhere. It unnerved him that she could disappear in plain sight. He had watched her get up from the fire, watched her cross the camp to the far side, but then she had vanished right before his eyes. *Where the hell does she go every night and how the hell does she do that?* He was a soldier, trained in the art of detection, yet he never saw Snake unless she wanted to be seen. It was starting to piss him off. The Reverend abruptly interrupted his private musings.

"Can't find her, huh? Don't worry you'll get use to it."

The Commander wasn't too fond of the mind reading skills of the Reverend either, "It's been five days and I'm still not use to it. It's actually starting to wear on my nerves."

The Reverend chuckled, "Try three years. I trained her, taught her all those tricks, and not even I can find her anymore. She's like a ghost and if she doesn't want to be found she won't be."

"So, how do you handle it?"

"I let it go, as should you. She can and will take care of herself and the more you worry about her, the farther away she will become. She's a perfect thief but a hard lady."

The Commander sensed that the Reverend was not just giving him advice. He looked like he was doing battle with himself on this one. Being smart, he decided to skip that part of the conversation but his curiosity got the best of him on another idea.

"What happened to her? Why is she so completely bitter?"

There was no storm of violence in his voice when the Reverend responded, just the sound of simple defeat, "To answer that would be to betray the only trust she has ever had in me. Since I value that which is so rare I can never answer that. I will say this, if you ever get her to tell you that, then you might actually save her."

Then the Commander saw it. For just a fraction of a split second tenderness flashed in the Reverend's eyes and Gabriel knew that this powerful man had only ever lost one fight; he loved Snake and that was a losing battle. Unsure of how to stomach weakness in one so strong, Gabe changed the subject.

"Okay. I'll let that one go. So, how about you? Why are you here?"

The Reverend cocked an eyebrow at the Commander's questions. He had never appeared that interested in other's business. That was one of the things the Reverend liked about him. *Maybe he's just making conversation.* It amused him so he answered . . . sort of.

"I owe Brennen a favor."

"See, that confuses me. I can't seem to figure out what a man like you would need from anyone, especially a Lord."

The Reverend smiled at the interesting compliment, "I wasn't always a man like me. I use to be more like a man somewhere between you and Lord Earin over there."

It was Gabriel's turn to smile, "Oh, you were young, driven, slightly confused, and pissed off at the world."

The Reverend shrugged with a grin, "Take it as you wish. I was Brennen's personal guard back when the Lords had personal guards. In my service I managed to provide Brennen with the opportunity to save my ass. So, now I'm going to try and save his."

The Commander eyed the powerful man. In the glow of the firelight he seemed almost unreal, like a figure you dream of or dream of being. *So, your past is closed, too. This is becoming a trend.* As much as he hated to be in the dark, the Commander could respect the need to keep some things private. After all, his life wasn't exactly skeleton-free. He shrugged.

"Well, I hope you get your chance to repay the debt. It's not easy owing people; it wears on you."

The Reverend smiled. The more he got to know the Commander,

the more he was reminded of who he once was, and, although he could never be that person again, it was nice to know someone else could. For a brief moment, bonding in the glow of the firelight, he almost felt a fatherly compassion for this man . . . almost. Instead, he decided to return to the safety of solitude.

"Oh, I am certain that my debt will be repaid. I can only hope that more are not incurred along the way."

The Commander lifted his cup in a salute, "Amen to that, brother."

"You are indeed an interesting man, Commander. But, now I am going to retire until my shift. Wake me for my turn on duty."

Then, the mighty thief stood, stretched his legs, and walked off in the direction of the forest. *Retire, my ass.* The Commander might not have the wisdom of the Reverend, yet, but he could spot the obvious in a hurry. He knew that the master thief was on his way to try and find the mysterious Snake. It was actually quite amusing to realize that he too knew very little about the woman he had helped to create. Somewhere deep in the pit of his stomach Gabe had a feeling that, before this was all over, Snake was going to cause him a lot of pain. He pushed that feeling aside and returned to guarding the slumbering Lords. *Zippity-do-dah.*

*   *   *

Snake sat high in her perch, bottom lip pulled between her teeth, and thoughts of her new path running through her head. She had been sitting alone in the darkness of the forest for hours, just listening to the sounds of the world around her, watching the glimmer of the camp fire diligently tended by the Commander, and searching what was left of her soul for some reason for it all. Still nothing. She pulled her knees to her chest, leaned her back against the tree trunk, and watched the leaves of the tree rustle in the breeze. It was almost peaceful.

Then, from below, came the sounds of light footsteps and a heavy heart. Snake stopped her breathing and the beating of her heart to listen. The disguised breathing told her immediately who was seeking her out; it was the Reverend. She listened intently now. He was directly underneath her tree. She slowly slid her body onto her stomach and sank into the tree branch. Without a sound, she peered over the edge and saw the shadow of the giant man as his head turned this way and that, desperately searching for her invisible form. She grinned.

"Looking for me?" she asked, slyly.

Anyone else would have jumped out of their skin. The Reverend let his heartbeat return to normal, but showed no outward signs of surprise.

"My, aren't we arrogant. Why does it always have to be about you?" retorted the startled thief.

"Because I'm much more interesting than the local wildlife. Trust me, I know."

The Reverend looked up into the eyes of Snake as she lay across the tree branch with her head peeking over the edge. Her long blonde hair fell in front of her face like a veil. No matter how hard he tried to protect it, she continually made his heart skip a beat. It was all he could stand to be around her knowing that he had probably lost her forever. He sighed.

"What's wrong, boss? Problems back with the Lords? I didn't hear anything."

The Reverend shook his head, "No. They are sound asleep and the Commander is on duty."

Snake nodded, "They are safe, then. That man is not to be taken by surprise."

This was going nowhere, and fast. This was not why the Reverend had hunted Snake down. The truth was, he wasn't even sure why he had hunted her down. There was just something in him that was craving some kind of resolve. There was a continual and unspoken strain on their relationship ever since that night in his chambers. He longed to remove it and restore his sanity. But, as he stood close to her, he wasn't sure that was possible. *What the hell is a matter with me? I'm the leader of the underground. Cold. Calm. In charge. Then why do I feel like a child?* He looked up at Snake.

"Yeah, the Commander is tough. Look, Snake could you come down for a minute?"

Snake detected weakness in the Reverend's voice, it made her suddenly uncomfortable. "What's up?"

He grinned and attempted to regain his composure, "You are, but I need you down here."

Snake hesitated, but curiosity got the better of her. In a single, fluid motion she had silently slipped from the tree and was standing in front of her mentor and the closest thing she had to a friend.

"Okay, I'm down. Now what?"

Panic grabbed at the Reverend's stone heart for the first time in years as he formulated an answer to her question. But, he had no choice. If he was going to regain control of the man he was, he had to start here and he had to start with her. He fought back the urge to move toward her and stood his ground.

"I just wanted to say I'm sorry . . . "

Snake had a bad feeling about this, "Hey, it's not your fault. I stole the damn necklace against your orders, remember? This mess is my own doing and I'll find a way through it."

The Reverend shook his head, "That's not what I mean. I'm sorry for that night. I'm sorry for breaking down your wall. I know your anger is all you have and your walls are your protection. I know because the same has always been the same for me. And, I took that away and changed things . . . and I'm sorry for destroying that last part of you capable of trust."

For the second time in her life Snake felt as though she had the upper hand in a relationship with a man. Only this time it didn't bring her joy, this time the power gave her an odd mixture of calmness and regret. She had brought the Reverend to his knees, which gave her power. But, she had inspired weakness in the strongest person she knew, that gave her regret. Somewhere deep inside herself she found the compassion to be human.

"No. You are wrong. It was my cousin that destroyed the part of me that trusts others. He is to blame. All you did was remind me of what he has taken away. For a moment, I was just a woman, something I can never be again. My cousin took that, and he will pay for it. That moment was merely a reminder that everyone I trust either betrays me or dies. So, I choose to remain alone. There is less chance for true pain that way."

There was an eerie coolness in Snake's voice as she spoke. A chill ran down the Reverend's spine. He searched her eyes for some sign that she had forgiven him, but found only ice blue orbs staring back at him. Something had to be done.

"Can you tell me that you are honestly happy that way? Alone is a horrible way to live. Take it from an expert. I've been doing it for years. In the end, it leaves you cold, empty, and alone with your secrets."

"Some secrets are best taken to the grave," muttered Snake.

The sight of some sort of defeat in her eyes enraged the Reverend. He stepped forward in the darkness and seized Snake by the arms, determined to shake it right out of her.

"Do you trust me? Did you ever trust me? In all those years of training and protection, did you ever learn trust?" he demanded.

Snake stood firm and calmly said, "If I answer that, I will condemn one of us for certain."

That was not enough for the Reverend. After years of the self-imposed death that he now saw reflected in Snake, she had brought him back to life. He was not about to let her go so easily.

Again he demanded, "Do you trust me?"

The fury in his eyes and the strength of his resolve masked the weakness Snake had seen in the Reverend just moments ago. She knew he deserved the truth. For all the things he had done for her, he deserved at least that. But, she also knew that only pain could come from this. So, with a heavy heart, she told him the truth.

"You are the only man I have ever trusted."

The admission was too much for him. It was more than he had ever even dreamed to get from the lady of ice. All his anger flooded from his body and was replaced by an overpowering urge to have her close to him again. Without stopping to consider the consequences, the Reverend pulled her to him and kissed her passionately. And, as she allowed herself the joy of physical love, once again, a single thought filled Snake's brain, *One of us will die.*

* * *

The dying fire crackled and a single spark flew into the air and landed on the toe of a black boot. It's light quickly went out and its short flight of freedom ended. Snake stared deeply into the glowing embers at the base of the fire. Like the ember that had extinguished itself on her boot, she felt as though she were dying. With a fierce determination, she resolved to put her life back in order. She yanked her gaze from the hypnotic fire and glanced at the sleeping form of the Reverend.

His massive back faced the fire. She watched it heave with each breath he took. *This is getting ridiculous.* To say she cared for him would have been an understatement; to say she was afraid of him would have been a greater one. She had thought she had it all under control. *Just avoid him and it goes away, right?* But, she had been wrong and her had called her on it. Now, she was searching for normality. She wanted to be able to love him, but she knew she was no longer capable of such an emotion. She had perfected cold, angry, and alone. The last thing she needed was to try and remember how to love. Love had only ever brought her pain. She eyed his muscular back. Still, it was nice not to be completely alone. *Looks like I get to be confused for a long time.* She pulled her attention away from the Reverend and tried to shake the notion that one of them was going to die.

A movement to her left drew her full attention. Lord Earin shifted in his blankets but did not wake. It was still amazing to Snake how deeply the Lords were able to sleep. *Don't they have any idea what is going on around them?*

A voice just beside Lord Earin answered her unspoken question, "It is because we know exactly what is going on that we rest. We can only regenerate our powers with rest."

Fire shot from her eyes as Snake responded to Lord Anjalina, "What gives you the right to get into my mind?"

Lord Anjalina remained lying in her bed, "I did not choose to read your thoughts, they were just there. We only probe minds when an issue of trust or safety is at hand. But, rest easy, your thoughts are well concealed. That is why I cannot decide whether or not to trust you and why Lord Earin is so uneasy around you."

Snake unclenched her jaw, "Trust is never easy. To be fair, I don't entirely trust you Lords either. As far as I can see, if it weren't for your secrecy I wouldn't be in this mess."

Now the redheaded lady lord sat up, "If you had not been a Chosen

One, then you would be free. I told you before, that is not the will of the Lords . . . "

As small noise in the trees just beyond the sleeping form of the Reverend caught Snake's attention. She quickly tuned out Lord Anjalina, put her hand on one of her knives, and focused. There it was again, breathing. Snake slowed her own as she realized she was being watched. She searched for the form of whoever was watching her. There, just in front of the Reverend, eyes in the bushes. Keeping her eyes focused on that spot, Snake used her other senses to search for any other figures in the darkness. Her concentration began to slip at the sound of Lord Anjalina's confused voice.

"Snake? Are you listening to me?"

Shut up! She ordered mentally. Lord Anjalina's voice stopped and Snake immediately heard the other person. He was standing behind the horses and in the perfect position to take out the Commander. *Hello, we have been flanked.* With an unknown stranger on either side of the camp, Snake realized she could only protect one. She had to wake the Reverend. A friendly voice told her there was no need. It was the Reverend.

"I know that's you T, I can smell you a mile away."

The Reverend sat up. *T?!* Snake sniffed the air. *Well, no duh. Wait. What the hell is he doing here?* Quickly, Snake shifted her attention to the other unknown person and realized what was happening on the other side of the camp.

"Hey, Rock, you might want to show yourself before the wide awake Commander over there gets sword happy."

Snake was rewarded by the all too familiar sound of Rock's gruff voice, "Oh sure, give my position away. Some friend you are."

Then the two thieves emerged from the shadows. As the Commander rose to greet the new entries, he couldn't help but wonder how these two men had managed to be so quiet. Rock was literally a mountain of a man. He stood close to seven feet tall, had arms that appeared to be chiseled out of granite and ended in massive hands, shoulders broader than a bear's, and a chest that could only be rivaled by solid stone. T was less intimidating in size but not in stature. His dark skin and bald head gave him the look of a pirate, but his muscular form made him look like a wrestler. As they approached, the Commander had a real understanding of the power of the Reverend. *If he can train and command men like these* . . . He left that thought unfinished.

Snake remained at the fire. The Reverend and T embraced then joined her there. Rock came upon them with a grin on his face. He wrapped his arms around Snake, lifted her off the ground in a bear hug and returned her to the ground before she could protest. He then turned his attention to the Reverend with equal affection. Lord Anjalina woke Lord Earin and the two Lords stumbled to the fire to join the rest. The Reverend made a quick round of introductions as everyone seated themselves around the fire.

"Okay, T. I know you didn't come all this way just to make sure that I still love ya. What's going on and why were you hiding in the bushes for so long? Snake might have killed you," said the Reverend.

The smile faded from T's face. He looked at Rock for help. The massive man stared at the ground, uncertain of what to say. Snake felt an overpowering sense of fear. The Commander wanted to pry for information, but knew it was not his place. The two Lords linked minds for strength. T lifted his eyes to the face of the Reverend and spoke to the spellbound audience.

"We wanted to make sure that you were still in charge and not prisoners or anything," began T.

"Prisoners? Who the hell would have captured us?" asked the Reverend.

T took a deep breath, "The same people who slaughtered your men and friends in their own home."

Snake felt the world start to spin. Once again, her reality was about to come crashing down around her head. Once again, her safety net was yanked from beneath her. And, once again, fury filled her veins. She felt a tremor and looked down in shock to find that her hands were shaking. She clenched them into fists. She looked to the Reverend for strength. He sat completely stoic, a man without emotion. It was the scariest thing she had ever seen in her life.

An echo of his voice eeked from the emotional shell of a man, "How many survived?"

T searched his own trembling hands for strength, "You're looking at them."

For a moment the Reverend faltered, but he refused to die, "What happened?"

The Reverend listened in masked horror as T recounted the horrific tale of what had become of his underground city and army. He felt his heart shatter into a million pieces when he learned of Sam's treachery. *Sam, you bastard! I took you in and taught you everything!* He let pure fury course through his veins at the description of the scene of death in the dining hall. And, he wept inwardly at the knowledge that he had no home to which he could ever return. As T finished his story, the Reverend looked into the face of Snake and was mortified.

She had complete resolve set in her jaw, her hands trembled in anger, and the look of that lost child he had rescued so many years ago reflected in her eyes. Panic filled him as he realized that once again she had been betrayed by someone she trusted and those she had cared for, whether she would admit it or not, were dead. Her pain and fury reflected his own. The camp was silent. Then, the Commander spoke.

"You spoke of a wizard, what did he look like?"

T faced the Commander, "Like a disgusting, withered, old man. He was obsessed with finding the Lords and some damn necklace."

Snake nearly broke, "What?"

T shrugged, "They came to the city looking for some necklace that the Lords are suppose to have. For some reason they thought we had it. So, they stormed our lair and killed everyone over some fucking piece of jewelry that I've never even heard of!" T looked at the two Lords, "That makes me want to break your fucking necks."

It's my fault. Despair filled Snake.

The Reverend saw the thoughts that ran through Snake's mind and he could not stop them, but he had to stop T.

"That's enough. They are not to blame. They serve the Land. They have no control over the actions of that demented wizard. He is to blame, as is Sam for leading him to us." Even as he spoke, the Reverend felt his own support of the Lords begin to falter. Things had been different with Lord Brennen; he wondered if he had the strength for this.

The Commander spoke and tried to hide his own guilt as his necklace burned into his chest, "The wizard has to be Mongrel."

I killed them. They are all dead because of me. Snake felt like she was falling, again.

Feeling the very real threat in the air, and protected only by the slipping faith of the Reverend, Lord Earin finally spoke, "Yes, it must be Mongrel. This is most distressing. It can only mean that the Betrayer has grown in strength and is now seeking to destroy us before we can save the High Lord or find the Chosen."

"That's just great," snapped T. "Some demented wizard is running around looking for Lords and necklaces, and because you Lords stop by our town on your way, all my friends are dead!"

No! I stole the necklace. They are dead because of me! Snake began to search for stable mental ground.

The Reverend stood and placed a restraining hand on T's shoulder. "I told you to let that go and I meant it! I owe a Lord, that's why they were there. Redirect your anger, now!" *Yeah, but can I redirect mine?*

T looked into the eyes of the Reverend and saw his pain mixed with his resolve. He was right. There were better people to hate for this. The Lords seemed to be nothing more than pawns in this. Besides, if the Reverend was resolved to help and not blame them, he had no choice but to follow suit. He dropped his head.

"Okay, you win."

Lord Earin thought of his past and of losing his fellow Lords. He knew that would be too much. His heart ached to help these men with their sorrow. A mental message from Lord Anjalina attempted to stall him. *They are not sensitive people. You do not understand them. Best to leave it alone.* But, he knew he couldn't. He wanted to make some kind of amends.

"I am sorry for your loss. I do not pretend to understand the pain and anger you feel; I can only offer you hope that, if we succeed in our mission, they will not have died in vain." The silence that followed told him that Anjalina had been right.

Not in vain? Am I really that important? Can these necklaces really save the world? Snake struggled to follow that chain of logic out of the depths of her despair. All she could see was that she had been betrayed, again, and that she had no "normal" life to return to. All she had was the new path before her. She felt trapped, angry, and guilty. Someone would have to pay. She glanced at the useless Lords. Not them. They couldn't even control necklaces. *Then who?*

Rock wanted to strangle him. *In vain or not, they are still fucking dead!* Yet, he sensed real pain in the Lord and he knew that the Reverend would never permit it. As a matter of fact, he was shocked at how much he was protecting these Lords. He decided not to understand it and turned his attention to the plan at hand.

"Okay. It works like this. This Mongrel guy, Sam, about ten of the king's men, and some troops to be named later are tracking us as we speak . . . " began Rock.

"Trolls," stated the Commander.

"What?" asked Rock.

"The troops that Mongrel commands are always trolls, count on it."

"So, boss, what do we do?" asked Rock.

The Reverend had returned to his seat and was keeping a watchful eye on Snake as she dealt with yet another betrayal. She looked as though she was going to snap. He wanted to help, but there was nothing he could do. To reach out to her would only destroy what he had gained. Besides, he had other things to attend to at the moment. He contemplated the situation.

"Well, this really isn't my party. The Commander is the one in charge and obviously knows more about this Mongrel character than I do."

Snake pulled her mind from her own despair and listened. The Reverend was trusting this man with their lives. *Are these necklaces really so important?* It didn't matter. It only mattered that he was not blaming her. He was moving forward. She would have to do the same. In her new life there was no time for self-pity, guilt, or sorrow. Like she had so many times, Snake focused on the one thought that could keep her going, revenge. *Sam dies. And if anything happens to the Reverend . . .* She let that dangerous thought die and faced reality.

T and Rock exchanged confused glances. The Reverend never relinquished control of any situation. The Commander eyed him suspiciously. *What's this guy up to?* Soon all eyes were on him. *Lucky I'm a cool genius or all this attention just might bother me.*

"Well, here's what we can expect. Mongrel will keep his men moving pretty much day and night. The trolls will not need to rest and he, himself, will not care to. They may loose some of the men, but they won't matter as they aren't loyal to the wizard anyway and would scatter at the first sign of a fight. How far behind us would you say they are?"

T shrugged, "Day, maybe less. It all depends on when they met up with the trolls and whether or not they have stopped for a rest."

The Commander took in the information, then looked to the Reverend, "There are two ways we can handle this. We can run like hell and hope we reach Bodicia, locate the High Lord, who may or may not be there, save him, and try to get out of town before Mongrel reaches us or we are killed by the locals, or . . . "

The Reverend grinned, "Or, we ambush them and hope that we are smarter and more skillful than they are."

"Either way," said the Commander, "it's bound to be a laugh a minute. What do you think, Snake?"

The Commander had seen the panic and real pain in the ice-lady's eyes as she dealt with the knowledge that she was somehow connected to the death of her friends. It was a feeling he had been battling with himself. In an effort to help them both, he reached out to her sense of vengeance; she bit.

"I say they die."

Relief rushed over the Reverend, but he kept it under the surface.

"Great. Now all we have to do is come up with a brilliant plan of attack. Anybody got any ideas?" asked the Commander.

"Have you lost your mind, Commander?" demanded Lord Anjalina.

"What's the matter? Don't you like plans that are tactically simple and mortally dangerous?"

"You have lost your mind. We, with our seven people, are not going to attack Mongrel and his hordes of who knows how many. It's ludicrous!" yelled the fiery female Lord.

The Commander turned to the Reverend, "She has a point, we don't know how many there will be."

The Reverend sensed where the Commander was going and jumped right in, "Then we'll have to be really careful and use a lot of arrows, knives, and shit."

"What you are suggesting . . . " she began.

"Is the only choice we have," finished Gabriel. "There is no other way. If we run, we will be caught and we can't risk being caught in Bodicia. We are going to have to make a stand."

For the millionth time since she had met the cocky man, Lord Anjalina realized just how much she hated him. He was always so smug and far too eager to try dangerous tactics. But, she knew that he had a point and that she was not going to win this battle. Still, if they were to fail here, they would be sacrificing the High Lord and two of the Chosen. It was a loss she could not bear.

Lord Earin saw the thoughts that ran through Lord Anjalina's head. His heart went out to her and he shared his understanding with her. But, he too knew they had little choice.

"We stand to loose more than this battle if we fail. Make your plans solid and sure and we will aid in any way that we can," said Earin.

Commander Gabriel nearly fell over in shock. The Lords always backed each other, at least to the best of his knowledge. This was the first time any one of them had ever sided with him. He smiled.

"Great. Sounds like we can get this party started. Now, what the hell are we going to do?"

"I have an idea," responded the clever Reverend, "and I'm sure you are just all going to love it."

The tone of his voice told them all that they were not. However, since no one else had any bright ideas they had no choice but to follow his lead. He smiled, *Only when you are all out of options can you find a way out.* Then, he let them in on his brilliant plan.

*   *   *

What a beautiful plan. I'm so happy to be a part of this. Snake concentrated on her mission and tried very hard to ignore thoughts of anger, frustration and guilt. *Why do I always get the fun jobs?* It had been decided that someone had to go back and find out how many troops they were facing and how far away they were. That someone got to be Snake, *Because you're the sneakiest,* the Reverend had explained. So, Snake had disappeared into the forest to check out the rear and left the rest of them to set up the ambush. She was to do recon and return via the treetops; any other path could be deadly. She pushed her way back through the forest and listened intently for foreign sounds. All she could hear were happy birds, furry things, and the sounds of an ambush being set. *Could you quiet down? This is suppose to be a secret.* She crawled forward.

It was a heavily wooded forest and that helped the master thief quit a bit. There was no lack of dark, leafy hiding places or shadows. In fact, the sunlight that did shine through the canopy seemed to fall only on the single path down the center. According to T, the wizard and his men were marching right down the center of this path. *What idiots!* She hoped they remained that easy to spot. In the end, it wasn't the troops that revealed their own presence as much as it was the forest through which they were traveling.

Snake had been on recon duty for nearly half the day, now. She was getting hot, tired, and cranky. The trees shut out the sunlight and kept her gloomy like her surroundings. Critters of every size and shape ran past her and made annoying noises. She hadn't eaten anything all day, and her water supply was low. In addition to all that, she was tracking people that were looking for her so they could kill her and her friends. *This is not a good day.* She moved past another tree and was stopped dead in her tracks by the sudden stillness in the air. It was as if the forest life that had annoyed her so much to this point had vanished. Chills ran up her spine as she listened. No sounds reached her ears. No birds. No bugs. No furry things. The world around her was dead. All her senses came to life as she realized that there had to be bad guys approaching, and a large enough number to scare the forest into silence.

Snake quickly scaled the nearest tree to gain a look out position. Carefully, she peered through the branches and scanned the forest below. At first there was nothing and she began to wonder whether or not she had contracted a case of the Reverend's paranoia. However, something inside her told her to hold her ground. As always her senses came to her rescue. In the distance she heard the sound of heavy forced marching. She concentrated on the noises and tried to locate and describe them without getting any closer.

Judging by the faintness of the horses' footsteps, Snake guessed they were about three or four miles away. At their current rate she guessed they would be on them in a days time, maybe less. She could make out horses and other footfalls, but she had no idea how many. *I have got to get better at this.* She considered heading back to the camp, but didn't think the Commander and the Reverend would like to hear that they were up against "a whole bunch" of enemy soldiers. As it was, she wasn't even sure if they were trolls. *Not my fault . . . I've never actually seen a troll before.* Snake sighed. She was going to have to get closer.

She slid down the tree and moved forward as fast as she could, not too concerned about silence as the troops she was stalking were making enough noise. She covered a great deal of distance before another thought occurred to her, *If I go too much further, I won't be getting back in time to do any good.* She stopped. *Well, hell.* She was caught between a need to know and a need to return. She decided to climb another tree and try another look. Quickly, she bounded up a large nearby tree and peered, once again, into the distance. No luck. She could hear grunts and marching, but still could not see a thing. The only thing she was certain of was that there were a lot of them and that they were getting closer. *I could always wait for them.* As soon as she thought it, Snake realized how truly stupid that idea was. She had to keep moving forward. Now she was really getting pissed.

She leaped to the ground and moved toward the incredible sound as fast as she could. The exertion told her that she was wearing herself out, but she did not care. All she wanted was to find them, count them, and get the hell out of there. Suddenly, she realized that she was being totally reckless and acting like a scared child. The seasoned thief stopped dead in her tracks. *Whoa, what the hell is my problem? Now is not the time to revert.* She took a deep breath and began to calmly assess the situation with all the wisdom and training she had received over the years. She used the same devious thoughts that had gotten her into and out of the castle without a soul, save one, ever knowing she had been there.

Okay, I can't wait for them to find me and I need enough time to get back. What do I do? What would piss off the Reverend? A smile found it's way to the clever woman's face as she assessed the situation and scanned her surroundings. All around her was thick, deep forest filled with trees and undergrowth. To her left were several fallen trees and directly in front of her was the only path through the forest. *Only when you are all out of options can you find your way out. Maybe I can wait for them.* Snake smiled and went to work.

*   *   *

Sam controlled yet another urge to run. He had wanted to run the moment he had put himself into the middle of this. The Reverend would kill him if he ever found him and here he was following this despicable wizard right down the path of least resistance into the hands of the Reverend. Yet, he knew without the trolls and warriors that surrounded him he was as good as dead already. If he left not knowing whether or not the Reverend was dead he would spend the rest of his life wondering and fearing one of the Reverend's many connections would kill him in his sleep one night. But, if he saw the Reverend dead, then he would be safe to tell any tale. So, he followed the mangled old wizard down the path, knowing full well that by this time T and Rock had found him and warned him. *This sucks.*

Mongrel had been lulled into a semi-trance as his horse obediently followed the others through the forest. The king's men lead the way, followed by him and the thief, and then came the trolls. Fifty of the biggest, ugliest, smelliest creatures to walk the earth; creations of the dark magic of the Betrayer. They were unnatural, unholy beasts who needed little food and no rest. They lived in dark caves in mountains and were never loyal in groups unless under the control of the Betrayer. They were thick skinned with huge hands, arms longer than their bodies, and fierce jaws. Mongrel loathed the fearsome beasts, but none were better suited for this purpose.

Abruptly, the king's men stopped, sending a ripple through the force as everyone struggled to follow suit. Days of marching made it difficult to break the rhythm.

"Why have we stopped?" demanded the wizard.

The head of the guards approached, "The path ahead is blocked by several fallen trees. We need to go around."

Sam's hair stood up on the back of his neck. He scanned the trees for the eyes that had to be watching him. He could not see them, but he knew they were there. Panic seized him.

"No. It is a trap. We must not journey into the forest," Sam cried.

Mongrel stared at the paranoid thief, "What would you have us do then?"

"We need to carefully clear the trees and continue down the path. The path is open and we can see anyone coming. The second we step into the forest, we are dead. That I promise you." *Where the hell is she? I know that's you out there, Snake. No one else is this big of a pain in the ass.*

Mongrel looked ahead at the huge trees and wondered how they had gotten there. It seemed a waste of time and resources to move them, but the thief looked truly frightened. He decided it was best to follow his advice.

"Fine. Bring forward a few trolls and let's get these trees out of the way so that we can continue."

In response to the wizard's command, four of the trolls slowly made their way to the fallen trees. As he watched the huge beasts struggle with the massive trucks, Sam wondered how Snake could have moved them. Then, he questioned himself. *Maybe it's not Snake. Maybe the trees just fell there? Yeah, and maybe I'm the Queen.* The thief knew better. His instincts had kept him alive for years, he wasn't about to give up on them now. No, he was certain she had been here . . . nothing else in the world felt like Snake's presence. She could give the executioner the chills. He reluctantly turned his attention back to the trolls and the task at hand.

They had managed to move the first tree off the path and out of the way, but there were still three more cris-crossed on the path blocking the way. Without hesitation, the trolls went to work on the next trunk. Perhaps Sam should have seen it coming, but the truth was he had not been paying real attention to the trolls. His true focus had been on watching his own back. That is why it was too late to do anything but duck when the trap sprang itself.

As the trolls lifted up on the second trunk, a rope went tight. Sam saw the rope, thought, *Oh shit!*, and slid from the back of his mount to flat on the ground. He kept his head low as he heard the arrows fly. Like clockwork the arrows that had been released by the lifting of the log whizzed past his head and into the bodies of several trolls. Sam chanced a glance. Sure enough, in front of him several of the king's guard were dead or injured and behind him two trolls broke off the tiny arrows that were stuck in their limbs.

He climbed to his feet, "Son of a bitch."

Mongrel was furious, "What the hell has happened here?" He turned to Sam, "You knew this was happening!"

Sam calmly remounted his stead, "Don't look at me. I saw the trap about two seconds before it fired. Looks like someone has warned the Reverend that we are on our way. We should be more careful, like I said."

Mongrel did not like this answer, "We have wasted enough time on this. We will go around the trees and continue down the path on the other side."

Sam was shocked, "And what if there are other traps? Would you suggest we march right into that which we can't see?"

The old wizard hesitated for a moment, "Very well. You go first. If there are anymore traps you can point them out to us."

This deal is getting worse by the minute. Without much of a choice, Sam shrugged and slowly led the group around the trees. *I'm not incredibly stupid.* He knew to carefully inspect for traps would take hours and he didn't care. If the wizard insisted on being an idiot against his orders, he was going to have to do it on his time schedule. And so he led them inch by painstaking inch into the forest.

The good news that Sam could not possibly know was that Snake was long since gone. After rolling the fallen trees down a hill and into place, she had only waited for the group to appear in her field of vision from a nearby tree. She had counted them and left before they could even see the trees blocking the path.

CHAPTER 10

All was quiet in the forest. Leaves swayed gently in the breeze, small creatures ran to and fro, and six people lay in wait for a horde of trolls. *Just another day in paradise.* The Commander surveyed the scene, quickly picking out the Lords, slowly picking out T and Rock, and never picking out the Reverend. If he hadn't known exactly where he was, he never would have known the excellent thief was there. *At least I know where Snake gets it from.* He scanned the treetops for a sign of the recon team, a.k.a. Snake. There was still no sign of her and she had been gone all day. That was either good or bad. *That's a definite maybe if I ever had one.* Either it meant the bad guys were really far away or she was not coming back. Shaking that thought from his head, the Commander continued to wait.

Across the camp sight, the Reverend watched the Commander search for everyone. He smiled when he realized that he could not be seen. *I guess I've still got it. Not bad for an old man.* Then, he saw the Commander search the treeline and found himself doing the same. Still no Snake. He held his body in check as he wondered where she might be. She had been gone a long time. A small breath behind him stopped his wondering and let him know that everything was okay . . . within reason.

"Took you long enough," he said as he turned to face the calm form of Snake.

"Well, you know me. I had to rearrange the forest while I was away. Never did like making anyone's life too easy," she smirked.

"I don't even want to know. All I want to know is how many and when we can be expecting them."

Snake folded her arms across her chest and grinned, "Don't you think we should have the others join us first so that I don't have to repeat myself and so that I can be filled in on things?"

The Reverend couldn't help but smile. *You are truly growing into one hell of a powerful woman. Note to self: don't be on her bad side.* He signaled for the others to move out of hiding and approach the center of the camp sight. Snake watched as the rest of the party appeared from the hiding places she had seen on her way in. She hoped they had been easy to spot because she was trained in detection and deception and not because they were just obvious. Anymore, it was getting to where she could hardly tell the difference. Yet, she knew that she could be standing directly in front of people and not be seen. She opted for the option that it was her and not them.

The Commander grinned a kind of "I'm-the-center-of-the-universe" grin, the Lords approached in unison, and T and Rock sauntered up to the meeting of the minds.

"Okay," said the Commander, "Tell us what we are up against."

Snake felt the pressure of prying eyes and realized that, for the first time, she could handle it without that sick feeling in her stomach. She was surprised, but no one could see it. She spoke, "We are looking at fifty trolls, Sam, the wizard, and ten of the king's guards, give or take. The guards are leading, followed by . . . "

"Excuse me, but what do you mean 'give or take'?" asked the Commander.

Snake scowled at the interruption but addressed the question, "I mean there were ten but there might be less by the time they get here. I kinda left a trap behind."

Snake waited for the response that had to be coming from the Reverend. After all, she had done it because she knew it would piss him off . . . and because she knew it would work.

"You did what?" boomed the Reverend.

"I left a trap. Look, I had very little choice. It was the only way I could count them, slow them down, and get back in time to be of any use."

"Oh, I see. So, you had this brilliant plan to let them know that we know they are following us, thus rendering our ambush useless," grated the Reverend.

"No," said Snake.

"No? This I have got to hear."

Snake grinned, "Sam knows that T and Rock were not captured, so I'm certain he has already figured out that we have been warned, which would explain why he is still with the group . . . "

"Yeah, he needs to know if he is safe," interjected T.

"So, he knows that we know we are being followed. He will probably view my little trap for what it was, an attempt to slow them down and make them paranoid while we high-tail it for this High Lord guy. So, it really is brilliant, from a certain point of view."

"A certain point of view?" demanded the Reverend.

Gabe had to fight to control his laughter as *The Empire Strikes Back* ran through his head. He couldn't help jumping on a reference he knew no one else would understand. He loved it. "You will find many of the truths we cling to depend largely upon our own point of view."

The Reverend looked at him in confusion, "What?"

The Commander smiled, "Nothing. Just thinking that the lady is probably right, but even if she isn't that doesn't change the fact that this is still our best plan."

The Reverend had quickly and expertly regained his composure, "Of course it is, I thought of it. So, Snake back to the enemy horde."

Snake knew she was in trouble, but there was nothing she could do to help that. As long as she and the Reverend were teamed together, she was sure this was bound to be a reoccurring pattern. In an odd sort of way it was kind of comforting. Patterns imply some sort of normalcy; a rarity in her troubled life.

"So, I'd say we are going to have to face fifty trolls, Sam, the wizard guy, and around six or seven guards," she finished.

"How long do we have to prepare?" asked Gabe.

Snake tried to gauge Sam's level of paranoia. "We have about a day, maybe two."

The Reverend and the Commander exchanged glances.

"What do you think? Should we move on or stand our ground here?" asked the Reverend.

Gabe was getting uncomfortable making decisions for this man, but suspected it was the Reverend's only way of getting his men to follow his lead as the Commander. He turned to Lord Earin.

"How much farther to Bodicia?"

Lord Earin did the mental math, "At least two days."

The Commander nodded, "We stay."

The Reverend smiled, "Like I said, I did think of this plan."

Snake rolled her eyes, "Yeah, it's fabulous, but do you think you could let me in on the rest of it or should I take a nap until it is all over?"

The Reverend cocked his head to one side, "Touchy, touchy. I was planning on including you. It is really very simple. While you were away, the rest of us set up a brilliant system of traps."

Snake sighed, "Any chance of you losing the sarcasm and handling this like a job?"

The Reverend managed a small laugh. In the end, they were still teacher and student. "Of course. We dug a trench across the path at the far end of the clearing. It's as deep as I am tall. Once the first of the troops fall into the trench, we will close off the rear of the clearing by releasing the trees we have cut through so that they fall across the path on that end. This will momentarily prevent them from moving either direction and will cause mass confusion for a while. At that moment, we will hit them with arrows, stones, and knives. If there is anyone standing after the initial onslaught we go after them with swords. Questions?"

Snake thought long and hard about the thousands of things that could and probably would go wrong. "Yeah, what if something goes wrong?"

The Commander jumped in, "We improvise. Anyway you slice it, it's going to be a laugh a minute. Rock and T are in charge of closing in the rear. They will then stand guard to prevent retreats. The rest of us will start the attack."

"Who's in charge of making sure they don't get out of the trench?" asked Snake.

"That would be Lord Earin," replied the Commander.

Snake eyed the troubled Lord and wondered if he was up to the task. But, it really didn't matter. It wasn't as though they had time to recruit better qualified people. She shrugged again.

"What if they don't fall for the trench?"

"The only way to avoid the trench is to enter the forest. If they do that we continue as planned, using the coverage provided to our advantage," answered the Reverend.

"Okay, I'm sold. So what do we do now?"

T decided to voice his opinion, "I have a marvelous idea. Since we have more time, let's eat, widen and deepen the trench, stock up on weapons, and get some rest."

Lord Anjalina sighed, "Finally, one of you has made some sense. Let's listen to the only voice of reason I have heard today."

"My, you certainly do get testy when you are about to set a major ambush, don't you?" teased Commander Gabriel.

She turned on him with fire in her eyes, but said nothing. *He sure takes great pleasure in irritating the hell out of her,* thought Snake. She wasn't sure whose side she was on in this dispute. *It's probably easier not to be on a side.* She decided to take that route. After all, she was only hanging around long enough to find this High Lord guy and get rid of the necklace. She had no intention of forming a lasting relationship with any of these people.

"I'm with T on this one. If I don't eat soon I'm going to get cranky," said Snake.

The Reverend grinned, "Meaning you are not cranky right now?"

"Very funny, boss. Interested in seeing the attitude change?"

The Reverend threw up his hands in mock surrender," Food it is."

*   *   *

The High Lord opened his eyes and looked around his small chamber. Weeks of maintaining his self-protection spell had worn him down to nearly nothing. Seeing that none of the wizards or warriors were in the room, he stopped the spell to give himself some rest. He knew it was dangerous to let the spell lapse, but his power was getting weaker and weaker and his resolve was being to falter.

He removed a small pouch from his robe and took out a root from the Alinith plant from the Lord's garden. Taking only a small bite, he returned the root to hiding and resumed his spell. Fortunately, the healing nature of the root could sustain him for months. But, he couldn't maintain the needed energy for his protection spell much longer. Lords need sleep and rest to regenerate their magic and he truly was not getting either. A sound from the hall drew his attention as the door to the chamber opened. A tall, thin, gaunt man in a long black robe entered the room.

"Resting, High Lord? For your sake, I hope so. You will not be able to resist us much longer. I have received word that Mongrel himself is coming to join us. You are doomed."

With that, the figure turned and left the room, closing the door firmly behind him. Lord Brennen felt true panic surge through his veins. At full strength he could withstand the withered old wizard, but not in his current state. He closed his eyes and searched for help. A single image passed through his mind, he smiled; the Reverend was coming.

*   *   *

Lord Earin paced the length of the camp, yet again. He stopped at the edge of the trench, examined its cover, walked to his hiding place, inspected his spot, and then paced back to the far end of the camp. Snake watched him with distaste. *Does he have any idea how annoying that is?* He had probably walked the length of the camp twenty times that day. It was obvious to Snake that he had never been a thief. *He has no patience. That boy needs to learn to calm down, or I may have to kill him.*

"They will get here soon enough, don't worry," chided the cool lady.

Lord Earin shot a nasty glance at the devious woman, "Are you always this unpleasant?"

Snake smiled, "This is pleasant."

Earin glared at her for a moment, but suspected that she was being truthful. The fact of the matter was he couldn't bring himself to trust or like this woman. She was far too cold and uncaring. And, she could disappear at will—that was completely unnerving. At least the Reverend, who was equally devious, had an emotional attachment to the High Lord. Snake seemed to have no emotions other than anger. Still, she was loyal to the Reverend . . . Earin shook his head and resumed his pacing. *I will never figure that one out.* For the millionth time since they had met, he wondered if the pendants still retained their natural black magic.

Lord Earin quickly crossed the camp to where Lord Anjalina was sitting in silent meditation. He knew he should probably do the same, but he could not seem to bring his thoughts to peace. He watched as she breathed slowly, calmly. He envied her.

"She is Chosen, you cannot change that," said Anjalina as she opened her eyes.

Earin sighed, "I only hope that the pendants are no longer true to their nature."

Anjalina ran her tired hands through her fire red hair and took a deep breath. This mission was wearing her down. She wasn't sure how much more she could take. All she wanted was to find the High Lord, return to the Lord's Palace, and resume the search for the last of the Chosen. She was not sure she had the energy to be a source of constant reassurance for Lord Earin. Still, she tried.

"We have to trust that High Lord Brennen knew what he was doing and that his magic was pure. We have long known that magic works in mysterious ways and that we must follow the path before us. Have faith."

Lord Earin smiled, "I will." *I just hope it is enough.*

Knowing that he was probably just telling her what she needed to hear, Anjalina smiled, "I know."

Then, it happened. Without warning the last moments of peace came to an eternal end. One moment the two Lords were conversing about the quality of magic, the next Snake was standing beside them with an evil look on her face.

"Get in a tree and keep your mouths shut—the bad guys are on their way."

They had scarcely digested her words before the specter of a woman was gone. The two Lords spent one last moment staring at each other for strength before moving to their predetermined places of concealment. The battle was about to begin. Lord Earin searched the clearing for a trace of the others. His eyes were met with the eerie sight of an empty forest.

Trees surrounded him on all sides; massive, towering trees that blocked out the sun and sucked up the sounds of the living world. Earin felt his heart begin to pound against his chest as anxiety filled him. *Relax. Nothing new. Just one more time.* It hadn't always been this way for him. There had been a time when the tame Lord was no stranger to battle, when he looked forward to controlling the battlefield. That time had long since passed. Now, he was a healer and protector and very afraid. He scanned the forest path for a sign of the enemy he knew must be fast approaching. Nothing.

Snake sat high in her perch as lookout and did a quick scan of the team. Lord Earin was at the far end of the clearing just beyond the trench. He was mostly concealed but stood out like a white dot on a black shirt to the seasoned thief. *He looks like he's just about to burst.* Lord Anjalina was hidden in a tree centered in the clearing. She was surrounded by projectiles of every nature. Oddly enough, she looked as though she could handle the situation. Rock and T were calm and composed as they flattened themselves against the forest floor and disappeared. They had done this sort of thing before.

As she watched them prepare for the battle, it occurred to Snake, for the first time ever that she had no idea who they had been before they were thieves. To her, they had always been the Reverend's henchmen. Looking at them now, she had the overwhelming sensation that this was routine to them and that they had been on many a battlefield before now. *Note to self: If we live through this, find out who they really are.* But, as fast as that thought entered her head, it vanished. She knew that as long as she wasn't willing to let anyone in on her past, she had no right to pry into theirs. *Besides, I am Snake now and they are T and Rock. No sense in confusing who we are with who we were.* A sound from the forest path ripped her from her thoughts and forced her to face reality. *Oh, that's right, a war is starting here.*

Snake shook her head and quickly completed her search of the clearing. The Commander lay in wait directly across from Lord

Anjalina. He looked calm, cool, collected, and excited. That failed to surprise her. That done, she focused on the Reverend. He looked like a man awaiting a reckoning. She understood. Life as he knew it had come to screeching halt and the only man he could safely hold responsible was marching this way. *Then again, maybe I'm projecting.* Snake blended into the tree and slid her hand down to the handle of one of her daggers. Gripping it firmly, she attempted to steady her hand and her nerves as she realized she was about to kill someone.

The air felt heavy and dangerous as the small team awaited the forces of evil that were steadily approaching. Hearts pounded against rib cages, breathing became fast and shallow, and the world teetered on the edge. Then, the waiting came to an end.

Snake held her breath as the first of the king's men rode his horse into the clearing. *Only seven left . . . Looks like my plan worked.* As the rest of the force began pouring in, she immediately spotted Sam. He looked like a child afraid that something might jump out of the dark at him. Snake smiled. She had every intention of being that thing. The first of the troops were quickly approaching the trench and the rest kept coming. There was no apparent end to them. As she watched, Snake had a horrifying revelation. They were not all going to be inside the parameters of the trap when the king's men hit the trench. That was bad. No, it was about to be a tragedy.

Snake knew that she had to do something. Instinctively, she wanted to signal the Reverend for some help on this, but she couldn't take the chance with Sam watching. He might not have seen them yet, but he would if she tried to get the Reverend's attention. *Looks like I'm on my own.* Hoping that the Lords could handle this end on their own, Snake slid to the ground and made her way through the forest until she was behind the tail end of the enemy horde. She wasn't entirely sure what she was going to do, but she had to do something. So she watched, waited, and planned.

The Commander counted the trolls for the millionth time. *Damn!* Only about half of them had entered the clearing and the king's men were nearly at the trench. That meant that they wouldn't have them all inside the clearing when it was time to spring the trap. That would be a tragedy. The beauty of this plan relied heavily on the timing of it.

If they had to hesitate, for even a second, there would be time for part of the enemy horde to escape. And, if not all the enemy were in the clearing, they might be able to break the trap. This was not going to work; he had to do something.

Not entirely sure what that something would be, the Commander slipped out of his station and made his way through the forest to where the enemy horde ended. What he saw shocked him. Across the path, slithering through the forest was Snake. *Maybe there is something to these necklaces after all.* Then, an insane notion hit him. T and Rock would have to spring the trap exactly as decided and he and Snake could deal with those not caught inside. *Brilliant! Just how do I let the rest of the world in on this idea in the matter of seconds I have . . .* He never finished that thought. Without warning a scream went up from inside the clearing along with the sound of several large horses falling into a cleverly laid pit. *Fuck! We are all screwed now.*

But, the chaos the Commander was expecting never came. Instead, the next sound and sight to reach his over-active senses was that of massive trees falling across the path only to block the trolls and other bad guys into the clearing. The Commander watched as Rock and T disappeared into the fray as planned. It all felt like they had somehow read his mind. But, now was not the time to stare in amazement; now was the time to kill or be killed. There were still about a dozen trolls that had not been caught in the trap. The Commander pulled his sword and made a mad dash toward the enemy.

He nearly ran into Snake. She simply materialized beside him as he rushed out onto the pathway behind the troops. At that moment he understood. She must have seen what was happening and let T and Rock in on it. That was why they followed the original plan.

"You just couldn't resist a moment to hang out with me, could you?" teased the Commander as he and Snake came up behind the enemy.

Snake grinned a sly grin, "I just knew you'd fuck this all up if I left you alone."

"Ready for this?" he asked.

"Of course."

"Good," he replied raising his sword, "let's get this party started.

Snake mimicked his behavior and calmness, all the while dying inside. As she rushed forward, side by side with the seasoned warrior, a single thought attempted to control her very being . . . she had never actually killed anyone before. She hesitated as the Commander thrust his sword through the torso of one of the trolls. Immediately, the rest of them turned to face this new challenge. It had been only seconds since the trap had been sprung, but it felt like years to Snake as she watched the battle begin. However, there wasn't much time to reflect on her fears. The Commander's action had sent the enemy horde into full force.

Suddenly, she found herself face to face with several hideous creatures with swords that wanted to kill her. One charged at her. She brought her sword up by reflex and the years of training began to take over. Without thinking she countered the first blow; the force of the impact nearly knocked her to her knees. *Shit! These guys are huge . . . and they stink too.* Wide-awake, she brought her sword up to counter the next blow. It didn't take her long to figure out that she could not afford to trade blows with this creature. He was stronger and would eventually win. She had to get nasty, and quick because the others were fast approaching. Reaching into her belt, she drew a dagger. As the troll lifted his arms to deal another blow, she jabbed the dagger into his chest with all her might. The troll shrieked and stumbled away, blood oozed onto her hand, and the world froze.

For the first time in her life, Snake had killed. Her heart raced as she watched him fall to the ground; her senses reeled as she saw him take his last breath; and, she found she was excited by the power she now had. Somehow, looking at the hideous beast, she didn't feel anything. He was simply an evil creature that needed to die. That was the easy part. The slow motion didn't last long. If it hadn't been for the Commander, it might have been over.

"Snake! Your left!" came the Commander's voice from out of the darkness.

Snake ducked and a troll flew over her head. *Oh, that's right, there's a battle going on here.* She came up and sent a dagger flying into that one's heart as well. She was beginning to like that plan. Daggers took a lot less effort than the sword. She pulled two from her brace and sent them flying into the fray; one into the heart of the bastard charging her and one into the eye of the troll the Commander was fighting . . . to make them even.

The Commander watched as a dagger sank itself into the eye of his newest enemy. *What the?!* He turned to see Snake smile and then disappear into the battle. That was a relief. For a moment, she had looked like a new soldier who have never killed anyone before. He had nearly panicked at the thought. Obviously, he had been wrong. *Or else she has done the quickest bit of character changing I have ever seen.* Now, she was flowing through the fight, killing and hacking apart trolls as fast as she could find them. The Commander calmly turned his back on her and finished off the newest troll to engage him.

It didn't take long, however, for the few outside the trap to realize they were being attacked from behind. They all turned with a vengeance to enter this fight. It was about to get really ugly. The Commander didn't waste any time. If the trolls got the upper hand he and Snake would be finished. He ran at full speed toward Snake, taking passing shots with his sword at the few trolls in his path.

"Snake!"

Snake turned to see the Commander closing in on her. Quickly, she scanned behind him and realized why he looked so concerned. The remaining trolls had turned to fight and were rushing them.

"I hope you have a brilliant plan," she said.

He smiled as he reached her, "Of course I do. We cover each other's backs."

"Duh. How?"

"We stand back to back and don't let them separate us. That way we can protect ourselves, each other, and limit their ability to attack."

As their time was up and there seemed to be no other options, Snake agreed to this plan. There was only one part she really didn't care for, she was going to have to trust him. It went against every fiber of her being, but she leaned her back against his. Both were momentarily shocked by the power of the other. That moment soon passed as the real fighting began. With swords extended, the dynamic duo fought for their lives.

*   *   *

The Reverend did a fast count of the number of enemy soldiers still standing. None of the king's men had made it to this point, and only sixteen of the trolls who were in the trap when it was set still stood. The wizard was nowhere to be seen, dead or alive, and Sam was hiding behind any troll he could find to avoid the arrows that had been flying over his head. To this point, the plan had worked pretty well.

As soon as the first line of the king's men hit the trench, T and Rock had released the trees and closed in the back door of the clearing. The Reverend had realized that several of the trolls were not going to be caught in the trap when it was time to spring it, but he hadn't worried long because he saw the Commander and Snake disappear through the trees. With that handled, he had decided to stay and make sure the rest of the world didn't fall apart. It hadn't.

As soon as they had released the trees, T and Rock had charged the rear trolls and taken them by surprise. With hardly any effort, they had managed to kill four of the nasty beasts. At the same moment, the Lords had sent the fury of hell raining down upon the heads of the front lines. The Reverend had been slightly stunned by the fury of Lord Anjalina and the accuracy of Lord Earin, but he recovered swiftly and concentrated on killing trolls all the while tracking his favorite little traitor. Come hell or high water that bastard was going to die.

Now, with only sixteen trolls left, Sam darting through bodies for cover, and an illusive wizard running around somewhere, the Reverend decided to jump in and try sword to sword combat. After all, he was out of things to throw. *Besides,* he grinned, *this is more fun.* Carefully, he jumped from his hiding place and landed on a rather large and nasty troll. Quickly, he pulled his sword across the stunned stead's throat and ended that fight. *I wish they could all be that easy.* But, they weren't, as he well knew from all his years of service with the Lords. So, he thrust himself into battle with all his might and prayed for a miracle.

Across the clearing, Lord Anjalina searched frantically for Mongrel as she launched projectile after projectile into the crowd of ugly trolls. Although she knew she needed to focus on the task at hand, which was to kill as many of the enemy as possible, she could not tear her attention from her search. Mongrel was a bigger danger than all the trolls and enemy soldiers in the land. If he escaped, he would head straight for the High Lord and then they would be out of time. She let another arrow fly into the crowd and held her breath in anticipation of the outcome.

Lord Earin stood on the far side of the pit and fired arrows and spears into the dwindling mass of the enemy. He was growing tired and it seemed that, although the numbers were shrinking, they would never end. He watched as Anjalina searched for Mongrel, but he felt the truth. Mongrel had disappeared as soon as the fighting started and was now on his way to the High Lord's hiding place. As much as he wished it not to be so, the young Lord was too smart to think otherwise. So, he fought on with a heavy heart.

The Reverend sidestepped another attack and lunged forward, bringing his sword into contact with the arm of a troll. Using his free hand, he pulled a knife and sent it flying into the face of another. A thud on his right drew his attention. He turned to see Rock pummeling a troll with his massive fists. Rock was the only man he knew who was powerful enough to go hand to hand with a troll. The Reverend grinned as Rock beat the troll back and then ran him through with his sword. *Ahh, the best of both worlds.* But, now was not the time to admire his men's handiwork. Now was the time to find and kill Sam . . . preferably slowly, although he'd take it any way he could get it.

Sam was harder to find than the Reverend thought, but, after killing or slicing up several more trolls, the Reverend spotted his target. Sam was making his way to the far side of the forest. *Oh no you don't, you bastard.* There was no way the Reverend was going to let Sam escape. True, he had enough connections to have him killed at a moment's notice in nearly any town, but this was a matter of personal vengeance and was to be settled as such.

Trusting his men and the Lords to hold their ground, the Reverend quickly pursued the fleeing traitor across the battlefield and into the waiting forest. This was about to get very interesting.

Sam felt no relief as he finally reached the forest. What should have served as protection, seemed to only be a trap with the enemy hiding behind every tree. He knew the Reverend could not be far behind. He could almost feel his breath hot on his neck. *I don't know how the hell I'm going to get out of this one.* He had let himself be lead into a trap and he knew it. If he died here, he had only himself to blame, although he found it much easier to blame the gnarled old wizard whom he had followed. For an instant he let his mind wander to the whereabouts of Mongrel, but he knew that was a lost cause, and so he ran on.

Cautiously, he stepped through the massive trees, careful to cover his trail and watch over his shoulder. He was so intent on looking back, he nearly missed the shadow that moved beside him. At the last moment, his heightened senses saved his skin . . . for the moment, at least. A small absence of sound to his left caused him to drop to the ground as a dagger flew above his head. He rolled and came to his feet with his sword in hand, only to be face to face with the man who had both given him everything and taken away his glory. Sam stifled his terror and concentrated on his anger.

"You must be slipping, Reverend. There was a time that dagger wouldn't have missed." Sam slid his back toward a tree to protect it as he spoke.

The Reverend grinned as he watched the terrified man maneuver for protection, "Who says I missed? I just wanted your attention. I wanted you to know who killed you."

Sam gritted his teeth in an attempt to control his fear, "We shall see who leaves this forest alive."

Sam lunged forward bringing the Reverend's sword into combat. The Reverend calmly and expertly countered the first blow. But the sword was not where the fight really lay for Sam. He knew that if he traded blows with the Reverend he would loose, horribly. No, for him the true battle rested in the tricks up his sleeve. As he and the massive thief banged swords, he prepared to release the trick he had up his sleeve. As soon as the Reverend struck his next blow, Sam pushed his back against the tree, brought his knee up, and shoved the Reverend back with all his might. The Reverend stumbled back and Sam brought his arm up and released the mini-crossbow he had up his sleeve. It had saved his ass many times. This was not to be one of them.

He heard the spring of the release, felt the snap of the string, and saw the Reverend start to laugh out loud. Sam stood in shock as the Reverend held up a tiny arrow.

"Looking for this?" he asked the perplexed traitor.

Sam felt his heart sink to the pit of his stomach. He was about to die.

"What's a matter, Sam? Did you forget that I'm a thief, and a damn good one, too? Now, I'm done playing with you. Let's finish this."

Sam brought his sword up to defend himself as he watched the Reverend charge. He was certain that it was all over at last. What happened next shocked him and the Reverend both.

"Reverend!" came the yell from the camp, "We need you."

Still fighting with Sam, the Reverend chanced a look back toward the fighting. He saw a flash of red and white. Immediately, he knew it was Lord Anjalina. She would not call unless something had gone horribly wrong. He knew he had little choice but to return to his duty. Yet, his heart ached to kill Sam, now. Sam seized the opportunity.

"You can't have it both ways. They will be destroyed without you. Where do your loyalties lie?"

The Reverend wanted to strangle Sam with his bare hands, but knew he didn't have the time.

"Reverend! Rock has been injured . . . more troops . . . the Commander is still out . . . " came the muffled yells. That was enough. The Reverend broke from the fight and began to run like hell back to the clearing.

Sam turned and ran the other way, his victory fresh on his mind. So confident was he in his win that he failed to look where he was going. It was too late when he saw Snake standing on the path in front of him. He turned to run back the way he came but soon felt a fiery pain shoot up his back. He stumbled and fell to the ground. With his face in the dirt and intense pain coursing through his body, he could only listen as Snake approached and leaned over his still form.

"You made a mistake, Sam. You assumed that you could escape my anger, my hatred, and my vengeance. That, as everyone will soon discover, is not possible."

Sam lifted his head to beg for his life, but he never had a chance. Snake used that opportunity to slit his throat. As his head fell to the ground with a thud, Snake felt that tiny place inside her that was still human shrink. She had finally killed another human being, and she had done it brutally and swiftly. She attempted to feel remorse, but could not. *Am I really that dead? Have I really lost who I am?* She stared into his vacant eyes and was surprised that her hatred for him was gone; she simply felt nothing as she watched the blood from his throat form a pool under his body. He was no more; she was no more. Somehow, the trade didn't seem fair. Almost as an afterthought, she reached down and pulled her dagger out of his back. Wiping it on his tunic to remove the blood, she put it away and headed at a run for the rest of the battle.

*   *   *

The Reverend reached the battle about two steps ahead of the Commander. Both men were sweaty and covered with blood, but neither looked as though he was defeated. They simply nodded acknowledgments to one another and then focused all of their attention on the battle before them. What they saw nearly broke them.

The dwindling troops were no longer dwindling. Instead, they had multiplied. The Reverend checked, again. Yes, they had definitely multiplied. When he had left this party there had been under sixteen. Now, there were at least twenty-five of the hideous creatures running around trying to kill the Lords and his only two surviving friends. The Lords had taken positions opposite one another in the trees and were throwing everything they could find at the trolls, but they weren't getting very far. T was engaged in sword to sword combat with several trolls at the far end of the clearing. Rock was nowhere to be seen.

The Reverend stepped into the fray with the Commander at his side. Immediately, both men began to slice through trolls as they worked a path towards T. They had to dig him out of the corner he was stuck in at the moment. As he hacked at nasty body parts, the Reverend tried to get information out of the Commander.

"Are the outside trolls taken care of?" he yelled through the fight.

"They were," screamed the Commander, "but it seems we can't be sure of anything."

The Reverend kicked a troll in the gut and slammed a dagger into his throat, "Yeah, there were a lot fewer of these guys here when I went in pursuit of Sam. It's like they multiplied."

The Commander had thought that there were too many trolls running around alive for the Reverend to have left the others to their own devices, but he wasn't sure about his need for revenge. That same need had sent Snake into the forest in an attempt to sneak up on this Sam character.

As if he had read his mind, the Reverend asked, "Where the hell is Snake?"

As though on cue, a sinister figure appeared along side the Reverend to answer, "Right beside you boss."

Both men experienced relief at the sight of the bitter bitch and the slew of weapons she had with her. After placing several daggers in strategic body parts of the many trolls running around, Snake calmly asked, "Where did all these guys come from? There were not this many inside and we killed all the ones outside the trap."

The Reverend smiled to himself at the thought of Snake and the Commander wiping out so many bad guys by themselves. *Maybe there is something to those damn necklaces after all.* But, now was the time to figure out what had gone wrong. He was not going to loose this battle. He had to live to kill Sam in his sleep some dark night.

"Listen, I'll make my way to T. You and the Commander get to the Lords and find out what the hell happened here and if there is anything they can do to stop it!" ordered the Reverend.

At this point in the fighting, neither of them needed to be told twice. All they wanted to do was get the hell out of this mess alive. There was no time and no need to argue about who would be in charge. *Besides,* thought Snake, *this combination has worked before.* So, Snake and the Commander began working their way back through the bodies toward the Lords in hopes that they had some answers.

The Reverend never turned to see whether or not his orders were being carried out. He knew they would be. At this point in the game, it seemed they had little choice. He slipped to the edge of the forest and ran up behind T's position. Bursting through the trees, he was just in time to slice through the arm of the newest troll to attack T.

"What the hell took you so long? I'm not a one man army you know," said T.

"Sorry. I was attempting to take care of that other business," replied the Reverend.

"How did it go?" asked T calmly as he hacked apart yet another nasty troll.

"I made an appointment for a later date when I realized you needed babysitting," answered the Reverend as he ran his sword through the guts of the nearest bad guy. "What the hell happened, and where is Rock?"

"Trolls started coming out of thin air, the Lords hit the trees on my order, and Rock took a slice. He's alive, but out of commission. I dumped him in the trench and made my way back over here in an attempt to keep them away from him. Then, you show up to try and steal all the glory."

The Reverend's head clicked through all the possibilities as he fought for his life. Then, it hit him like a ton of bricks; Mongrel had to be running some kind of regeneration spell. He had to be stopped.

"T, we have got to get to the Lords," said the Reverend.

T sighed as he looked at the mountain of trolls between them and the Lords. Most were charging the trees that now held the Lords and Snake and the Commander. They had started hacking at them with their swords in an attempt to bring them down, forcing the Lords to leap trees, leaving most of their weapons behind.

"Okay," responded T, "but this is going to suck."

The Reverend nodded in agreement. This was indeed going to suck, but it had to be done if they were going to pull this one out of their asses. With all their might, the two master thieves pushed their way through the battlefield and to the newest tree filled with Lords and other good-guy types.

Snake looked down at the mass of trolls swarming the tree. They had their swords drawn and were starting to chop at this tree, too. She could see that this was going to be an annoying pattern for the rest of this battle unless they did something about it. The problem was figuring out what. She looked at the frazzled Lord Anjalina beside her in the tree. She was worn beyond recognition. She looked as though she had fought the entire battle by herself. And, now, as she held onto the tree branch for dear life, ready to leap to the next tree, she looked defeated. Snake had no idea how to comfort her; sympathy was not her strong suit. All she wanted was to get out of these trees, find the wizard that Anjalina had said was causing this mess, and move on with this painful mission. She didn't see that happening anytime soon.

Snake looked across the clearing to where the Commander was pushing Lord Earin on to the next tree. For a split second, the Lord looked more like a skilled soldier than a Lord. Snake shook her head. It had to be time and place. She watched as they jumped into yet another tree. At this rate they were going to run out of trees and end up in the trench. *End up in the trench . . .* Suddenly, the light went on in Snake's head. They were all out of options and so she had a plan. All she had to do was get the others to follow along. *This would be a whole lot easier if the Reverend and T would magically appear.* In answer to her thought, a familiar face appeared in the tree next to them.

"Hello, my dear. Did you miss me?" asked the Reverend.

"I wasn't aiming for you," quipped Snake.

"Can't you be serious for just a moment? We are in no condition to play games!" yelled the exhausted Lord Anjalina.

Both thieves knew better than to play with her. They sobered up immediately.

"I have a plan, boss."

Snake was interrupted by the shaking of the tree as the trolls pounded on it with their swords. Anjalina lost her grip on her branch and slipped. Almost as a reflex, Snake reached down and grabbed her arm. Several trolls below howled madly and tried to grab the lady Lord's legs and pull her out of the tree. Without hesitation, the Reverend let some daggers fly into the trolls' eyes in an attempt to give Snake time. Snake wrapped her other arm tightly around a branch above her, braced her legs, and yanked Lord Anjalina back into the tree. Anjalina seemed relieved and sad all at the same time.

"Please tell me your plan involves getting us out of these trees in one piece," she mumbled.

Snake grinned, "Of course it does. I say we all make for the trench.

We join Rock inside, make sure he's still alive, and give the Lords cover until they can find Mongrel and make him stop with the regenerating of dead trolls."

Lord Anjalina nodded. She had informed Snake that, when the Reverend went after Sam, Mongrel had started bringing trolls back to life. She and Lord Earin could only find him if they were together and unoccupied with the fighting. That had not been possible so far and so Mongrel continued to use his magic from wherever he was hiding. She agreed with Snake's plan.

"I think that is the best option. How do we get the Commander and Earin to follow along?" she asked.

"It's done," smiled the Reverend.

Snake and Lord Anjalina followed his gaze to see T darting across the battlefield to the tree next to the one Lord Earin and the Commander were now in. That was enough for them. With the Reverend leading the way, the small group made its way from tree to tree until they were next to the trench. The trolls had not wasted much time hacking away at any more trees. When they saw the small band on the move, they began running toward the trench at full speed. There was only a matter of seconds between the moment they reached the trench and the moment the trolls were upon them.

As they leapt in for cover, Snake saw the Commander, Earin, and T reach their final tree. She hoped they wouldn't be too late to be of any use. They weren't. Instead of jumping straight for the trench the Commander and T jumped down behind the charging mass of uglies and Lord Earin dove for the trench and his fellow Lord. Snake grinned. It seemed the Commander was totally crazy. *That helps.* T wasn't too far behind on the nut-case scale as the two men attempted to engage and kill as many of the trolls as possible.

The Reverend decided to take advantage of the small relief. Crawling over dead bodies and maimed horses, he made his way toward the back of the trench and the semi-conscious figure of Rock. Rock had a gash across his abdomen; he looked like a man who wasn't going to make it. The Reverend quelled those thoughts and bent over Rock's form.

"Can you hear me?"

Rock mumbled in reply.

"Dammit, Rock! Don't you fucking die on me! You're not getting out of this one that easily!" yelled the Reverend as he attempted to wrap the wound to stop the bleeding. There was only moaning from Rock in response.

That was enough for the Reverend. He didn't have enough friends left for one of them to die. He wasn't sure that any cause was worth the death of one more good man. He yelled for the Lords. Seeing the pain and anger in his eyes, they responded without hesitation. They ran through the trench to the relative safety of his position, leaving Snake to handle the defense of the trench.

"I don't care what it takes or who has to die, you find that bastard wizard, NOW! I want him stopped and I want this over. Then, I want you to find a way to save his life," commanded the Reverend pointing to the near lifeless form of Rock.

Lord Earin took a deep breath as he realized there was a good chance Rock would not make it. The last thing he wanted was to incur the Reverend's wrath. "We will do it," he said as Lord Anjalina pleaded with him mentally.

"Good. Snake and I will give you all the time we can."

Then he was gone and the Lords were left alone to try and find Mongrel and stop him. Lord Earin was painfully aware that this was the most precarious situation of his life; Lord Anjalina was painfully aware that this was the most important moment of hers. If they could not find and stop Mongrel, this battle would be lost, and so would the lives of two Chosen and the High Lord. She could not let that happen. Briefly she glanced back across the trench to where the Reverend and Snake were fighting for all their lives. They had cleverly barricaded themselves behind several dead horses and the bodies of the king's soldiers. Any trolls who approached the trench met with knives, arrows, and spikes. Any who were unfortunate enough to jump in met with the Reverend's sword. *So far, so good . . . I guess.* Lord Anjalina quickly turned to the task at hand.

"Ready?" she asked Earin.

He nodded with complete determination on his face. Swiftly, as the time they had was disappearing, the two Lords began the incantation. It started as a low humming in the back of their throats and worked its way into a mumbled chant. The Lords joined hands, closed their eyes, and let the magic flow over them. Once they were completely enveloped by the power, they turned their attention to Mongrel. Slowly the magic oozed from the pair and spread out in search of resistance. This spell was designed to feel around for other magic in use. When it came into contact with other magic there would be resistance on the spell, thus locating the center of the other spell.

The Lords continued to chant, trusting those around them to keep them safe as they were totally defenseless in this state. Sweat begin to pour down their faces; the longer they kept the spell going, the worse it would become for their physical state. Lord Earin willed the spell to move faster. Lord Anjalina matched his surge of energy. The magic flowed outward, and, just when they thought they could go no further, they hit a magic wall in the forest just to the right of the trench. Abruptly, the two Lords released each other and let the spell die. Breathing heavily, they attempted to regain composure and to signal the Reverend.

Earin took a deep breath and tried to yell, "Reverend . . . Rev . . . er . . . end!"

It was no use. The sounds of the battle prevented him from hearing the meek voice of the exhausted Lord. Lord Earin tried to stand, but his legs did not yet have the strength to support him. They did not have time for the weakness that accompanies magic use. Every second was precious, and Mongrel would now be alerted. *We have come too far for this to happen. Get up!* Lord Earin clamored to his knees and began to crawl toward the Reverend, his sheer will power keeping him in motion.

Lord Anjalina watched him go. *Good luck.* Then she turned to the injured Rock. His breathing was shallow and blood oozed from his wound despite the wrap the Reverend had put around it. It looked bad. Still he was alive when others should have died. If his will to survive was that strong, then perhaps there was a chance that they could save him. With the little energy she had left, Anjalina reached into her robes and pulled out a small piece of Alinith plant from the Lord's garden. It had great healing and nourishing properties. She forced a small piece into Rock's mouth and stroked his throat until he swallowed it. Then, she broke the remainder open and applied it to Rock's wound. *I hope this works.* Having done all that she could for the physical wound, Lord Anjalina laid her head upon his chest and began to pray for them all.

*   *   *

The Commander kicked the troll on his left in the knee and jabbed the one on his right in the stomach with his sword. He and T had been fighting non-stop since their decision to not join the others in the trench. It was tactically simple and mortally dangerous, just the way the Commander liked them, but it was also getting old very fast. The Commander moved closer to the trench with T at his side.

T looked over at his fellow warrior, "Going in?"

The Commander grinned, "I was thinking about it."

T glanced over his shoulder, "Think again."

The Commander looked over his shoulder to see Lord Earin edging along the ground on his hands and knees. *Mother-fucker . . . what is going on here?!* He faced forward to deal with the fight before him and yelled over his shoulder, "Earin! Are you okay?"

The Lord was startled by the sound of the Commander's voice, but recovered quickly as relief flowed through him. "We have located Mongrel. He is just behind the first line of trees to the right of the trench," eeked Earin.

The Commander had to strain to hear the Lord, but he heard him and that was enough. They had the wizard and that was all they needed to turn the tide of this battle . . . if they could get to him in time. Commander Gabriel turned to T, "You heard the man, let's go."

T needed no prompting for this one. Since the moment he had discovered that this wizard was in part responsible for the death of his friends, he had despised him and wanted him dead. The opportunity to confront him and end this ridiculous fight sounded golden to him. Throwing a troll over his shoulder and onto a spike in the trench, T kicked himself into high gear and followed the Commander to the far side of the trench.

The two men were moving at high speeds, now, intent on the sole purpose of finding and destroying Mongrel. They scarcely slowed down to confront any number of trolls in their way. They were on a mission. The trees loomed before them, trolls were in their path and on their tails, and then they were through the trees. At the sound of the two men crashing through the forest, Mongrel came to his feet in fear.

"Times up you old bastard," said the Commander calmly as he charged for Mongrel.

T circled around the outside and tried to block the wizard's escape path. Mongrel, though caught off guard, simply smiled and waved his hand above the cauldron at which he had been working. Then, he was gone. Commander Gabriel found himself face to face with the ground as he leapt to tackle the vanishing man. He was too late. Mongrel was gone. T stood in shock.

"Where the hell is he?" he panted.

Commander Gabriel picked himself up off the ground, "Beats the hell out of me, Roy. With magic like that he could be anywhere. I just hope he disappeared himself to a far off location."

"How are we suppose to kill someone who can vanish in thin air? I wasn't trained in the art of hand to hand combat with ghosts."

"Well, we can't do much good here. Let's get back to the kind of battle we were trained for. I don't know how I'm going to get us out of this one," said the Commander.

The two men sighed, picked up their swords, and headed back to the battlefield only to encounter nothing but dead trolls. They exchanged confused glances and cautiously stepped out into the clearing. All around them lay dead trolls. There wasn't a sign of life. Unsure of what to think, they made their way to the trench and peered over the edge. Snake and the Reverend stood poised and ready to fire.

"Hey! Don't shoot! It's us," said the Commander.

"Where are the rest of the trolls?" asked the Reverend.

"Well, that's the funny part. You see, apparently they are all dead," replied Commander Gabriel.

"How did you kill all those trolls?" asked Snake in amazement.

"See, now, that's even funnier. We didn't. When we went to look for Mongrel, like Lord Earin told us to, there were plenty of trolls still hanging around ready to kill us. After Mongrel disappeared and we came back, they were all dead."

The Reverend sighed, "So, I take it Mongrel got away."

T shrugged, "Don't blame us, the guy just disappeared. At least he's gone."

"Yeah. I guess. Let's just hope he doesn't decide to return right away," said the Reverend. "Now, get down here and let's check on Rock and the Lords."

The two men jumped into the trench and followed the Reverend and Snake to the little hiding place of the Lords and Rock. To their amazement, all three were fast asleep.

Snake thought she had seen it all, but this was unreal. "Must be nice not to care how the battle ends."

The Reverend looked at the Commander and the two shared a smirk. "It's a Lord thing. When they use too much magic at once, they fall asleep."

Snake threw her hands in the air, "Well that's just great. Some help these two are going to be. What good does it do to have Lords around if they need a nap every time they help us out? I'm so glad they are in charge of the safety of the Land."

While Snake went off on her bitter tirade, the Reverend bent down to check on Rock. Surprisingly, he looked better. The ghostly pale of only moments ago was beginning to subside and his wound had stopped oozing blood. He let a small sigh of relief escape his lips and then pulled himself together. *This 'aint over yet.*

"Well, I guess someone had better wake the Lords," said the Reverend.

"Oh let me," said T as he kicked them both in the legs. "Hey! Wake up!"

Lord Anjalina slowly opened her eyes and glared at the thief, "Weren't you ever taught any manners?" she mumbled.

T grinned, "Yeah, I have manners. I didn't spit on you or anything."

Commander Gabriel suppressed a chuckle. It did his heart good to see Anjalina angry. He wasn't really sure why he derived so much pleasure from her anger, he just did. "It's not that we really wanted to bother you, it's just that we'd like to know what the hell is going on."

Lord Earin managed to sit up and look around, "Did you get Mongrel?"

"Not exactly," replied the Commander.

Lord Earin sighed, "Let me guess. He disappeared in a puff of smoke."

The Commander nodded, "You got it. And, then all the trolls died. It was the weirdest thing."

"Not really, Commander. That is a property of the regeneration spell. If the magician is no longer present to maintain the spell, those under it return to their former state of death. The good side of that is Mongrel is gone and the fighting is over. The bad side is . . . "

"Mongrel is gone and probably heading straight for the High Lord," finished the Reverend.

"Now what?" asked Snake.

The Reverend looked at Rock and then at the Lords, "What about Rock?"

Lord Anjalina responded, "I treated him with Alinith. He should improve, but he will need rest and care."

"Can we move him?" asked the Reverend.

Anjalina sighed, "You will do whatever you deem necessary. I suggest that we move him carefully until he regains consciousness."

"That still doesn't answer my question," interjected Snake. "Now what do we do?"

"We continue as planned," said the Commander. "Before you all try to kill me, remember that we have to get to the High Lord. That is our purpose in being here. That has not changed."

"Yeah, but now that Mongrel character is way ahead of us and knows exactly what we are up to. What's to stop him from heading straight for the High Lord and killing him?" demanded T.

Lord Earin answered, "Make no mistake, Mongrel will make his way straight to High Lord Brennen. However, he cannot just kill him. He must sacrifice him to prevent him from returning in spirit form. This he cannot do as long as the High Lord can continue to run a protection spell. Though he must be weakening, the High Lord can still be protecting himself. The greatest danger we have is that Mongrel gets to the High Lord soon and moves him. If that happens, we are right back where we started and will have lost precious time."

There was silence as each member of the small and beat-up team took in the truth behind Earin's words. It seemed that for each step forward, they were forced to take twenty steps back. Things were going from bad to worse in a hurry. Then, just when the train was about to hit, a small miracle set them all in motion again.

"Sounds like we had better get moving then," came the whispered voice of Rock.

All faces turned to see the damaged thief laying there with open eyes and a crooked smile on his face. They were all speechless.

"What did I miss? You all look like you just saw a ghost?"

T slapped his leg and laughed right out loud, "Son of a bitch. Do me a favor, the next time you want out of a battle, don't try getting killed to do it."

T walked over to his friend and patted him on the shoulder. The Reverend was close behind, followed by Snake.

"You scared the crap out of me. Don't do that again," said the Reverend.

Snake couldn't help herself, she was smiling. Rock looked up at her and grinned.

"What? No kiss?" he teased.

Snake laughed, "Not for lazy people who miss battles by playing dead."

"Great. The one time I could use a little sympathy and it backfires in the romance department."

The Reverend, filled with a new sense of hope, stood and turned to face the Lords. "You heard the man, we had better get moving."

The Lords found themselves smiling with hope and relief as they stood to join the Reverend. This was not going to be easy, but it had to be done. With the last bit of courage and hope they could muster, the small band of warriors picked up the pieces and moved forward into history.

CHAPTER 11

L ord Brennen knew something was terribly wrong, and that was a good thing. For some inexplicable reason those who were holding him had suddenly been filled with overwhelming panic and had began preparations for something in a panic. At first, he had thought that the Reverend had found him. However, had that been the case he would have found out from the Reverend and not because the guards were alerted to his presence. The Reverend was much too talented to be discovered by these goons. Still, whatever it was it had them all panicked.

With his remaining strength, the High Lord decided to reach out to the outside and see if he could get some information other than just the senses and sounds of mass confusion. He closed his eyes and calmly sent forth his mind to explore the darkness. It took only a matter of seconds for him to find the source and the center of the panic. *Mongrel!* Mongrel was here, but he was not prepared to battle the High Lord. Instead, Lord Brennen sensed urgency and exhaustion. He probed further. *The Reverend, the Commander, Earin, Anjalina, and . . . who are you?* There were others with them, but he could not tell who they were. All he did know was that Mongrel had met up with them, but had been beaten. Now, he was here, they were on the way, and he was about to move the High Lord.

Immediately, Lord Brennen knew the problem that was about to arise. He would be moved to a new and unknown location, his friends would be lead here, and if they survived the trap, they would be right back where they started in trying to find him. He had to do something.

There had to be a way to warn his friends. For a moment he considered ending it all, but that notion was too ridiculous to consider. It would only put the Betrayer one step closer to his goal. Then it hit him. He needed to find out where they were taking him and leave a message for his fellow lords, but there wasn't much time.

Swiftly, he began to search the minds of the guards and other non-magic captures, hoping that one of them might hold the knowledge. If he had to, he would probe the magicians, but that ran the risk of letting them know he was searching. As it was, he was dangerously close to losing consciousness now. He searched in vain. It seemed that no one low enough had been given the pertinent information. He pulled back his mental searching and began to prepare himself for a mental battle with the less powerful wizards. But, that moment never came.

Instead, his prayers were answered by the guards right outside his door. Lord Brennen had heard them approaching and knew his time was running out, so he had began to scribble a message to the Lords on his cell floor with the invisible juice of the Alinith plant. Suddenly, he heard one of them raise his voice in confusion.

"The island of Tay-yah-nay?! Why in the hell would anyone want to go to that fuckin' place?"

The other guard responded with just as much enthusiasm, "Not me, but those are the damn orders."

"Yeah, well they stink. Who came up with this bright idea anyway?"

"That new wizard that showed up today."

"That's just great. He shows up all in a panic and now we got to drag the high and mighty prisoner off to Tay-yah-nay island. I hate this fuckin' job."

"Me, too. But, it's either this or no job."

"I hear ya on that one. Well, come on. Let's get this guy onto the boat."

When the door opened, the two guards found the old prisoner sitting calmly in the center of the cell with a look of peaceful calm on his face.

"What are you so happy about? Don't you know that you are scheduled to die a slow and painful death? I wouldn't be happy about that," said the bigger guard.

The High Lord smiled, "And yet, you are seemingly happy."

The bigger guard looked at his companion, "Can you believe this guy?"

The second guard laughed a nervous laugh, "Yeah. Let's get him out of here. He gives me the creeps."

As the two men dragged the gentle High Lord away, they could not see the reason for his content. In letters that only Lord could see, scribbled on the cell floor, were the words "the island of Tay-yah-nay". And so, he held on to hope and moved forward.

*   *   *

T rubbed his eyes and yawned, but refused to fall asleep. They had been marching non-stop all day. Only the setting of the sun and Rock's need for rest had ceased the endless walk. Since the battle had begun, this was the first time that any of them had rested. T had volunteered to take the first watch so that the rest of them could rest, a plan he was starting to regret. He let out another yawn, shifted in his post, and willed himself to stay awake. He was nearly asleep when Snake tapped him on the shoulder and sent him leaping into the air.

"I'm sorry. I didn't mean to scare you."

"For the love of . . . Shit, Snake. Why do you insist on doing that?" demanded T as he attempted to regain his composure.

"I can't help it. It seems that, anymore, I don't have the ability to make noise even when I want to. It's as though silence is a habit," replied the stunning thief.

T had recovered by this time and was now wide awake, "Maybe you should get a hobby. Ever think about cooking?"

Snake rolled her eyes at her friend, "Yeah and perhaps you should start going to church."

"Point taken. So, what brings you out to my neck of the woods?"

Snake hesitated, but then spoke, "It's my turn on watch."

T didn't fall for it, "Try again. The Reverend is next on watch and that's not for another hour. So, what's up?"

Snake grinned, "I am."

"Ha, ha. Fine don't tell me. See if I care."

Snake grimaced, "Pathetic does not become you."

T smiled, "I know, but is it working?"

Snake shrugged her shoulders. She didn't really know what to say. "I can't sleep."

"Neither can I," responded the Reverend as he walked up to join the others. "That's why I thought I'd let you get some rest early, T."

"Great," said T, "now we are going to have a little family reunion. Why can't you sleep?"

The Reverend sat down next to his two favorite people and sighed, "I can't stop thinking that Sam got away and we nearly lost the battle because I wanted to kill him, so I failed twice."

Oh shit. I forgot. In all the action and the aftermath of marching forward, Snake had forgotten to inform them that Sam was dead.

"Actually, that's not entirely true," said Snake.

"What do you mean?" asked the Reverend.

"Sam didn't get away. I came up on him in the forest and I killed him. I slit his throat. That's why I can't sleep."

There was dead silence as the two men absorbed what she had said. Sam was dead. She had killed him. He had paid for what he had done. T was ecstatic.

"You are my own personal goddess. Unbelievable! You killed that slimy, back-stabbing, no good son-of-a-bitch. Now, I can sleep."

T suddenly noticed that the other two were silent. For a moment, Snake looked like the child she really was and the Reverend looked like he was in pain. A second later it sank into his thick skull. Snake had never killed anyone before. As hard as she was, it had been easy to overlook. He tried not to feel like a complete ass.

"Hey, what you did was right and justified. It had to be done and he deserved it. If he had lived, he would have killed us. Don't beat yourself up over this."

Snake looked over at T and saw real tenderness in his eyes. She attempted a smile, "Thanks."

For a moment there was an awkward silence as everyone tried to sort out their emotions and figure out how to survive this one. Finally, it went as far as T could stand. *I guess I had better leave and let them sort this out on their own. That seems to be when they do their best.*

"Well, I guess I'll get some rest then so that we aren't all exhausted tomorrow. Reverend, have a good watch. Snake, get some sleep. Night."

"Sweet dreams," mocked the Reverend.

"Screw you," came the loving reply as T crossed the camp to his bed sight.

The Reverend turned all of his attention to Snake. He struggled to remember what it felt like to have killed another human being for the first time, but found he couldn't. He had known that feeling for so long that he had become totally deadened to it. He searched his remaining soul and reached out to Snake.

"I'm sorry that you have to go through this. I know how you must feel," offered the Reverend.

"How?" asked Snake with a quiet desperation in her voice.

"Sad, confused, angry, depressed . . . "

"Oh, is that how I'm supposed to feel?" asked Snake.

The Reverend was taken aback, "What do you mean? How do you feel?"

"I feel nothing. I am completely numb. He is no more and all of me that was human is gone. That is how I feel."

The Reverend was mortified. Had it finally happened? Was she finally dead? Had she finally lost herself in her despair and reached that point where no one could bring her back; that place that he had lived for so many long years? He couldn't believe it was true. He was unable to think of the right thing to say, so he said nothing.

Snake raised her eyes and looked at him pleadingly, "Somehow I thought revenge would taste better."

Then it hit him like a ton of bricks. Her whole life was about revenge; her desire for revenge gave her the strength to get up in the morning. If this numbness was all there was, what did she have to live for? Revenge was suppose to bring her happiness and peace and now she knew it would not. At last, he understood.

"The problem with revenge is that it can consume you for so long and then be over in a matter of seconds. The energy the hatred requires is a hundred times greater than the energy the act requires, and so we often feel unfulfilled when it is all said and done. The real trick is to find another reason to live."

She heard his words, understood them, and even saw the truth in them, but she simply could not accept them. Revenge was all she had and she didn't know how to find something else. *Am I destined to feel dead? Is there no joy left for me to feel in this world?*

"Yeah, like what?" she asked.

"Are you serious? Like me, of course," he said with a grin.

She couldn't help it. In spite of herself, Snake smiled. "You really are a cocky son-of-a-bitch, aren't you?"

"That's why they call me the Reverend."

"No, they call you the Reverend because Lord-High Son-of-a-Bitch is too long," smirked Snake.

The Reverend grinned, "You know you love me. You can't help yourself; I have such a charming personality."

Snake groaned, "No matter what happens in the world, you will always be the same smug bastard who is madly in love with himself."

"And what, my dear, is wrong with that?"

Snake shook her head, *what indeed.* For a brief moment she let herself think about it. *Why not live for another reason? Why not make it him?* She knew her answer to those thoughts before she ever finished them. *Have you forgotten, stupid. Everyone you care for either dies or betrays you.* Her mood quickly returned to dark. All smiles disappeared from her face and she stared fast at the ground.

The Reverend watched as Snake did some sort of mental battle with herself. In the end, he wasn't sure whether she had won or lost. The only thing he was certain of was, if he couldn't bring some of her human side back, they would all be lost. He approached it as calmly as he could.

"T is right. Sam deserved to die. Perhaps you feel numb because he doesn't merit any feeling," tried the Reverend.

Snake looked up into his eyes and was hit by the pang of mixed emotions. Something inside her wanted to love him, but the rest of her was conditioned to know better. She shrugged and resumed staring at the ground.

"Maybe you're right. I don't know anymore. All I do know is I want this to all be over soon so that I can work on my reason for living."

As Snake stood and walked away, the Reverend wondered which

reason she was working on. He hoped for one, but knew it was the other. *I could kill the King myself for making her so bitter. Maybe I should . . .* He let that thought go, too. If he took that away from Snake, she would never forgive him. There was nothing else to do. He turned all of his attention to guard duty and waited for the night to end.

* * *

It was morning, of that the Commander was certain. He had been sitting, watching, and waiting long enough for that to be so. The only problem was there was no sun to awaken the rest of the world. Instead, the sky was filled with dark and ominous clouds. Instead of coming alive, the rest of the world tucked itself in and prepared itself to battle the storm that must be coming. The Commander surveyed the dark forest, glanced at his traveling companions, and stood to face the day. *Guess I'd better get this party started. But who to wake first?* He glanced at the Reverend. *Not a chance.* He looked at Rock. *Nope.* Then his eyes fell on Snake. *Only if I'm feeling really suicidal.* A grin slipped across his face. *I'm certifiable, that's for certain.*

For no other reason than he thought it might be fun, the Commander attempted to sneak up on Snake and wake her. It was the first and the last time he ever tried anything so stupid. He watched every step as he approached. He moved slowly and silently. He held his breath. He leaned down over her and . . .

"One more step and you will never be able to pee standing up again," hissed Snake's voice.

The Commander heard the threat in her words, but more importantly he felt the threat of her dagger against his groin. He took a step back and grinned.

"Easy, Nitro. I was just coming to wake you. It's morning and time to get going. No need to cut off any body parts. We are all on the same team here."

Snake sat up and returned her dagger to its hiding place. "Is there a special reason you insist on provoking people, or are you just generally an asshole?"

He shrugged, "I guess I'm just an asshole."

Snake sighed. The Commander was hopelessly arrogant and insisted on making life less serious than it truly was. It was a quality that could have been endearing, but ended up being chronically annoying.

"Well, I suppose you had better wake up the Lords since that little trick of yours roused all my friends."

The Commander turned to see all the thieves up with weapons ready and big grins on their faces. He never even hesitated, "So my plan has worked; you are all awake."

Rock snorted, "Your plan, my ass. Your lucky that Snake is faster than the rest of us."

T laughed and the Reverend stood and stretched. He looked out into the morning and sighed. "Is this really morning? Looks like we are in for a fun day of walking in the rain."

Commander Gabriel began to sing, "Singin' in the rain, I'm singin' in the rain . . . "

The others looked at him like he had lost his mind, and life was back to normal. By the time they had roused the Lords, consumed some food, and packed all the gear for the march, the rain had started to fall. At first it was a light drizzle; just enough to make everything damp, slippery, and generally annoying. Soon, however, it worked its way into a massive downpour. It was like a wall of water that they were struggling to pass through. It wasn't long before they could not hear each other and could barely see each other through the constant sheets of water. Snake, who had taken the lead, called a halt. She worked her way back to the Reverend who was bringing up the rear and supporting an exhausted Rock.

"This is not going to work. I'm afraid I'm going to loose someone," she yelled over the pouring rain and constant rumbling of thunder.

The Reverend produced a rope, "Here!" he yelled as he shoved it at her. "We'll tie together with this!"

Snake looked at Rock as she took the rope, "Is he going to be okay?! Should we stop and wait out this storm?!"

The Reverend shook his head, "We can't afford to stop! Keep moving and I'll make sure he makes it!"

Snake knew better than to argue with the Reverend on this. She also knew he was right. She took the rope that he had secured to himself and Rock and made her way forward to where the others were. First, she looped the rope around Lord Earin, he nodded in understanding. She then secured T, Lord Anjalina, and finally the Commander. Wrapping the last length around herself, Snake started the drenched company forward into the dark and wet unknown.

They hadn't gone far when Snake felt a sharp tugging at the rope. She braced herself. Someone had fallen. The entire group came to a stop and she worked her way back to find out who it was. She carefully searched the near complete darkness for the signs of the others. The Commander was directly in front of her but squatting over someone. It was Lord Anjalina. Snake moved in close.

"Is she okay!" she yelled over the fury of the storm.

The Commander nodded. "She's not injured, but she is exhausted!"

Snake knew that was the truth. Marching would wear them out on its own, but the added pressure of marching through this weather was almost too much. She wasn't sure what to do. Gingerly, Lord Anjalina returned to her feet.

"I'm fine!" she screamed. "Keep moving!"

Snake hesitated, but then returned to her post. *This is getting ridiculous!* But, there was little that could be done about it. With hope and energy dwindling, the rag-tag group pressed on into the violence of the storm.

*   *   *

Mongrel paced his chamber in complete frustration. There seemed to be no end to the problems he faced. They had loaded the High Lord and all of the supplies onto a ship and were waiting to set sail when this violent storm hit from out of nowhere. The captain of the ship refused to sail until the storm passed, no matter what the threat the magician made. He knew they had to wait, but his patience had been worn away. No doubt the High Lord's friends were still pressing forward in that sickeningly dedicated manner. The thought of the trap he and his men had fallen prey to inflamed his anger and his frustration. He debated whether or not to make contact with the Betrayer, and decided against it. He would know already that they were not moving, and Mongrel didn't have the fortitude to deal with Him when He was angry. So, he continued to fume and pace.

On board the ship, however, the mood of its only passenger was quite different. Despite the rocking and swaying of the sea vessel, the High Lord was smiling and in good spirits. He knew that as long as the storm persisted they could not set sail. This delay might be all his friends needed to find him in time. At the very least, it would prevent the forces of evil from getting too much of a head start. It had also given the High Lord one more gift. Because the magicians were afraid to wait on the ship while the storm raged, he had been left alone with the chance for some rest. For the first time since he had been taken, the High Lord closed his eyes to sleep, trusting his magic to wake him when the storm ended. *Perhaps we have a chance after all.*

*   *   *

Snake circled back to the Reverend. *He's not gonna like this one.* The treacherous trek of the faithful few had just taken a turn for the worse. *And I thought it wasn't possible.* At first, Snake couldn't hear the danger, or even see it; it was more like she sensed it. Something just wasn't right. No matter how hard she tried, she hadn't been able to shake that feeling. So, she went with it and, as always, her senses did not betray her. It wasn't long before the roaring sound of water got louder, the wind increased, and the water that was hitting her seemed to be coming from more than one direction. She had called a halt, untied herself, and moved slowly forward until she found exactly what she had expected—a raging river. Now, as she moved back to tell the Reverend, her only thought was *at least we get to rest for a minute.*

The Reverend looked calm and composed as usual, "What's going on?!"

Snake slid up close to him so that he could hear her better, "A river! Right ahead! I can't see a way around it in this weather!"

The Reverend sighed inwardly. He had a feeling something had to be coming. Something always went wrong, not that the storm itself wasn't taxing enough. He started to calculate their options, but he already knew where this was going.

"Did you see any shelter?!" he yelled in response.

Snake shook her head, "I can barely see you!"

At this point, the Commander appeared out of the darkness, "What's the hold-up?!"

The Reverend pointed forward, "River!"

That's just great. Maybe next we can all get struck by lightening, for fun. As soon as he thought it, he wished he hadn't. Now he was going to be looking toward the sky for the next attack. He faced Snake.

"Did you see any shelter?!"

"What is this, interrogate a thief week? No! I wasn't looking for shelter!"

"Okay! Let's bring everyone in closer and I'll scope for shelter!" yelled the Commander.

Since he couldn't think of a better idea, and the weather made it next to impossible to carry on a prolonged banter of smart-ass comments, the Reverend nodded. The Commander untied himself from the group and started to move away, but Snake's hand on his arm stopped him.

"And just how the hell do you expect to find you way back to the rest of us in this weather?!"

Oh yeah, there is that. "I guess I'll take the rope with me! Who is going to anchor it?"

The Reverend jumped on this one, "I'll anchor it! Pull the Lords in and get moving!"

Snake slid forward and located the rest of the party. A burst of lightening lit up the entire world as she reached T. He looked forward, caught a glimpse of the river, and nodded. Untying himself, he made his way back to the Reverend. Snake quickly brought in the Lords and the Commander made his way off into the darkness. As he left the small, huddled group, he wondered how they were going to make it out of this one. *Hell, the good guys always win, even in another dimension.*

Another burst of lightening nearly sent the Commander diving for the ground. *Maybe I am going to get struck by lightening in my lifetime.* The deep rumble of thunder told him he was about to see the light, again. Suddenly, a thought that should have occurred to him before struck him like lightening. *Sometimes I am soooo dense.* When the next flash lit up the sky, he scanned the horizon for some kind of shelter. At first, it seemed they were in the middle of nowhere, even the trees seemed to have disappeared. It looked like a barren and desolate world of water and blackness. But, to his right, there was a mass of darkness, darker than the rest of the world. He moved in that direction.

He didn't get very far, however. He had run out of rope. *Well, so much for the trail of bread crumbs.* He felt around for something to anchor the rope to and found a tree. He untied himself, tied the rope to the tree, attempted to get his bearings, and then stepped into the unknown. The ground was slick stone and he had trouble keeping his footing. He inched his way painstakingly forward. Suddenly a blast of lightening slammed into the ground just a few short feet from where he stood. The blast threw him to the ground and the shock jarred his entire being.

For what seemed like forever, the Commander laid on the ground and attempted to stay conscious. *This has been such a long day at the office. I really need a coffee break.* This was getting ridiculous and appeared to be getting them nowhere. Commander Gabriel lifted his head and scanned his surroundings, again. This time he nearly jumped to his feet in joy. Directly in front of where he lay prone on the ground was a cave entrance. *What are the odds of that?* His joy was cut short by the memory of the others he had to find and then bring back to this location. *Just great. One day I'm going to have to retire.* But, Gabriel had never been one to give up just because the world was about to come to an end. Instead, he dragged himself to his feet and started on his way back to where the rest of his team was waiting.

The Reverend listened as the Commander explained where he had found apparent shelter. It was a cave to the west. They were going to try to get everyone to it, wait out the storm, and attempt to find a way around the river. As everyone was exhausted, soaked, and probably on the verge of developing a horrible sickness, this was the only option . . . and that made the Reverend nervous. He hated to have his course of action dictated to him by the world around him. Nonetheless, there was no other way to go but forward. So, with as much caution as he could spare, he grabbed Rock and followed the Commander.

Twice on the trek lightening shattered trees within a body width away from the party, and twice they found themselves lying on the ground in a state of semi-consciousness as the trembling of the earth subsided. Yet, somehow, they all managed to pull themselves back up to their feet and move on along the path Commander Gabriel mapped out for them. Still, the more they walked, the less it felt like they were getting anywhere.

The Reverend had just begun to work out other options when the Commander yelled out over the never ending storm, "There, just ahead!"

The Reverend strained to see through the darkness and was rewarded by the sight of a small cave in the face of a hill directly in front of them. Although it was not possible over the raging storm, the Reverend was certain he heard a collective sigh of relief from the rest of the team at the Commander's announcement. Re-energized by the sight of shelter from the non-stop rain, the tough team rushed forward into the dark but dry cave.

For the first time in hours there was no water. Oh sure, they were all still soaked, but there was no rain falling on them and keeping them perpetually drenched. The Lords collapsed against a cave wall just inside the entrance. The Reverend gently dropped Rock next to them and then joined the rest of the suspicious types still standing at the entrance, scanning for unknown dangers.

"Well, here we are. Trouble is, none of us know exactly where here is," stated the Reverend.

Snake felt the truth of that statement. *The more time I spend on this trip, the less like myself I feel.* "Looks like we are going to have to have a little recon party," she sighed.

The Commander nodded, "We definitely need to check out our surroundings and make sure that there is nothing living in the caves that would mind having uninvited guests."

"Well, then it's settled. Some of us are going to have to look around while the rest get rested and dry. We must also have someone to watch over the Lords and Rock. Marching through the storm was too much for all of them. Want to draw straws?" asked the Reverend.

"For which?" asked T, "Walking around cold, dark caves while soaking wet, or babysitting duty?"

The Reverend shot a look over his shoulder at the Lords. They just sat there trying to catch their breath. *Guess they aren't going to set up camp on their own.*

"I'll scout," said Snake before the Reverend could answer. All eyes turned on her. *Good, at least that part is normal.* "Truth be told, I could use the time away from you guys. Too much warm and fuzzy stuff for me."

The Commander grinned, "Yeah, real warm and fuzzy. Which part made you choke up on your emotions? Was it the horrendous rain storm, or the fabulous accommodations?"

"Mostly the charming people."

The Reverend grinned. It was probably best to let Snake go on this one. She wasn't one for social contact and she'd had a lot of it lately. As much as he wanted to go with her, he knew he needed to stay here and watch over things. *Who else will come up with a brilliant plan if this all goes to hell?*

"Okay, Snake scouts. I'll pull babysitting duty. T you guard the front entrance, and Commander you can go with Snake."

Commander Gabriel nearly laughed out loud. He and Snake alone together in the dark, *That would only happen under orders from the Reverend.* He looked at the soaked beauty and let a dangerous thought cross his mind for a split second. However, the flash of fire in her ice blue eyes quickly quelled any further thoughts in that direction.

"Okay, sounds like a plan. Ready to get this party started?" asked the Commander.

Snake sensed something in the Commander's tone of voice that she didn't like. But, then again, she nearly always sensed something she didn't like about the Commander. There was just no getting around his cocky and irritating personality. She shrugged. She just didn't have any fear left of men and there was only one she truly respected.

"Okay. You go first," replied Snake.

Gabriel shrugged and moved forward into the dark unknown. Snake glanced at the Reverend and T, sighed, and followed the intrepid Commander into the dark.

As he watched them disappear into the dark, T asked the Reverend, "Do you really think that was such a bright idea given Snake's general feelings about men?"

The Reverend shrugged, "It was the best option given our current situation. Besides, better him than one of us."

Following the Reverend over to the Lords, T muttered under his breath, "'Aint that the truth."

As the Reverend approached, Lord Earin opened his eyes and scanned their surroundings, or attempted to scan them. The first thing he noticed was that there wasn't much to notice. The cave was nearly completely black and no light came from outside, except for the occasional burst of lightening. Lord Anjalina sat next to him on the cold, hard rock floor. They were just inside the entrance, but at least they weren't being rained on anymore. Lord Earin sighed. This journey kept getting longer and longer. He was beginning to believe it would never end.

It has to end, one way or another all things do, came Anjalina's soft mental voice.

When?

Soon, you'll see.

He hoped she truly believed that. However, now was not the time for wallowing in misery. Now was the time for getting up and setting things in motion. Lord Earin forced himself to his feet to greet the Reverend.

"Where are the others?" he asked.

The Reverend smiled at the Lord's effort to move forward, "The Commander and Snake are checking out the cave and T is standing guard."

"How are the Commander and Snake looking around without a candle or a torch?"

"Pure talent."

That conversation wasn't going anywhere, so Lord Earin decided to let it go and move on to something more constructive.

"I suppose that we should attempt to start a fire so that we can dry ourselves," said Lord Earin.

"Good idea. How are you going to pull it off?" asked the Reverend.

"Magic."

Earin reached into the folds of his robe and produced a small stone. The Reverend recognized it immediately, a thermal stone. Thermal stones were created by the Lords centuries ago in an attempt to reduce the number of trees burned to make fires. They were used throughout the Lords' home. Lord Earin sat the stone on the ground, waved his hand over it, and muttered a brief chant. Instantly, the stone bean to glow with life. It was an odd glow with an eerie green tinge, but it gave them light and heat.

"That's a great trick," said Rock as he began to come around. "I thought we would be wet and cold for the rest of our lives."

"It appears that we Lords are not entirely useless," grinned Lord Earin.

Rock shrugged, "Not entirely."

At that the Reverend laughed out loud. Lord Anjalina even smiled. With the world somewhere close to normal, for this group anyway, they began to dry off, warm up, and set up a small camp. The prospect of food, dryness, and warmth lifted their spirits and for a moment they all forgot where they were. However, things were a little different for the last two members of this team. They were up to their eyeballs in dark, cold, and wet.

The Commander closed his eyes and listened for the sound of Snake's breathing. Nothing. If he didn't know she was behind him, he would never have known where she was. Even then, he was wrong.

"There's something in the back west corner," came her whispered voice from directly in front of him.

The Commander nearly jumped out of his skin. He snapped his eyes open and tried to calm his frazzled nerves, "Jesus, Snake. Why do you do that to people?"

"I can't help it if the rest of the world is completely unobservant. Keep your voice down. There is something large, hairy, and sleeping at the back of the cave."

"How do you know?" whispered the Commander as silently as possible.

"I said keep you voice down," replied Snake is a barely audible voice. "Listen. You can hear it breathing. And, if your sense of smell is any good, you can smell its breath. Not to mention the fact that I got as close to it as possible and could make out its figure in the dark."

Gabe tried to keep his temper in check. *God, this woman is infuriating.* "Must you always be so pleasant? Some of us are human and have trouble walking on water."

"What are you talking about?"

"Nothing. Okay, so there is a big, hairy beast in the back corner who will hopefully sleep out the storm. Anything else?"

"Just a feeling. It's as though I can smell the rain better back here and it feels like the breeze has increased."

Gabe stood still and concentrated, "I sense that, too. You thinkin' there's a back door to this place?"

"Don't know. But, I think we should check it out."

"Fine, but do me a favor this time."

"What?"

"Stay where I can find you."

Snake grinned in the darkness, "I'll try."

Snake started forward into the dark, following the smell of the rain and the sounds of the storm. It wasn't long before she realized that they were heading directly towards the creature she had spotted earlier. *Yeah, I could have told you that. Why is it life is only predictable when bad things are about to happen?* She took a few more silent steps forward before reaching back to see if the Commander was still close enough behind her. Her hand touched his chest. *Guess so.* She moved on.

Gabriel was just starting to wonder if Snake had left him when he felt her hand brush against his chest. *Yes, I'm still here.* Oddly enough, there was something comforting about her touch; it was almost like the handshake of a long lost friend. Once again, he was forced to think that there just might be something to these necklaces after all. *And, she hasn't slit my throat and left me for dead or anything, either. That's got to be a good sign.* Gabriel shook off his private musings and focused on the task before him. It took about two seconds for him to hear the low growl. He froze and reached forward to see where Snake was.

At that precise moment, Snake had stopped dead in her tracks and reached back to stop the Commander. They joined hands. The world stopped. What happened next could only have been explained by the magic in the pendants each wore around their necks. Without warning, the darkness disappeared and they could see all clearly, but they weren't seeing it with their eyes; they were seeing it in their minds. They saw the rest of the team by the entrance sitting around a glowing stone drying themselves; they saw the massive beast a mere inches in front of them; they saw the back entrance that lead out into the thunder storm; and, they saw the raging river just beyond that opening. It happened all at once and was gone in a fraction of an instant. The two Chosen dropped hands and gasped for breath. The world was dark and silent once more, as were they.

Snake's mind raced. *What the hell was that?! Think, girl, think. Okay, first you have got to calm down.* She took a deep, but silent breath, and let it out slowly as her mind began to grasp what had just happened. It had to be the pendants, of that she quickly convinced herself. They had all these weird magical properties and both she and the Commander possessed, or were possessed by, them. *It must have been the magic, the emotions, and the contact.* Snake shook herself out of the after effect and turned to face the Commander, who had reached the same conclusions simultaneously.

"Let's not do that again, whatever that was," she whispered.

"Do what?" asked the Commander.

Snake hesitated. Was he serious? It was hard to tell. Commander Gabriel felt Snake tense up and realized his sarcasm had misfired. He quickly attempted to rectify the situation.

"Look, it was probably just some magic trick of these damn pendants. I won't tell if you won't."

Snake relaxed and fired back, "Tell what?"

Gabe grinned from ear to ear. *That's my girl.* "Nothing. Let's get back to camp and tell them all about our new neighbor."

"Right. You go first."

"Oh no, I'm not falling for that one again. You go first and stay where I can find you."

"Okay," said Snake with a shrug, "Just try and keep up with me."

Relying on the image that had been seared into their brains only moments ago, the two explorers made their way quickly back to the entrance where the rest of the team was waiting. By this time they were mostly dry. The Reverend was noticeably surprised to see them so soon.

"Back so soon? Don't tell me you're afraid of the dark?" asked the Reverend.

Fire flashed in Snake's eyes, "Can I help it if I'm that much better at this than you are?"

Gabe felt the temperature in the cave rising, "What Snake is trying to say is that there wasn't much to see. Just a monster, a back entrance that leads to the river, and a whole lota rocks."

Lord Earin started, "A monster?!"

"Take it easy. It's sleeping and will probably stay that way as long as the weather is nasty. Most animals have sense enough to stay out of the rain, unlike those of us on quests," replied the Commander.

Lord Earin attempted to look relaxed, but failed miserably. Lord Anjalina comforted him mentally as she picked up the conversation, "So, this monster is merely an animal."

"Just like this storm is a summer shower," mumbled Snake.

"What was that?" asked Anjalina.

"Not a damn thing," replied Snake. "Any chance we could get some food? I am starving."

The Reverend sensed that something strange must have happened but he couldn't put his finger on just what it was. All he knew was that Snake was on edge and the Commander seemed very distracted. *What the hell happened back there in the dark?* He knew he wasn't going to find out right now. He would have to wait and try to get it out of Snake at a later date. So, he resolved himself to that plan of attack and resumed the conversation as read.

"Sure we can provide food, if you tell us a little more about this animal slash monster in the back," said the Reverend as he moved to unpack some provisions.

"Big, hairy, smelly, with long claws and sharp teeth. It's sound asleep next to the back entrance that leads directly to the river. It would appear that is how it goes in and out. Perhaps it doesn't even know about this end of things," said Snake as she sat next to the thermal stone in an attempt to warm herself.

"Not likely," replied T. "Cave dwelling creatures are usually familiar with their surroundings. Still, if it is asleep we should be okay until the storm is over . . . as long as we are quiet."

"Yeah, and as long as we don't cook anything that smells like food," broke in Rock as he watched the Reverend breaking out the supplies.

"I'm way ahead of you on that, Rock. For our dining pleasure we have bread, cheese, and some dried fruit. Yum, yum," grinned the Reverend.

Snake rolled her eyes as her stomach growled, "Fabulous. I can't wait for desert."

The thieves shared a brief laugh at Snake's dry humor. Every once in a while she surprised them with something resembling a human side, but not too often. It did seem, however, for a split second that all was right with the world. That second didn't last long as Lord Anjalina played her part and brought them all crashing back to the moment.

"You never cease to bewilder me. Here we are sharing a cave with a monster, in the middle of one of the worst storms ever, on a blind quest for the High Lord so that we can stop the return of the Betrayer, who is probably searching for us at this exact moment, and you are all making jokes about the food. It must be nice not to carry the weight of the world on your shoulders."

Commander Gabriel sensed the complete desperation in Lord Anjalina's voice. Her assessment of the situation was much more about her own fears than about what the thieves were doing. "Laughter is the best way to deal with that weight. If we stop all emotions and wallow in the seriousness of the situation at hand, we will all have to give in to despair. It is these brief seconds of normal human behavior that keep us all from losing our minds. Perhaps you should try it some time, before it is too late.

The Lord dropped her head and sighed, "And you I understand least of all."

The Commander grinned a "well-no-duh" grin, "That, my dear Lord Anjalina, is my plan."

Snake listened intently as the two exchanged theories of their plight. She was amazed that they had not tried to kill each other yet. While she could not agree with either of them entirely, she knew that they both had valid points. This mission to save the High Lord of the

Land was getting worse and worse and she felt trapped in the middle. All she could do at the moment was move forward. The problem was that with every step forward she felt as though she was losing ground on establishing who she was. That thing between her and the Commander seemed to be just one more intrusion into her soul. *What the hell happened back there?*

Snake shook her head and turned her attentions to the Reverend. *That's a whole different set of painful emotions there. What the hell is going on? Are you people trying to drive me crazy.* The Reverend sat munching on his "fabulous" meal and discussing the lay-out of the cave with the Commander who had joined him. The two were running over every angle of approach a creature that size would have. T interjected an opinion here and there, Rock dozed in and out of consciousness as his body fought to heal itself, and the two Lords sat in quiet contemplation. Snake was struck by an overpowering sense of aloneness. The scary part was that it hurt. Quickly, she squelched that feeling and renewed her eating with a fierce determination. They were not going to be the end of her. For that reason, she was very annoyed when Lord Anjalina struck up a conversation.

"And what about you, Snake? What is your assessment of things as they stand?"

Snake glared at the latest intrusion into her aloneness that she was trying to remember how to enjoy, "No assessment needed. It is what it is."

"That is not an answer," replied the annoyed Lord. Somehow she felt that Snake held all the answers if she would only share them.

"You were expecting one?"

"Why else would I ask?"

Why, indeed? Snake sensed that there was more going on here than Anjalina cared to share. "Fine. I think we have all lost our minds. This quest is dangerously close to impossible. Even if we make it to Bodicia alive, this High Lord of yours is sure to be somewhere else and then we will be on the chase, again. Only this time there will definitely be a lot more troops to contend with."

"If that is truly how you feel, why do you continue?" asked Lord Earin.

"That part alone is easy. One, the Reverend goes, so I go. And, two, only the completion of the pre-determined task will enable me to get rid of this damn necklace. So, I will continue and do my best to find the High Lord to get me and the Reverend out of this alive."

"I don't agree with you," braved Lord Earin. "I truly believe there is nobility in you than you are unwilling to admit, even to yourself."

Snake's ice blue eyes flared to life. The kind Lord had unwittingly chosen the worst word possible. *Nobility! Does he know? How could he know?* Searching his now very scared eyes, Snake saw the truth. He had no idea what he had said. Using every ounce of self-control she possessed, Snake pulled back into her emotional shell and gave him a response, "Don't search for things that aren't there. Do not seek to see yourself anywhere in me. The *noble* side of me died long before you came along."

Lord Earin watched as Snake removed herself from the gathering. She moved just outside the light of the stone and perched herself on a large boulder. Although he did not trust or like her, Lord Earin stood firm by his opinion of her. There was something good about her, he could sense it. As much as she wanted the rest of the world to believe it was not so, deep inside there was a heart. He just hoped they could tap it before it was too late for the Land. She was, after all, Chosen.

"That was not wise Lord Earin," said Anjalina. "She could have killed you."

"But she didn't."

"Ahh, and you think that small fact makes you right."

"No. I think that combined with her loyalty and love for the Reverend makes me right."

Lord Anjalina knew he was right. Any warmth from Snake was always directed towards the Reverend. It was painfully obvious to her that Earin spoke the truth. But, that truth also brought another, "Yes, but may the fairies protect us if anything happens to that man."

Lord Earin sighed. She was definitely right. Snake's relationship with the rest of them was, at best, precarious. She would never forgive any of them if something did happen to the Reverend. Once again, he found himself wondering what had happened in her past to make her who she was. There was so much anger in her. It was as though she was balanced on an emotional fence and leaning toward the side that was less human, but every once in a while she looked back at the other side to see what she was missing. At those moments Earin was certain she was looking at the Reverend. *And that's a whole different enigma.* He shook his head. He didn't even want to try and figure that one out. Instead he took his share of the meal and tried to rest. *This journey's not over yet.*

And so the mighty band sat as the world raged on around them. They may have remained in the cave long enough to fully recover and continue rested if the rest of the cosmos would have allowed. However, it was not to be. Rock had finally dozed into a fitful sleep, the Lords had finished their meal and were joined in mental contemplation, the Commander, Reverend, and T were engaged in a discussion of proper battle tactics, and Snake had just decided to rejoin the group when the world came crashing down around them . . . literally. A boom that sounded as though the sky had shattered and crashed to the earth sent shocks through the cave that sent everyone flying. It was followed by a burst of lightening that lit up the inside of the cave as though it stood in the noon day sun. The entire scene was concluded by the crackling sound of rock being forced apart. T had the presence of mind to yell, "Duck!" just seconds before the front of the cave was smashed into fragments by the bolt and came crashing to the ground.

Snake lay on the ground and waited for the dust to settle and the world to stop shaking. She opened her eyes to complete darkness. Taking a deep breath, she calmed herself and began listening for signs of life. Coughing to her left let her know that someone else was still alive. *Lord Earin?*

The Reverend's voice broke through the darkness, "Snake?"

"Alive and uninjured," she replied.

"T?"

"The same," came his strong voice.

"Rock?"

"Alive and still injured," responded the sarcastic thief.

"Commander?"

"I'm not dead yet."

"Lord Anjalina?"

"I'm fine," she responded in a very shaken voice.

"Lord Earin?"

"I'm fine, I think."

"Okay," said the Reverend. "We are all still functioning. But, this is a bad situation. Earin?"

"Yes?"

"Do you have another thermal stone?"

"I have one," responded Anjalina in his place.

"Great. Can you please shed some light on the situation for us?"

"I'm already on it."

As she finished her sentence, an eerie green light illuminated her haggard face. She was covered in dust and grime, but she was alive. Slowly the light made its way outward and the members of the quest were able to see each other again. Each looked as though he or she had been through a battle, but no one seemed to be injured except for Rock. They pulled closely together and began to assess the situation. Where the entrance had once been, there was a mountain of stone and debris. It appeared they were not getting out that way. They turned their attentions to the back of the cave. Although a few of the boulders had shifted and the ground was covered with dirt and debris, it did not look blocked.

"Looks like we have to go out the back door," said the Commander. "Still, I'm not thrilled with the idea of walking past that creature back there. What do you think, Snake? Snake?"

"Where the hell is Snake?" demanded the Reverend.

"Calm down. I'm right here, boss," said Snake as she jumped down off the pile of rocks that was once the cave entrance. Having reached the same conclusions as the Commander, she had decided to see if there was any possible way to go back out the way they came.

"Well, what did you find?" asked the Reverend when he figured out what she had been up to.

"Looks like we have no alternative. There is a small gap at the top, but the only people getting through that would be Lord Anjalina and me. We are going to have to sneak past that creature."

A low growl froze them all in their spots. The sound of claws scraping on the ground behind them caused them all to turn and face the rear of the cave. Something was coming towards them.

"Unless, of course, the sound of the cave collapsing woke it up. Then we will just have to run," muttered T.

As though he knew what he was talking about, all hell broke loose, again. Almost as if it had materialized out of nowhere, the massive creature appeared out of the darkness and charged towards them. Somehow it was worse than Snake and the Commander had remembered. It stood nearly ten feet high on all fours. It was covered with a thick mat of nasty brown hair that reeked of old dead things. Its shoulders slumped forward and ran into its enormous head that ended in a tangle of razor sharp teeth. Drool flew from its disgusting mouth as it roared in what must have been a cry of attack, and its claws, which had to be a foot long, scraped through the very rock with each step. The members of the quest scattered as teeth, drool, and claws flew past them.

Snake dove towards Rock and pushed him out of the path of the beast. The Lords jumped to the side. T moved to Snake and Rock and grabbed hold of him.

"Let's get him out of here!" he yelled to Snake.

Snake hesitated only to see where the Reverend was. She found him quickly. He and the Commander had drawn their swords and were facing the creature; doing their best to keep his attention away from the rest of the team. Snake grabbed Rock's other arm and helped T get him to his feet.

"Here, take him out the back. I'm going to help the Reverend," said Snake.

The Reverend, who was standing side by side with the Commander facing big and ugly, had other plans. "Snake, you lead the others out the back. They can't find their way without you. The Commander and I will be right behind you!"

Why does he have to be right all the time?! "Shit," muttered Snake. As much as she wanted to protest, she knew better. Grabbing Rock, she headed for the Lords and the back exit. As she went past the Lords she yelled, "Grab onto me and each other and don't get lost. We are getting out of here, now!"

No one argued. They just latched onto one another and blindly followed Snake into the darkness.

Meanwhile, the Reverend and the Commander were busy trying to keep the creature engaged and to not get killed. It was easier said than done. The Reverend moved to the left and front of the beast while the Commander moved to the right and front. This didn't seem to confuse the monster at all. It reared up on its hind haunches and swiped at both men simultaneously. Bringing their swords up, both men blocked the swing. However, the force of the blow drove them back and to their knees. Quickly, looking like a rehearsed battle, both rolled backwards and came up in a crouch with swords poised.

It didn't take long for the creature to make its next move. Ignoring the Commander, it rushed the Reverend with front claws flying. He blocked with his sword and desperately swung at the gigantic claws. The Commander wasted no time. While the Reverend tried to keep the claws from ripping him apart, the Commander charged the creature's exposed side. He struck at the hairy beast with all his might, but nothing happened. It was like beating on a stone castle with a feather. His sword merely bounced off into the air. The Commander took a few more swings for good measure, but he didn't even succeed in getting the creature's attention.

Things were reaching a critical level for the Reverend. His arms were weakening and the creature was coming at him from two sides at once. He watched in disillusionment as the Commander tried to hack through the tough hide and got nowhere. *Well, this has reached the ridiculous stage.* Praying that the others had reached safety, the Reverend decided on a new approach. Sliding through the grasp of the beast, he rushed to where the Commander was looking for a weakness.

"New plan," he panted. The creature turned. "Run."

The Commander needed no coaching on this new tactic. Instead, he grabbed the Reverend and began to drag him through the maze of the dark cave at high speeds. *Memory don't fail me now.* He hoped he could get them safely through before the beast caught up with them. They would be no match for it on its home turf of darkness and close quarters. It would probably be able to see in the dark and they were relying on feel to find their way. The smell of rain and the sound of a rushing river reached the Commander and pulled him forward. The roar of the beast and the sound of his monstrous claws pushed the rushing men faster toward their destiny. Finally, the dim light of the outside world reached their weary eyes. Both men lunged through the opening and both men were quickly stopped by the force of arms grabbing them and pulling them to the sides of the entrance.

The Reverend looked to see Snake standing beside him, holding his arm with all her might. At the confused look on his face, she motioned to the river that he and the Commander had come only feet from plunging into at high speeds. It was right outside the entrance. The Reverend glanced to the other side to see T helping the Commander regain his balance and grasp of the situation. Suddenly, Snake was thrusting a piece of rope into his hands.

"Hold on tight," she yelled over the noise from the raging river.

It took only a fraction of an instant for the Reverend to understand. *Shit!* He wrapped the rope up his arm and braced his body. At that precise moment an enraged hell-beast came charging out of the cave opening. The rope went tight. The four anchors held their ground for a moment. Then, the beast lost its balance and began to stumble. The four let go in an effort not to be dragged down with it. It appeared to nearly regain its balance, but then it hit some loose rock and slid down into the river. A agonizing howl followed its form down the mountainside and into the cold water below. The four rope bearers stood and walked to the edge to see where it had gone.

"Great plan," mumbled the Commander as he caught his breath. *Except that I think my arms are two inches longer than before.*

"It was Snake's idea," replied T. "Myself, I thought she was crazy."

The Reverend shook his head. *I might have known.* "Who says she isn't?"

"Ha, ha, very funny. Crazy or not, I saved your ass."

"What? We were doing just fine with my plan," said the Reverend.

"And what, precisely, was your plan then? To fall head over ass into the raging river and hope the beast would follow you in? And, of course, you had a brilliant plan for dragging your pathetic forms out of the river if you survived the fall and the rocks, right?" smirked Snake.

"No one said it was a good plan," replied the Reverend.

"Yeah, your welcome," said T.

"Now what?" asked Snake.

"Now we must hurry to Bodicia," came a familiar voice from behind. They turned to see Lord Anjalina standing beside Rock and Lord Earin. "For in case you have not noticed the rain has stopped and the storm has ended."

With the weight of Lord Anjalina's words still hanging in the air, the members of the quest for the High Lord shouldered their burden and started the journey once more.

*   *   *

Mongrel was smiling. *It won't be long now.* The storm had finally ended. He and the other wizards had finally boarded the ship. They were finally taking the High Lord to the island of Tay-yah-nay. And, the trap had been laid for the Lords that followed them. It finally seemed that things were as they should be for the wizard. However, all good things must come to an end.

"Mongrel," came the sinister voice from the depths of the dark cauldron. He nearly jumped out of his skin and the smile faded fast from his face. He slunk to its side and peered in.

"Yes, Master?"

"Once the others are captured, you must return and find the pendant. If you loose that pendant I will be forced to rely on the prophecy. Do not fail me."

Then, just as every time before, the voice and the power of evil behind it were gone. Mongrel collapsed in despair. *Come back for the pendant! What if it is not there? What if it is lost?* The thought of what might happen should he fail terrified the pathetic old man. So, he turned his attentions back to the task at hand. The ship was moving forward with ease and soon he would have the High Lord alone on that horrendous island. That, at least, he would have done right. He smiled, again.

CHAPTER 12

Snake stood in the corner of the cell and stared at nothing. There was nothing to stare at in the dark room. *Why do I always have to be right about the bad things?* The rag-tag band of High Lord hunters had reached Bodicia in the late hours of the night. After finding a place to eat and rest the Reverend had gone in search of the needed information. Through his many informants he had discovered where the High Lord was being held. However, the fact that everyone was certain he had not been moved and the fact that they all knew the exact same information, with no variation, made the Reverend nervous. So, he had decided to check it out by himself. The others had decided against that. If there was something sinister going on, and there probably was, the Reverend would be watched . . . as much as that was possible. So, after a lengthy debate Snake had been volunteered for the job. Now, as she stood alone in the empty cell of the castle dungeon she knew that they had been correct. *Great, now how do we find the High Lord?*

She shook her head. This wasn't something that she was about to decide for herself and the longer she stood there the greater her chances of discovery. She had to get back to the others and figure out what to do next. As she moved through the shadows back to the cell door, however, something struck her senses as just not right. She scanned the room with her eyes, nothing. She closed her eyes and listened intently, nothing but the rodents. *What is it? Something is . . . familiar.* Then she placed it. It was a very subtle smell. It smelled vaguely like Rock smelled after Lord Anjalina had patched him up.

Maybe it's a Lord thing. Still she couldn't be certain without a Lord. *Well, hell. Now what?* The course was obvious. She was going to have to get a Lord in here. *This sucks!*

* * *

The Reverend stared at the sleeping Lords. It never ceased to amaze him how quickly they could fall asleep and how deeply they could sleep. That was why they had always had personal guards; he had never fully understood the decision to eliminate the position. But, it wasn't his decision to make or even to worry about anymore. *No, now all I have to do is find him now that he is gone because no one was watching over him.* It was an endless circle of fun and excitement.

He stretched and looked over at Rock and T. They slept much more lightly. The slightest suspicious sound would wake them and they would be alert and ready to fight if necessary. They were two of the best thieves he had ever known as well as very good friends. The fact that they were all that was left of his mini-empire broke what was left of his heart every day. He had known from the minute that Snake had entered his life that things would change. He just hadn't realized how drastic it would be. *And we are back to this, again.* The mere thought of Snake clouded his mind whenever he had a few moments to think. She was either going to save him or be the death of him.

"All is quiet out front."

The Commander's voice roused the Reverend from his deep thoughts.

"No sign of Snake," said the Reverend. It was a statement, not a question.

The Commander shook his head, "She could be standing right in front of me and there wouldn't be a sign of her."

"Scary, isn't it?"

"More like frustrating."

"That she is, Commander. What about our other friends? They still waiting for me to do something?"

The Reverend was referring to the soldiers pretending to be guests at the tavern. Once the Reverend had made his presence known to his underworld friends, he had promptly been sold-out and soldiers had shown up in the tavern across the street. He wasn't certain why they hadn't approached him yet, but he suspected some sort of a trap.

"Yeah, their still out there. Sooner or later we are going to have to give them something to do."

"Let's hope we have all our players present before we have to accommodate them."

"Are you all still waiting on me?" asked Snake as she stepped out of the shadows. Both men let their heart beats return to normal before greeting their ghost.

"Just once you could try coming through the front door, Snake," said the Commander.

"Who says I didn't and you just missed it?" asked Snake. "Besides, the front door is being watched by some "guests" at the tavern across the street. But, you guys knew that."

"Yeah, we knew that. We really are going to have to give them something better to do before they die of boredom," replied the Commander.

"It may be sooner than any of us are really ready for," said Snake.

The Reverend leaned back in his chair and studied his protégé's face. He didn't like what he saw. Things were about to get complicated, again. "What did you find?"

Snake sat down across from her mentor, leaned forward, and simply stated, "He's not there. It's a trap for certain."

"So, we are right back where we started, and with all my informants in town either paid off or mislead we aren't getting any useful information from that source," sighed the Reverend.

"Great," added the Commander. "Now what?"

Snake shrugged, "There is something else."

Both men looked at her in anticipation, eager to grasp at any lead that could get them out of this lovely mess.

Snake sighed and continued, "I don't know if it is anything or not, but at this point it is better than nothing. When I was in the cell I was struck by a familiar smell. It smelled like Rock smelled right after Anjalina patched him up. I have no idea what it means, or even if it means anything at all. For all I know, it's just what old Lords smell like. However, it seems to me that the only way to be certain . . . "

" . . . is to get one of the Lords into the chamber," finished the Reverend.

"Well, there goes a perfectly good evening. Thieves sneaking in and out of a trap is one thing; Lords have a hard time sneaking in and out of a convention of the deaf and blind."

The Reverend couldn't help but chuckle. The Commander had a point. Lords were not known for their stealth. Yet, Lord Earin might be able to pull it off. There was something about him that the Reverend hadn't been able to put his finger on; something different. The only thing that was for certain was that Earin had not always been a Lord. He seemed to have some sort of military training. Perhaps, with proper guidance, he could get in and out of the cell without blowing the whole thing.

"Well, this entire mission has been next to impossible so far, why break a trend? Let's get the Lords up and moving and see what can be done," decided the Reverend.

No better option jumped up to present itself, so they moved on the one they had. After what felt like a military effort, they had the Lords awake and all filled in on the situation along with T and Rock. When Snake mentioned the smell, both Anjalina and Earin appeared excited. They exchanged looks like children anticipating a present.

Anjalina pulled the Alinith root from her robes and held it under Snake's nose.

"Is this the smell?"

Snake sniffed cautiously, not entirely trusting anything that came out of a Lord's robe since the whole necklace fiasco. "Yeah, that's the smell. What the hell is it?"

Lord Anjalina looked as though she was about to burst with joy, "That, my dear Snake, is Alinith plant. It has great healing and nourishment properties and only grows within the Lords fortress."

"So, we are now really certain that the High Lord was in that cell, big deal."

Anjalina could not be daunted by the negativity of the somber woman, "Alinith root also has another property. Its juice glows in Lord's light."

The Reverend lifted an eyebrow, "So, if a High Lord were to write a message in this juice, it would be invisible to others but not to say, oh I don't know, a Lord on a desperate quest to find him."

"Exactly!" exclaimed Anjalina in great joy.

In all the time that he had known Lord Anjalina, this was the first time that Commander Gabriel had ever seen her excited. *Excited, hell. She's downright giddy*. It was actually quite sickening. He could, however, understand her joy. If this played out as it should, they were that much closer to the High Lord, provided they could get a Lord in and out of an obvious trap.

"Well, all this does is reinforce what we already know. Meaning we have to get a Lord in and out of that cell," said the Commander. "Anybody have any brilliant plans?"

"It just so happens that I do," grinned the Reverend.

"Why am I not surprised?" muttered Snake.

"Oh, but you are going to looove this one. It goes a little something like this. Snake, you take Earin back to the cell and see if Brennen did, in fact, leave any secret messages. T, you take Rock to the harbor and procure transportation . . . "

"What if they didn't leave by boat?" interrupted Lord Anjalina.

"In case you missed it, this entire area is surrounded by water. There is the river and the ocean. The best and quickest way out of here is by boat. So, even if they didn't we shall in hopes to make up for lost time. Now then, Anjalina, the Commander, and myself will play decoy and occupy the guards while the rest of you attend to your duties. We will all meet up in the harbor. Any questions?"

"How long do we wait?" asked T.

"I suspect that if one of the groups doesn't make it the whole town will know, but just in case the alarm doesn't go up, don't wait past sunrise. If the sun comes up on us it will be too late anyway."

T nodded. Somehow, the Commander suspected that order would never be followed if it should come to that. He couldn't see T leaving the Reverend behind, even under orders to do so. Still, it wasn't a point he wanted to debate. It didn't seem like it would be a healthy debate. Instead, he began to think through his new roll as a decoy. He smiled when he discovered he liked the idea. *Besides, this plan is tactically simple and mortally dangerous, just as all good plans should be.*

"Okay, I like this plan, it's a good plan, I'm excited to be a part of it. When do we get started?" grinned the cocky Commander.

The Reverend joined him in that grin, "Why now, of course."

Snake sighed and looked at the two craziest men she had ever met, "I just know I'm going to regret this."

*   *   *

Earin stayed as close to Snake as possible. He was terrified that she would disappear at any second, which she had a long history of doing. It really wouldn't be in anybody's best interest if she did, but he wasn't anywhere near figuring her out anytime soon. So, he clutched after her in the dark like a scared child. However, the sad truth of the matter was he didn't really need her to find his way to the castle dungeon; it was a route he knew all too well. For a moment he let himself remember the soldier he had once been, guarding the very man whose castle they were now invading in the dark. His skin crawled. He shook his head and tried to concentrate on Snake. He might know the way, but she knew how to get there safely and quietly. *Pay attention to the present, Earin. You'll get nowhere holding on to the past.*

Snake stopped and pressed herself up against the stone wall in the castle garden. As gently as she could manage, she reached behind her and pushed Earin to the wall. It had taken twice as long to get this far this time and her temper was starting to rise. *I hate babysitting.* Still, if she was going to get through this she needed the Lord, so she held her temper in check and concentrated on the task at hand. There were guards just around the corner, two of them. She listened for the sounds of alertness, but all she could hear was Earin breathing. That had to be dealt with. She put her mouth right up against his ear. The feel of her breath and the vague sound of her voice sent shivers down his spine.

"I need you to hold your breath for a moment."

He nodded and took a deep breath. Snake moved closer to the

edge of the wall and listened. Nothing unusual. No extra guards, no shallow breaths, and no really alert people on the other side. *Are all guards so complacent on duty?* Her mind flashed back to the guards that failed her and the guards that had failed to protect her cousin. Her blood ran hot. She shook her head to clear it. *Stay here, now. There will be another time for the past.* Remembering Lord Earin, she tapped him on the chest to let him know he could breath, again. The sound of the air escaping sounded like a scream in her ears. She waited for the guards to hear it. They hadn't. Controlling the desire to slap Earin, Snake lead them forward.

It was just a few yards from the garden wall to the guards' entrance, but it seemed like hours before they were beneath the small window that Snake had used on her first trip. Silently she lifted herself up and peered inside. It was all as she had left it. The window was just above and behind the main guard desk, which faced the only door in and out of the room. That door lead to the hallway to the cells and to the outer entrance. As before, there were no guards in the room. They were all positioned elsewhere in the castle. *Probably waiting to spring a trap on the Reverend and company. Won't they all be surprised, I hope.* She lowered herself to the ground and pulled Earin close.

"You go first. Slide through the window, quietly. Wait for me behind the desk."

The Lord was shocked. *She wants us to go through the main guard room. Is she crazy?* Then he calmed himself. They would only be going in this way if there weren't any guards. *That makes no sense. There were always guards in there, except for special occasions.* All at once he understood. There were no guards in the guard room because they were probably all being used to track the Reverend and spring a trap. The bad news was that the hall to the dungeon cells would be swarming with guards. Earin decided against debating with Snake and let her help him to the window.

As he slid through the very tight squeeze, Earin was very thankful that he had left his Lord's robe with Lord Anjalina. It would have been snagged somewhere causing noise and confusion, not to mention the bright white color would have given them away in the dark. The down side was most of his magical supplies had been left with her as well. He hoped they would not need them. When he turned to help Snake through the window and found that she was already inside and checking the entrance of the chamber for guards, he realized they wouldn't. *How does she do that? I swear she is not human.* He moved to her side. She turned and motioned him back to the desk where she promptly joined him.

"When I tell you to wait, I mean it. I'll let you know when to follow me," she whispered in a barely audible voice.

Lord Earin swallowed his pride and said nothing. There was something different in Snake's voice. It was as though her anger was being taken over by another emotion. Earin tried to place the feel of her words. Searching her eyes, he caught a glimpse of what he knew to be fear. It was there for only a split second before it was quickly replaced by ice cold nothing. But, it had been there. *So you are human after all.* He decided not to push her and kept his mouth shut. That decision most likely saved his life, for if Snake had been exposed to pity at that moment she probably would have killed him. The similarities between this place and her once upon a time home were almost too much for the scarred beauty. She took a deep breath, sized up the Lord, and motioned him forward.

The hall leading to the cells was dark, narrow, and sparsely lit by torches. The close quarters and heat from the torches created a humid and mucky feel. Each breath sat heavily in their throat and lungs as they worked their way further and further down into the depths of the dungeon. Every so often a moan, groan, or stirring caught their attention as they passed a cell. Earin's heart longed to free those inside, but Snake shut down all emotions and never paused. They were on a secret mission. Letting prisoners out of their cells does tend to get one noticed in a place like this. They had no choice but to keep moving.

As they moved deeper and deeper into the dungeon, Earin began to get more and more worried. There just weren't enough guards around. He tried to reassure himself by thinking that they all must be looking for the Reverend, or even setting a trap, but his mind would not be put at ease. He wondered if Snake shared his reservations, but the need for silence dictated that he couldn't ask. *How did I get myself into this? Oh yeah, I'm a Lord.*

As they turned the next corner, Snake pushed Earin firmly up against the wall and then promptly disappeared. Uncertain about what he should do, the Lord stood as still as possible and chose not to make a sound. For a split second he wondered if Snake might be in danger and if he should check on her, but he quickly realized that if he had to come to her rescue it was all over for both of them. He didn't have to wait long, though. In a matter of mere seconds Snake returned and backed him down the hall. When they were in front of the nearest cell she put her mouth to his ear and spoke.

"I found the guards. They are all just around the corner from the cell that we need to get into. They will hear us going in and they might even see you. I have a plan. I will distract the guards, you get in and out as fast as possible and then high-tail it for the guard room. Don't wait for me. If I don't meet you there get out and find the others. Do you understand?"

Lord Earin put his mouth to Snake's ear, "I don't like it."

"You don't have to. It's gotta be this way." Snake didn't know how or why, she simply knew that Earin knew his way around this place. It wasn't going to be a problem for him to find his way as long as he could get in and out of the cell in one piece, and that was up to her.

"When do I move?" asked the apprehensive Lord.

Snake grinned, "It will be painfully obvious."

"Good luck," muttered Earin and then Snake was gone. Earin moved back to the corner and waited.

Snake swallowed her fear and slid down the hall with her body pressed into the wall. *How did I get myself into this one.* The pendant brushed against her chest. *Oh yeah, I'm a thief.* She knew that this plan felt like suicide to Lord Earin, but she couldn't see any other option. Nearly every guard in the castle was waiting just down from that cell hoping to catch them. If she had tried to sneak Earin passed them they would have been caught for sure. At least this way they had a fighting chance. *Besides, this won't be the first castle I broken in and out of.* She shook the memory from her mind and concentrated on the here and now. The swarm of guards was directly in front of her now. She pushed herself further into the wall as she prepared to walk right through them. *Just a walk in the park . . . past people who want to kill me.*

As she approached them, she noticed that most were bored to tears. In fact, the only ones that were actually paying attention were the three directly in front of Snake. Those behind them were napping, eating, and even playing cards. It was obvious that they were watching the cell on shifts, had been doing so for quite some time, and were ready to go home. It meant something else as well, they would jump at the chance for some action. *I just hope they are stupid.* Snake worked her way right under their noses and came out behind them. *Now all I have to do is get them to chase me.* She thought about jumping out at them and running, but decided against the suicide path.

Instead, she moved further down the hall and started making the sounds of someone trying to sneak down the hall but doing a very bad job. She kicked a couple of stones, brushed against a cell door, and breathed heavily. Then she listened. Nothing. She tried harder, kicked some bigger stones, stumbled into a cell door, held her breath, and then had a whispered conversation with herself. Then she listened. Success.

"Did you hear that?" whispered a voice from down the hall.

"Shhh, listen," replied another.

Snake moved again and tried whispering to herself.

"They are coming in behind us, from the castle. Follow me. One, two . . . "

Snake moved closer. The guards seemed to be holding their breaths. She whispered, loudly, "You guys wait here, I'll go check." She heard the guards tense and prayed she would time this right. She stepped into view. The guard who had been counting cried out, "Three!" She turned and yelled, "Run! It's a trap!" And then it was chaos as Snake, pursued by every guard in the hall, ran into the dungeon maze.

Lord Earin watched in amazement as Snake took on the castle guard system. *She is crazy. I hope she doesn't get killed.* He thought about following them to help her but he knew that if he did she would kill him. He also knew he didn't have a lot of time, so he went straight for the cell. It was unlocked, just as Snake had said it would be. *Another part of the trap, no doubt.* Lord Earin slid inside. Immediately he could smell the Alinith plant. There was definitely a message somewhere in this cell. Earin scanned the surroundings for the what would be the most likely place for the message. Sounds outside told him he didn't have a lot of time to search. There appeared to be only one option. He was going to have to light up the entire room. *Snake is not going to like this one bit.*

Snake turned yet another corner at high speeds, taking care to make as much noise as possible. She yelled out to herself, "Which way?" Followed by a lower voice of, "They're right behind us!" That much was true. The guards were closing in on her. She would have to do something brilliant and fast. Turning into a new row of cells, she stepped into the entrance way of one and disappeared. Only seconds later a sea of guards rushed past her. *It's not going to take them long to figure out that they are chasing nothing.* She eased back into the hall and started back towards Lord Earin, but she didn't make it far before the entire dungeon lit up in an eerie green flash. It only lasted a second, but the damage was done. *Son of a bitch! What the hell is that idiot doing?!* Snake wasn't sure what had just happened, but she knew one thing for certain, the guards would be turning around and heading straight for the cell and they would be doing so now.

She took off at a dead run, determined to reach Earin first. *If anyone is going to kill him it will be me.*

The guards stopped dead in their tracks as the flash of green light subsided. They all looked at each other in shock and confusion.

"What the hell was that?" asked one.

"It looked like magic," responded another.

"We've been tricked; everyone back to the cell!"

Snake reached the door of the cell within a matter of seconds. Earin was gone. *At least he listens.* She paused long enough to listen for the sounds of pursuit. The guards were coming up fast. It would be mere moments before they arrived at the cell followed by alarms being raised all over the city. *Shit! Think!* Snake scanned the area for something to use to slow them down. Nothing but cells. *Cells? And what is in a cell?* Well, it was all she had left. Snake ran a few feet further down the hall, then stopped and picked a lock. Swinging the door open she yelled, "You're free!"

Without ever stopping to see if the person inside had responded,

Snake moved on to the next cell and opened it. She was working on the third when she heard the guards reach the High Lord's former cell. "Search it!" Snake opened the third door and moved on to the fourth. "It's empty! They must be heading back out!" The fourth door sprang open. Snake moved to a fifth door. "There's one of them!" Snake knew she had been spotted. There was no time to loose. She popped open this last door and turned to face the guards. She had to give Earin time to get out, which meant she had to keep the guards occupied as long as possible.

Three guards rushed her. She pulled two knives and let them fly into the right and left guards. Then, she pulled her sword and charged the third. At the sight of two of their companions dying, three more guards drew their swords and rushed forward. As Snake traded blows with the guard in front of her, she wondered how she would counter the next three, but she never had to. As they ran past the first set of open doors, they were tackled by what appeared to be two very angry men. Suddenly, the guards who had been intent only on reaching Snake, were being pummeled to the ground by very pissed off and extremely filthy prisoners. *That's one for our side.*

Snake kicked the guard she was fighting in the groin, hit him over the head with the hilt of her sword, and then ran like hell. The last thing she saw was prisoners wielding swords and guards fighting for their lives. She had no idea how it was going to end and, truth be told, she had a hard time caring, but she knew one thing for certain she had to find Earin and make sure that he had made it out in one piece. The few extra moments she had spent engaged in battling with the guards had to have given him time to escape, especially since he seemed to know where he was going.

Snake slid into the main guard room and stopped to listen. No guards were in pursuit yet but they would be soon enough. There were only five prisoners at best and they couldn't hold out against all those guards for long. They were little better than the distraction she had used them for. She also knew that once the guards got out of the dungeon they would be sounding alarms all over the city. That meant that she had to find Earin, get to the harbor, find the others, and skip town at high speeds before the world came crashing down around their heads. *What I really need is another delay.* Scanning the room, she found precisely what she needed.

Two torches next to the hall entrance and a single candle on the desk dimly lighted the small room. The entire castle was made of stone with only a few minor exceptions, namely the desk, the chairs, and the straw on the floor in this room and throughout the dungeon. It was a very simple plan, really. Gathering some of the straw off the floor, Snake made a pile on the desk. *I hope that's enough.* Noises in the hall told her she didn't have the time to mess with it. If the fire wasn't going when the guards reached the room they might be able to put it out instead of evacuating. That simply would not create enough confusion. She grabbed both torches, threw one on the floor in front of the door and put the other on the pile of straw on the desk. She then used the candle to set the floor under the desk alight. All three burst into flame. It would take time for the underlying wood to catch, but she wasn't about to wait for the end result. Instead, she was out the window and running through the gardens before the room got hot.

She had just about reached the point of the fence where she and Earin had come in to this mess when she saw a shadow approaching. Sucking in a deep breath, she melted into the surrounding foliage and waited without making a sound. The person was nearly upon her now. *Just keep on walking, boy. No need for you to die tonight.* She put her hand on a dagger, just in case, and held her breath. Suddenly, he stopped and muttered, "Oh my god!"

Snake nearly leapt out of the bush at the familiar voice, "Earin."

Lord Earin did leap out of his skin in response, "Shit, Snake! What are you trying to do? Give me a heart attack?"

"Keep your voice down. Do you want us to be discovered?" responded the cunning mistress of the dark.

Earin shook his head and pointed back to the castle, "I don't think they'll notice."

Snake looked back at the castle. What she saw startled her for a moment then made her proud. The entire guard room was ablaze, fire leaked out the window and had set the surrounding grounds on fire, and thick black smoke was rolling out of all above ground prison windows. Snake allowed herself a smirk. *I love it when a plan comes together. Sometimes I amaze even me.* That was enough of that. She stopped admiring her handiwork and focused on the task at hand.

"Okay, so they won't hear us, but that doesn't mean they won't find us when they all come running to put out the flames. Let's go."

Lord Earin was amazed. *Does she ever loose focus?* It seemed to him that no matter what was happening in the world Snake always had one goal and that one goal was all she had. For what must have been the millionth time he wondered if she was human. *How did she escape that fire . . . Oh my god!*

"You started that fire?" asked the perplexed Lord.

Snake came to a halt and turned with impatience, "And this is a problem because?"

"People could die."

Snake rolled her eyes, "Yes, people like thieves and Lords hanging out in the enemy's backyard when they should be running away."

"How can you be so cold?"

Snake thought she would finally snap. For a brief moment she visualized stabbing him through the heart; her hand itched for a dagger, but she maintained. In a split second she was up against him, her face in his. Her hot breath brushed his cheeks as she spoke.

"You didn't leave me much choice, did you? When you lit up the world with your magic did you even stop to consider that those guards might turn around? Did you realize that I was going to have to confront them to keep them from finding and killing you? And, did you ever consider the possibility that your actions would lead to our discovery and death? Well, I did. Now we are out, we are alive, and we have to go."

Then, she turned and started into the night. Earin was numb as he blindly followed her. She was right. He hadn't completely thought things through. He had needed the information, for him that had been justification for his actions. But, he never finished that train of thought. He hadn't truly considered what would happen next. His only thought had been that Snake would be upset. He had not contemplated the lengths she would have to which she would have to go in order to save him. *Dammit! I'm tired of people having to cover for me and save my ass! Earin, you idiot! You know how this works.* And that was the worst part of all. He was not naive. He knew what happened in situations like these and he had screwed it all up only to have Snake pick up the pieces. Anger at his own actions surged through him. *Never again!* With his jaw firmly set, he swallowed his oath and followed his tainted savior out of the garden and into the shadows of the street.

*   *   *

The Reverend peered around the corner of the tavern. It was just as he suspected; the small band of troops that had been following them since they "snuck" out of their hotel was still just a few feet behind. *Following a little close, aren't we?* They were all huddled in the shadows trying not to be noticed but failing miserably. They were also simply following. No swords ready. No attempts at a surprise attack. *What are you waiting for?* He didn't like it, but he had little choice but to deal with it for the time being. Judging by the amount of time that had passed, the Reverend guessed that Snake and Earin would, at best, be just entering the castle now. It was his job to keep these guys entertained. Silently, he walked past them and rejoined the Commander and Lord Anjalina.

"Well, they're still right behind us," said the Reverend as he stepped into view.

Anjalina started, "Must all thieves creep in and out of the dark giving people heart attacks?"

The Reverend smirked, "Yes."

As much as he enjoyed watching Anjalina suffer, Commander Gabriel jumped to her rescue, "I have a feeling that as long as we are heading in the direction of the castle we will have these "sneaky" guards right behind us."

"They are definitely herding us in that general direction. At least it is clear that they currently have no intention of attacking us for any reason. I suspect that their job is to lead us into a trap at the castle," said the Reverend.

"That appears to be the case," responded the Commander in a rather pensive tone.

"What is it, Commander?"

"I just don't like it. Wouldn't they save a great deal of time if they just killed us? I don't understand the trap thing."

"I think I do."

Both men turned in surprise to Anjalina.

"Remember what dragged you all into this?"

"Yeah, you came looking for me," said the Reverend.

"In part, yes. However, Mongrel came looking for you, too. He came looking for the pendant."

"Son-of-a-bitch, he's still trying to get his hands on it. He knows that one of us has it and he is trying to trap us to get it!" exclaimed the Reverend.

Gabriel brought a hand up to grasp his own pendant. *All this trouble over this little piece of metal.* "Why not just kill us and search the bodies?" asked the Commander.

"He can't risk that we have it hidden somewhere or that we would banish it before that could happen," explained the lady Lord.

"Well, let's not disappoint them, then. Time to get moving towards the castle and continue this game of cat and mouse. We need to give Snake and Earin time," replied the Reverend.

"I just hope we don't have to give them too much more time. I can only play the bumbling idiot for so long before it isn't believable anymore," said the Commander with one of his famous grins plastered across his face.

"Oh, please," muttered Anjalina.

"Okay, I think the castle is this way," said the Reverend in a slightly too loud voice.

"Yeah. We should hurry so that we can find the High Lord before it is too late," responded Gabriel at the same volume.

"But, we have to be careful in case someone is following us," replied the Reverend, trying desperately not to break into a fit of laughter.

"I didn't see anyone when I checked. But, you are right, we should be careful," continued Gabriel.

Lord Anjalina rolled her eyes as the two men carried on what they seemed to regard as some sort of comic routine. This was getting downright painful. *How did I end up with these two?* As unpleasant as it was for her, she knew it could not be helped. There had to be a Lord in the decoy party and she was it. She wasn't sure why Earin had been sent with Snake, but the Reverend knew best where that one was concerned. So, Anjalina chose not to question his judgement on this one. She sighed and motioned the men forward.

"Can we go now?" she whispered.

"Alright, alright. Follow me," replied the Reverend.

And, then they were off yet again with the local morons hot on their tail. It was painfully obvious that, not only were the guards there, but that their job was to make sure that they made it to the castle and could not get out once they were in the "trap". This being the case, the Reverend decided to take the agonizingly long scenic route through town. First, he moved them into a closed alley way behind the local taverns. When they reached the dead-end, he loudly announced that they would have to go back out the way they came. Then, they waited a few moments for the guards to get out before retreating themselves.

Next, Commander Gabriel took the lead announcing that he knew the way. He led them on a zigzag trail through the merchant section of town, making sure to hide behind every building at least once. When that got them nowhere, they consulted a piece of paper that they declared to be a map of the town. After several minutes of staring at this blank piece of paper, the Commander suddenly announced that he thought he had heard something and went to check behind them to see if they were being followed. The Reverend and Lord Anjalina hid, but not too well, in the shadows while Gabriel investigated.

Slowly, so that the fabulous guards would have time to hide, the Commander made his way to the edge of the building he and the others were hiding behind. Peering around the corner, he could make out the shadows of the guards as they pressed themselves against the black smith's shop. Controlling an urge to laugh out loud, he peered into the darkness for a few moments before returning to the others where he loudly proclaimed it must have been the wind.

A great deal of time had passed now and the Reverend, though enjoying this game, was worried that the guards might get bored and do something stupid or that the trap may leave the castle and come to them. He decided that they had played around enough and needed to get serious about heading toward the castle. His natural concern for Snake's well-being helped him make the decision. He knew she could take care of herself, but taking care of Lord Earin as well might just be too much. He produced the "map" and looked it over a second time.

"Oh, I see our problem. We need to go that way," he said as he pointed in the direction of the castle. "It's time to get serious," he added in a muted whisper.

The Commander nodded in understanding then said, "So I had it upside down, so what? It's an honest mistake."

"Would you two stop bickering and get going!" exclaimed Anjalina with just a tad too much enthusiasm.

For the first time that night they were actually heading for the castle. They moved carefully so as not to loose their escort, but quickly to make up some time. The Reverend, ever mindful that they would have to get to the harbor at some point, took a route that would make that possible. He tried to keep them on roads that also lead out to water. It would seem, however, that being between the castle and the water supply would not turn out to be the best idea.

"Do you smell that?" asked the Commander in a very low voice.

The three of them stopped and sniffed the air.

"Smoke," replied the Reverend, "and a lot of it."

The three of them turned toward the castle. In the sky there was an eerie red glow and big black clouds that blocked out the stars and were trying for the moon as well. It could only mean one thing. The castle was on fire. That could only mean one thing as well . . .

"Snake," whispered the Reverend.

The Commander immediately knew that the Reverend was right. Whatever was going on back at the castle had to be her doing. That meant they didn't have a lot of time to decide what to do. Snake was either on her way out or needed help. *Shit! This would be so much easier if I could read minds.* That not being an option, he opted for the "she can take care of herself" attitude and decided that they should make a break for the harbor.

"Looks like we should split," he said.

The Reverend stared at him while doing a mental battle with

himself. He knew that Snake was probably doing just fine, but parts of him refused to take that chance. He was stuck. *Damn her!* He felt a hand on his arm.

"Reverend, we have to go."

He looked into the pleading eyes of Lord Anjalina and knew she was right. They had to get moving. With the castle on fire it would only be a matter of moments before guards were swarming the area in an attempt to get away and to put out the fire, and they were directly between it and the nearest source of water. He put his emotional wall back up and did the only smart thing.

"Right, let's go."

Unfortunately, they hadn't made the decision fast enough. While they had been trying to decide what to do, so had the guards behind them, and it appeared that the guards had reached their decision first. When they realized that smoke was coming from the castle, they quickly decided that their new job was to kill the people they had been leading into a trap. After all, the trap was no more. They drew their swords and charged.

As the Reverend turned toward the harbor, he caught movement out of the corner of his eye accompanied by a flash of silver. It only took a split second to register. *Oh yeah, the morons are behind us.* They were nearly on them. Shoving Lord Anjalina to the side, the Reverend pulled his sword and yelled, "Commander!"

Commander Gabriel turned to see the Reverend encounter the first of the guards with a shove, sending the man flying onto his back. He then turned and punched a second one in the face, followed by bringing his sword up to fight the next one to arrive. The Commander rushed to his side as the two men traded blows. Never one for a fair fight, the Commander threw a dagger into the one the Reverend was battling and charged another, promptly running him through with his sword. The first one was up off his back now and looking very pissed. He and the guy who had been punched in the face both charged the Reverend who had finished off the guard wearing the Commander's dagger.

But, the Commander was unable to help as he was faced with his own problems at the moment. The last two guards charged him with swords flying. He ducked to miss the first one. As he went down, he swept the guy's feet out from underneath him, which would have been a great trick in a one on one fight. This, however, was not one on one. The second guard was on top of him before he could get up and finish off the first guy. Lying on the ground, he was just able to get his sword up to block the death blow. As the guard made another swing, Gabriel rolled out and up to his feet. At this point the other guard was up and swinging. *This is getting ridiculous.* The Commander traded blows with them as long as he could.

Next to him the Reverend had managed to run through the first of his attackers and was busy trying to beat the life out of the second one, which was hampered by the huge gash in his sword arm. He swung with all his strength, but he was quickly running out of force. His arm ached with the strain of holding the sword and sustaining the blows from his enemy. He had to think of something brilliant . . . and he had to do it fast.

Suddenly, the guard let out a scream, dropped his sword, and fell to the ground with a dagger deep in his back. *That'll work.* The Reverend turned to thank the Commander and found himself face to face with a bewildered man. At the Commander's feet were two dead guards with daggers in their backs. This all had a very familiar feel. Both men had just put two and two together when their hero materialized.

"I swear, I can't leave you two alone for even a minute. I take one little trip to a castle, only to return to find I have to save your asses, yet again."

They were so relieved to see Snake that they almost let that one slide, almost.

"What are you talking about? I was only prolonging the fight to get some practice. Things have been mighty dull around here," shot back the Commander.

"And I knew you were coming and wanted to give you something to do," grinned the Reverend.

"Fine. Have it your way. At least the rest of the world will know the truth. But, we are in a bit of a hurry, so . . . "

They knew she was right. They had to be going.

"Where's Earin?" asked the Commander.

"Right here," said the Lord as he stepped out of the darkness. "Where's Anjalina?"

"Right here," replied a grim male voice.

They all turned to see Anjalina being held by a big, nasty guard. He had a knife pressed against her throat and his sword against her back. Snake eyed him carefully. He was a tall and stocky man with a wide chest area and about a foot of height on Anjalina.

"Now, give me the necklace or I will kill her!" demanded the guard.

Snake smiled an evil smile, "I don't think so."

"What?" asked the man, leaning forward exposing more of his broad chest.

Before anyone else could blink, Snake shot a dagger into his chest. He stumbled back, releasing the terrified Lord, and fell to the ground. Snake pulled her sword, walked over to the guard, and leaned over him.

"I said, I don't think so."

With the same evil grin still on her face, Snake slit his throat, removed her dagger, and rejoined her companions. The Lords seemed to be in shock. The Reverend looked like a proud father, and even the Commander finally had something nice to say.

Handing her the other daggers he had retrieved from the dead guys, he smiled and said, "Okay, now I am impressed."

"It's about time. Now, can we go?"

"Yes, let's," replied the Commander. "Oh, and Snake?"

"What?"

"Thanks."

Without another sound, the five members of the High Lord's rescue squadron high-tailed it out to the harbor in search of T, Rock, and their freedom.

*   *   *

The captain eagerly scanned his seemingly unending hordes of treasure. His cabin was stuffed with chests of gold, jewels, ale, and silks. There was scarcely enough room for him to walk around and inspect the take. His heart swelled with greed and power and he let out a snarl. This had been an incredible stroke of good fortune for him and his crew. They had pulled into this harbor only to pick up some supplies, borrow some funds from the local drunks and tavern guests, and spend some time with the ladies. What they had found seemed too good to be true at first. But, after the first couple of days in port they had discovered that the world was theirs for the taking.

Apparently, there was a high value prisoner in town and all the guards were busy with a trap to capture some thief that called himself the Reverend. The captain had heard rumors about this man, but didn't pay much attention to them. The truth was he didn't care who the guy was as long as he was keeping all the authorities busy. He and his men had relieved this town of all the wealth they could carry. He grinned, again, at the sight of all he had. Nothing could stop him now, or so he thought.

"You've done well for yourself, Tarvis."

The captain spun around to face the voice in the dark, sword in hand and ready.

"Who are you?!" he demanded. "How did you get in here?!"

"I came to this harbor looking for a ship. Imagine my surprise at seeing the Falcon moored here in all her glory, and imagine my shock at finding you alive and well as her captain."

Here Rock stepped into the light, allowing the terrified traitor to see his face. Tarvis nearly collapsed.

"Captain Davis? That's impossible," he muttered trying to find a way out of this nightmare.

"Oh, no more impossible than you still being alive, my ship still being in one piece, and you being the captain. You sold me out, you fucking bastard!"

Then it hit Tarvis. The only way out of this one would be for him to kill his former captain. He lunged.

Rock laughed as Tarvis hit the floor. It seems he was tripped by a large, dark figure hiding in the shadows.

"Thanks, T."

"Don't mention it," said T as he came out of hiding. "So this is the bastard that betrayed you? Seems to be a lot of that going around lately."

T helped the man to his feet and then threw him into the nearest chair.

"You want me to break his neck?" asked T, using Tarvis' own sword to keep him in the chair.

Rock grinned, "That would be fun, but not nearly painful enough. No, we have some catching up to do, don't we, Tarvis?" The name dripped off Rock's lips like poison.

"How?" mumbled Tarvis in utter despair.

"How am I still alive? I was sprung from prison on my execution day by a man looking to start a colony of dregs. But, that's not the fun part. The truly exciting story is how you sold me out, faked your own death, destroyed what I thought was my ship, and sailed away with my crew." Rock leaned in close to the traitor's face. "Did I miss anything you low-life piece of shit?"

"Fuck you!"

"Now, now Tarvy. That's no way to speak to your captain. After all, I imagine you are so glad to see me that you are just going to hand me back my ship, right?"

Tarvis glared at Rock as his mind tried to work out an escape. He couldn't find one. He couldn't even call for his men. If they came in now, they would know what Davis had already figured out and he would be dead anyway. It looked like the only choice he had left was how to die. If he could get Davis to kill him here he wouldn't be strung up by the men. That, at least, was something. Without warning, he jumped for his sword.

T slapped him back into his seat without flinching. "Sit down. Your captain is talking to you, you worthless hunk of mule dung."

Rock laughed out loud, "Thanks. You just answered my final question. I wasn't sure before, but now I know. The men don't know what you did, do they? No need to deny it. If they did you wouldn't have tried to get yourself killed in here. Say, I have a crazy idea . . . Let's go talk to the men. Everybody loves a reunion."

"You're goin' ta have ta kill me here. There 'aint no way you get me out there with them. I 'aint stupid."

"Am not stupid, Tarvis. When will you learn that if you sound like a pirate, people will treat you like a pirate. Oh well, you always were an incredibly slow learner. Now, get up!"

"Not on your life," growled the desperate man.

"Have it your way. T."

T dropped the sword and proceeded to beat the man with all the fury he had saved up for his other favorite traitor. When Tarvis was nearly unconscious, T dragged him out of the chair and tied his hands behind his back.

"After you," he said as nonchalantly as if he and Rock were on their way to a dinner party.

Rock, who had been looking over the ship's records and treasure, went to the door.

"I'm pretty sure things will work out the way I plan. Tarvis' actions tell me my men are still loyal. But, fifteen years is a long time. There are bound to be changes. Some men will be gone, some will be new, and some might never have cared for me to begin with."

"So, what do we do?"

"We play on the pirate's code of ethics," smirked Rock.

"Great," replied T, "The Pirate's code of ethics. There was one?"

"It's not much to look at, but one thing is for sure, pirates don't like mutiny behind their backs. They all want a piece of it."

"That's reassuring."

Rock grinned and slapped T on the back, "Whatever happens, you can't say I'm boring."

T shook his head. That was certain. This trip had been anything but boring. Terrifying, painful, long, and a general pain in the ass, but not boring. As it was, he was still trying to come to terms with the knowledge that Rock had a past. Not that he thought Rock had always been a thief, he knew better than that, but no one in the underground had ever asked any questions. It was unnerving to know who Rock had been before he was Rock. He thought about his own past for a split second. He had also been saved by the Reverend; he had even given him that name because he seemed to always be saving some desperate soul. Now was not the time for reminiscing. Now was the time for finding out just how strong ethics were among pirates. *Oh joy.*

T followed Rock up the stairs from the Captain's chambers to the main deck of the ship, dragging Tarvis' limp form behind him. The ship looked better from on board. When they had first seen it in the harbor, T had thought it was a hunk of junk. Rock had nearly fallen over at the sight of it. He knew it was his ship immediately because, as he had said, he had made a great deal of special modifications to it himself. When they hit the open air, they found the men of the ship drinking, counting loot, drinking, gambling, and drinking. *At least they are consistent with all my preconceived notions,* thought T.

Rock surveyed the ship shaking his head, "Tarvis, what have you done to my men? They have lost their culture and, more importantly, their edge. T, get their attention, will ya?"

"Right," said T, and he threw the beaten captain down the stairs into the center of the main deck.

What followed was chaos. Men jumped to their feet, dropped their drinks, and ran to the captain's side. Cries of panic and confusion filled the air. Men began to draw swords and ask what happened. Slowly, they started to sober up and look for an explanation. Finally, one older pirate found it.

"Over there!" he cried out to the rest of the men that were scrambling to the scene. "By the helm. Two strangers!"

As the men drew their swords and charged, Rock stepped forward and boomed, "Stranger?! Do you not know your own Captain, Mr. Cliff?"

Suddenly, the ship was as quiet as a graveyard as all the charging men stopped dead in their tracks. Mr. Cliff's face was frozen in shock.

"Captain Davis? But how? You're dead."

"If I am, then the afterlife isn't much to look at," replied Rock.

A few of the older pirates laughed. Mumbles of 'Captain Davis', 'That's him, alright', and 'How is that possible?' ran through the crowd of stunned pirates. The younger ones looked confused and scared. Rock jumped into the moment.

"Aye, it is me. I have returned to call out the man who betrayed me and stole my ship."

A wave of shock ran through the crowd. Betraying people was part of pirating, but stealing another man's ship was worse than stealing someone's wife. That was an act that demanded retribution and the crowd knew it. Rock had given himself grounds for the challenge even among those pirates who did not know him.

He stepped down into the crowd, leaving T to watch his back. "That's right. Tarvis sold me out, told you I was dead, and ran off with my ship. But, I escaped my execution and have come back to claim what is rightfully mine."

While he had been laying in a heap on the deck, Tarvis had been racking his brain for a way out of this mess. His first thought had been to flee, but that didn't seem possible. Now, his devious little mind formulated a plan. There were several new, young pirates on board; pirates that had never seen Davis. All they knew of him was the legends that they had been fed. Tarvis had lead them and brought them success. He decided to take a gamble. He pulled himself to his feet.

"You say I betrayed you and stole your ship, I say you abandoned us and left the ship to my care," here he turned to the young ones, "In the time you have been with me, have I brought you anything but money and power? Do you want to risk it all with a new captain, a captain who disappears when the going gets tough?"

As Rock listened to the last desperate attempt of this pathetic worm to save his skin, he nearly laughed right out loud. *Ignorant bastard. You've just played your last ace.* Before Rock had a chance to respond, however, Mr. Cliff shouted out to the crowd.

"Tarvis is a lair! I knew Captain Davis. I was with him from the beginnin'. There 'aint no way he abandoned us. James, you remember how he risked the whole ship to go back for you when you was captured by the guards in Port Beacon? And you, Fredrick? How many wives have you set up in ports all around the world with the treasure we made? Did you ever know a braver, fairer Captain? Even you young lads have heard the legends. How can you doubt . . . "

Rock stepped forward and silenced Mr. Cliff, "That's alright, Mr. Cliff. No need to sing my glories. My actions will speak for themselves. If *Captain* Tarvis here wants a true challenge, then I suggest we give it to him. How 'bout it Tarvis? Are you willing to face me?"

And now Tarvis knew he was finished. He had walked right into this cleverly laid trap. He had no doubt that this is what Davis had planned from the beginning. He wanted a fight, and Tarvis really had no choice but to accept. If he backed down now, all would know he was a traitor and he would be strung up for sure. Yet, he was damn sure he couldn't take Davis in a fair fight. He hesitated, but his pride soon caught up with the rest of him. *Davis is gettin' old. He's probably out of practice. I can take him.*

"I thought you'd never ask."

"Bring the swords! Clear a space!" cried Mr. Cliff.

Quickly the orders were followed and the two Captains stood facing each other in the center of the ship's main deck. The crowd of pirates was divided into those cheering Davis and those chanting for Tarvis. It had all the makings of a great epic battle between two emperors fighting for control of a single empire. T stood at the helm and shook his head. *I hope Rock hurries the hell up. We've got a secret mission to finish.* The fight was about to begin. Rock turned to T and gave a wave. *Good idea.* T grinned. Rock turned to his opponent.

"Ready?"

Tarvis tried to appear calm, "Anytime, old man."

Rock smiled, "Pirate's Rules." Then, he turned his back to Tarvis. Shock ran through the crowd. Tarvis lifted his sword. There was the distinctive thud of metal hitting flesh. Rock turned to see T's dagger sunk to the hilt in Tarvis' chest. Tarvis fell dead. Rock grinned up at T. There was a brief pause as the pirates all took in the situation. Then, the crowd of on-lookers broke into cheers. At once the old-timers knew that this was their devious Captain of old. He had fought this battle as only a true pirate Captain would. And, the young ones were suddenly certain that all the legends they had heard were true. This man was the Captain of Captains.

T made his way through the cheering crowd toward his pain in the ass friend.

"Pirate code of ethics, huh?" he questioned over the many voices asking hundreds of questions and cheering their Captain.

Rock laughed, "Never mess with another man's ship."

"Guess there is nothing about fair fighting in that code."

"Pirate Rule of fighting number one, cheat to win," replied Rock with a grin.

T laughed, "Pirate's Rules, my ass. You stole that one from the Reverend."

Rock put his hand on his chest in mock offense, "What? Me? I am shocked that you would . . . Okay, you got me. Pirate Rule of fighting number two, steal the best ideas from others."

"Well, you got your ship back. Now, can we get back to the whole saving the universe thing?"

"Let's."

As his first act as re-instated Captain of the Falcon, Rock had Tarvis' body unceremoniously dumped over the side of the ship into the sea. Then, he had the bed coverings burned. He ordered the men to get the ship ready to evacuate the harbor in a hurry. T helped where he could and Rock ran from one side of the ship to the next reclaiming his territory and taking hold as Captain. The men never hesitated in following his orders. They obeyed as though he had never left. Occasionally, they hit him with questions about where he had been and what he had been doing. He would just smile and tell them that all would be explained later. Now was the time for preparing.

In the middle of these massive preparations, a cry went up from one of the look-outs, "FIRE!"

All hands immediately turned their attention to the direction he was pointing, to the castle. Smoke rose above the buildings and covered the night sky, an eerie red glow tinted the harbor giving it a hellish appearance, and the sound of alarms being raised filled the air. At once, every man on that ship knew the same thing, guards were coming and they would be there any second. But, only two understood what was really happening.

After assessing the situation, T and Rock turned to each other and said in unison, "Snake."

"Captain, we must set sail immediately. The castle guards will be here any minute," said Mr. Cliff.

Rock looked around at the faces of his crew. Each and every one was filled with the desire to flee. Rock knew they were right. The smart thing to do was high-tail it out of there before they had to deal with any guards, but that was something he could not do. He had friends to rescue. However, that was not something this crew would understand. He had just returned to take command, if his first act was to put all their lives in unnecessary danger this crew would mutiny for real this time. He had to come up with something and it had to be fast.

"Breathe easy, Mr. Cliff. Hold the anchor, lads! Don't look so confused, I haven't lost my mind. I have only thought about this like a castle guard. These men won't be looking for pirates. They will be looking for water to douse that hell fire. If we take off at the first sight of trouble, we will only be drawing unwanted attention to ourselves. No, I say we make ready but hold steady. Let them wear themselves out fighting that inferno." *God, I hope this works.*

T stood directly behind Rock and muttered, "That had better work or we are going to be joining Tarvis."

"It'll work . . . I hope."

Mr. Cliff looked at his Captain suspiciously. Although he had made sense, this was not his normal way. Fifteen years ago they would have run at the first sign of trouble and been out of the harbor before the guards ever arrived. He sensed something was up, but he held his tongue. If he knew anything, it was that Captain Davis never did anything without a good reason. So, Mr. Cliff decided to back his Captain now and get the true answers later.

"The Captain's right, lads. We will do as he says and sneak right out from under their bleedin' noses."

Rock nodded his thanks to Cliff.

Cliff leaned close and whispered, "I'll be expectin' my explanation as soon as we set to sea."

Rock grinned, "And that you will be gettin', my dear Mr. Cliff. That you will be gettin'."

Moving like men relieved by Mr. Cliff's support of their new but old Captain, the crew continued with the readying of the ship as swarms of guards reached the harbor and began hauling water to fight the now massive fire. As Rock had promised, their actions and their ship went completely unnoticed as the guards struggled to move enough water fast enough to do any good. Bolstered by the fact that the Captain had been right, the men returned to their earlier passion. Questions resumed, those who had sailed with Rock before told stories to the younger sailors, and Rock renewed friendships with those he had lead before.

Smoothly, with the ease of a man firmly in command, Rock moved from man to man dropping words of encouragement, phrases of times past, and greetings to the faces he did not know. T watched from the helm. It somehow seemed very right that Rock was in charge of these pirates. He at once felt joy for Rock and a pang of sadness as he remembered the last group of men they had belonged to. That life suddenly seemed so long ago and far away as the quest for the High Lord had consumed them all. *All this over some stupid pendant. How can something so small make changes that are so big?* T shrugged off the serious thoughts. There was no time for that now. He had more immediate things to handle, like finding his boss, getting the rest of the team on board, and moving forward.

Leaving Rock to handle the pirate side of things, T went back down to the Captain's quarters to find something useful like a shit load of weapons, or perhaps something to eat to take the edge off the hunger that he suddenly realized was gnawing at his stomach. As he stepped into the dark room, he immediately sensed he was being watched. He moved his hand to the hilt of his sword and searched out the intruders by the sound of their breathing. There were two in the corner crouched behind the desk. Their were others, of that he was certain, but he couldn't quite place them. He nearly jumped out of his skin when they let him off the hook.

"Is it safe?" asked an all too familiar voice.

T refused to show that he had been caught off guard, "Not with you around, boss. Where the hell have you been and why are you hiding in the shadows trying to scare people?"

The Reverend stepped out of the shadows along with the Commander. The Lords stood up behind the desk and Lord Anjalina lit a lamp that was hanging in the room. T nearly fell over when the light reached where he was standing because Snake was standing directly in front of him and he had, had no idea that she was there in the dark. *How the hell does she do that?!*

"We are hiding to be sure that you don't need rescuing and we have been skillfully avoiding a cleverly laid trap," replied the Reverend with a grin.

"Oh please, an eight year old could have avoided that trap. It was not that clever."

The Reverend plopped into the chair that had earlier been occupied by the deceased Tarvis. "Leave it to you to take all the fun out of my egotism. So, whose fancy ship is this?"

T sat down on the desk and grinned, "It's Rock's."

Snake grinned, "Yeah, now. I believe the Reverend wants to know who you had to kill for it."

The grin on T's face attempted to consume the whole of it, "This you are going to looooove. We killed a guy named Tarvis, who used to be first mate to a Captain Davis. It seems that this Tarvis betrayed his Captain and took over the ship, leaving his Captain to be executed. Only this Captain Davis was rescued and managed to come back and reclaim his ship."

Snake nearly fell over, "Are you saying that Rock is actually a pirate captain and this is truly his ship?"

"That's precisely what he is saying."

Everyone turned to face Rock as he entered the room.

"Well, don't just sit there staring at me, say hello to your friendly, neighborhood pirate captain," declared Rock.

The Reverend stood up and embraced his friend, "Well, you have outdone yourself. I tell you to find transportation and you bring me a ship and crew."

"What can I say, I'm an over achiever."

The Commander, who had been having a conversation with the Lords in the corner, now jumped into the conversation.

"Yeah, but the question is now how much of an over achiever?"

"Why?" asked Rock.

"Because you need to be the kind of Captain whose crew will follow you to hell and back for no other reason than you say so. Unless, of course, these are all the kind of pirates anxiously waiting to do a good deed and save the world by joining our quest."

The Reverend didn't like the tone of the Commander's voice, "What's the problem, Commander?"

"Lord Earin just told me what the High Lord's message said. He apparently left the name of where they are taking him."

"Which is?"

"The island of Tay-yah-nay."

There was dead silence in the room. Rock felt sick to his stomach. This was not good. The Commander was right; they were going straight to hell. No one in their right mind ever went to Tay-yah-nay. Years ago it had been used as an island prison for the worst society had to offer. At some point the prisoners managed to take over the island and set up their own mini-kingdom. But, greed and power ran the men, and soon they were fighting among themselves. A small group made it off the island to tell of a massacre that left no one standing. Since that time, several attempts were made by authorities to reclaim the island, but all failed. Boatloads of men were never seen again. Rumors of trolls and other dark creatures had circulated throughout the sailing world. Whatever the truth was, one thing was certain, no one ever voluntarily went to Tay-yah-nay. *This is going to be harder than I thought.*

Rock spoke in a shaken voice, "Maybe if I had been with these men all these years . . .

Maybe if there were rumors of treasure . . . Maybe if pigs were to fly . . . I just don't know. Only a handful on board are left from my original crew. They may be coaxed into a journey such as this. But, the others . . . I just don't know."

Then, as the room filled up with tension, an answer came from a surprising source, "That settles it then. There is only one way to handle this. We don't tell them where we are going, for now. Then, we set sail, get as close as we can to that cursed island, and use the time to figure out a brilliant solution to this problem." Snake waited for what she had said to sink in around the room.

For a time no one spoke, then T grinned, "What the hell? It's the best plan I've heard so far."

"It's the only plan you've heard so far," piped in Rock.

"Exactly my point."

"Okay, it's a winner," said Rock. "Only I'd like you to add one thing."

"And what is that?" asked Snake.

"While you are working on a way to convince my men to visit the fabulous island of Tay-yah-nay, do you think you could come up with a way to convince me?"

The Reverend jumped out of his seat and slapped his friend on the back, "Oh, hell. That one is easy. You'll go because you are nuts, just like the rest of us."

The Reverend, Rock, T, the Commander, and even Snake laughed. Each one aware that they had lost their minds and that there was nothing they could do about it. The Lords simply looked confused and prayed that this would work, all the while seething with doubt. All in all, they were right back where they had started.

"Okay, then. I guess I had better weigh anchor before the whole town burns down. Excuse me, there is some pirating to be done," said Rock as he clothed himself in his old identity of Captain Davis and made his way to the deck.

The others watched him go in silence. It was as though they all understood the fine line he was now walking between two conflicting realities. The Reverend was the first to break the somber silence.

"Okay, assuming no one here gets seasick, I say we find some rooms to sleep in and get some true rest for the first time in a long while. It may be the last chance we get until this is all over."

Lord Anjalina actually smiled, "Now, at last, you make sense."

*   *   *

CHAPTER 13

The High Lord looked out the small window in his prison room. As far as he could see there was only water. *I am truly in the middle of nowhere.* For the millionth time since he had been imprisoned in this cell, he wondered if he would ever, could ever be found. It seemed to him that Mongrel had found the perfect prison. Mongrel. There was another puzzle for the High Lord to attempt to piece together. He knew the wizard was there and that he had orders to destroy the him, but he had not seen or heard from Mongrel since his arrival. It just didn't make sense. Time would be of the essence to the twisted old man, yet he did nothing.

The High Lord sighed and looked out the window towards the horizon. *Perhaps I should just accept this precious gift of time.* But, he knew better. Something devious was being planned somewhere and he could do nothing but wonder. With time running out and Mongrel refusing to make sense, all Brennen could do was pray for his savior. *Hurry, Reverend.*

*　　*　　*

The castle dungeon stood in complete devastation. Mongrel surveyed the scene. All around him were burnt out, empty shells that use to be cells. The floor was littered with burnt corpses of the king's guard and dungeon prisoners. Nothing remained alive. Nothing. And still, with all the damage and death, there was no sign of the one thing he needed, the one thing that would set him free. There was no cursed pendant.

Mongrel turned to his escort of scared and haggard guards, "Have you found any trace of the outsiders?"

"None. The only thing we have found is the dead bodies of the guards who were to trail them here and catch them from behind," replied the guard, trying to sound detached.

Mongrel snorted, "It figures that the entire guard could be wiped out by a small band of misfits. You make me sick."

However, the truth was that Mongrel was just a tiny bit relieved by their failure because it made him less of an idiot. He may have fallen into their trap, but he escaped with his life and the prize of the High Lord. These morons were completely destroyed and they were the ones who had planned the trap. This knowledge brought him comfort for a few short moments before he realized something else; those who were tracking him were clever, skilled, and lucky. He could waste no more time looking for what he knew was not there. He had to get back to the High Lord and his only chance at redemption.

"Should you find any remains of the group, contact me immediately."

As the wizard slunk away, it occurred to the guard that he had no idea how to contact him. He almost yelled out to him when he realized that he didn't really need to know how. They both knew that there was nothing to find. Totally demoralized, the guard returned to his duty.

Mongrel walked to the end of the hall and entered an empty cell. Taking a deep breath, he pulled out the cauldron. For a moment he hesitated. He did not really want to talk to the Betrayer. He didn't want to tell him that he had lost the pendant, again. He didn't want to tell him that all that remained for them was the High Lord. And, he sure as hell did not want to tell him that the prophecy was all that remained. But, he had no choice. He leaned over the cauldron and waited for the murky waters to clear. Slowly, the eyes appeared; the eyes that controlled every second of his life.

"Well?" echoed the sinister voice.

"It is not here, Master."

There was nothing but a horrible silence in response. It felt like an eternity passed before He uttered another word.

"Destroy the High Lord."

Then, just as he had appeared, the Betrayer faded away. Mongrel breathed a small breath of relief. He was still alive. Now, however, he must hurry. It had been twelve days since they had left Bodicia with the High Lord. That meant that, if they had any clue where to find him, that dedicated group of rescuers would be very close to the island by now. He had no time to waste. Using the same sinister spell he had used to escape them in the forest, Mongrel disappeared in a puff of smoke and sent himself back to the island of Tay-yah-nay.

*   *   *

Mr. Cliff sat back in the chair in shock; a heavy sigh escaped his lips. He had known there was more to the Captain's story than he had told the rest of the men. He had been completely aware that something more than the promise of a payment bound the Captain to the strangers he had brought on board. In the past twelve days, the Captain had explained where he had been and introduced them all to the Reverend, who had saved him from execution, T who was the Reverend's right hand man, Snake, another thief that terrified them all, and the Commander and two Lords. He had told them that, for a price, they were helping the Lords find another Lord. Cliff knew there had to be more to this story, but in his wildest dreams he had not expected this.

"Well, say something, Mr. Cliff, or at least breathe," said Rock, a.k.a. Captain Davis, in genuine concern.

"I would if I could only think of something to say. I just can't believe what I am hearing. That you were a part of a secret underground group of thieves, I can believe. That you are part of a quest to save the world . . . Well, that takes some gettin' used ta."

"Tell me about it. I'm still not sure what is going on. All I know is we have to do this. I owe my life to the Reverend, and if this is something he tells me we need to do, then we do it. The only problem is I really need the help of the crew on this and I don't know them well enough to know how to get them to follow me on some damn, fool, idealistic crusade. Do you?"

"To Tay-yah-nay? Hell, Capt'n', I'm not even sure I want to follow you there."

"Well, that makes us even, Mr. Cliff, 'cause I'm not sure I want to lead you there."

Mr. Cliff looked around the room at the faces of those who were anxiously awaiting some sort of brilliant answer from him. The Reverend stood behind the Captain with a look on his face that said he understood everything. The Commander stood at his usual post just a step away from the two Lords. He was always close enough to protect them from anyone. Not that they really needed any protection from the pirates. Pirates, like thieves, understood that there were inherent dangers associated with doing anything foul to Lords. The Lords themselves looked tired, desperate, and confused.

Then there was Snake. She sat in the back corner of the room, concealed in shadows. Since she had been on board, she had spooked the entire crew with her ability to be there one second and gone the next. They whispered among themselves that she was a witch. Mr. Cliff was certain she was not a witch, but he wasn't sure whether or not she was human. She never spoke to any of them. She just watched from the shadows as she was now. *I wonder what it is that she knows and the rest of us don't.*

As he contemplated those in the room, the initial shock of the new knowledge began to wear off and Mr. Cliff began to search his devious mind for a way to convince the crew to join this crazy quest.

"Okay. You got me. But, I'd follow ya to hell and back, and it looks like I'm goin' ta. Truth is I 'aint never had the respect for another man that I hold for ya, Capt'n Davis. You saved me neck plenty of times, you did. I owe ya my life, but I'm not sure how we will be gettin' the rest of the men to follow us to that cursed place. Not without treasure to find."

Lord Anjalina couldn't take it anymore. She had sat on this ship for twelve days watching the pirates prepare themselves for plunder and she had listened to Rock become the Captain. Now, as she listened to him explaining away their mission, she just couldn't believe that there existed people in the world who were so self absorbed that they could not be persuaded to stop the Betrayer from destroying everything. Her fury flowed from her mouth in the form of venomous words.

"Why not try the truth?! Do you honestly mean to tell me that every man on this ship cares so little for the world that he would let it be destroyed? How about the fact that if they do nothing and the High Lord dies . . . " here her voice faltered and tears formed in her eyes but she refused to let go," . . . the whole world will be destroyed and there will be nothing left for them to plunder?! Why not just tell the selfish bastards that?"

T, who was at the end of his rope as well, jumped on Anjalina's lead. "I'm all for the truth. Tell them what those bastards did to our friends, our home, the only family any of us has known for fifteen years. Tell them about the cowardly sneak attack lead by that fucking wizard. Tell them that this is about revenge!"

In the shadows of the back corner, Snake cringed at the idea that this was about revenge. Her whole life was about revenge and it had left her so empty. But, until that very moment, she had not realized that this quest, no matter how annoying, was the only pure thing in her life. Somehow, that warm spot somewhere deep in the center of her heart wanted it to remain as such. She wanted to cry out to T and make him understand, but her ice cold shell prevented it. So, her soul took another blow that she silently wrapped in her emotional wall and she bit her tongue.

Lord Earin listened patiently to the others explain, debate, and vent. This was getting them nowhere. He remembered his days of fighting pirates as a guard. They cared little for anything but themselves. All of his memories of pirates were of them killing, stealing, drinking, and telling their exaggerated tales of might and conquest. *Their tales of conquest . . . That's it!*

"Or, perhaps we could appeal to the heart of their nature," said Earin in a low voice.

"I suppose you have a great and wise insight to offer us on the ways of pirates," said Rock with massive amounts of sarcasm dripping from his words.

Earin ignored his tone, "As a matter of fact I do. It seems to me that one thing pirates love to do is tell others how close they came to dying, how tough they are, and how they have done things that no one else would ever dare to do. So, I was thinking that we offer them something grand to go along with this quest. We offer them the ultimate in bragging rights."

Jaws all around the room dropped. A chuckle broke the silence and everyone turned their attention to Mr. Cliff.

"Where did you find this Lord, Capt'n? He sure 'aint like any Lord I ever 'eard of. I seems he understands us pirates a great deal better than we understands him."

Rock shook his head with a smirk on his face, "Well, once again Lord Earin, it would seem that you Lords are not entirely useless."

Earin grinned in response, "Not entirely."

"Okay, then. It would seem we have a plan. Mr. Cliff call all hands on deck and let's get this party started for real."

"Aye, aye, Capt'n."

Snake stood, "Well, I guess I had better go and get ready, too."

"Ready for what?" asked Rock.

"I was going to get a life boat filled with supplies for when we are laughed right off the ship."

"Oh ye of little faith," responded the Commander. "What's the matter? Don't you believe that a crew of cut-throat pirates wants to help us save the world and all that noble junk?"

Snake stared at the Commander with an evil grin, "Do you want to check for leaks, or should I?"

"I'll do it."

Lord Anjalina's voice flared, "Can't you two ever be serious?"

"Who says were not?" asked the Commander.

"Oh, come on guys. What could possibly be more entertaining than convincing dregs to do good?" joked the Reverend.

"Oh, I know. We could take on an entire horde of trolls and a wizard . . . No wait. We could sneak into a trap in a hostile dungeon . . . "

"Alright, T. Point taken. But this will be fun, trust me."

"That is exactly what I am afraid of," mumbled T.

The crew was already assembled as the members of the quest for the High Lord followed Rock out onto the main deck. Rock moved to the front of the helm balcony to address his men. The others took strategic positions behind him, just in case. The Commander couldn't help but think, *Just because you're paranoid doesn't mean people aren't out to get you.* The whole world seemed to hold its breath as Rock surveyed the crowd and prepared to speak.

As he moved forward to address his men, Rock felt torn between his two lives. This pain was nothing new for him now. Since the moment he had stepped aboard his old ship he had felt it. It was impossible to just step back into his old life, yet he longed for the freedom of the man he used to be. For the man he once was this problem would never have existed. He would have dumped the pesky Lords at the nearest port and sailed off with his crew to claim all the treasure they could lay eyes on. But, that was then.

Now, he had more to care about then himself and his crew of undesirables. Now, he had to look after the Lords, his friends, and the fate on the known world. However, for all the pain it had brought him, Rock knew that he would never change a thing given the chance. For his new life had taught him the true value of friends. And though they required a huge amount of saving, he knew that they would go to hell and drag him out if he needed them. That made all the difference. Rock swallowed the pain of two lives colliding and addressed his crew.

"I know I have only been back with you a short time. For some, this is the first time we have sailed together. For others, it feels just like another adventure together. In truth, I wish this was just another voyage seeking treasure, but the fates have made it much more than that. The fates brought me back to you after fifteen years of me believing you all gone and you believing me dead. And now, I must tell you that we were brought together for a reason greater than any of us, and I'm not talking about a shit load of treasure."

"What could be greater than treasure?!" cried a voice from the crowd. It was followed by a round of laughter.

Rock grinned, "What indeed. Well, I will tell you. I'm talking about a chance to save the world so that we may continue to terrorize it. I'm talking about revenge of epic proportions. And, I'm talking about the tale to end all tales in any tavern in any port!"

"Tell us! Tell us!" was shouted out among the crowd.

"We're going to need to get out of here fast if they don't go for this," Snake whispered to the Reverend.

"I've already got an escape worked out with T," he replied.

"I'll grab the Lords," said the Commander.

Then Rock began his tale of mystery and intrigue. He told them about the underground world of the Reverend. He told them about the kidnapping of the High Lord. He told them about the bastard wizard who had his fellow thieves murdered in such a cowardly attack. He told them about Sam. The battle in the forest. The quest. He told them everything, including that he intended to take them to the island of Tay-yah-nay. And, he had them, too. That is, right up to where he mentioned Tay-yah-nay.

"Tay-yah-nay?! Are you crazy? No one dares go to that cursed place," mumbled many in the crew.

Snake braced herself, "Ready, Reverend?"

"Give Rock a little more time to do something brilliant."

"That's exactly my point," replied Rock without missing a beat. "No one dares to go there; not even the toughest pirates around. Now, imagine if we went there and brought back the High Lord. We would have to be seen as the craziest and most fearless band of pirates to ever sail the seas. No one would dare challenge us. There would be those who would lay down their swords rather than fight "those crazy bastards who went to Tay-yah-nay". And, we would have something that most pirates don't have to go with their tales, witnesses. The honest kind. We would have Lords to tell our tale."

Most of the crew mumbled in approval at Rock's logic. Truth be told, they were mostly in awe of him as they had been raised on his legends. Most wanted a chance to have a grand pirate adventure with such a legend and they were willing to go to hell to do it. Those who had sailed with him before felt some loyalty to him as most did owe him their lives in some way or another. So, most were willing to take this on. But, there was one who was not convinced.

Jones had been first mate to Captain Tarvis. He had quickly lost his spot and his chance at ever being Captain when Davis returned. So, legend or not, he was determined not to go on this quest. He saw this as his chance to try and regain the ship. Mutiny was, after all, only a breath away.

"That only works if we survive!" yelled Jones. "No one who has ever gone to that island has come back alive." Here he turned to the crew, "He says there is great glory and revenge to be had. I say we have nothing to seek revenge for and glory 'aint no good if you're dead. I have made up plenty a tale of my might, as have you all. I don't see the need to risk death to tell a tale I can make up by myself."

The Commander leaned over to the Reverend, "And so it begins. The few on the edge are about to change sides unless we do something brilliant."

The Reverend nodded as he watched and listened. The crew was beginning to split in two, those with Davis and those against him. Mumbles of the suggested mutiny started to fill the air, and Rock looked stuck. He had played all his aces. There was only one thing left to do. The Reverend leaned over to Snake and said, "I'm sorry." Before she could even ask why, he was at Rock's side about to make her life hard, again.

"You bunch of yellow-bellied cowards! I have seen some pathetic things in my life, but you take the cake. A group of murdering, thieving pirates and not one among you is man enough to go to an island. And why? Because you've heard some scary stories. It's pretty fucking scary that not one of you tough guys has the courage of this woman behind me. I can't wait to hear that story in a tavern. How a woman made it there and back and you were all too scared of ghost stories to go."

Has he lost his mind? What the hell is he doing? The last thing I need is these men hating me any more than they already do. I'm going to fucking kill him! Snake glared at the Reverend with all the hate she could muster towards him; it wasn't much. While her mind raced to figure out a way out of this one, a small part of her worked on a way to pay her darling Reverend back for this. However, she was rudely interrupted by the Commander.

"Easy, Nitro. Think this through. The Reverend may have just found a way to salvage this."

"Yeah, by throwing me to the lions."

"Only if you think any of these men can beat you. He doesn't."

Snake was now torn between her desire to kill the Reverend and slap the shit out of the Commander for making sense. But, make sense he did. The Reverend was playing on the macho nature of the crowd. He knew they would take the bait and he knew he would never let her lose. She bit down on her anger and decided to do something almost against her nature; she decided to help the situation along.

Stepping forward and looking at the crew she said, "Save your breath. These cowards aren't going to go. Hell, there isn't even one among them that would dare stand up to me. Fearless pirates, my ass." Here she turned to Rock, "It appears that your men have gone soft in you absence, Captain."

Now the crowd did split, and with force. Those who had already decided to follow their Captain spoke up with a loud voice. Cries of, "We are with ya, Capt'n!" and "No ghost stories will stop us!" and even, "We were goin' long fer *that witch* ever was!" echoed through the crowd. But, those were the ones who had been coming all along. The shouts to worry about came from Jones' side of the crew. "*That witch* 'aint braver than us; she's stupid, that's all!" and "You'll lead us to our deaths!" came from that side.

Jones stepped up with a grin on his face and silenced the crowd, "The only way she could ever tell that tale would be for her to make it there and back alive. I says that I can end her chances of ever doin' that now. I says I can kill her. She's just a little girl. Not so tough without her body guards."

Jones felt a chill run down his spine when every member of the Captain's new found group grinned sly grins. Something told him that he had just made a huge mistake, but there was nothing he could do about it now. He had made the challenge—the challenge that he now guessed they had wanted him to make. If he stepped down now, he would be seen as a coward. *Besides,* he told himself, *she can't possibly be as devious as I am.* He attempted to give them the same grin in response. He failed.

Snake stepped forward and said in a voice that they all strained to hear, "Alright, little man. I'll take that challenge. I hope you aren't afraid to die."

Gasps and nervous chuckles filled the air as the pirates tried to figure out how to react to this woman who was not afraid of any of them.

"Before this fight ever happens," shouted out Rock, "two conditions will be met. One, if Snake wins you all agree to follow me and if Jones wins I will agree to give up my ship, take a long boat and leave. And, second, this will be a one on one fight. There will be no Pirate's Rules or I will kill you all myself. Agreed?"

Jones thought it through carefully, but he really had little choice but to agree. His arrogance had already placed him in that corner. "Agreed. I look forward to being Captain very soon. I'm not afraid to die, witch. Are you?"

Snake simply smiled an icy, evil smile in response. *Yes, as a matter of fact, I am afraid to die. That, you worthless piece of shit, is why I am going to win. I'm not ready to die.* Jones could not possible begin to fathom what he was up against.

As she prepared to descend to the arena, the Reverend pulled her to the side, "I am sorry for putting you on the spot. I didn't see any other way."

Snake stared into his soul, "I know. But, I still intend to pay you back for this, ten-fold."

Relief washed over the Reverend and he smiled a genuine smile, "I know. Now, don't get killed or anything."

Snake shrugged, "You better hope I don't, because if I do, you will be the person I haunt with a vengeance."

As she walked away, they both knew that he would never let that happen.

While Snake moved into position, Rock asked the Reverend, "You're sure about this?"

"She killed Sam, didn't she?"

Rock nodded, "Just checking."

A mixture of jeers, cheers, and uncertain grumbles filled the crowd as Snake descended to the deck and into the circle that had now formed. On the far end stood Jones with his sword in hand. Quickly, Snake surveyed the crowd and picked out Jones' accomplice. He was a short, stocky man just behind the front row of people and a little to the left. He was almost too easy to spot with his hand on a knife and sweat on his brow. She would have to keep her back away from him. She couldn't kill him unless he showed himself, or she would be seen as breaking Rock's rules. She wouldn't do that. With all the patience of a good thief, she would wait.

The traitor located, she focused all of her attention back on Jones. His hand twitched. At that second, Snake knew he was about to attack. *Alright, let's go.* He charged with sword flying; she ducked. *Well, that was easy.* Her lack of fear and intelligent maneuver enraged him. He turned and charged, again. Knowing that she could play this game forever, but that it would accomplish nothing, Snake held her ground this time. And, where seconds ago there had been only her bare hands, there appeared a sword that she used to counter his blow. The crowd gasped in amazement. For a few minutes, the two combatants exchanged furious blows. Excitement filled the crowd, and the Reverend smiled as he kept an eye on the short, stocky man with his sweaty hands on a dagger.

Snake quickly realized that Jones was actually very skilled with a sword and a great deal stronger than she was. She needed a moment to think of something brilliant. Stepping into his next blow, she brought her knee up and dealt him a blow to his groin. He pulled back in pain and she caught her breath for a second. She also did a quick check to make sure that her traitor was still where he had been. The Commander, watching from the helm, caught Snake's glance to the left. He followed it, picked out Jones' friend, and stealthily placed an arrow in his bow.

Snake's second was up before she had completely worked out a brilliant plan of attack. Jones quickly recovered from his blow and charged, again. However, this time he came at her head on, and instead of swinging at her with his sword, he wrapped his arms around her and drove her to the ground. The force of his body weight falling on her knocked the breath out of her. Pinning her lower body by sitting on her legs, Jones punched her in the face to keep her stunned. The Reverend itched to kill this man right now, but he could not unless he was willing to forfeit Rock's ship. *Come on, Snake. Do something amazing.*

With her head still spinning, Snake was having trouble focusing on the man on top of her. *One things for certain, he stinks.* The feel and smell of him made her want to vomit. She shook her head and tried to catch her breath. A flash of silver caught her eye and her instincts came alive to save her ass. Jones had pulled a dagger and was bringing it down towards her chest. Snake's left hand flew up to block the blow; she caught his arm just inches away from her body. Knowing he had the better position for this battle, Snake did something amazing. Just as she caught his hand with her left hand, her right hand pulled out a dagger and slammed it into his thigh up to the hilt. Jones cried out in pain and loosed his grasp on his own dagger. Snake took that opportunity to pull his dagger from his hand and, in a split second, slam that one into his other thigh. Now, Jones screamed in terror.

The Reverend watched in pride. *That's my girl. Now finish this.* Almost as if she had heard him, Snake moved to finish the fight. She returned Jones' blow to the face. He fell to the side. She pulled herself to her feet and kicked him in the face. He fell to his back. Snake picked up her sword from where it had fallen and moved towards his fallen figure. As she approached him, a movement in the crowd drew her attention. With hardly an upward glance, she let a dagger fly in the direction of the traitor. A gasp went up from the crowd. She turned to look, and what she saw only made her want to laugh out loud.

The traitor lay on the ground with two daggers and an arrow piercing his heart. His dagger was still in his hand, and T stood behind him with a bloody sword. Snake knew that when they turned the man over they would find a sword had cut through his back. The Reverend, the Commander, and Rock all joined her and T on the deck.

"What's the matter? You guys felt left out?" asked Snake as they all inspected the body and removed their daggers.

"What? I was cleaning my crossbow when it accidentally went off," responded the Commander.

"Yeah, and when that arrow hit the poor bastard, he stumbled back into my sword that I was inspecting for defects," piped in T.

"And you?" Snake asked the Reverend with a smile.

"Me? I'm afraid of ghosts." The rest looked confused as Snake and the Reverend shared a secret laugh. But, it didn't really matter that they didn't understand. It only mattered that everything was back to normal . . . in a manner of speaking.

"Well, what do we do with him?" asked Snake, pointing to Jones who was being carefully watched by Rock.

Rock grinned, "Oh, him? Why he dies."

That being the final word on the matter, Rock ran him through with his sword. Jones had, after all, broken the rules that he had laid down for the fight and he couldn't have that on his ship. Then, for a few moments, there was an eerie silence on the ship as the crew tried to make sense of what had just transpired. Snake's fearlessness and skill both scared and awed them. But, that was nothing compared to how they felt about the death of the traitor. The pure skill of the small group caused a sense of fear and respect to fill the crew. They all knew at once that these people would do whatever it took to finish their quest, and they doubted that anyone could stop them. The actions of their Captain, the way he had simply killed Jones without the slightest hesitation or remorse, only strengthened his growing legend. The silence was filled with pressure of every man reaching these realizations at once. Then, it was over.

A sudden cheer went up from the crowd of spectators. People rushed forward to congratulate both Snake and the Captain. Backs were patted, hands were shaken, and loyalties were pledged. Men took it upon themselves to lift the bodies of Jones and his accomplice over the side of the ship and dump them into the ocean for the sharks. Several remarked that it was cruel to feed men such as them to the sharks for the sharks would certainly get belly aches from the meat. More than she liked, Snake was touched by men eager to show their approval and welcome her to the crew. She moved closer to the Reverend as she accepted their compliments. He knew she was approaching the limit of what she could handle. So, he rescued her.

"Well, it's time to take Snake to our friends the Lords over there and patch up her injuries from the fight. We leave you to the care of your Captain."

The crew called out their understanding as they turned to look to the Lords still standing on the helm. They had all but forgotten the Lords were there. Lord Earin couldn't help but wonder what they would all think if they only knew that he and Anjalina had spotted the traitor as well and that they had sent a protection spell to Snake. As the Reverend and Snake approached, he thought about mentioning it to better their relationship. He had only to look into Snake's eyes to know that, that would only strain things further. So, like the good Lord he was, he bit his tongue.

Anjalina smiled as Snake and the Reverend approached. Though she often found them irritating and painfully secretive, she always admired what they could accomplish together. She knew, that as long as they both wanted to, they would reach the High Lord. She also couldn't help but feel some sense of pride that another woman had stood up to and bested a macho pirate. It gave her a sense of sisterhood with Snake. A feeling she knew would not last.

"Well done. Now, if you will allow, I will give you some Alinith to help you heal," said Lord Anjalina.

Snake searched Anjalina's face for a sign of deception. There was none. Still, it was very hard for her to trust a Lord. "Won't that stuff knock me out?"

"It does cause you to sleep to speed the healing. That wouldn't really be a bad thing for you, you know. When was the last time you truly rested?"

"There will be time for rest when I am dead. Right now I have things to do."

Here the Reverend actually took Anjalina's side, "Guess, again. You can't do a damn thing until we reach that island, and I suspect that you will need more strength there than you have ever needed in your entire life. So, you will take the Alinith; you will sleep; and, I will watch your back."

Snake stared intently at the Reverend. Somewhere inside his eyes was a deep pain, and next to that there was resolve. She knew he would fight her on this. She also knew she could win if she had to, but now was not the time. He was right. There was nothing to be done for now. *Besides, if I'm asleep I won't have to listen to the incessant babbling of this crew.*

"Okay. I'll rest, for now, but not for long."

"Come then," replied Anjalina as they disappeared into the Captain's quarters.

Back on the deck, Rock assumed his role as Captain Davis and began the process of taking back his ship for real. He barked out all the necessary orders to set the men in motion. He didn't waste a minute in getting started because he knew that if they had time to think this through, there was always the chance of another attempted mutiny, but he also knew that they had to be running out of time. He didn't know much about this High Lord or the situation he was in, but he had seen what the wizard was capable of doing and he knew that the longer they waited the worse off the High Lord would be.

T slipped into the role of first mate without ever being asked. It seemed to be understood by all that he and the Captain had an inseparable bond. Mr. Cliff never even hesitated in letting that happen. He could sense that there were powers bigger than piracy at work, powers he did not want to mess with. So, he did all he could to help ready the ship, her crew, and her Captain for what lie ahead.

The Commander watched as Snake, the Reverend, and the Lords disappeared below deck. His natural instinct was to follow the Lords and watch their backs, but he had a funny feeling that was not needed on Rock's ship. He turned his attention to Rock. He looked like he had always been a part of this ship and crew. *I guess piracy must be like riding a bike. There are a lot of things like that . . . I wonder what riding a bike is like.* He shook his head. No sense in going off on that tangent when there was work to be done. It had been a long time since they had set to sea. The danger to the High Lord increased with every passing second. He knew they didn't have much time left. So, he did the only useful thing he could think of, he reported to the Captain.

"Well, what are my orders?" he asked Rock.

Rock tried not to let his surprise show as he stared at the Commander and processed his question. *You are taking orders from anyone? That I believe.* "Gather the Reverend, Mr. Cliff, and any other pirates that have any idea what this island might look like and meet me in my chambers. We are going to have to have some kind of brilliant plan when we get there, don't you think?"

The Commander nodded, "Oh, yeah. And, brilliant plans seems to be our specialty."

Rock grinned from ear to ear, "Yeah, but let's not build any more ditches."

"Wouldn't dream of it."

Still trying to work out a way to build a ditch on the deck of a ship, the Commander turned to his newly assigned task and left Rock to wonder just what he would do with a ditch on his ship.

*   *   *

The pulsing stopped and the High Lord opened his eyes. Mongrel stood in front of him, panting in exhaustion. If he had, had any energy left himself, he would have smiled. Instead, he closed his eyes against the pressures in the air and meditated. For a moment, all he could sense was the sound and feel of Mongrel sucking in air in huge gulps like a man who had just climbed a mountain. He pushed that distraction aside and concentrated on his own healing. Somewhere deep within his soul he possessed the creative healing power of the fairies. All he had to do now was reach that place and release that power. He was pulled from his inward search by the sound of Mongrel's raspy voice.

"You can't hold out for ever, old man. Your powers are weak, and I have all the resources of my Master to call upon. In the end, you will fail."

Despite the venom in his voice, the High Lord heard something else behind the words. He heard a quiet desperation in the wizard. He sounded like a man who was certain his own death was just around the next corner. Brennen could not help but take pity on the miserable creature.

"Be that as it may, Mongrel, I intend to resist you to the very end."

Enraged by the stubborn resolve of the High Lord and his own inability to break him so far, Mongrel stormed out of the prison cell, slamming the door shut behind him. Lord Brennen breathed a small sigh of relief and took a bite of the Alinith plant still carefully hidden in his robe. There wasn't much left. Mongrel had been right about one thing, he could not hold out much longer. For two days the wizard had been attacking him with the dark magic. And, although his protection spells were strong, they would not last forever. Not when Mongrel could go replenish his strength and he could not. Brennen took a deep breath, closed his eyes, and began his healing, again.

*   *   *

CHAPTER 14

Mongrel looked into the murky waters of the cauldron and smiled like a kid with a new toy. They were coming, but he was ready for them. For days, he had searched for them on the seas. He had known that they would follow. He had guessed that somehow the High Lord was able to let them know where he was. At first, he had been angered and even scared by that knowledge. But, that had changed. Now, he longed for their arrival. Let them come. He was ready for them.

He had moved the High Lord to the highest tower of the prison ruins and surrounded him with, guards, traps, and his fellow wizards. He had called forth hundreds of trolls and filled the island with them. He had set traps along every possible landing spot on the island. He was ready to do to them what they had done to him. As he watched the approaching ship on the cauldron's water, he nearly burst with the excitement of knowing that they were sailing into his clever trap. They were sailing into their own doom. Finally, he would win.

*   *   *

Snake listened intently to the plan the others had devised while she was resting. So far, she was sure of two things: one, they were completely insane; and, two, she should never let them plan things while she was sleeping. Unfortunately, the plans were laid and, given the current situation, there didn't appear to be any better options.

Not that the one they had chosen was all that great, it was just the best they had. As they ran though it one more time, Snake contemplated every hole and each little snag. *Here we go, again.*

"Okay, just so we are all clear, let's do this one more time," said the Reverend. "Thanks to the magic of the Lords, we know that we have been discovered. They know we are coming. So, Mongrel has undoubtedly set traps at all landing sites. That means we can't pull into the harbors or move in too close to the island. It also means he can see us sneaking in. That means another round of "distract-the-bad-guys". We send in a decoy boat of pirates, thieves, and Lords. That will be the Commander, T, Rock, the Lords, and a handful of pirates. You guys will take your time moving to the island and find a place to land safely. Do what you can to secure the area and wait.

Snake and I will swim in under their noses and pop up at the prison. Where we will successfully find and rescue Brennen. Then, using a location spell, we will meet the rest of you and return to the ship where we all sail away happily ever after. Any questions?"

"Yeah, what do we do if this doesn't work?" asked Snake.

Rock gave her a sly look, "Why then we simply use Plan B."

"Which is?"

"A fabulous alternative escape route that I am certain I will be able to think up given enough time."

"Great. I feel so much better."

"Look on the bright side," said the Commander.

Snake raised an eyebrow, "There was one?"

"If anything goes wrong there is a very strong possibility that none of us will be around to deal with the aftermath."

"And I thought you were a pessimist."

Lord Anjalina was at the end of her rope, again. "Must you two do this before every terrifying situation?"

"Yes," responded the two Chosen in unison.

Anjalina rolled her eyes in disgust, "It's not bad enough that we are embarking on an impossible task. You two have to drive me crazy with your sarcastic comments."

"It could be worse," said the Commander.

"Oh really? How's that possible?"

"Snake could be coming with us on the boat."

"I still wish you would take one of us with you, Reverend," said Lord Earin, choosing to end the discussion between the Commander and Anjalina.

"Sorry. Can't do it. You guys just aren't sneaky enough. This job calls for ghosts and you guys don't qualify."

Lord Earin knew he was right, but he still couldn't bring himself to like this plan. There were so many unknowns, too many. He was beginning to wonder if the Reverend's seemingly miraculous luck could get them through this one.

"I still don't like it."

"Hell, none of us is crazy about it, but we have few other options open to us," said T, sounding like he was trying to convince himself to go along with it.

"Right. We don't have much time left, so I suggest we get packed, eat something, and catch a nap before we do this," said Rock.

The others all nodded in agreement and moved off to take care of their individual assignments. As the cabin emptied, the Reverend pulled Rock to one side.

"When all hell breaks loose, we are really going to need a Plan B."

Rock looked into the eyes of his friend and saw a flash of something that looked like fear for a second. It was gone faster than it had appeared. Rock nodded. "I'm working on it, boss."

"That's all I needed to know."

"You better get a move on, boss. I'm pretty sure that Snake it waiting for you. I don't think she likes this plan."

The Reverend grinned, "I'm pretty sure she doesn't like much of what I do. But, that can't be helped. Just have a miracle ready when I need it, okay?"

Rock noticed that the Reverend said "when" instead of "if". Then, he knew they were in trouble. He was definitely going to have to think of something, and fast. "I told you, I'm working on it."

The Reverend nodded in understanding. He was aware that he was asking Rock to do the nearly impossible, but that was all they had left. This quest had started out as highly improbable and made its way to next to impossible in the first five minutes. Yet, they had managed to get this far. Something told the Reverend that the pendants worn by the Commander and Snake had something to do with it. *Oh yeah, Snake? Time to deal with her. What joy.* Knowing that Snake was most likely waiting outside the door, the Reverend decided to do the only thing he could, he moved forward.

"So, here we are, again. About to attempt the impossible, again," came Snake's voice out of the darkness.

The Reverend turned toward the sound and made out Snake's form in the shadows. He took a step in that direction. "Would you expect anything less?"

"No. Not any more. I just wish that once the world would surprise me with good news."

"There is good news. This time it is two professional thieves sneaking into a trap. That means you don't have to baby-sit."

"Yeah, on the way in. But, somehow, I suspect that getting back out alive might present the real challenge. If I get my hands on this High Lord and then can't get out, I may just kill myself."

"Not to worry. Brennen is different than the rest of the Lords."

"He had better be. I'm not sure I'd do all this for the other two." *Sure you would.* "Fair enough. I still owe this guy."

There was an awkward silence for a few minutes. Neither one spoke. They just stood in the dark corridor and waited for something. Finally, Snake gave form to a thought that was on the minds of every member of the quest.

"Suppose he's dead?"

The Reverend cringed inwardly, but shrugged outwardly, "Then getting back out will be a cinch."

"I'm serious. What if we go the distance on this one and he is already dead? Then what?"

The Reverend sighed as Snake put voice to all his greatest fears. "It doesn't really matter. There is no way to know whether or not he's dead without completing our task. Since we have no definitive proof that he isn't still alive we have to act as though he is. There is just no other way around this. We have to get on that island."

Snake knew he was right. They truly had no choice. If they were going to see this thing through, they were going to have to take this step. "You really owe him that much?"

"It's gone way beyond what I owe him, Snake. This quest has entered a whole new realm for me. It's all I've got left. Because of this quest, my entire world has been destroyed. In case you forgot, there is nothing to return to. The saving of Lord Brennen is all that remains."

Snake couldn't help but feel she should be shocked by the Reverend's revelation. Yet, she just wasn't. It had occurred to her some time ago that this quest was his new life. She had known it deep down inside but had left it in the shadows of her soul. So, as he spoke, the knowledge surfaced like a familiar friend and she absorbed its meaning. There was something else as well. Unless she made it otherwise by choosing him, this quest was all she had to live for, too.

For a moment, the Reverend thought he saw pain and compassion doing battle in Snake's eyes. He dared to imagine that she was fighting to find a reason to live other than the cold and empty life of vengeance; he dared to imagine she was thinking of making him her reason for living. What he had said to her was the truth, but not the whole truth. This quest had become only one of his reasons for living, the other was her. But, without her permission, he couldn't say it was so. Their relationship already bore the weight of their past attempts at intimacy; attempts that she had not been ready to handle. He stared intently at her, heart aching and soul on fire, and waited for her to say something.

Snake felt the Reverend's eyes probing her as though he was on the edge of a grand discovery. She pushed her feelings of desire and confusion back into the ice cold cage of her heart. The quest it would be . . . for now.

"Okay. We will finish this, together."

The Reverend was overwhelmed with relief and joy as Snake told him they would do this together. His joy must have reflected in his face, for Snake slipped back into character and added, "Besides, you'd only screw things up without me."

"There I would have to disagree," said the Reverend as he slid his body up against hers. "I think I'm much better at screwing things up with you."

For the first time in her life, Snake did not resist or hesitate. Instead, she responded to the urges in her body and her heart openly, almost desperately. Yet, as he carried her off to find a place where the two of them could be alone for a brief while, in the back of her mind pulsated a single thought, *One of us is going to die.*

*   *   *

The Commander watched the shivering form of Lord Anjalina as the small boat they sat in swayed with the rolling of the night sea. Was it the cold or the situation that was sending chills up and down her spine? He couldn't tell. It was a cold night, as it should be for an undertaking such as theirs. The wind rushed by unrelentlessly causing a constant mist to spray their faces as they sat waiting in the darkness. *I'm really beginning to hate being wet and in the dark. It's like being stuck in a bad horror movie.*

Lord Earin and Mr. Cliff sat in the stern waiting for T and Rock to finish lowering the remaining supplies from the ship. The Commander turned his attention from the preparations back to the shoreline. He was to watch for any sign that they had been spotted by the enemy and were in danger of attack. Deep inside, he knew that Mongrel had already spotted them. He also knew that there was no attack forthcoming. Not yet, anyway. They would make it to the island safely. Of that he was certain. It was what was waiting there for them that made him worry. This was a trap. It was going to take a hell of a lot of skill and luck to get them out of this one alive. And, something told him they would need a great deal more luck than skill.

"See anything?" came Snake's voice as she materialized out of the darkness.

This time, the Commander was unable to play it off in a composed manner, "Jesus, Snake! You scared the shit out of me! What are you trying to give me a heart attack?!"

"Relax, Commander. I just came down with the supplies. It's not my fault you didn't see me. Besides, I don't really do it on purpose. Sneaky is just sort of habit."

Now that his heart beat had returned to normal, the Commander quickly composed himself and was better able to deal with the invisible lady. "Take up drinking."

"Very funny. Now, back to my first question. Do you see anything?"

"No. I don't imagine we will either. We are meant to get onto the island, just not off, again."

Snake nodded, "That's obvious. I guess it's a good thing that bad guys are so predictable."

"Yeah, let's just hope that we aren't as predictable ourselves."

"It doesn't matter much now," said Snake. "We have to do this. Well, see ya on the other side."

"Yeah, try not to get killed or anything. Then I would be all alone in this nice Chosen One hell," responded the Commander.

"I'll work on it."

Then there was silence. Not the kind of silence that comes before a grand realization, or even the brief kind that comes at the end of a conversation. It was the kind of silence in which the entire weight of the world slowly lowers to your shoulders and the pressure surrounding you makes it impossible to speak even if you wanted to, but you don't because you can't think of anything to say to the darkness and all you want to do is scream. It was that kind of silence that descended on the small group in the boat.

"Ready?" came the Reverend's voice out of the darkness.

Snake didn't even flinch as the others nearly jumped out of their skins. She grinned. *Looks like I'm not the only ghost on this ride. We may just make it, yet.*

"Ready," she whispered.

He nodded and slipped over the side of the boat into the freezing and turbulent waters. She followed without making a sound. Then, the two thieves were gone, like shadows in the darkness. Gabe shook his head. *Unreal.* He searched the water with all his senses, but could not find them anywhere. For all he knew they had been eaten by some horrible sea creature as soon as they hit the water. *Not likely. They would have put up a fight.*

"Do you think they will make it?" asked Lord Earin with childlike fear in his voice.

"Or die trying," responded the Commander.

"That's what I'm afraid of."

Commander Gabriel looked out towards the ominous shoreline, "Me, too."

They both searched the water for a few more minutes in silence as the remainder of the supplies and crew were brought aboard the small boat. The Commander turned his attention away from the unknown fate of the two thieves and back to the task at hand. He was about to lead a small band of pirates and two uneasy Lords into a definite trap. He needed his mind on the task at hand and not on things he could not control. He double checked to make sure everyone and everything was there and secure. It was. He waited a couple more minutes for good measure. Then, he had no choice, it was time to start the final leg of this journey. *What the hell. We might as well get this party started.*

"Ready, Captain?" he asked Rock.

"No, but when has that ever stopped us?"

"True. Then, I guess we had better cast off, but let's not be in too much of a hurry."

Rock nodded and turned to the pirates manning the oars, "You heard the man. Let's move, but let's do it slow and steady."

"Aye, aye, Captain," responded the two men.

And, just like that they were jumping into another trench in an attempt to save the world. The Commander couldn't help but smile.

*   *   *

Snake slid up against one of the massive boulders that were crowded around the shoreline like dangerous, silent guards against incoming ships. She reached out and found a crevice to hold onto with her numb fingers so that she could float and catch her breath instead of treading water with her cold and aching muscles. The Reverend was directly in front of her, looking as though he was simply out for an afternoon swim. *Either I'm out of shape or he's a fabulous actor.* He turned towards her. His heaving chest told her that she was not out of shape. The swim from the ship to the rocks below the prison had taken its toll on them both.

He signaled to a gap in the rocks where they might be able to climb to shore. She tried to take a deep breath and still the shaking in her hands. She didn't have time to be this cold. Cautiously, watching for trolls and making sure she didn't slip, Snake followed the Reverend up the jagged path and onto the small strip of beach above. As they approached the top of the boulders, Snake heard a small sound. She froze as did the Reverend. Both strained their senses to hear the sound, again. After a few moments it was there again, barely audible above the sound of the water rolling up against the boulders to which they were clinging, but it was there. It was the unmistakable sound of someone shifting after sitting in one position for too long. That meant guards. That meant trolls.

The Reverend brought himself back down to Snake as she clung to the boulder just beneath him. He placed his mouth against her ear and whispered, "They are right above us. Kill or sneak?"

Snake carefully considered the options. It would be easier to take them by surprise and wipe them out, but that could leave a hell of a mess to clean up. With no idea when or if the guard switched, they had no way of knowing when the dead guards would be discovered. They simply could not risk Mongrel knowing there were two groups on the island. They would have to find a way around them.

"Sneak."

"That's what I was afraid of," grinned the Reverend.

He repositioned himself on the boulder just below the top. Snake moved in just below him and tried to calm the beating of her over-exerted heart. She was cold and tired, but she didn't have time for the weakness that came with either. She needed all of her wits and skill and she needed it now. She closed her eyes and concentrated on breathing silently. When she opened her eyes the Reverend was on the move. She watched as he disappeared into the dark. Quickly, she moved into his former spot and peered over the edge. He was gone in the shadows, but there were two ugly trolls "hiding" in the trees directly in front of her. She searched the Reverend out with her senses.

It took only a moment for her to find him. He was in a tree on her left. She listened intently and guessed that he was positioned to let a knife fly into the heart of the nearest troll should she be spotted.

What's the matter, boss? Don't you think I'm as good as you? Her pride and competitive nature got the best of her. She dropped back below the ledge and moved to her left along the boulders until she was certain that she was behind the Reverend's position. With every ounce of skill she could muster, she slid onto the beach and worked her way to the Reverend's side.

The Reverend kept his eyes firmly fixed on Snake's position. Nothing. He listened to the guards. Nothing. He went back to concentrating completely on Snake. Nothing. *Where the hell is she? What is taking her so long?* Then a thought occurred to him that probably should have long ago; she was being sneaky. Quickly, he switched to his sixth sense. He made the adjustment just in time to realize that Snake was right behind him. He reached out and snagged her tunic, pulling her close. An evil smirk filled her face. He put his mouth up to her ear.

"Very funny."

She shrugged and put her mouth to his ear, "Just in case you thought I'd lost my touch."

The feel of her hot breath only excited him so he broke away in order to keep his senses. *What the hell is the matter with me? One sexy woman and I loose all sense of business.* He laughed at himself on the inside, but on the outside he motioned for her to move on towards the prison. She slid out of the tree and he followed close behind her specter-like form as she disappeared into the darkness. *It's a good thing I taught her all she knows, or I would think she had just vanished.*

Snake moved through the dense foliage scarcely disturbing a leaf. She was on a mission. She kept her eyes focused on the prison tower that shot up out of the island jungle like a mistake by the gods and her ears focused behind her, listening for signs of danger. She more felt the presence of the Reverend behind her than anything. It seemed that the longer they were together the less she needed her outside senses to find him. She just kind of *knew* where he was at all times. She tried to clear her senses and move on without the thoughts that plagued her mind. They were on a mission, after all.

The two apparitions moved swiftly with hardly a backward glance. They knew where they were going and they knew they had to get there before the rest of the crew was discovered. It was crucial to get in before all hell broke loose on the island. Walking into a trap was one thing; walking into a sprung trap was something else. As soon as the confusion started, the High Lord would be even harder to reach. The loose guard that would be allowed to entice a trap would be tightened to prevent an escape. They were working against time and they knew it. Snake took a deep breath and hoped they would make it. The Reverend took a deep breath and hoped Rock had worked out a miracle for the last stretch of this suicide quest.

Then they were there. Snake called a halt to their speedy trek as she examined the crumbling stone wall before her. The Reverend moved to her side and began his own scan of the situation. The wall seemed to be that of the outer courtyard. It stretched as far as they could see into the darkness on either side, was about twenty feet tall, and surrounded the tower on which they had fixed their determination. It appeared they would have to go over it. Snake pressed up against the Reverend.

"So, how does one quietly scale a twenty foot wall?"

"Very carefully," came his hushed reply.

He motioned to the nearest tree attempting to overgrow the prison ruins. It stood higher than the wall. If they climbed it they would definitely be above the obstacle, but it was also pretty far away from the wall. The nearest branch still missed the wall by at least six feet. *Why does this not surprise me,* thought Snake.

"Let me guess," she whispered. "Climb the tree, jump, and pray."

The Reverend nodded with a grin.

Great, she thought, *I wouldn't want this to be easy at all.*

With great reservation, she followed her mentor to the base of the tree. Like two panthers they scaled the tree and found perches on the branches. Before making any attempt to leap from the safety of the branches, they scanned the scene below them. A long dead prison is an eerie sight. Below them, just beyond the wall were scattered remains of what must have served as rooms at some point. The buildings, which had been constructed out of stone, were crumbling and overgrown with dark and dense vegetation. Small creatures skittered among the ruins, knocking over pieces of human remains. None of the skeletons gave the impression of having died in peace.

All were contorted, run through with swords, bows, or knives. The fire from the torches lit by the new masters brought the shadows of the past to life. Despite herself, Snake shuddered.

As powerful as the images of the history of the prison of Tay-yah-nay were, that was not what they were looking for. They had to locate the enemy and figure out where they needed to land. They both knew where they had to go; the High Lord would be in the high tower. That was definite. There was no harder place to reach or easier to protect on the island. Snake scanned the area for trolls, guards, anything that would suggest the enemy was around. She didn't see anything. Her senses came alive and the hair on the back of her neck stood on end. There had to be someone on guard. *If there are no guards, then who?* As soon as she had the thought she wished she hadn't. To her knowledge there was only one other type of person on the island, wizards.

Having reached the same conclusion, the Reverend put his mouth against Snake's ear, "One of the wizards must be here somewhere."

Snake whispered into his ear, "But where? I can't see a thing."

"You are going to have to *feel* him."

Snake nodded her head and closed her eyes. Without ever knowing why, she wrapped her hand around the pendant she had come to need and hate all at once. Like a shockwave her senses all magnified. Suddenly, the beat of the Reverend's heart pounded loudly in her ears, the night breeze was a gust of hot air, and an uneasy person shifted his weight on the other side of the fence directly beneath their position. Snake had found the wizard. Her eyes snapped open and she dropped her hand from the pendant. Her head was reeling.

The Reverend stared intently into Snake's dazed eyes. She had the look of someone who was waking up from a drunken stupor. He had watched as she grabbed her pendant. He had seen pain flash across her brow. And, he had seen as realization consumed her. When she released the pendant and opened her eyes, he didn't know whether to be scared or relieved. He grabbed her shoulders and silently made her look into his eyes.

The Reverend's touch grounded Snake. She quickly composed

herself and looked into his pleading eyes. She nodded to his unspoken question. Then she mouthed, *One wizard. Just below. We can't cross here.* The Reverend nodded in understanding then proceeded to start his mind racing to conceive a new plan quickly. They had to be running out of time. He was going to have to come up with something quick and he was pretty sure that killing the wizard, although tempting, was not the best idea when trying to go unnoticed.

While the Reverend went to work thinking about a new plan, Snake scanned the area for another way over, through, or around the wall. Nothing. As she brought her gaze back across the tree tops she saw something that made her smile. *Perhaps we shall cross here after all.* Her gaze had fallen upon the form of a panther sleeping in a nearby tree. In the same tree, just above him were the remains of whatever creature he had caught earlier in the night. Snake devised a simple, albeit, dangerous plan in just seconds. She tapped the Reverend and pointed to their savior. His eyes picked the creature out of the dark and then flashed back to her with a questioning look.

She pressed her mouth up against his ear in an attempt to speak without being heard. He listened intently. "Be ready to jump and run on my signal."

The Reverend faced Snake and mouthed, *What signal?*

She responded with, *You'll see.*

He was sure it would be obvious. He made ready to leap. Snake pulled a dagger and a rope out of her small pack. Quickly, she tied one end of the rope to her dagger. She looked at the Reverend's now understanding face. *Ready?* He nodded. *She is crazy. God, I hope this works.* Then it began. She threw the dagger with pinpoint precision. It sunk into the hide of the panther's kill. The panther lifted its head. It was now awake and completely alert. Snake pulled with all her might. The kill came loose and hit the ground. The panther leapt to its feet and searched the ground for its dinner.

Realizing the danger of the situation, the Reverend grabbed a hold of the rope and helped Snake pull the carcass towards them. The panther pounced to the ground. The two thieves pulled frantically. The panther charged the moving food. They pulled it into the air. The panther stopped and began searching the trees. The dead creature reached their hands. The smell made Snake want to vomit. Grabbing the animal, she pulled her dagger loose. The Reverend grabbed the other side and together they heaved the animal into the air and over the wall. The panther hardly hesitated. It leapt into the air, touched the top of the wall only long enough to use it as a springboard, and dove down the other side in pursuit of its dinner.

The wizard would have two choices; stand and fight the panther, or disappear himself out of the way. A gasp, a scream, and a puff of gray smoke told the two troublemakers everything they needed to know. The wizard was a coward. Moving fast, they made their way over the wall and headed off in shadows away from the panther and towards the tower. This night was just getting started.

* * *

The Commander held is hand in the air for the troops, okay pirates, to hold as they beached the small boat. He didn't want anyone on the beach making noise until he was certain that they were either alone or not going to be ambushed just yet. He stepped onto the sand and scanned the vegetation all around them. It was dark and he couldn't see anything so he listened intently. The wind in his ears, the water lapping the shore, and the breathing of those behind him made it almost impossible to distinguish any other sounds. *How hard does this have to be?* He waited a few more seconds and then decided that the trap must be elsewhere because they had not been attacked yet. It was the only logic he had. He turned to the crew and motioned for everyone to get out of the boat.

Rock stepped to his side and whispered, "No sign of them?"

The Commander shook his head, "Not yet. But, they are here somewhere."

Rock didn't doubt that for a second. The fact that they were still alive merely meant the trap was further inland, which actually made sense from a tactical point of view. There were more hiding places inland and their small crew would be cut off from escape and aid from the ship as they moved further inland.

T joined them, "Well?" he whispered.

"We move as planned. We head straight for the tower, and we watch each other's backs," whispered the Commander.

T nodded. He wasn't sure he liked the idea of marching into a definite trap, but they had no other choice if they were going to give Snake and the Reverend time to find and rescue the High Lord. *If he is even alive.* T let go of that thought immediately. It didn't really matter whether or not the High Lord was alive at this point. They could only act as though he was. *Oh well. It's not like we haven't been walking into traps this whole damn journey.* He grabbed his bag of tricks out of the boat, double checked to make sure everyone else was ready, and took up the rear.

Commander Gabriel led them into the trees with Mr. Cliff right behind him. They were followed by the Lords, five pirates, and Rock. Rock smiled as T stepped in behind him. *At least my back is safe.* He would do his best to keep the rest of them alive and he knew that T would protect him no matter what. Slow and steady the group moved forward further into the island and closer and closer to the trap they knew was coming.

Lord Earin could feel sweat dripping down his face. He wiped at it with his robe. The island was hot, that was certain, but it wasn't the temperature that was making him sweat. It was pure fear. He couldn't understand why this time was any different than the rest of this trip. Perhaps it was because for the first time they were not in control. Maybe it was being so close to the High Lord. Or, maybe he was convinced that their luck was about to run out.

Lord Anjalina's voice entered his mind, *Do not despair. We will not fail.*

Are you so sure, or are you just trying to reassure me?

Perhaps both. I do know that only our faith will save us, so that we cannot afford to loose.

Lord Earin knew she was right. He had to hold to the faith. He had to believe that they would make it through this quest successfully. Yet, somewhere deep inside of his soul he couldn't shake the feeling that something horrible was going to happen.

The Commander moved as slowly as his will would allow. His senses yelled at him to run to the prison, grab the High Lord, and make a mad dash for the boats. This slow and painful trek into certain doom was about to kill him. He wanted to get it over with and he wanted to do it yesterday. Then, just ahead of him, he heard something. He threw his arm up to signal a halt. Then he motioned for everyone to get down and dropped to the ground. He searched the area for something to explain the noise he had heard and the chill running down his spine. He wasn't let down. Ahead of him were two trolls on guard duty. *We must be close to the prison.* There was no other option but to eliminate the threat.

As quietly as he could, the Commander pulled out his bow. Slowly he cocked two arrows. Mentally crossing his fingers that he could still pull off this stunt, he let the arrows fly. Like a scene choreographed in a movie, the arrows found their marks and both trolls dropped dead with a thud. *Just like riding a bike.* The Commander motioned for the group to continue forward. They did.

A mere fifty feet from the dead trolls the island jungle broke open and the small crew found themselves staring at the entrance to the old prison. Even now in its dilapidated state it was ominous to look upon. Two huge iron doors hung from their hinges barely attached to the stone wall that stretched out on either side as far as they could see. The inside edge of each massive door bore the signs of having been rammed down. Inside the gate they could make out skeletons of a battle scattered throughout the inner yard. Guard towers on either side of the entrance stood as empty reminders of the mutiny by the prisoners. For a second, each member of the quest wondered if any wild prisoners still survived, but that was a thought for another time.

The Commander moved the group back into the trees and pulled them into a tight circle.

"This is definitely it. This is the perfect place for an ambush. We will probably make it to the center of the yard before they attack and then they will attack from all sides. Be ready. When they attack form a circle with swords out and backs in. Anjalina, Earin, stay inside the circle . . . "

"We will not," interrupted Lord Anjalina.

The Commander hesitated. He could not afford to be worried about their safety, but he could use the extra fighters. "Fine. Join the circle, and don't get killed. Is everyone ready?" They all nodded slowly and uncertainly, all except Rock and T. That was enough for the Commander. Time was up and now they were going to have to save the world. He put on his "thank-god-I'm so-damn-awesome-or-this-might-be-hard" face and led his crew into a trap.

* * *

High Lord Brennen looked from his window down into the courtyard below him. He could see that Mongrel had set a trap. Trolls lined the outer wall and hid in every shadow. That could only mean one thing, the Reverend had found him. His joy was tempered by great fear, for even if he was found they would still have to survive a vicious trap. It seemed that every ray of hope was soon covered by shadows of evil. He turned from the window and stared into the darkness of his cell. It wouldn't be long now.

"So, this is the High Lord?"

Brennen nearly jumped out of his skin at the sound of the voice in the darkness. He stumbled back in fear.

"Who . . . "

Then a familiar face stepped out of the darkness and into the moonlight that came from the window.

"Easy, Brennen, it's just me."

Joy and relief rushed over the High Lord as he looked into the eyes of the one man capable of saving him. He rushed forward and the two embraced one another like long lost brothers.

"Reverend. I knew you would come. How did you get in here?"

"We just walked right in."

"We?"

Snake stepped out of the shadows and eyed the High Lord with caution. Somehow she had expected there to be something more grand to him, but there wasn't. He just looked like another Lord, a little older perhaps, but just a Lord nonetheless.

"This is Snake. She is a master thief, a trusted friend, and . . . "

"One of the Chosen," finished Lord Brennen.

Snake wasn't sure she liked the way he had figured that out on his own, "How did you know?" she asked guardedly.

"I can feel the presence of the pendant. It is an honor and a privilege to meet you," said Brennen with a bow.

"Don't be so sure," replied Snake.

The Reverend shot her a look that told her to tone it down. Obviously, he trusted this man and that meant she should, too.

She shrugged, "I mean don't be so sure until we get you out of here alive. It's one thing getting in but quite another getting back out, again."

"That is very true. There is a massive trap awaiting below," responded the now composed Lord.

"We know. But we have a plan. Can you locate Lords Earin and Anjalina with a small location spell?" asked the Reverend.

The High Lord nodded. "I can. Then what?"

"Then we get the hell out of here, hook up with them, and fight our way out of the trap so that we can successfully rescue you," said the Reverend with a smug grin on his face.

"You haven't changed, my friend," said the High Lord.

"Oh, but I have. I have a far greater opinion of myself than I used to."

Snake rolled her eyes, "Oh please. Are you quite done? Because, you see, I'd like to get out of here sometime this century and it can only be so long before the others spring the lovely trap below."

High Lord Brennen looked at the unlikely Chosen One and wondered what about her had drawn the pendant to her. There had to be something more than her rough exterior. Somewhere within her there had to be strength and passion; there had to be a real and loving human being. He just couldn't see it right now. He searched her face and probed at her mind. Her eyes flared as she sensed his probing and she closed herself as skillfully as a person with private pain would. The only thing he now knew about her for certain was that she was linked to the Reverend by ties stronger than love. He smiled warmly.

"Of course, Chosen One . . . "

"Snake," she said abruptly. She had only one identity and she needed it intact.

"Of course, Snake. We shall move very swiftly."

The two thieves watched as the High Lord closed his eyes against the world. Indistinguishable words flowed from his lips in a rushed whisper. Snake tried to catch any of them, but they were gone with the wind as soon as they were uttered. For a brief moment, the High Lord's body radiated a faint green glow, then he opened his eyes and smiled.

"The Lords Anjalina and Earin are just outside the main gate of the prison. There are several others with them."

The Reverend nodded, "Then we had better get moving because this trap it about to be sprung."

Snake started for the door, but was stopped by the High Lord's voice.

"There is something else. Mongrel and the other wizards are down there as well. He means to finish this."

Snake turned back towards the door, "Then we had better get moving so that we can save everyone."

As she disappeared into the darkness, Brennen turned to his friend and asked, "Is she always like this?"

The Reverend smiled the warm smile of a proud parent and shook his head, "No, some days she is mean."

* * *

CHAPTER 15

The entire world seemed to be holding its breath as the minimal force of eleven stepped across the threshold of the broken down prison gates and into the perfect ambush. Sweat rolled down their faces and splattered to the dusty ground as they moved towards the center of the courtyard. The Commander searched out every possible hiding spot for the enemy; there were just too many. *This is going to be real ugly.* He began to wonder if they could truly pull this off or if they were just delaying the inevitable. He knew it didn't matter much, though. They had no choice but to keep going, and so he took another step forward.

That step took the team to the center of the courtyard. Then, just like everyone had planned, all hell broke loose.

Trolls came flying out of the shadows and rushed the small band of warriors, but they were ready. Quickly they formed a circle as per the Commander's orders. Swords flew up just in time to connect with swords and bodies of charging trolls. In an instant the night had gone from silent and sneaky to a full-fledged war zone. The first round of trolls were easily dispatched by the talented and vicious band. The pirates had a definite skill for hacking things apart without remorse and for fighting dirty. The next wave of brutes took a little more handling.

The Commander swung at anything and everything that was moving in front of him. Sweat poured down his face and arms as he used every trick he knew to stay alive. A troll rushed him. He sliced through its torso, kicked a second one in the leg, and brought his rapier up to pierce the heart of a third. To his left, Rock was beating on trolls with his sword and his fist. Jabbing one through the heart, he lifted the body into the air and sent it hurling towards the others. He managed to knock down a sizeable group of the enemy in that manner.

Next to Rock, T dispatched the horde with a smooth ease that made it look like he was bored. He chopped limbs and heads off of bodies like he was playing a child's game. He never stopped and he never hesitated. Next to him, the pirates hit, kicked, slashed, and even bit their way to victory. They fought with the ferociousness of a mama bear backed into a corner and separated from her cubs. They were definitely holding their own against the crowd. In fact, the only weak link was the area occupied by the Lords.

They were fighting valiantly and with all their heart; they simply did not have the necessary speed and tactical skill to handle so many enemy troops at once. They were in danger of being overwhelmed. The Commander called out to T.

"T! Get between the Lords. Help them hold that side!"

T didn't even hesitate. One second he was standing firm beside Rock, the next he was in between the Lords. That worked for a moment, and the pressure lessened on that side. But, as talented as they were, the small band could not hold out forever. *Well, now what?* thought the Commander. *We can't just hang out and trade blows all night.* Then, with all options gone, an answer presented itself in the form of a dagger . . . or two. The Commander almost cried out in joy as a dagger sank into the eye socket of the troll directly in front of him and nearly laughed as a second one hit the troll to his left in the heart.

A familiar voice reached his ears over the horrible scream of battle, "Commander! Behind you! Move this way and we will cover you!"

Without so much as glancing behind him, the Commander ordered the group to move towards the Reverend's voice.

"You heard the man, move!"

T called out, "They are just in front of me. They are standing on an old building throwing shit at the trolls! How the hell did they get up there?"

"Around the back!" yelled the Reverend, "Snake will guide you!"

The small band ran at full force towards the Reverend's location.

The trolls hesitated for only a second before they charged in full pursuit. Seeing the obvious dilemma, the Commander stopped and turned to fight off the advancing trolls in an attempt to give the others more time. He was not the least bit surprised when T joined him.

"I told Rock to get the Lords on that building and that we'd be right behind them."

The Commander nodded. "Then we'd better kick some ass so that we don't make a liar out of you."

The two warriors stood against the enemy horde and fought with all their might, wielding swords, knives, and even arrows with unmatched skill. The Reverend and the High Lord continued to throw anything they could get their hands on at the trolls in order to keep the two men alive. The rest of the crew had reached the back of the building only to find Snake waiting at the top of a rope. Rock thrust the two Lords forward.

"You guys first. See if you and that High Lord of yours can do something spectacular."

Much to the amazement of the pirates, both Lords climbed the rope like pros. Snake helped them to the roof of the building. "Get everyone else up and don't leave the rope hanging over the side." Then, as was her custom, she turned and disappeared. The Lords shrugged and turned to their new duty.

The Reverend was very relieved when Snake appeared at his side. She quickly loaded her bow and began firing arrows into the horde of trolls that were nearly consuming the Commander and T. Both men moved with lightening speed and skill, but they could not hold out forever.

"The others are coming up behind us. It's time to save those two," said Snake.

The Reverend was glad to hear it. He had no desire to sacrifice anyone on this mission.

"T!" he yelled. "Move!"

That was good enough for the dynamic duo. They sliced through the most immediate threats, threw a couple of more knives, and even drop-kicked a troll or two, and then bolted from the scene at top speed. The trolls found themselves fighting with thin air and being bombarded from above by arrows, knives, and an assortment of heavy rocks. Enraged, they charged forward to the stone structure on which the small group was perched. But, they were too late to catch them, and the Lords had done as they were asked, the rope was no more.

For a brief moment, the band came together unmolested. The Commander and T reached the rest of the group to see the Lords embracing with tears streaming down their cheeks, the pirates standing and staring at Rock as though amazed that they were all still alive, and the Reverend and Snake looking entirely too smug. The two warriors rushed to their side.

"I swear, Snake. Doesn't feel like we are always having to save these guys' asses?" quipped the Reverend.

"Makes you wonder why we even brought them along," replied Snake with a grin.

"You brought us, my dear, so that we could get caught in a trap so that you wouldn't have to," retorted the Commander.

"Yeah, so be nice and shut the hell up about it," finished T.

The Commander motioned to the Lords, "So I see Lord Brennen is still alive."

"Alive and well, all things considered," replied the Reverend. "But, that won't be for long if we don't get the hell out of here. Those trolls aren't just going to walk away from us. They are either going to find a ladder or come up the back way."

"The back way?" questioned T.

"Yeah, how do you think we got up here? The back way is just a hop, skip, and a jump away," said Snake.

T looked past her towards the other buildings and figured out very quickly what she was talking about. If they jumped two roofs, they could then hit the cliff that ran along the back of the fortress. Then, they could make their way back down to the wall where Snake and the Reverend had entered this mess and head out the back. That was all contingent upon them getting past the really pissed off trolls below. He sighed, *Here we go, again.*

"Alright. Let's get this party started", responded T.

Snake smiled, "Commander, you come with me. The rest of you, gather the Lords and keep up."

Then, she bolted off at top speed. Never even slowing down, Snake leapt into the air and sailed onto the roof of the second building. The crowd of trolls below came to life with mad howls and ran to the base of that building. They threw rocks and daggers into the air in an attempt to reach her. They missed. The Commander shrugged, *Guess I'd better join her*. Taking a deep breath, he ran as hard as he could and launched himself into the air. He hit the rooftop hard and rolled to a stop beside Snake.

"Nice," she smirked.

"Hey, I'm alive aren't I?"

As they watched a second person make the leap, the trolls became even more enraged and increased their frenzied attack on the second building. A group even wedged itself between the two buildings and began throwing things into the air. That was going to make getting the others across very tough, but they had no choice. They were going to have to risk it.

Snake yelled across to the Reverend, "Send a couple pirates over first so they can help defend against those trolls!"

He nodded and told the first two to go. They hesitated at the jump, but knew there was no other way. Against their better judgement, they took the flying leap. Rocks and knives flew at their bodies as they soared through the air, but they hit the other side unscathed. Immediately, they joined the two chosen in attacking the forces below. The Commander looked to see who would be next. What he saw nearly knocked him off his feet. The High Lord was soaring through the air towards them as easily as an eagle flying through the air. He landed next to them softly and gracefully and then joined in the fight.

Snake brought Gabe back to his senses, "Yeah, I know. He did that on the way over. Shocked the shit out of me, too."

Commander Gabriel shook his head, "I guess the High Lord has skills we didn't know about."

Just when they had composed themselves, the amazement continued. They turned to see Lords Earin and Anjalina gliding through the air towards them. They also landed gracefully and joined the High Lord. The Commander couldn't let that one slide.

"Now wait a minute! You guys never pulled a stunt like that before. What gives?"

Lord Anjalina smiled, "The more Lords you bring together, the more powerful each individual Lord becomes."

"I guess I'll buy that."

"Commander!"

Commander Gabriel whirled around to see what had Snake so worried.

"What is it?"

"Nothing much. It's just that the trolls seem to have figured out where we are heading. Look."

He followed Snake's arm to where she was pointing. Indeed, the trolls had figured out their plan. At least half of the group was leaving and moving in the direction of the back entrance. They were going to have to speed up the process if they were going to beat the trolls out of here.

"Reverend!" called the Commander.

"I see it!" replied the Reverend. "Okay, gentlemen," he said to the others still on his roof, "It's time to go."

T said to the Reverend, "We can't all make it at once. Rock and I will stay behind to watch your backs."

"There's not much time," replied the Reverend.

"Don't worry, we'll be right behind you," said Rock.

Snake looked across the buildings and saw five men running for the edge. "Move back!" she yelled at the others. "There's a bunch coming!"

The others did as they were told without hesitation. Then, the five men were in the air. At first it looked as though all five were going to make it, but it was not to be. As they flew through the air, a rock slammed into one of the pirates. As the other four landed on the roof, he hit the side of the building. The Commander dove for him and managed to snag his arm. Then, Mr. Cliff and another of the pirates were there, holding the Commander's legs and helping him to pull the limp man onto the roof.

As they pulled the pirate to safety, they realized that all their efforts were in vain. The rock had crushed his skull on one side. He had been dead when he hit the building. The Commander nearly lost his cool.

"Son of a bitch," he mumbled feeling futile.

"It's not your fault," replied the Reverend.

"We done what we could. Taint nothin' can be done when your time's a come," added Mr. Cliff.

Then, T and Rock were there. They had been as good as their word and were right behind the men. Rock walked over to the dead man's side.

"Poor, Trevor. But, he did die in battle as all good pirates should. Come on. It's time to go."

For a moment they all just stared at Rock, but they knew what he had said was true. There was no time for mourning now. They had to keep moving, or risk more dead than just Trevor. As they headed for the next jump, the High Lord uttered a small blessing over the dead form of Trevor to send him into the next world in peace. But, that was all there was time for; they had to keep moving. They still had one more leap to make before they would be able to get down the cliff and out the back way down the cliff and through the jungle.

Snake moved to the edge of the second roof and looked over, only to have daggers, swords, and rocks come whizzing past her head. *Goddamn it! Why do I always have to be right?*

"Well, they are definitely ready for us," she said as the others joined her at the edge.

"Got any bright ideas?" asked the Commander.

"Yeah, let's get out of this without getting killed."

"Thanks."

"It was all I had."

The Reverend took control of the situation, "Okay, here's what we are going to do. We shower them with anything we can get our hands on, then we go four, five, and four."

"Do you think we can get that many over safely at once?" asked Snake.

"I don't think we have a choice."

"Fine. Who's first?"

"Same order. I want you and the Commander over there with a

couple of pirates just in case the trolls come sneaking up on us from behind. Then the Lords, Mr. Cliff, and one more pirate, followed by T, Rock, the last pirate, and myself."

"All the Lords at the same time? Do you think that's wise?" asked the Commander.

"The odds are better that way. They probably won't all get hit at once, but if we send them one at a time, they may all get hit," said the Reverend.

"Still sounds very risky to me."

"I'm not crazy about the idea either, but it's all we've got," replied the Reverend.

"Fine. Let's do it, now," said Snake.

The lead four moved to the center of the roof and prepared to run. The other members of the group filled their arms with everything they could throw.

"Now!" yelled the Reverend.

They threw all the projectiles over the roof at the enemy below, then they stepped to the sides and out of the way as the four jumpers came rushing past them with all their might. They seemed to hang in the air for hours as knives and rocks flew up at them. But, it was just a matter of mere seconds before they had all reached the other side. Not all the landings were graceful, but all the landings were successful and that was all that mattered.

Snake helped a pirate to his feet and watched as the Commander was helped up by the other pirate. She couldn't help but grin. The Commander looked down and got the look on her face.

"What?! I made it, again," he said.

"Graceful," was all she replied.

Great. A million thieves in the world and I have to get hooked up one who thinks she's a comedian. Fabulous. He thought about entering a battle of wits with Snake just then, but they had more pressing matters to take care of, namely getting the others across the gap. The four on the cliff loaded their arms with anything that wasn't rooted to the ground and moved to the edge. The Reverend and his men were ready on the other side. This crossing would be crucial. They could not afford to let a Lord get killed.

Then, the Reverend gave the signal. The two groups threw everything they had on the hordes below, then ducked. The Lords soared through the air like angels, with Mr. Cliff and another pirate flanking them. It was an odd sight. The dark, rough pirates contrasted sharply with the pure, white-robed figures of the Lords. The landings reflected the differences as well. While all three Lords touched down with ease, the pirates hit the ground hard and came up stumbling. But, they had all made it and now only four members of the brave band remained. Quickly, the pirates and Lords began to ready themselves to bombard the trolls.

However, as Snake turned to look for ammunition, she was faced with a far greater problem. The trolls had found the back entrance and were charging across the plateau at full speed. And, to make matters worse, they had apparently picked up a few friends on the way in because their numbers had at least doubled. Snake dropped her rocks, pulled her sword, put her hand on her daggers, and called out to the Commander.

"Commander!"

Gabriel turned to the sound of Snake's voice, "Jesus!" He pulled his sword and rushed to Snake's side. The trolls were almost on top of them.

Over their shoulders they heard the Reverend's voice, "Help Snake! We can handle ourselves!"

Then the trolls arrived with a vengeance just as the pirates reached their side. Snake dropped and sliced through some kneecaps. The Commander thrust his sword into the first chest that reached him, elbowed a troll to his right, and chopped an arm off of some troll to his left. Mr. Cliff led the pirates into the chaos with a sick grin on his face. When the pirates attacked, the trolls actually looked afraid for a split second. The pirates charged with their entire bodies. They knocked trolls onto their backs, beat on them with fists, stabbed them with knives and swords, and even bit into flesh. Snake was impressed. *Now that's what I call fighting dirty.* She shot a look back to where they had left the Lords and discovered that they were no longer there. She shifted her gaze forward to the fighting and quickly spotted all three wielding swords. *What the hell are they doing?!* She had not come this far to rescue the High Lord just to see him chopped to bits by an angry troll. Taking out as many bad guys as she could along the way, Snake rushed to cover the Lords.

As soon as the trolls attacked, the Reverend and his group made the leap. They knew they had no other choice as they watched the wave of hundreds of trolls wash over the small band of warriors. And, although the pirates looked like they could take out all the trolls, the Reverend knew there was no way they could fight and protect Brennen at the same time. The four men hit the ground hard, rolled to a stop, and came up fighting. The Reverend scanned the field for Brennen. He found him right where he didn't want him, up to his elbows in trolls. *Son of a bitch! Won't he ever learn.*

"T!"

There was a small delay in a response as T dispatched a troll or two. "What, boss?"

"I'm going to cover the Lords. You save everyone else."

Then, the Reverend was gone. T shrugged and looked out into the sea of enemy. *Save everyone else? Sure. No problem.* As daunting of a task as it seemed, there was really nothing else to do but save some people. So, the talented fighter charged with Rock and the last of the pirates right behind him.

The Reverend reached the Lords at the far side of the battle just in time to see Snake jump between them and the trolls, sword and fists flying.

"What the hell is your problem?!" she yelled over her shoulder at the shocked Lords as she chopped up trolls. "We didn't rescue your sorry little ass so that you could get killed!"

Before Brennen could say something the Reverend was sure he would regret, the Reverend jumped into the scene and the conversation.

"See," he said as he pushed the Lords back away from the fighting, "I told you that some days she could be mean."

With the Reverend in charge of the Lords, Snake knew she could go back to concentrating on the battle instead of babysitting duty. She would leave that to him. *Besides, he is nicer than I am.* The Reverend watched as Snake disappeared in the jungle of nasty enemy types, but he didn't worry much. He knew she would be okay. It was the Lords he was worried about. He turned to his wards.

"Don't do that, again," he said with no laughter in his voice.

"I will not sit back and watch while others' lives are in danger," replied Brennen.

"You don't get it, do you? Our lives have been in danger from the moment we started this crazy crusade to find you. We do not need all the sacrifice to mean nothing because you choose to get yourself killed now. Like it or not, you will not fight."

Brennen looked into the eyes of his old friend and saw the power behind his words. Frustration coursed through his veins as he realized that his friend meant to keep him out of the fight at all costs. His words made sense, of course, but Brennen had never been one to sit back and let others take care of him. He wasn't sure what he should do. He looked toward the frenzy of fighting and felt the hopelessness of the situation.

"Do not despair, Lord Brennen. We will stand and fight, no one can prevent that. And, with your strength, we shall be victorious," said Lord Earin.

The Reverend smiled, "Sure, you can fight. Just don't move more than two steps away from Brennen. I got news for you. It is up to the three of us to keep him safe, because here they come."

Earin, Anjalina, and Brennen all turned to look at what the Reverend had already seen. The small band of fighters was simply too tiny to hold back the enemy force. Groups of trolls had broken past them and were now heading straight for the Lords. The Reverend pulled out his rapier so that he now held a weapon in both hands. Anjalina and Earin moved to his side with their swords ready. Brennen centered himself behind them and began to mutter a small protection spell to give them strength. Then, it hit with the force of a landslide.

Trolls seemed to come from every angle. The Reverend countered every attack. He expertly wielded both weapons, cutting apart any troll who came near him. The Lords fought valiantly at his side, though neither could hold with the same force as the Reverend. Slowly, they were being pushed back towards the edge of the cliff. Things were quickly turning from worse to down right ugly.

Across the plateau, the rest of the group was barely visible in the swarm of hideous trolls. They appeared only as flashes of light in the otherwise dark mass. Things were desperate on all sides of this battle. The Reverend knocked a couple of trolls down, sliced through another one, and kicked yet another in the gut. To his left, Lord Earin fought like a trained soldier, cutting through the thick bodies that came within reach. Lord Anjalina fought like a woman possessed. She knew the importance of the High Lord, but she knew something else as well. She knew that she was next in line should the High Lord die and she was not ready to lead. She fought for his life and her sanity.

As the Reverend countered attacker after attacker, he suddenly became very aware that the trolls were doing everything in their power to reach the High Lord. They were all heading straight for him. In fact, they didn't even seem interested in those that were in the way. He and the other Lords were merely an annoyance. Something in the pit of his stomach told the Reverend that Mongrel was behind this phenomenon. *Things just keep getting better and better.*

The Commander ran his sword through the nearest troll and then turned to look for the Lords. The Reverend was with them. *At least they are safe . . . for now.* When he turned to look at the Lords, he all of a sudden saw something that he cursed himself for not seeing any sooner. The entire army of trolls was surging in that direction. They weren't really interested in fighting with or killing him or the pirates; they were after the High Lord. *This is about to be very bad.* He knew he had to change plans and fast. He scanned the battlefield for Snake. Somehow he knew that she could get the message across.

"Snake!" he barked over the sounds of battle.

He was just getting ready to call for her again, when she appeared beside him. *Even now, she is a ghost.*

"What?" she asked in between sword thrusts.

"They are after the High Lord. We need everyone to fall back and form a new defensive line, one designed to contain."

Snake glanced towards the Reverend and immediately saw what the Commander had seen. *Idiot! How the hell did I miss that?!*

"Right. I'm all over it."

Then, just as she had appeared, she disappeared. The Commander did not doubt for a moment that she would reach the others. Snake had a way of always coming through when she was needed. So, he took out one more troll and then bolted to a fall back position. He was not disappointed. One minute he was breaking through to a point just in front of the trolls by himself and the next he was a part of a defensive line of pirates with Snake right in the middle of everything.

Rock's voice rang out above the roar of battle, "No one gets through! Understood?"

The pirates all acknowledged that they did understand, and then the fighting began, again. The trolls rushed the small line of defenders in an attempt to break through to the Lords, but the line held. The Reverend watched in relief as the Commander brought the band of warriors to a defensive stance in front of him and the Lords. If the line held, he would only have to contend with those trolls he and the Lords were already fighting. If he could eliminate them, he could get the High Lord on the move to the ship and the others could follow. Things were starting to look up for them, but it failed to last.

Five very big and nasty trolls rushed the Reverend and the Lords. One charged Anjalina. She brought her sword up to strike him, but he never even slowed down. Instead, he rammed her into the ground. She struggled to free herself. At that same instant, a second troll charged Lord Earin. He managed to move out of the way, but found himself locked in a furious fight of his sword against the trolls battle ax as another troll joined in the attack. Together, they seemed to be too much for Lord Earin. He was being forced away from the Reverend's side.

The last two trolls rushed the Reverend at a full run. He collided with one and sent him flying. Then he turned and threw his sword at the other troll who had rushed past him, heading straight for the High Lord. The sword hit its mark directly between the shoulder blades of the troll, but it was too late. The troll would finish his mission before he died. He took the last few stumbling steps towards his target and pushed with all his might as he fell to the ground. The Reverend watched in horror as the High Lord went flying over the edge of the cliff.

He leapt forward, arms outstretched, and caught the High Lord's hands as he hit the ground. The Reverend thought his arms were going to be pulled out of their sockets, but he held on as he felt the pull of Brennen coming to a stop.

"Hold on!" yelled the Reverend as he attempted to keep them both from falling.

Lord Anjalina fought desperately to regain her feet as the troll she was fighting tried to crush the life out of her. She pulled a knife and stabbed at his side until he rolled off her. She pushed herself to her feet and was immediately faced with his battle ax in her face. She struck at him with all her might. Then, she saw the Reverend. He was laying on his stomach holding hands that could only belong to the High Lord dangling below the cliff's edge. She knew at once that they were in great danger and that she could not help them. She glanced toward Earin and saw that he too was locked in mortal combat. As she fought for her life, the situation got worse. The troll that the Reverend had knocked out of play earlier was now on his feet and heading for the two men with his sword drawn. Anjalina did the only thing she could think of, she called for help.

"Snake! The Reverend! Help him!"

Snake turned from her fighting at the sound of Lord Anjalina's desperate cry. What she saw made her heart stop. The Reverend was laying on his stomach trying to pull the High Lord back up onto the cliff, Earin and Anjalina were consumed with combat, and a very large troll was bearing down on the Reverend with a sword. She swallowed the panic that welled inside her and calmly reached for a knife. Panic overtook her when she her hand found an empty brace; her knives were all gone. Knowing she could not possibly make it in time, Snake did the only thing she could, she took off at a dead run toward the troll.

Snake had covered half the distance.

The troll lifted his sword.

Snake was nearly there. She lifted her sword.

The troll struck with all his might, driving his sword into the Reverend's back.

Snake sliced through the troll's neck, neatly cutting his head from his shoulders, but it was too late. The damage had been done. Snake kicked the troll's body out of the way, pulled the sword from the Reverend's back, and dropped to his side.

"No, this can't happen," she cried.

"Snake," said the Reverend. "Get Brennen. I can't hold him."

Without hesitation, Snake reached over the cliff and grabbed the High Lord's wrists. As she pulled him back up, the Reverend rolled to his back, grabbed a sword, and killed the troll that had broken from the attack on Lord Earin to finish the job. It was all the Reverend had left. The sword fell from his weak hands. He lay gasping as Snake dragged the High Lord to safety. One look at the Reverend told her she didn't have much time. She threw the High Lord to the ground at his side.

"Save him!" she commanded.

The High Lord looked at her with sad, pleading eyes that told her a truth she was not going to hear. His eyes called out to her that there was nothing he could do. Snake charged the troll fighting Anjalina and dispatched him with ease as the fury of her pain flowed. She grabbed Anjalina and dragged her to the Reverend's side.

"I don't care what you have to do, you will save him." The words grated across Snake's teeth as unbearable agony consumed her at the sight of the Reverend. She had to lash out in anger to save her sanity and probably keep from killing the Lords. Her fury was so great, she hardly noticed when Lord Earin joined the others at the Reverend's side.

"T!" she yelled.

It was only a matter of seconds before T arrived. He had seen Snake leave and had seen the Reverend fall. Like Snake, his own heart had nearly burst with rage and pain. He reached her side gasping, but not because he was out of breath. One look at the Reverend's pale face told him all he needed to know.

"Dear God, no," he muttered.

"Protect him. Nothing happens to him while they save him. Understand?" Snake spoke with an anger that could only be the sound of her soul slipping into total darkness. T dared not argue with her.

"What are you going to do?" he asked.

Snake motioned towards the battle, "Kill them."

Then, she was gone. With the Reverend's head cradled in his lap, the High Lord watched her go. There would be no stopping her, of that he was certain. She would seek to end the pain in her veins by killing everything in her path and there simply were not enough trolls to fill her empty soul and end her suffering. Lord Anjalina's voice entered his tired mind.

He is not going to make it, is he?

No.

Then we are lost, for she will never forgive us.

I know.

What can we do? asked Lord Earin.

We ease his suffering and we wait.

God help us, came Earin's muted reply.

Commander Gabriel watched in amazement as Snake broke from the group surrounding the Reverend and came charging. He was amazed that the Reverend had fallen, amazed that Snake had not killed a Lord, and completely stunned that she had left his side. When she reached the first of the trolls, however, he understood everything. Like a madwoman, she hacked through troll after troll. She did not hesitate and she did not deviate; she simply killed. It was as though she had been created to destroy and was consumed by that mission. He continued to fight, to help her in her mission, but suspected that in her frenzied state she needed no one's help.

Snake barely saw as she exploded into battle. Though she was looking at trolls with her eyes, all she could see in her mind was the fallen form of the Reverend. Her rage was more complete than it had ever been in her short and painful existence. She wanted to cause as much pain as she was feeling; she wanted someone to pay the price; she wanted to die. So, she chopped down anything standing in her way. If she could have seen the look of pure hatred and anger on her own face, she would have been terrified. But, she could not. She could only see the Reverend's pale and dying face. *No! Not dying! He will not die!*

And then, it was done.

Suddenly, there were no more trolls left to kill, no more pain to inflict. Snake stood, chest heaving, in the middle of a dead battlefield. The only things standing were the pirates, the Commander, and herself.

"I don't believe it," muttered Lord Earin as he stared at the carnage.

"I do," replied T as he looked at the Reverend. *Come on, boss. Pull through.*

"Snake?" said the Commander. "Snake? Are you alright."

Snake stared blankly at the Commander, unable to stop the pain and needing something else to kill. She couldn't speak. Her chest was too tight with pain. The Commander moved towards her.

"Come on. We have to get the hell out of here."

Snake didn't budge. The Commander started to wonder if she had finally snapped. Then, they heard the laughing. It was low at first, but grew in volume quickly. They turned to see Mongrel and four other wizards appear at the far end of the plateau.

"Well, met. But, it will not be enough."

Before, anyone could react, Mongrel sent a bolt of light exploding into the air. The blast lit up the night sky as though it was mid-afternoon and the force of the blast knocked them all on their asses. Then they heard the laughing, again.

"Now, feel my wrath as you face the remainder of my army of trolls!" screeched the maniacal wizard.

The small band of warriors climbed to their feet and turned to face what was coming. The Commander knew they were in deep trouble. The pirates questioned their own sanity for the millionth time since they had left themselves be talked into this. And, Snake smiled an evil smile. The sound of things crashing through the trees reached their ears. They readied themselves for battle. Mongrel grinned with glee. Then, it happened.

A fighting force bolted out across the plateau and headed straight for Rock.

"What the?!" exclaimed the Commander as he watched an army of pirates, not trolls appear.

Snake was shocked back into communication, "Where are the trolls?"

Rock greeted his men and replied, "Plan B, just like I promised."

When the others were leaving the ship, it had occurred to Rock that he really didn't need anyone to stay behind at watch the ship, since it would do them no good if they failed in this mission. So, instead, he had arranged for everyone left to sneak to shore shortly after he and the others left. Their mission had been to come up from behind and kill any trolls they came into contact with, and to do so quietly. He had a pretty good idea it would be fairly easy since most of the focus would be on the inner island and the trap. It appeared he had been right.

"What took you so long?" teased Rock.

"Ah, the water was choppy, there was no place to land, and, oh yeah, that's right, we had to kill about a hundred trolls just to get this far," came the sarcastic response from Fredrick, whom Rock had put in charge of the whole night raid party.

"No! That's not possible!"

The scream from Mongrel brought all their attention back to the group of wizards. Snake looked at the Commander.

"Ready?" she asked.

"Always," came his smug reply.

Like synchronized swimmers, the two Chosen picked up their swords and charged. The wizards took a step back, but held their ground at Mongrel's command. As they passed the pirates, Snake removed two knives from one man's brace without ever stopping, while the Commander helped himself to a bow and arrows from another. Both men barely had time to notice what had happened before the Chosen acted. As if listening to some unheard cue, they dropped their swords and let their other weapons fly. Two daggers thudded solidly into the chests of two wizards at the precise moment that an arrow reached the heart of a third, only to be followed a split second later by another arrow piercing the eye of the fourth. Mongrel stood all alone. The Chosen retrieved their swords and took up the charge. Mongrel could see that he had no choice remaining. In a total rage, he wrapped himself in magic and disappeared.

"Son of a bitch!" yelled Commander Gabriel. "I hate it when he does that!"

Snake muttered, "Coward."

It appeared the battle had come to an end. The warriors stood in near disbelief. This part of the mission was over, at least. Now they could move on to the next step, getting the hell out of here before Mongrel came back with more friends. Yet, even now, reality came back to haunt them one more time.

"Snake!" came T's desperate voice from across the field.

Her heart broke at the sound of his voice. She knew the truth before she ever turned around, but she refused to believe it. She turned and ran back to the Reverend as fast as she could as though if she only got there fast enough the inevitable would not happen. That, of course, was not to be. When she reached them and looked down at his ashen face, she knew it was already too late. She knew that he was leaving her. She knew that she had been right. She had dared to love, again, and death was all that followed. She looked to the Lords.

"I'm sorry," said the High Lord softly, "There is nothing we can do."

Snake snapped and lunged for the Lord. "No! You can't let him die!" she yelled as she yanked his body into the air.

He showed no fear, only understanding as he stared back into her cold and angry eyes. "I'm sorry," he said, again.

"Stop saying that! I don't believe you!" she yelled back into his face.

Now she had a hold of the front of his robe with both hands and it looked as though she meant to toss him off the cliff herself. Panic surged through the other Lords and they leapt to his aid, pulling at Snake's arms and screaming. "Let him go! It's not his fault!" But, she could not be reached. And, although he completely understood her anger, Commander Gabriel knew he had no choice but to intervene and save the High Lord. He rushed Snake from behind, swept his arms up under hers, and pulled her off the High Lord in a full nelson. Her body was tight with the tension of anger coursing through her veins, but she did not resist him. Still, he didn't think it was safe to release her. The High Lord stood calmly and faced her as though he was about to repeat his apology.

"If you say it again, I swear that I will snap your fucking neck," said Snake in a tone that everyone knew to be truth.

Commander Gabriel whispered in her ear, "Please, don't make me have to kill you. You are a better person than him."

For a few more minutes the world stood paused on the brink of total destruction. Then a weak but firm voice brought it all to and end. When the Reverend spoke, Gabriel felt Snake's body go slack in his arms and her released her.

"Snake. Stop and listen to me," said the Reverend.

Snake fell to the ground at his side, "Please don't die," she whispered, "What will I live for?"

The Reverend smiled, "Promise me you will protect Brennen. Repay my debt. And, promise me you'll fulfill your destiny."

Snake could not stand it any longer. An emotion she had locked away so many years ago as unattainable came flooding over her; her heart shattered into a million tiny pieces, and, for the first time in years, hot tears ran down her face. If she could have lifted her head, she would have seen the shock register on the faces of all those around her as they realized that she did have a heart. The Reverend lifted a weak hand and wiped a tear from her face.

"Snake, promise me."

She nodded, "I promise."

"I love you, you know," he said with the conviction of a dying man.

Snake leaned down so that her lips nearly touched his face, "I love you, too."

The Reverend smiled like a newborn babe, Snake placed a gentle kiss on his lips, then, as peacefully as an old man in his bed, he exhaled his last breath and died. Snake felt her heart and soul die, too. Around her, all the others felt their own sorrow. T even wept.

She had no idea how long she had been sitting there when she heard the Commander speak, "Come on. We have to go before Mongrel returns with more troops."

Snake sucked in her tears and closed off her soul one last time. Then, strong as the north wind, she stood.

"Yes, let's leave. But, not without him," she commanded, daring only to glance down at the Reverend's body.

"He will not be left behind," said Rock firmly as he bent down to lift his former boss in his arms.

"I'll lead. Rock, you and your men protect *him*," she pointed to the High Lord with a nod of her head, scarcely hiding the disgust she felt for the Lord. "He lives, no matter what. The Reverend will not have died in vain."

No one uttered another word as they followed Snake and her pain back to the waiting ship.

*   *   *

A cold wind blew in from the north and stung the somber faces of the crew of the Falcon as they stood in silence listening to Lord Earin's prayer. It seemed fitting that the temperature around them should run cold. It was a just mirror of the way they felt on the inside. It had only been a day since they left the island of Tay-yah-nay, but it seemed like an entire lifetime had come and gone. Snake, at least, felt as old as the sea they now sailed upon.

Indeed, to the rest of the crew she seemed to be barely alive. Since the death of the Reverend, Snake simply sat and stared out into the vast nothingness that surrounded them, barely speaking to those who passed by her, eating nothing, and never moving. It wasn't until the funeral arrangements had been made for the Reverend that she moved from her spot. She followed the Reverend's body to the starboard side of the ship and watched with a cool, blank stare as he was prepared for burial at sea. No one was sure that she heard a word that was said by Lord Earin, but everyone knew she felt the power of the moment. For, more than the Reverend had died on that cliff. The last human part of Snake had died with him.

Commander Gabriel watched that death in silent sorrow. Though he really knew nothing about her, he understood that losing what was human in her was a dangerous thing for the rest of the world. She had been hostile before, now she would be evil. But, it was more than that. Something very beautiful had just left the world and there wasn't enough beauty left for that to happen. As he listened to Lord Earin and stared at the suffering Snake, he couldn't help but wonder if she could ever be reached, again. *God help us all if she can't.*

T and Rock stood like phantom guards behind Snake's weary

form. The death of the Reverend had been terrible for them as well. He had been more than their leader. He had been a friend, a mentor, and a savior. Each of them was very much aware that, had the Reverend not saved them, they would have been dead long ago. He was a legend. *Legends aren't supposed to die.* T let that thought bounce through his brain for a few seconds while he tried, yet again, to believe that the Reverend was really dead. He found he could not come to grips with it, so he went back to watching Snake and waiting. *Just what am I waiting for? The Reverend to rise?* Truth be told, that was precisely what he was waiting for.

Rock, on the other hand, was simply angry. They had come all this way, accomplished so much, and even come back with all the necessary men and equipment to start a new life, and the one man who had made it all possible was gone. He moved his gaze from Snake to the stoic form of the High Lord. *You had better be worth it, old man.* He wasn't sure that was possible.

Then, Lord Earin was finished. The sound of silence filled the air and everyone seemed to hold their breath forever. Then the High Lord stepped forward and placed his hand on the Reverend's shrouded figure.

"Go in peace, my friend."

Snake's hand itched to strike him. Then, Rock moved forward to do his duty.

"Raise the plank," he said.

Two pirates lifted the plank on which the Reverend was laying. He slid off into the sea, and was gone. Snake thought she was going to vomit. One last time, hot tears ran down her face. She wanted to jump into the sea and follow him, but she was bound by her promise to him. *Not to mention, he would kick my ass.* The thought of him being angry enough with her to come back from the dead just to put her through some extra training made her smile a tiny smile for a split second. It didn't last long. The High Lord was approaching her with a determined look upon his face. He stopped just in front of her.

"Words cannot begin to express the sorrow I feel for you. The world is a darker place with his loss. I can only offer you the small comfort of knowing that he will suffer no more, and to let you know how pleased I am that you will be joining us in our battle to destroy the evil that has taken him from us."

Although what he said rang true and his voice oozed with sincerity, Snake felt bitterness welling up inside her until it exploded in the form of angry vengeance. She grabbed the High Lord and slammed him up against the mast. She put her face right up in his and spoke in a voice that was barely even a whisper.

"I'm here because I made a promise to the Reverend. You are alive because I made a promise to the Reverend. Make no mistake, his death is your fault. He is dead because of you. Get it?!" Her eyes burned through his and down into his soul. Then, she dropped him and walked away, disappearing into the shadows.

The High Lord did get it. He felt her sorrow, her anger, and her guilt. Somehow she blamed herself. Of that fact, he was certain. Her own pain was more than she could bear, so she made it his fault in order to cope. *That's okay,* he thought, *I blame myself, as well.* And, so, each savior of the land wrapped themselves in their own personal guilt and attempted to find a way to move on.

*   *   *

EPILOGUE

"Are you sure you won't come with us?" T asked Snake for what seemed like the millionth time.

Snake shook her head, "You know I can't do that. I have a promise to keep. Besides, who wants to hang out with a bunch of disreputable pirates?" She smiled.

It was good to see her smile. In the two week it had taken them to sail back to a mainland port, T was certain that she had not smiled once. He had known that she would pull through and keep moving; she had always been the strong one, but he wasn't sure how pleasant it would be.

"Who you calling "disreputable"?" asked Rock with a grin on his face.

"Who do you think?" Snake responded.

"Yeah, well, at least I have the good manners not to deny it," he replied.

As he watched Snake prepare to leave with the Lords, perhaps never to be seen again, Rock felt overwhelmed with sadness. She had become such a huge part of all their lives. The world was not going to be the same without her. He decided to let her know that, in his own way, of course.

"Anyway, who is going to get us into big messes when you are gone?"

Snake raised an eyebrow, "Are you kidding? Have you seen your crew?"

Then, the three of them laughed. Watching from their horses, the Lords and the Commander felt warmth and love re-enter the world for just a moment. *Those three together is just right,* thought Gabriel. He glanced at the Lords and thought about what lie ahead for them. *And us taking her away from them is just so wrong.* Still, it was his job to keep things moving, no matter how much it killed him to do so. *Funny, my job was so much easier before Snake.* Choosing to separate himself from the Lords, Commander Gabriel dismounted and approached the trio.

"I hate to break up this party, but we have to be going. The High Lord 'aint gettin' any younger. Rock, T." He held out his hand to each in friendship, and each man shook his hand heartily. "It has been an honor knowing you."

"You 'aint half bad yourself, Commander," replied Rock.

"Yeah, you would have made one hell of a thief," added T.

Rock snorted, "You mean pirate, of course."

T grinned, "There's a difference?"

"Yeah," said Rock, "We work on water, now."

Then, there was silence. Long, painful silence. Snake wasn't sure if she could stand one more good-bye. Rock didn't give her a choice. He wrapped his arms around her and lifted her from the ground in a huge bear-hug.

"You be careful."

She smiled at him, "I will."

He released her and T took over where he had left off. He gave her a hug like a father watching his daughter go off to college for the first time. "If you need anything, find us. We will be there, always."

Snake choked back her emotions, "I know."

With so much left unsaid, but nothing else left that she could say, Snake turned and mounted her waiting horse. She waved one last time and then followed the Commander and the Lords away from her past and towards a new future. As she felt her past falling away behind her, Snake had a single thought, *And so it begins . . .*